The
Baby-Catcher
Gate

Wendy Jo Cerna

The Baby-Catcher Gate

Copyright © 2017 Wendy Jo Cerna

This is a work of fiction. Any similarity to persons, living or dead, is not intended by the author. The places, incidences and circumstances portrayed are the product of the author's imagination.

Cover design: Delaney Cerna
Photo credit: Martha Stejskal

ISBN-13: 978-1979995061
ISBN-10: 1979995060

For Carmen & Taryn
Joy & Caroline
Gail & Amy
Jen & Baby W

and

mothers everywhere
whose children
live beyond the gate

But as the Scriptures say,

No eye has ever seen and no ear has ever heard
and it has never occurred to the human heart
All the things God prepared for those who love Him.

God has shown us these profound and startling realities
through His Spirit.
The Spirit searches all things, even the deep mysteries of
God.

I Corinthians 2:9–10
(The Voice)

Soli Deo Gloria

THIN PLACES

I come from a long line of baby catchers, but I never wanted to be one, and I never wanted to be named Pearl. Funny how God can turn things like that around. Not funny in a 'ha-ha' way, but in a way so beyond the imagination, it's hard to describe. Maybe you haven't encountered God like that—I certainly hadn't, nor did I expect to. He simply showed up one stormy August night in 1982. I have no idea why He chose me, a lanky, twelve-year-old girl living in a two-stoplight town in the northern woods of Minnesota. All I know is that He did, and it changed me. And not only me, but my family, my friends, and pretty much my entire town.

☐

"Pearl, are you ready to go?" Mother's voice pierced my bedroom door.

"Just grabbing my stuff," I yelled back.

A girl born in my era wasn't supposed to be named Pearl. Jennifer or Amy or Michelle, perhaps. But Pearl? It was a name for grandmothers, great-aunties, or second cousins twice removed. For women with silver braids wrapped around their heads and watery eyes. Not for girls with long, chestnut hair and clear, amber eyes, like me. Mother's explanation? God gave her my name.

I was what she liked to call her late-in-life baby. My siblings, Susan and David, were fifteen and twelve years old when I arrived. Mother had just turned forty. The pregnancy was difficult and the delivery complicated. But she said that when Grandma placed me in her arms, a still, small voice whispered, "This is a pearl of great price." How could she name me anything but Pearl? I accepted her explanation, even secretly relished it, but I still disliked the name itself. Once I asked my friends at school to call me Patricia, but somehow Mother found out and put an end to my scheme. So, I was frustrated with Mother and irked with God. Why would He give me an old-lady name? Did He lack imagination? Was He unaware of my discomfort with my identity? Turns out, the answer to those questions was a resounding no. But for the first twelve years of my life, I was oblivious to that fact.

"Do not lollygag. This is Mrs. Norquist's third baby."

"Baby number three, in a hurry will always be," I said.

What twelve-year-old girl would know that? One who lived in my house—that's who.

It was simply assumed that if you were a female born into my family, you would participate in the family business—the baby-catching business. My grandmother Ilsa was a baby catcher, and my great-grandmother Edna before her. My mother, Elizabeth, had earned a nursing degree and worked in the maternity clinic at the hospital. She also offered private midwifery services in the county to women who either couldn't afford a hospital delivery or simply preferred to give birth at home. My sister Susan went to grad school to become a doctor in obstetrics and gynecology. I thought that was just a fancy way of saying "highly educated baby catcher." Stories were told of prior generations also being baby catchers, but no one had documented proof. For me, four generations of women wrapped up in the business of labor and delivery were enough. I had determined that I wanted nothing to do with it.

"Make sure you pack an overnight bag, just in case," Mother said as she popped her head around the doorframe of my room. "Third babies are generally in a hurry, but—"

"Every delivery is unique," I finished Mother's mantra.

"Good girl," she said as she marched off.

Before her death, Grandma stayed with us for extended visits, and oh, the stories that passed between her and Mother. By my seventh or eighth birthday, I knew more about possible childbirth scenarios than most mature women. It's not as if they sat down and taught me; I simply couldn't help but overhear. Some kids might have been intrigued by this insight into birthing babies. Not me. I thought it was gross. Words like *cervix*, *placenta*, *effacement*, *preeclampsia*, *dilation*, *transition*, and *perineum* were part of everyday conversations in our house. One time I asked if I might soundproof my room so that when my friends came over I could close the door and pretend I lived in a normal household. My request was denied.

"Pearl, have you seen the new pair of umbilical scissors I just bought?" Mother hollered from the kitchen.

"In the pantry. By the box of lubricating jelly," I hollered back.

"Found 'em."

Whenever someone asked me what my mother did, I said she was a nurse. I had learned that saying "midwife" or "baby catcher" only seemed to conjure up images of hippie earth mothers in people's minds. This had often led to awkward questions accompanied by looks of concern for my welfare. Of course, if they had met Mother, there would have been no such worries. She didn't have a wardrobe of flowing skirts, fringed leather vests, or tie-dyed T-shirts. In fact, her closet was full of medical scrubs and mom clothes that were more out-of-date than bohemian. And though her spiritual roots were in a Pentecostal church, she had long ago agreed to worship at Our Savior's Lutheran Church. That was the church where my Daddy's family had worn indents into the fourth pew from the front, on the right side. She had learned to embrace the traditional liturgies and revel in the age-old hymns. But every now and then, when we sang "Holy, Holy, Holy" or "A Mighty Fortress Is Our God," I saw her stuff the hand not holding her hymnal into her pocket, as if to restrain it from shooting heavenward.

For her, being a baby catcher wasn't about rebelling against the establishment. It was about fulfilling the task she felt God had put her on the planet to do. She was passionate about giving mothers and babies the best care possible, which in her mind included the option of home birth. Many in the medical world viewed this option as old-fashioned and risky, but she didn't seem to care. Okay, maybe in that sense she was a bit of a rebel. But she wasn't the kind that carried protest signs or stuffed daisies into gun barrels. She was the kind that quietly went about doing what she was convinced was right, regardless of what others thought. She admitted to me that being a midwife was often inconvenient, exhausting, and difficult, but most of the time, she extolled it as being exhilarating and purposeful. She loved that it positioned her in what she liked to call life's "thin places"—places where the distance between heaven and earth became so small, you could see into one from the other.

I raced across the hallway to the bathroom, snatched up my toothbrush, threw it in the bag, and met Mother in the front entry. She was dressed from head to toe in blue scrubs, with a matching bandana wrapped over her short, blond curls. Not the most attractive outfit, even on her petite frame. But I always admired the way the blue matched the color of her eyes.

"Ready to go?" she asked.

"Did you call Mel's mom?"

"Yes. They're expecting you."

She gripped her leather satchel as she strode out the front door, a quiet prayer already on her lips. Prayer was as vital to her as the instruments that filled her well-worn satchel. That's what she told me, at least. Answers to her prayers came in unusual ways. Sometimes she sensed God's hands covering her own and guiding her to do things she had never done before, especially during a difficult birth. Other times she heard a voice drop instructions into her mind. Once she saw angel wings hovering above the scene like a heavenly shield. Not surprised by this interaction with the divine, she actually relied on it. She loved feeling connected to eternity. Of course, she loved the mothers and babies, but the thing that fueled her inner passion remained this direct cooperation with the workings of God.

I didn't quite know what to make of it all. God and I were definitely on speaking terms, but mostly it was me speaking and Him listening. I believed what Mother described about hearing from God and working with Him, but I wondered if He only did those things with certain people— like Mother.

"I may be back before bedtime, but I'd rather you be settled at Mel's for the night," Mother said as she stood in the driveway behind the opened car door.

"That's cool. We've already got plans."

I slung my bag on my back and mounted my bike.

"I'm sure you do. Be good," she said before dipping inside the dingy tan station wagon and speeding off.

I took my time riding down 7th Street to the stop sign at Sycamore. The day was warm, but not stifling, a welcome break from the humid weather we'd been having. House after house along our tree-lined street had windows and doors stripped open to the screens to welcome the clear afternoon breeze. I took my time winding my way to Mel's house. It was easy to navigate the well-plotted streets of St. Gerard. Those that ran north to south were numbered one through twenty-seven, and those that ran east to west were alphabetically ordered tree names: Ash to Yew, with the notable exception of Main Street, which fell between Hemlock and Iris (which, of course, was not a tree, but understandable in light of the lack of trees beginning with the letter *I*). My detour that day looped over to the corner of Oak and 10th Street, where the three-story brick edifice of Edison Junior High School confronted me. I stopped my fuchsia Schwinn and stared at the double doors I would pass through on the day after Labor Day.

Everyone had told me, "It's going to be an exciting time in your life." But I had heard the stories. This was the place where it all began—the separating and dividing into cool kids and nerds, jocks and burnouts, pretty and awkward, popular and not so popular. None of those labels really fit me—except maybe awkward. I didn't have a great need for popularity, but I did want to be known for something besides my oddball name. What I longed for above all else was to find the place that belonged just to me. Not just a label, but an identity.

A mosquito landed on my hand. I smashed it flat and flicked it away.

I put my feet back on the pedals and resumed my journey, wishing I could as easily flick away the familiar ache that had begun to grow in my heart. It was the ache that longed for him, the person in my life who was supposed to help me figure this kind of stuff out.

The ache helped me understand why Mother loved the thin places. They were her way to feel close to heaven and to Daddy. He had been a mechanic and truck driver for the paper mill down the river. Routes that had him gone more than a night at a time were not to his liking. He preferred to be home, and Mother preferred to have him home. But one night, he didn't come home. On his way to deliver paper products during a snowstorm, he lost control on an icy highway and slid down a steep embankment. He died on impact at the bottom of a ravine. I don't remember much about his death; I was three years old. The one clear memory from that time still lodged in my brain is the image of my mother leaning on her dresser, her blond curls shaking as her slender frame convulsed with sobs. It is one of the few times in my life I have ever seen her cry so desperately.

My bike tires rumbled across the defunct Northern Pacific railroad tracks in the middle of 26th Street just before the turn into Whispering Pines Estates. Mel's split-level house was situated near the end of the street on a lot twice the size of any on 7th Street. She hopped up and down on the front stoop and waved with both arms when I came into sight, her dark braids swinging wildly.

"Hey, Pearl, what took you so long?"

As I pulled into the driveway, she swooped over to give me a hug, which I couldn't return since I was in the process of steering my bike into the two-car garage. Just as well. I wasn't as keen on hugs as she was. Nobody was. Mel hugged everyone, regardless of whether or not they hugged back. I was used to it, but I had witnessed on more than one occasion some very startled responses from the generally nonhugging Scandinavian/German population of our town. Mel's own mother couldn't understand it. She had once told me, "The only thing we can attribute it to is that her father's great-grandfather was Italian."

Mel may have lived only a couple miles away, but it felt like she lived on a whole different planet. Whispering Pines was the newest neighborhood in St. Gerard, the only one with an actual name painted on a carved wooden sign at its entrance. Mel's father was a banker, and her mother was an accountant who worked out of their house. I wasn't quite sure why they needed such a big house when Mel was their only child, but I enjoyed the fact that they had reserved one bedroom just for me on my frequent visits.

Mel's mother stuck her head out the front door.

"Melissa, come and get the cookies out of the oven before they burn—oh, hello, Pearl! There's pop in the fridge. I've got a client downstairs. Don't leave this door standing open. You'll let all the cool air out."

Two other things I enjoyed about staying at Mel's: an abundance of sugary goodies and air-conditioning.

Our plan for the evening was to immerse ourselves in *The Wonderful World of Disney*. Mel had all the latest videos. Her mom didn't just rent them; she flat out bought them.

"Okay. So, here's the plan," Mel said, her green eyes alight with the internal energy she seemed to perpetually possess. "We'll start with a short cartoon and then you choose—*Mary Poppins* or *Dumbo*?"

Mother called in the middle of *Mary Poppins*.

"Baby Girl Norquist has arrived safe and sound," she said. "Everything okay there? You can meet me at home in an hour or so if you'd like."

"Nah, I'm fine here. We're in the middle of a movie," I replied from the comfort of my oversized beanbag chair. "See ya in the morning."

And so, another baby had entered the world under Mother's capable supervision. I wish I could say I was overjoyed by the news, but my greatest emotion was relief - relief that I was nowhere near the blessed event and relief that there were no complications. I hated hearing about all that stuff. Mother tried not to burden me with the details. But the reality was, she and I were the only ones left at the dinner table of our three-bedroom, one-bath rambler on the other side of the tracks.

My sister Susan was a full-time medical student at the university in the Twin Cities, 200 miles south of St. Gerard. She had more homework and work than hours or days. We heard from her once a week, when she made her obligatory check-in phone call after supper on Sunday evenings.

We didn't hear from my brother David at all anymore. After graduating from college, he'd landed an engineering job in Billings. He and Mother had not parted on the best of terms.

It was a drippy afternoon in late May when David came to pick up some of his belongings before heading west to Montana. His girlfriend Miranda was in the car, which is how we found out she was moving with him to Billings. It seemed she had secured some kind of job for a newspaper there. Mother was not pleased.

Mother's issue wasn't with Miranda. We all liked her—at least, we liked what we knew of her.

"Nice."

That was the word Mother used to describe her after the one weekend David brought her north to meet us. The sticking point between mother and son wasn't the girl it was the living arrangement with the girl.

"Living together is neither a good nor a godly idea," Mother had stated in her closing arguments as David headed out the front door that day. David didn't agree. I know because he disagreed loudly.

"This is the 80s, Mom!" he had yelled. "Get a clue. Your old-fashioned standards might have worked for you and Dad, but the world is changing. Miranda and I are grown adults, and we will live as we choose. Stop trying to dictate my life."

Those were David's last words as he stomped off the front porch toward his '71 midnight-blue Chevy Nova, which was jam-packed with all of his and Miranda's worldly possessions. She sat staring into her lap in the front passenger seat, her face hidden from us by a curtain of long, blond hair. I felt bad for her and embarrassed for us all at the same time. We were not a yelling sort of family, let alone a yelling-on-the-front-porch-for-the-entire-neighborhood-to-hear sort of family.

As I stood inside the screen door, barely breathing, David slammed his car door and peeled out of the driveway, the tires smoking and pebbles flying. Mrs. Schmidt, our "easily excitable" neighbor across the street, popped her head up from her gardening and shook her spade. Mother waved at her. Mrs. Schmidt simply tamped her large straw hat tighter on her head, shoved the spade into the dirt, and returned to her labors.

I didn't move until Mother finally lowered her head, sighed, and turned to come inside. She managed a weak smile and a shrug when she saw me standing there, as if to say, "I have done all I could do." Not an easy admission for her.

We had not heard a word from David since that day.

So, with Susan busy and David gone, who else was she supposed to share with?

☐

The summer of 1982 was not overly busy in the baby-catching business. Mother had only two home deliveries in all of June and July. She had reduced her hours at the clinic to be home with me more during summer break. Most days she didn't leave the house until after lunch. The number where she could be reached was tacked prominently above the phone in the kitchen next to the list of chores she expected me to accomplish before watching TV or meeting up with friends. She had informed me of the boundary lines beyond which I was not allowed to stray and the friends with whom I was allowed to hang out. It was not like I was a wild kid or anything, nor did I have a long list of friends. But when David or Susan had been home for the summer, they had always juggled their work schedules to make sure I was supervised. Mother missed their help; I missed them.

My summer routine was this: get out of bed by ten or eleven, eat Cheerios with banana slices on top, get dressed, do chores, call friends to make plans, and go from there. On nice days, I met Mel and El at the city pool. On not-so-nice days, we congregated at Mel's house. El, or Elspeth as her mom still called her, lived halfway between my house and Mel's, in a duplex with her mom and two younger brothers. It was pretty crowded, and she was only there every other week during the summer. The rest of the time she had to stay with her dad at his farm three miles out of town. We were never invited out there. And even if we had been, Mother wouldn't have let me go. El's dad had a bit of a reputation.

The only scheduled place I had to be that summer, besides church on Sundays, was a community art class Mother had signed me up for on Wednesday afternoons at First

Presbyterian Church. My pals elected to remain poolside. El would situate herself under a beach umbrella with one of her four-inch-thick novels, her unruly, red hair tucked into a floppy sun hat, while Mel preferred to slather on baby oil and stretch out on her towel in her unfairly filled-out lime-green bikini. Her reading material of choice? The latest copy of *Teen Beat*. So, I went to art class myself.

The first day of class, I locked my bike onto a tree next to the church's brick façade and followed the signs. An arrow pointed down the stairs into the fellowship hall. When I checked out who was in the class, I considered turning around and heading back out into the sunshine. It wasn't just my friends who weren't interested in being part of the class—it was every person in town under the age of fifty. Actually, it was every person in town, period, except two women who appeared to be about the same age as Mother and a gentleman who looked ancient—he was probably seventy years old.

The teacher seemed familiar for some reason, but I couldn't pinpoint why. She was a tall, willowy woman with frothy, salt-and-pepper hair, dressed from head to toe in a floral-print dress topped off with an embroidered jean vest. Clearly, she did not shop in St. Gerard. When she spotted me, she strode across the room to meet me, her clogs pounding out a steady rhythm on the concrete floor. She pulled me into the space with a friendly but professional handshake. An aroma of oil paints, homemade bread, and Shalimar perfume wafted from her presence.

"Bonjour. I'm Teacher Anne. Your mother told me to expect you. I'm so pleased you could join us. We are few, as you can see, but we are mighty," she offered with a final strong pump of my hand and a wink. "Let me introduce you to the others."

Good manners demanded I stay for at least the first class. Besides, I was intrigued by the chance to learn more about art. I sort of had a feeling it could help me find that place I was looking for—the place I belonged. In school, my teachers praised my art projects, although they were few and far between. Our school district didn't place much emphasis on development of the fine arts. Most of the attention and money went to athletics. And although I was tall for my age and looked like I might be good at basketball or volleyball, I pretty much stunk at any activity that had anything to do with a ball.

As Teacher Anne led me toward the others, I suddenly remembered why she looked so familiar. Once during the previous summer, Mother and I had ventured out on one of our rare nights on the town. After we ate burgers and drank root beer out of tall, frosty mugs at the Corral Drive-In, we went to see a movie at the Uptown Theater. That night there was a display of artwork in the lobby, with a picture of the artist alongside the paintings. It was Teacher Anne. Mother told me that she and Anne were old friends. I didn't bother to dig any deeper at the time, though the wistful look on Mother's face begged for more details. The paintings had stolen my attention. Teacher Anne made canvas and paint seem like living things. The colors, the lighting, the movement all sucked me into the frames for so long that we missed the previews of coming attractions.

I wanted to learn how to paint like that.

Teacher Anne and I approached the other students, seated in a row behind a long table with art pieces spread out in front of them.

"I asked your classmates to bring samples of their favorite artwork to share with the class," Teacher Anne said. "But don't worry if you didn't bring anything. Now that I think about it, I can't remember if I even mentioned it to your mother." She bopped her forehead with the palm of her hand. "It was a very brief conversation."

The first woman stood from her chair and reached out her hand. She looked familiar too.

"Pearl, this is Mrs. Grant," said Teacher Anne.

The word *roly-poly* came to mind when I looked at Mrs. Grant's flushed cheeks and friendly, blue eyes. She was nearly as round as she was tall. Her denim jumper strained around her tummy, and her ankles puffed out over the tops of her sensible, brown shoes.

"Hello, Pearl. So lovely to see you. You probably don't remember me then now, do you?"

Mrs. Grant encased my hand in both of her plump hands, and the ends of her silver, bobbed hair swung forward along her rounded chin line.

"Uh, I kinda do."

"Oh, dontcha worry about it," she laughed. "You were just a baby when I used to take care of you in the church nursery."

The lights went on. She was the lady who always stood inside the double door of the nursery, shuttling babies and their bags of goodies in and out of their mothers' arms before and after services. I always thought she was much taller.

"These are her charcoal sketches. Aren't they remarkable?" Teacher Anne said as we perused three sketches laid out on the table before Mrs. Grant.

I could only nod in agreement as I gazed at her work. The pictures were so detailed, I had to bend closer to see whether or not they were photographs.

Next to Mrs. Grant's sketches lay two vibrant watercolor paintings. One depicted a field of wildflowers and the other a lake at sunset.

"Are these yours too?" I asked Mrs. Grant.

"Oh no, no. Those beauties flowed from the gifted hands of my friend Delores here," she said, indicating the athletic-looking woman in the chair next to her.

"Pearl, this is Mrs. Wilson," said Teacher Anne, continuing the introductions.

"Hello. Pleased to meet you," Mrs. Wilson said with a nod.

She remained seated in her chair, which sat several feet back from the table, her long legs extended in front of her. Discarded tennis shoes and socks lay on the floor. She leaned forward with hands on her thighs, as if stretching with Jack LaLanne. Her crisp, khaki pedal pushers and vibrant-yellow polo shirt were completed by a matching yellow visor stuffed into her abundant, auburn hair.

"You'll forgive me if I don't stand up," said Mrs. Wilson. "I just got off the golf course. My lower back is aching, and my dogs are barking."

"Pleased to meet you too."

At the end of the table sat the old man. When he got up, he didn't seem quite so old. Yes, the crown of hair around his head was pure white, but he was lean and muscular, like the kind of guy that still chopped his own firewood. In front of him stood the sculpted head of a woman. I moved closer to inspect it.

"That there's a sculpture of my wife," he said.

I stared at the stone's lifelike features. His voice was softer than I'd expected.

"She's very pretty," I said.

"Ya. She was." As he extended his hand, he added, "You can call me Fritz."

The moment our hands touched, his eyebrows furrowed and his lips tightened. His eyes held mine, and I caught a glimpse into his inner world. He was sad—very sad. He dropped my hand and bowed his head.

"Nice to meet you, Fritz," I said, trying to sound as if I hadn't noticed anything unusual.

"You too."

He sat back down without lifting his head.

Teacher Anne suggested I take a seat next to Fritz. She took her place on a stool in front of us and began to talk. I don't remember what she said. My brain was swimming. I wondered why Fritz was so sad, what dogs had to do with golfing, and when I should make a break for the door. Why was Teacher Anne's conversation with Mother "very brief"? I thought Mother said they were friends. The chatter in my head was like a flock of crows over a cornfield.

"Pearl, are you okay? Would you care to join us?" Teacher Anne stood directly in front of me on the other side of the table. How long she'd been there, I had no idea, but long enough for the others to leave their seats and move to the back of the hall. "We're going to get started on our first project."

I nodded and attempted an eager smile. She nodded, too, and turned to catch up to the group. I slipped from my chair, still uncertain if I should follow her or flee the premises. Then I caught sight of what awaited the class at the far end of the hall. Easels with blank canvases, paints, brushes, and palettes for five stood at the ready. A sudden hunger sprang up inside me, more desperate than any physical hunger pang I had ever experienced. It was as if I had an art stomach inside of me that had functioned up until then on tidbits and morsels and it was growling for something with more substance. And I knew. Not only would I stay—I had to stay.

Every Wednesday that summer, I reveled in the hours spent in that basement hall pursuing my budding love affair with the world of art. Wednesday after Wednesday, my classmates and I donned the aprons Teacher provided to spare our clothing from flying substances and dug into whatever project she had planned for us. I wasn't sure if Mother would call it a thin place or not, but for me, it was the closest thing to heaven on earth I had experienced. At least until the night of August the third.

STORM CLOUDS

A muggy silence hung outside my opened bedroom window that night. The frogs and crickets had ceased their chirping hours before. Grandma used to say that was a sign stormy weather was headed our way. The only interruption to the calm was the occasional thud of a moth thwarted in its efforts to reach my bedside lamp by the mesh of the screen window. I should have been asleep, but I sat atop my blankets, back against the wall, knees pulled up close with my sketchbook propped on top of them. Still in my shorts and T-shirt from the day, I was absorbed in a sketch for art class the next day. In my determination to make my pencil scratches resemble actual bird wings, time slipped by unnoticed until the telephone's jangle disrupted my concentration. A peek at my alarm clock told me it was 12:48 a.m. Baby call.

I stopped drawing and listened. Mother answered the extension in her bedroom on the second ring. I heard a muffled version of the usual list of questions. Her ability to be alert and in control when she emerged from a deep sleep always surprised me. When her feet hit the floor and the hall light flicked on, I knew the call wasn't just a preliminary update or premature panic. It was time. I picked up the colored pencils scattered across the bedspread and reached for my tote bag hung on the footpost at the end of the bed.

My door creaked opened, and Mother poked her head around the corner. Her eyebrows rose when she found me awake and moving toward my sweatshirt.

"I heard," I said. "I'll get the blankets."

"Good girl. We need to leave as soon as possible. We have some ways to drive, and it sounds as though this baby is in a hurry to arrive."

Since our numbers were thinned to just Mother and me, it meant, among other things, that I had to accompany her if she got called to a delivery in the middle of the night. Before, I had simply stayed home with David. Mother allowed me to be home alone for several hours during the day, but not at night. If she had time, she tried to make arrangements for me, like she did the day of the Norquist delivery. But in my experience as the daughter of a baby catcher, I found babies didn't always allow for advanced planning.

I had gone with her before when necessary, but I wasn't very helpful. If I had shown any interest, she would have found a few simple tasks to keep me involved. Instead, my one assignment was to be in charge of the receiving blankets, to make sure we had several along and to keep them warm. One would be used to quickly dry the baby before placing him or her on the mother's bare chest for what Mother called "skin time." Another would be used later to swaddle the newborn snugly in a bundle to be passed around to dads or grandmas or aunties or whoever else attended the birth.

"Give her a kiss. Hold her close. Whisper a welcome," Mother would gently coach those new to the world of parenthood. She believed newborn babies needed a sense of security, welcome, and love as soon after arrival as possible.

I took the blanket-keeper assignment seriously. My simple technique to keep them warm was the use of body heat. I found a cozy place where I was close enough to hear Mother's voice when she called but far enough away to avoid the nitty-gritty of the birthing business. Sometimes I read or sketched, but since it was usually the middle of the night, I often just snoozed with one ear open for Mother's voice. When she needed the blankets, a firm, calm command came: "Pearl, I need you now." And "now" meant *now*.

By the time I had zipped up my sweatshirt, swept my hair into a ponytail, and packed my art supplies, Mother was in the front hallway. Garbed in green scrubs and a navy windbreaker, she wrapped a scarf around her freshly permed hair and grabbed the leather satchel from its post atop the bookshelf in the entryway niche. I retrieved two cellophane-wrapped blankets from the tidy stack on the shelf below.

"Looks like we've got a thunderstorm headed our way," she said as she opened the screen door.

A wind gust whipped it from her hand and smacked it against the house's wooden siding, emphasizing her forecast. I stepped out into the night behind her, locked the front door, and jammed the screen door back in place before running to the car. The neighbor's beagle barked and ran along the fence, sending up an alarm that could be heard blocks away.

"That'll make Mrs. Schmidt happy," I said as I crawled into the passenger seat.

I wondered how long it would take for Mother to get a call from our self-appointed neighborhood overseer.

We backed down the driveway and turned north toward Main Street. The dog continued to howl. Mother didn't respond to my remark. Her lips moved in silent prayer. I assessed her grip on the steering wheel. It was a notch above firm.

"Where're we headed?" I asked.

"The Furness farm."

"I thought you said her baby wasn't due until September."

"True."

"Is she alone out there?" I asked, although I knew it was a sensitive question.

I had overheard, as one often does in a small town, that Mr. Furness had packed up and disappeared a few months back. No one knew why, but that didn't stop them from guessing. Mother probably knew the reason, but she wouldn't say. She wasn't fond of gossip.

"No. Her mother has come to help," Mother answered, her eyes straight ahead.

When we reached the two-lane road we called a highway, she zoomed to seventy-five miles per hour—in a fifty-five zone. I felt prompted to join her in silent prayer. The leather satchel sat between us on the seat. The blankets covered my lap, and my tote bag rested at my feet. Mother turned on the wipers when the first large plops of rain exploded on the windshield. The night grew darker as clouds raced past the moon and small branches skittered across the road.

Soon raindrops pounded on the roof and sheets of rain flew past our headlights. Mother reduced her speed to sixty as water filled the grooves made by years of trucks, tractors, and trailers on our obscure county road. It was not a good night to be out and about. It was the sort of night when the town's tornado sirens interrupted the thunder peals and we headed for the basement, packing flashlights and radios. I didn't enjoy these kinds of nights; I enjoyed being out in them even less.

After what seemed an eternity, we pulled into the Furness farm's long driveway, our tires crunching over the gravel bumps and ruts. The two-story farmhouse sat back from the road, hidden behind a row of thick spruce trees. After we passed the windbreak, it was still hard to distinguish the house's outline from the surrounding darkness. All was pitch-black.

"Power must be out," Mother said more to herself than to me.

I guessed she was making allowances in her mind for this new variable in her delivery strategy. As always, I was glad she was in charge, not me.

Our headlights flashed past the large front windows as we drove around the side of the house. A shadowy figure stood inside the back door, illuminated by a flashlight. Mother pulled in next to the back steps, threw the gearshift into park, and turned off the car. She grabbed the leather satchel and ran, head bowed, into the rain toward the back door. I put up my hood, stuffed the blankets and tote bag under my sweatshirt, and dashed full tilt through the storm after her.

Mrs. Furness's mother flung the door open as I approached, and the wind slammed it shut behind me. She acknowledged me with a terse nod. A small wisp of a woman, a thick, silver braid hung halfway down her back atop a sleeveless, button-down shirt. Mother removed her sopping wet windbreaker and head scarf and hung them on a peg by the back door. She slipped off her muddied shoes before the two women headed toward the bedroom at the end of the hallway, where a faint glow seeped under the door. A stifled moan betrayed a woman in labor.

"Glad ya made it," Mrs. Furness's mother remarked. "Quite a storm out there. Haven't had power for about twenty minutes now. Found a big lantern and some candles. Hope that's enough light for ya."

"We'll make it work. How's she doing? Have things slowed down, or still moving pretty fast?" said Mother, her voice beginning to fade as they moved away.

"Well, contractions are starting to pile one on top of the other . . ." Their voices muted as they shut the door behind them and left me in the dark.

It was fine with me to be left out of the actual work of labor and delivery. I preferred it that way. But to be in the dark without a flashlight or candle in a strange house was a bit awkward. I slipped my shoes off and shuffled to the kitchen table that I had seen by the glow of the flashlight. I removed the blankets and tote bag from under my sweatshirt and set them on the table. A sharp cry came from the bedroom. I stiffened. Mother's muffled instructions reached me through the closed door. Her calm voice soothed my nerves. My soaking wet sweatshirt chilled my neck and shoulders. I took it off and stretched it over a chair back.

I plopped down on a chair next to the table and wondered what to do next. I knew there was probably a more comfortable chair in the living room, but where that was and what I might have to maneuver around to get there were unknown. I decided to stay put, scooting the chair back to the wall and resigning myself to trying to sleep upright. Goose bumps broke out on my arms and legs. I made an executive decision to unwrap one of the blankets from its packaging and swaddle my own shoulders.

The wind continued to howl. I couldn't sleep. Outside the kitchen window, the treetops whipped dramatically from side to side. The rain came down in windswept sheets and pummeled the roof. The storm's racket partially masked the clamor of labor in the bedroom. My eyelids grew heavy, mesmerized by the dancing treetops. Just as I closed them, the bedroom door opened. Purposeful footsteps headed my way. I opened my eyes in time to see Mrs. Furness's mother reach for the phone on the kitchen wall. The shadows from the flashlight made it hard to read her expression, but the phone shook in her hands. After one or two punches of the buttons, she stopped and rattled the receiver. She tried several more times and gave up.

"Lord, have mercy," she muttered as she headed back to the bedroom without a glance in my direction. I think she had forgotten I was there.

This was not good. A pit of worry settled in my stomach. I drew the blanket tighter around my shoulders and decided it might be a good time to pray. I wasn't exactly a prayer warrior like Mother or Grandma, who seemed to know just what to say to God on every occasion. But I knew the basics, like, "Now I lay me down to sleep, I pray the Lord my soul to keep," which didn't quite seem appropriate for the occasion. So, I started with another tried-and-true opener.

"Our Father who art in heaven, hallowed be Thy name," I whispered. "Uh, we could really use some help here. I know You already know that, but I know You like us to ask. So, I'm asking. Please give Mother wisdom and Mrs. Furness strength. Please keep the baby safe and, uh, let Thy kingdom come and Thy will be done on earth as it is in heaven. If you could arrange for the storm to stop and the lights to come back on, we sure would appreciate that too. For Thine is the kingdom and power and glory, forever, amen."

No sooner did I say "amen" than the bedroom door flung open. Mrs. Furness's mother came down the hallway at a trot. She grabbed keys from a hook near the back door, swooped up her jacket, and catapulted herself out into the storm. A gust smelling of wet dirt and hay blew in before the door slapped shut behind her. The flashlight beam bounced across the yard as she darted to the garage. She yanked the door up in one heave and disappeared inside. A split second later, a white Chevy pickup backed out and sped down the driveway, spewing water and gravel in its wake.

In that same moment, the call came.

"Pearl, I need you now."

I froze. Was it time for the blankets already?

Then a bit louder, "Pearl, I need you now."

Defrosted, I unfolded myself from my perch by the table. I grabbed the wrapped blanket and moved warily toward the light at the end of the hallway. At the bedroom door, I halted in midstride, unsure where to step next. A large, metal lantern on the floor emitted a strange uplighting. Bizarre shadows danced on the walls and ceiling. Several candles flickered on bedside tables. They gave off a mingled pine and vanilla scent, mixed with the unmistakable odor of a body hard at work. Mrs. Furness lay on her side in the middle of the bed, with one leg draped across Mother's shoulder in the side-lying position. I surmised from my file of unsolicited midwifery knowledge that Mother had arranged her in this position because the baby had been coming too fast.

Mrs. Furness gripped the headboard slats, her eyes clamped shut. She let out steady swooshing breaths. Beads of sweat dampened her face and dripped down the creases of her neck. Her cotton nightgown was scrunched above her waist, clinging to her upper body like a wet washcloth. At Mother's feet lay a dark-colored towel. A sticky-sweet odor arose from its heaped folds. My stomach lurched. I fought down the gag reaction in my throat.

"Pearl," Mother commandeered my attention. "Set the blanket down on the chair next to the door and go into the bathroom." She pointed down the hallway. "Bring me as many towels as you can find."

I snatched up a candle and jumped into action. I was relieved to have an excuse to leave the room. I found several towels hung on a towel bar and an entire stack in a linen closet. I gulped in the fresh air in the hallway before stepping back into the thick, heated atmosphere of the bedroom.

"Hand one to me," Mother said evenly as she eased another dark towel from under Mrs. Furness.

She reached for the towel I held out. Her gloved hand dripped with darkness as well. I realized it was blood. The towels were saturated with blood. Lots of blood—too much blood. I swayed and leaned back against the doorjamb.

"Pearl, stay with me," Mother ordered. "Set the other towels down on the bed where I can reach them, and hand me the Pinard horn off the dresser."

I followed her instructions. She pressed the trumpet-shaped opening of the Pinard horn to Mrs. Furness's belly and bent her ear to the smaller end of the metal cone to listen for the baby's heartbeat. I held my breath. Mother's brow was creased when she handed the instrument back to me.

"Come. Quickly. Sit here," she said, indicating the spot she occupied. "You will need to help hold this leg up when the next contraction comes."

"But, but I don't know—"

"It doesn't matter, sweetheart. I will tell you what to do."

Mrs. Furness moaned and tensed as a fresh contraction overwhelmed her. There was no time to ask where her mother had gone. My legs felt wooden as I stepped obediently to take Mother's place on the bed.

"Good. Stay right there," Mother instructed. "Get underneath this leg and hold it steady."

Gingerly, I lifted the leg off Mother's shoulder. It was heavier than I'd imagined and slick with sweat. I arranged my shoulder to serve as a prop. Mother got down on her knees next to the bed and positioned herself to see the baby's approach.

"Okay, Violet, it's time to push. Baby needs out now. Let the contraction do the work, and push when you feel ready," she instructed in a controlled voice.

Violet. That's a pretty name, I thought.

Mother continued her encouragement in a practiced, steady tempo.

"Good, Violet, good. Now push. Breathe. Push. I can see the head. You're almost done. Here comes the head. Good. Good. Relax and breathe. One more contraction, and we'll be done."

Violet went limp, her eyes closed, breath shallow, one sweaty leg still propped on my shoulder. She seemed to have given up. My mind raced and my heart pounded. Mother interrupted my internal panic.

"Pearl. Look at me. When this next contraction comes, the baby will arrive. You will then carefully set Violet's leg down. After I cut the cord you need to have a blanket ready. Do you understand?"

"Yes, I, uh, think so," I stammered, still shocked to be doing what I was doing.

Mother returned her full attention to Violet as a new contraction shook her back into action.

"One more, Violet. One more." Mother's guidance and reassurance continued unabated.

Violet gripped the slats with a ferocity that came from who knows where. A guttural cry burst out as she gave everything for this last push. I braced my hands under her leg and watched in utter amazement as Mother guided a tiny, messy newborn out into the world. Violet collapsed into her pillows, her hands still attached to the slats. I eased her leg down and stealthily backed off the bed, unwilling to disturb her after her epic struggle. She didn't move.

Mother stood next to the long, low bureau where a plastic drape lay strewn with her instruments. Next to the plastic was a small mattress covered with a sheet where she placed the infant. She was so intent on her task, she didn't feel me behind her. I peered around her side to catch a glimpse. It was a boy; he was stone-still.

Mother reached for a suctioning bulb and inserted it into his mouth. She extracted it and checked his pulse. Then she turned him over and laid him on his belly across her forearm as she briskly massaged his back and feet. His arms hung limp, and his legs slipped floppily off Mother's arm. She turned him over again, placed him on the mattress, and started chest compressions. He remained motionless. Silently she worked, trying one thing after another as the minutes piled up. I watched and willed him to move. He didn't. Finally, a moan from Violet drew Mother's attention. She turned to me, the lifeless infant in her hands, a glint of tears in her eyes.

"Wrap him nice and tight and hold him while I tend to Violet. Can you do that?"

"But, Mother," I whispered, "he's not moving. Is he, uh, . . . ?"

Mother set the baby in the blanket, placed him in my arms, and peered into my eyes. "Pray, Pearl. Pray." She kissed him on the forehead before she turned to the bed.

My mouth was dry and my palms sweaty. I placed the baby on the bureau to swaddle him as Mother had taught me. I couldn't tell for sure what color his skin was in the dim, flickering light; next to my skin, it appeared gray or blue. His little lips looked as though someone had applied a deep shade of burgundy lipstick. His hands and feet were perfect. I tentatively stroked his fingers. So soft. So cold.

"O Lord Jesus, please help," I whispered.

I wrapped him tightly. I had no welcome to whisper. He had passed us by and gone directly from the womb to some other place. I sat down on the straight-backed chair and stared into his face. The room and Mother and Violet and the raging storm outside all faded away. His face captivated me.

When I lifted my head to see how Mother was doing, the room began to spin. My heartbeat roared in my ears. Darkness closed off the light, like a slow-motion camera shutter. The next thing I knew, I was tilting off the chair, unable to stop myself.

My only thought: "Don't let go of the baby. Hold on to the baby. Hold on . . ."

INTERLUDE: JOHN

Massive evergreens line the rocky shoreline of the lake like sentinels. Echoes of the birds warbling from their heights bounce off the water in a fading fugue to places unknown. I settle onto the smooth grooves on the wooden bench where we meet for these types of conversations, and I wait for Him. He will come. He always does. No matter what else is happening with whomever, wherever, He will meet me.

I am still astonished by my access to Him. He is, after all, the King. The truth is, I am still astonished by a great many things. This limitless stuff takes some getting used to. Just when I think I have a grasp on it, the possibility boundary expands yet again. In another place and time and sphere, I might have described it as "a real trip."

"Hello, John."

He has arrived without a sound. I stand to greet Him, though my natural instinct is to fall on my knees. That was, in fact, what I did at our first meeting. But He gently drew me to my feet and insisted from then on that I stand and greet Him as a friend. I do as instructed, but my knees still buckle a bit at His presence. He kisses my cheek as He envelops me in a warm embrace.

"Good to see you, My friend," He says. "Let's sit."

After a few pleasantries, we sit in comfortable silence, shoulder to shoulder, and gaze across the vast, glassy surface of the water. There is an issue I want to discuss, but it can wait. There is, after all, no hurry in this place. And I have learned that if I wait, if I allow Him to lead the way, He always has something amazing in store—something designed, it seems, just for me.

What will it be this time? I steal a glance at His strong profile. His gaze remains focused on the middle of the lake. A slight smile tugs at the corners of His mouth, underneath the trimmed outline of His beard.

"Watch there, John," He says, pointing to a spot about a hundred feet from the shore.

I lean forward, my arms on my legs, my toes tapping.

Then suddenly, from that very spot, a wave alive with color erupts. Up and up it goes, until it crests and splashes back down into the water, sending giant ripples out in every direction across the lake's surface.

"What was that?" I say.

"Keep watching."

Up it rises again, fifty feet closer to the rocky beach. I snap upright against the back of the bench as I realize what is headed our direction. The wave is alive. Hundreds, if not thousands, of fish fly upward in a shimmering wall of flesh. Their bodies spin as they hover above the water, their scales brilliant hues of green, pink, red, and purple. For one breathtaking moment, they hang suspended in the air and then plunge back into the water, a foaming wake behind them as the entire school abruptly turns toward the right. A three-foot swell speeds our way and crashes on the rocks. I jump up, trying to avoid the spray that spews from their midst, but to no avail. The droplets shower me from head to toe.

The King throws back His head and laughs, His arms open wide to receive the drenching I had hoped to escape. I stare at Him. It appears as if a dozen paint cans in every hue of the rainbow have exploded upon His pristine garments. Colorful beads drip down His hair all the way to the end of His beard and fall to His chest as He rocks with laughter. He looks absurdly wonderful.

"Oh John . . . you should see yourself," He gasps between guffaws.

I glance down. My clothing and skin are doused in color too. And the funniness that has tickled His fancy tickles mine as well. I drop beside Him on the bench, and we laugh until we can laugh no more.

Finally, we sit in silence once again, His arm wrapped around my shoulder. Again, I wait. The warmth of the light all around us soon absorbs the multihued splashes, leaving no trace of dampness or color. Yet I know the experience will remain. Something new and extraordinary has seeped into my heart forever.

"So, John," He says, removing His arm and turning to face me, "what would you like to talk about?"

It's interesting to me that there are things He simply reveals to me, and in an instant I know what I had never known before. And then there are other things— things He likes me to seek out. This seems to be one of those things.

"Since my arrival, you've given me glimpses," I begin.

"Yes, everyone gets glimpses," He says, nodding.

"So I've heard."

"What exactly have you heard?"

"That windows open and we can witness certain occasions or accomplishments in the other realm."

"Does this puzzle you?"

I cross my arms and peer out across the water. Its surface is once again glossy smooth.

"Well, not exactly." I smile to myself as I remember some of the sweet glimpses I've been given. "I've thoroughly enjoyed the moments I've witnessed. Thanks."

"All just part of the plan, My friend."

He pats my leg.

"You've always got plans."

"True," He chuckles.

"So, I guess the thing I wanted to ask You is, what about a glimpse that showed me something troubling?" I return my eyes to His. "Is that part of the plan too?"

"Do you think anything could happen outside of Our plans?" He counters, His eyes alight with warmth and wisdom.

I shake my head.

"What did you see, My friend?" He asks.

"I saw Pearl, my youngest, crying in her bed at night."

"And?"

"And she was holding her stuffed cat. The one I gave her for her third birthday. And she was talking to it."

"Anything in particular?"

"She kept saying, 'They can't make me do this. I won't. I can't. I'm not gonna.'"

"Strong words for a young lady," He acknowledges. "Was that all?"

"Just one more thing . . . but I'm sure You already know that."

"Ah, yes." He nods. "I heard her cry."

He turns His gaze from my face to the panorama before us.

"John, what do you see here in front of us?"

I scan the vista, wondering if I am supposed to see something new.

"Uh, just the same lake we always see when we sit here."

"And what did we see a few moments ago?"

"An awesome wave of rainbow trout."

"Did you know they were there before they leapt to the surface?"

"No."

"But does that mean they weren't there?"

"No."

"And what happened when they went back under?"

I replay the scene in my mind.

"Great ripples of water spread across the lake."

"So great that we became participants in their bounty," He says, laugh lines crinkling around His eyes.

Gurgles of laughter threaten to bubble up from my belly, but I manage to tamp them down. My mind slips back to her, curled up under her blankets with tears dripping onto her pillow.

"I wish they could get glimpses into this realm," I say with a sigh.

"Who says they can't?"

"Hmm . . . my Lizzie used to tell me she could."

"Did you believe her?"

"I did . . . sorta . . . sometimes." I shake my head. "She was just so different from me. Why couldn't I see what she saw?"

"Each one is unique."

"But could You maybe . . ."

He waits.

"She was crying so hard, and I just thought maybe giving her a glimpse like . . . well, like her mother gets. Could that maybe be part of Your plan too?"

He sets His hand on my knee and peers through my eyes, into my heart.

"John, do you trust Me?"

BABY CHRISTENING

A *deep voice* sliced through a thick mist. "Pearl, I need you to hold the baby and come with me."

I stood up, relieved to find the swaddled bundle still in my arms.

"Is it time to go?" I asked. "Is Violet okay?"

"Yes, Violet will be okay. Come."

The room grew brighter, as if the power had come back on. My vantage point rose. Why was Mother kneeling at the foot of the bed? Was there a body on the floor? Poor Mother. How was she supposed to help that person and Violet at the same time?

Mother lifted her face skyward. Tears streamed down her cheeks and she cried out, "Help! Dear God, help!"

Violet stirred. Mother turned toward her but did not leave the side of the body on the floor. She leaned her head down over the mouth of the person. She pressed her fingers into the neck. Violet moaned and asked for her baby. Mother rose. Suddenly I was able to see the person on the floor—it was me. Flat on my back, the baby still in my arms.

"Pearl, we need to go," the gentle voice persisted.

Whose voice was it?

"But Mother needs my help. I can't leave her," I pleaded.

"Help is on the way. She will be alright," the voice assured me.

I ascended higher and higher, until the entire Furness farm spread out beneath me. Through the cloudy veil that enveloped me, I made out the flashing lights of an ambulance on the highway. It was speeding in the direction of the farm. A white Chevy pickup followed close behind.

"They will arrive soon. Help is near. It is time to go," the voice prompted me.

A warm hand rested on my shoulder and guided me upward. I saw no one but sensed the presence of a large being next to me. I was not afraid. In fact, I felt better than I had since I sat on my bed, sketching bird wings. I didn't know who accompanied me or where we were headed, but I knew I was going to be okay. The bundle in my arms stirred. I glimpsed down and piercing blue eyes peered back at me.

"He's alive! Oh, his cheeks are so rosy," I gasped. "And his hair . . . it's the color of shiny pennies!"

I leaned down and nuzzled his neck. He smelled of spring rain.

"He is handsome, is he not?" the voice remarked.

I nodded, unable to take my eyes off this glowing, fragrant baby.

"His name is Joseph," the voice continued.

"I think that suits him perfectly," I said as I studied his face. Joseph rewarded me with a tiny grin. "Mother will be relieved to see him so healthy. And Violet . . . oh, she'll be so happy. I can't wait to tell them. But where are Mother and Violet?"

I received no answer.

I looked around, but I couldn't see beyond the haze that surrounded us in a foggy tunnel. We glided so swiftly that a misty breeze blew past my ears with a low whistle. Despite the velocity of our travels and the mystery of how such a pace was possible, I sensed no danger, only peace and safety. Joseph began to coo in my arms. When I glanced down he stared back, a knowing look in his eyes.

"What do you know, little Joseph? What can you tell me?" I asked, mimicking Mother's best baby talk.

He stopped cooing and his mouth curled in a satisfied smile, the smile babies get right after they have eaten. "Drunk with milk and love," Mother would say. A tired delirium crossed his face, his eyelids drooped, and he fell fast asleep.

The fog thinned and a lustrous road materialized before us, stretching across a broad open plain. Bordering the road on both sides were fields of flowers squared off in a multicolored checkerboard. A soft wind blew across the blooms, and waves rippled the surface, producing brand-new hues in each section simultaneously. An exotic aroma accompanied the stirring, unlike any I had smelled before, heady, lively, and wondrous.

On the other side of the panorama loomed an enormous hill. It stretched from horizon to horizon and was made of countless layers of glistening, colorful stones—purple, green, amber, scarlet, turquoise, and other strange colors I had no names for. Occupying the entirety of its peak was a beautiful walled city. Cresting over the top of the wall were towering buildings that glowed as if lit from within. Colorful shafts of light reflected off their facades in all directions. Trees the size of skyscrapers spread their canopies between the towers, forming glorious arches of cascading green. Over the entire skyline, flocks of winged creatures flew intricate flight patterns. I stood in awe, unable to move until the presence at my side nudged me gently forward.

The being beside me was beginning to emerge from the fog. He was draped in regal garments that flowed down from a statuesque height in effervescent gold, silver, and white. His face remained far above me, obscured in the haze, but his hand rested on my shoulder, rings on each finger. Four were studded with jewels, and the fifth was engraved with the signet of a crown. Their colors swirled hypnotically. The rings seemed alive, like part of his hand, and they sparkled with a mysterious energy. For the first time in our journey together, I was intimidated by him.

"Sir, uh, can you tell me where we're going?" I said, swallowing my jitters.

He looked down at my upturned face as the mist around him melted away. I sucked in my breath. He was handsome beyond my wildest dreams. Greenish-gold eyes blinked at me, and sandy-blond hair tumbled in waves down to his shoulders. His bronze face was so smooth, I had to stifle the urge to reach up and touch it. He smiled at me with great kindness, and dimples appeared in both cheeks. Mel and El were never going to believe it—he was an absolute hunk. I swooned under his gaze.

"You can call me Gregory, not sir," he replied. "I am here to escort you and Joseph to your destination."

"And what exactly is our destination, uh . . . Gregory?"

He smiled.

"We are going to a reception."

"A reception? For who? I'm not dressed for a reception."

"Oh, I must disagree. I think you are clothed quite appropriately."

I glanced down. My shorts and T-shirt had been transformed into an exquisite dress. The sleeves draped down to my fingertips in fabric that sparkled with greens, pinks, and silvers. Small jewels were woven throughout the velvet of the bodice and skirt; any movement created a kaleidoscopic waterfall. A pure-silver belt circled my waist with a clasp overlaid by perfect pearls. Bright, polished silver slippers covered my feet. I gaped at Gregory, dumbfounded.

"I believe my assessment is correct," he said as another shockingly attractive smile lit his face. "Please hold tightly to Joseph. We are nearing our destination."

I peeked down, expecting to see Joseph's blanket transformed as well, but it wasn't. He still lay wrapped in the soft flannel receiving blanket from home. It was shabby in comparison to the things Gregory and I wore.

"What about Joseph?" I asked. "Doesn't he get new things too?"

"Soon you will see. Be patient and watch."

As we crossed the flower-filled space, other tall, stately escorts glided in beside us from all directions. With brown, yellow, black, red, and white skin and robed in shining garb, they were all stunning to behold. Soon we had become part of a vast parade advancing toward the city. Although our ranks continued to swell, there was no jostling or crowding. We all stepped at our own pace, yet each pace flowed flawlessly with the next. Some escorts accompanied human figures, but most appeared to be by themselves. Gregory knew many of them and nodded in acknowledgment to those on our left and on our right. No one, however, exchanged verbal greetings. When we grouped closer together I could see that the escorts who I thought were by themselves actually had small bundles in their hands. No matter how hard I tried, I couldn't get a glimpse of what they held. They cradled whatever it was close to their chests, as if to protect their packages from curious eyes—like mine.

Climbing with ease past the jewel-encrusted layers toward the city, we drew nearer and nearer the colossal wall. The closer we traveled to the wall, the higher it became, until it obscured our view of the skyline completely. We continued upward on the golden road, which had begun to emanate soothing warmth. I peered down into it, searching for the source of the heat, but all I saw was endless translucent gold.

Suddenly an escort next to me announced in a clear voice, "Her name is Naana." He spoke to both no one in particular and everyone at the same time.

Then another proclaimed, "His name is Axel," and still another, "Her name is Sasha."

More voices joined in all around us, declaring names. Akim. Claudia. Xiang. Lee. Svetlana. Chidike. Pikatti. Christine. Julio. Arnold. Doris. Leilani. Paul. Kojo. Elsie. John. Fatima. Josephine. Todor. Min. Kamini. Antoinette. Soobin. Omar. Jesse. Rajasi. Hideki. Eva. Jacov. Baako. Thierry. Einar. Johanna.

Name after name after name streamed past my ears in a harmonious symphony. Though the announcements overlapped each other, I could hear each name distinctly and clearly. Every tribe, every tongue, every nation was represented.

I tilted my head to Gregory. "Why are they saying all these names?"

"They are christening babies who left the planet unnamed," he said.

"Are they *all* carrying babies?"

"Certainly. Each one has been sent to escort a baby to The Gate. Many babies already received their name on earth but there are many who did not."

"Who names them? The escorts?"

"No dear one. We simply give them the name written in The Book of Life since before time began."

"And how do you know that name?"

"We are told their name before we go to retrieve them, but we only speak it when we get nearer to the Great City and the Gate."

"What gate? I just see one ginormous wall."

"Soon, Pearl, soon."

The sound of the christenings lessened as we continued our trek on the golden road. A holy quiet settled upon the throng as we progressed. We drew much closer to the wall, and I studied the stonework intently. Not one stone appeared to be the same as the next, yet they all were perfectly suited one to another. Some had swirling agate patterns, while others were striped or banded in brilliant reds, golds, and greens. I reached out and caressed the wall's glossy surface. The stones pulsed under my hand as if a heart beat inside them. I leaned in and pressed my ear against the stones. They weren't just beating; they were singing. Gregory stopped beside me.

"If you listen, you will find that everything here has a song."

"Everything?" I asked, one ear still tuned to the wall's melodies.

"Yes. The stones, the road, the trees, the grass— even the air carries a tune."

Eager to test this new knowledge, I knelt and bent my ear toward the road, careful to keep Joseph cradled near my chest. Gregory joined me.

"What do you hear?"

I held my breath and listened.

"I hear drums."

He nodded. I bent closer.

"And, um, a trumpet. No, lots of trumpets. And a harp, maybe?"

"Ah, yes. A chorus of harps, actually. You have a good ear. We call it 'The Song for the Redeemed.'"

We paused and listened. He seemed as enthralled by the music as I was. We stayed for long moments.

I would have stayed for more, but Gregory stood and said, "Come. There are more wonders to see and hear as we go. But we must continue."

Reluctantly I joined him, uncertain of how anything could be more wonderful than what I'd already experienced. I was eager to see the Gate but content to travel beside this remarkable wall. All the while, Joseph slept peacefully in my arms. He was not heavy.

"Gregory, why do some escorts have humans alongside them and some don't?" I asked, hesitant to interfere with the sweet music but too curious to remain quiet.

"Some babies leave the planet at the same time as another human, and when that happens, the King of the Great City prefers to have the babies held in human arms all the way to the Gate."

"But why is that better?"

"The nearness of another human in this journey brings comfort to both parties. He wants people to be comforted in every way possible."

"Are the babies who come by themselves lonely?"

"Oh no, the King would not allow that. He arranges for them to sleep all the way to the reception so they will never have a lonely moment. Joseph woke up because you were holding him and your face brought him comfort. Clearly, his face brought comfort to you as well. True?"

"Yeah, that's true. He's beautiful, isn't he?" I said, looking into Joseph's slumbering face.

Gregory smiled as he peered down at Joseph.

"Yes, indeed, he is beautiful."

We travelled together contentedly as the living wall and road serenaded our steps. Time seemed to both matter and not matter at all. We walked a great distance, yet we never grew weary. Gregory hummed along with the tunes from the wall. He was familiar with them all. I'm not sure when the light around us began to swirl in all the colors of the rainbow, but soon billowing hues encircled us. They danced in rhythm to the music, bouncing, skipping, twirling, and swooshing. Some colors intertwined and blended into colors I had never seen before. Oh, the paintings my class could have painted with this indescribable palette!

The beauty all around us was so delightful, it overwhelmed my senses. When I thought I could take in nothing more, a wafting scent tickled my nose. It was so marvelous, I tasted and smelled it at the same time. I closed my eyes and inhaled deeply.

"What is this smell?" I asked. Cookies? A summer breeze? Cinnamon rolls? Christmas morning? And then I knew. "It smells like home."

"That is because we are getting close to the Gate and to the reception," Gregory said. "We are close to home."

WELCOMING COMMITTEE

Ahead of the great mass of travelers, something magnificent and massive protruded from the wall. All the colorful lights appeared to originate from this one spot. It was the Gate. It reached far above the height of the wall, far above any height I had ever seen a structure rise to before. Its doors were flung wide open, with a grand archway spanning the mammoth opening. I'm not sure how, but I was able to see the lofty top of the gate as clearly as the bottom. Words were inscribed across the archway in an intricate script. They pulsed and glowed as if powered by an inner life. I didn't know what they said, but they were captivating. I was about to ask Gregory when a luminous winged creature appeared at the apex of the arch and hovered there. It had the face of a man, the mane of a lion, and the body of an eagle. The creature soared out over the crowd before the gate, shot upward, and circled back to its post. It left a brilliant jet stream in its trail. A delighted murmur rose from our ranks, and excitement swelled in our midst. We had reached our destination.

Gregory guided me closer to the Gate until we stood beside the edge of one of the great opened panels. I expected it to be made of a precious metal, such as gold or silver, but it wasn't. The ornate grillwork glimmered with iridescent silvers, greens, and pinks. Butterflies stirred in my stomach. I shifted Joseph in my arms in order to compare the material of the gate with the buckle on my belt.

"It's a pearl," I whispered.

"You speak truth," Gregory said. "It is indeed a pearl. It is, in fact, *the* Pearl—the Pearl of Great Price."

"Mother says I am a pearl of great price. That's why she named me Pearl."

"I know, little one. You are privileged to carry the same name as the Gate of the Great City."

I paused to absorb those words. All the years of spurning my name melted away in an instant. I embraced it for the first time, appreciating what an honor it was to share such a divine and ancient name.

Joseph began to stir, calling me out of my reverie. His arms wriggled free from the blanket. He reached up to a swirl of light hovering just beyond his fingertips. He let out a giggle when the light bounced on his tummy and circled above his nose.

"He's awake, Gregory, and he's so strong."

"Yes, they are all awakening. It is time for them to be received."

One by one, the escorts approached the Great Pearl Gate, dwarfed by its immensity. As they did, people came out from behind the Gate, frolicking and leaping. They gathered in groups to greet the approaching escorts. In the crescendo of noise that accompanied their movement and the sheer volume of bodies, order was maintained. Everyone seemed to know exactly which escort to advance to, as though participating in an elaborate choreographed dance. When a group was fully assembled at an escort's side, the escort reached forward and presented the baby he held with great reverence to a chosen person in the welcoming committee.

Gregory bent closer to instruct me.

"Watch carefully. Soon it will be our turn and you will deliver Joseph into the arms of the one assigned to receive him."

"M-m-me? I don't know what to do."

"Do not worry. I will not leave you."

An escort in front of us reached forward with his bundle into a crowd of people. I watched eagerly. The blanket wrapped around the escort's tiny infant was a shredded, grimy rag that gave off a terrible odor.

"Why is that baby wrapped in such filthy rags?" I asked.

Gregory hesitated.

"This escort gathered him from a slum in a large city. His mother wrapped him in these rags. They were all she owned. She left him in an alley."

"What? How could she?"

"People have many reasons, but the main one is despair. She already had children she could not feed, and this little fellow was sick and small. She had to make a choice. Do not think poorly of her. She has suffered a great deal. If you knew her whole life and the darkness she has lived, your heart would ache for her too."

My eyes fixed on the tiny figure being passed from the escort to a waiting woman's outstretched arms. She held out a blanket that was blue and edged by pure white light. It seemed to vibrate with the same eagerness that showed on the woman's face. As the escort placed the baby boy on the blanket, the filthy rags instantly became as white as snow, melted into the fabric, and formed dazzling crystal patterns on its surface. The woman swaddled him into a secure bundle, using a technique very similar to Mother's. The baby's face glowed as the woman kissed his forehead. She lifted him above her head and pivoted to face the Gate. The people who had gathered around her also turned.

"You are welcome here, little one. You are welcome," they cried out in unison.

While the woman held him aloft, all eyes watched in anticipation. A Dove filled with light shone forth from the Gate and swooshed above the throng. It came to hover right above the child's face. The people cheered exuberantly as a voice came from the Dove, a voice so deep and profound that the road beneath us shook.

"Welcome home, My son. Welcome home," the Dove declared in deep, soothing tones.

The Dove's light encompassed the men, women, and children in the group in a crystal-like portal. They passed the babe tenderly from one pair of outstretched arms to another. Each one took a turn cuddling and cooing over the child. When at last he rested in the original receiver's arms, the group maneuvered back to the opening in the gate, singing, skipping, and dancing.

Gregory nudged me and pointed to another group gathered near the gate.

"Watch over there now," he said.

At our side, an escort moved forward, accompanied by a young woman. She held an infant in her arms wrapped in a pink, crocheted blanket. This was not a tiny baby but a chubby, rosy-cheeked eight- or nine-month-old. She faced forward and leaned out across the woman's forearm. Her hands and feet bounced in rhythm to the music from the wall.

The mother laughed and spoke into the baby's ear, "Hold on, Emma. We're almost there."

A large crowd came out to meet them, led by a gentleman who looked young and yet seasoned at the same time. His eyes twinkled as he approached the young woman.

"Hello, Rosemarie," he said. "We are delighted you are here."

"Grandpa," Rosemarie gasped. She flung herself and her child straight into the grandfather's outstretched arms. Her muffled voice drifted out through the crowd. "I can't believe it's really you. Oh, how I have missed you!"

The grandfather held them close and kissed the top of Rosemarie's head as if she were a child. They stayed that way for some time, savoring their reunion. The assembly around them waited in patient anticipation. When Rosemarie drew back from the embrace, her grandfather touched the shoulder of the woman next to him, urging her forward. She held a delicate, lacy blanket in her arms.

"Rosemarie," said the grandfather, "I want to introduce you to your grandmother." He bent down close to the baby girl. "And, dear little one, this is the woman who bears the same name as you. Emma, meet Emma."

"Oh my goodness," Rosemarie said. "I am so pleased to finally meet you. You are even more beautiful than your pictures. And you are so young."

Grandmother Emma laughed.

"You will soon see that everyone here is young and everyone is beautiful. You have your mother's eyes. What a joy to see you face-to-face! May I hold her?"

"Yes, yes, please do. But may we keep the blanket she's in? My mother crocheted it for her, and it's Emma's favorite. She had it in the car today before . . . before . . . I don't remember what happened, but everything changed."

"Certainly, my dear," assured Grandmother Emma as she reached for the baby. "You will see how He takes our favorite things and weaves them into something marvelous."

As the mother placed little Emma into her grandmother's arms, the crocheted blanket and the receiving blanket merged together into a marvelous quilt. Pink and frilly, the squares were edged in golden zigzags and shiny tassels hung from each corner. Baby Emma grabbed the sides of her freshly woven coverlet and pulled them up, immersing herself in its softness. The entire crowd laughed at her antics, which caused her to peek out, an impish smile on her face. Grandmother Emma kissed her on the forehead and lifted her high overhead. She squealed and kicked as the group shouted out its welcome. When the Dove filled with light flew toward her, she quieted and reached eager hands forward to hug Him.

He, too, seemed tickled by her antics, and there was a smile in His voice as He proclaimed, "Welcome home, My daughter. Welcome home."

The Dove shifted and hovered above Rosemarie. He repeated His welcome as golden droplets showered her in light. She lifted her arms straight above her head and dropped her head back to bask in the brightness. As she did, the Dove's light enveloped her completely and twirled her around in a gentle waltz. The reception committee watched and swayed to the rhythm of the dance, riveted by the luminous duo before them. When the last step was taken, the group applauded and cheered as the light from the Dove expanded to include them all. Each one came forward to greet the newcomers. It seemed Rosemarie knew them all personally, and cries of sweet reunion flew up from their midst.

Gregory tapped me on the shoulder.

"They will be here awhile," he said. "Many family and friends are eager to participate in their reception."

Another question flitted across my mind.

"If this gate is only for babies and those with babies, where do all the other people go?"

"There are twelve gates around the Great City: three on the north, three on the south, and three each on the west and east. Each gate is separate from the others, but all are made of the same Pearl of Great Price. Every gate has a guardian similar to the one we saw fly out from the top of the archway. And every one is named for a different purpose. This one is called The Baby- Catcher Gate."

"The Baby-Catcher Gate?!"

"Yes," he continued, unfazed by my stunned exclamation. "The King of the City is concerned for the comfort and care of these little ones. Every soul who comes to the City is equally precious, but these infants come with such pure hearts and vulnerable souls that He takes special care to see to their needs. These first moments are important. It is a thin place where the world's residue can persist if we are not intentional in receiving them with great love and wholehearted welcome. The workers at this gate were baby catchers or teachers or nannies or doctors on earth. Those who devoted their lives to the care of little ones on the planet delight to do it here as well."

"All the women in my family would love it here," I replied. "In fact, you sound a lot like them. I never imagined their work would be important here too. But then again, I never imagined any of this."

"He has prepared things no mind has ever imagined. Even those of us who live in this realm have not seen the height, depth, width, and breadth of all there is to see in Him. There is no end to His creativity, power, and wonders. He is awesome."

"Do I get to meet Him?" I was becoming more and more curious about the *He* behind all the marvels I had experienced.

"I do not know yet. Come."

RECEIVING LINES

We walked away from Rosemarie and Emma's reception and to the Gate's right side. Here the escorts formed two long lines that advanced forward at a steady rate. The lines were headed by two women, one robed in deep purple and the other in vivid blue; diamonds and amethysts shimmered in their curly, ebony hair. Beside each one stood an imposing escort whose luminous garments mirrored the colors in the women's robes. The escorts held large open scrolls in their hands. As the women met the baby escorts at the front of each line, they peered into the tiny bundles held out for their perusal. Then they turned to the tall escorts with the scrolls, who pointed to a particular spot on the parchment-like surface. They held a short consultation. The women then directed each baby escort to individuals who stood waiting near the Gate.

There were no large groups here. The atmosphere was quieter than at the other side of the Gate. But this didn't translate into a lesser sense of love or excitement; rather, it seemed to intensify it. The bundles the escorts held were very small. Some were so tiny that the escorts simply cupped them in their hands and cradled them close to their chests. No hand-knit blankets, quilts, or even rags wrapped these little ones. Only the escorts' hands covered the babies' naked skin.

"What is this place? I feel as if I should tiptoe here," I whispered.

"It is called the Preborn Entry. Here babies are received who never drew a breath on the planet," he explained. "The only life they have known is in their mothers' wombs, and for many even this life was very short. These are the most vulnerable."

"Who are the women at the front of the lines?"

"They are called Shiphrah and Puah."

"Well, those are good names for baby catchers. There were two Hebrew midwives in the Bible who had those names. Did you know that? Mother used to tell me the story."

"I am familiar with this history," Gregory responded with a smile.

"Mother always says they are her heroes because of how they stood up to Pharaoh. They risked their own lives to save the Hebrew babies. Pretty crazy, huh?"

"Oh yes. It is truly remarkable. I am glad you know their earthly story. It will be a real privilege for you to meet them."

"You mean they are *the* Shiphrah and Puah?"

"Yes, indeed, the very ones. They were willing to lay down their lives to save babies on the planet, so the King has entrusted this special task to them here."

I peeked at the head of the lines.

"Are they here all the time, every day and every night? They must be exhausted."

"There is no night here, and the gates never close, but time is not part of this realm, and neither is weariness," Gregory said. "You still carry some worldly residue in your thoughts."

"Worldly residue"? I decided to not try to figure it out, but to instead focus on my upcoming assignment.

"What are they reading from those scrolls?" I asked.

Gregory replied with the patience of a saintly tour guide, "The scrolls tell the exact times, places, and circumstances of these precious ones' lives. From these facts, Shiphrah and Puah determine where the little ones must be whisked to behind the Gate. The tiniest ones go to a pavilion called Marvelous Kindness, where they will receive intensive care. Others may go to the fortress called the Secret Place or the refuge called Under His Wing. It depends upon the particular needs of each little life."

"Is this where Joseph will be received? He's so big compared to most of the babies here."

"Did he breathe a breath on the planet?" Gregory asked.

"No, he didn't," I said. "Mother tried her best, but he didn't."

"We are in the right place," he assured me. "Let us see where they will send him and who will receive him."

Joseph squirmed as if he were ready to be held by a fresh set of arms.

"Hold on, buddy. I think we're almost there," I whispered.

He settled down, but his gaze flitted back and forth.

Before I knew it, we were at the head of the line and I was staring into the remarkable, dark eyes of the one named Puah.

"Ah, Gregory, my friend, I see you have brought us Joseph and his baby catcher."

She shifted her attention and smiled directly at me.

"Ma'am, uh, Miss Puah . . . I am not really a baby catcher," I protested. "I just had to go out with my mother to the Furness farm, and when things went the way they went, I just happened to be the one who wound up holding

Joseph in my arms, and then, well, somehow, I'm not sure how, we came here . . . together . . . ma'am."

She listened intently. A gentle smile lit her flawless, olive-complected face.

"Yes, I see," she said as she glanced back at the unfurled scroll. "But it does say here Baby Joseph and Pearl the Baby Catcher. We will have to look into that, Gregory." She peered up at him and winked. "But for now, Pearl, I need you to move straight forward. Take Joseph to the young woman in the blue dress standing by the door marked 'The Secret Place.' I am delighted to meet you. I have seen your mother's work, and I look forward to co-laboring with her in the age to come."

"You have seen my mother at work?"

"Oh yes." She laughed at my shock. "Sometimes the great cloud of witnesses gets to watch and cheer on our earthly cohorts. Your mother happens to be one of my favorites."

With that, she turned her focus to the next escort in line and the next precious bundle.

I stood there for a moment, dazed by this revelation. Gregory moved ahead of me toward a broad double door marked "The Secret Place." It stood wide open, yet I couldn't see what existed beyond the door besides more of the golden road. A single woman was positioned in front of the door. She had a brocade blanket hung over one arm. Gregory greeted her and waited for us to catch up.

"Pearl and Joseph, I would like to introduce you to Margaret," he said when we arrived. "She is of Joseph's family. She has been chosen to receive him."

Margaret's gorgeous black hair hung down one side of her neck all the way to her waist in a twisted, thick cord, like a Disney princess. Woven into the lustrous cord were sapphire, emerald, and ruby strands. Her dress was a deep cobalt blue, the bodice dripping with the same colorful gems as those in her hair. But all this faded in comparison to the startling blue eyes set in her porcelain face. When she spoke, her loving words flowed into my soul and set me at ease.

"Pearl, I want to thank you for caring for Joseph on his journey to this reception," she said while peering into my eyes. "We have been eager to receive him and get him settled in the Secret Place. I see he has grown stronger by being in your arms and drawing from your tender comfort. You were the perfect baby catcher for him."

If I had been at home, tears would have streamed down my face in relief and gratitude for her kind words. But no tears came, only a warm, joyful sensation in my belly. I felt as if I knew Margaret somehow, but I also knew that couldn't be true. What was true was that I wanted to know her and I wondered if I would get that chance.

"Thank you, Margaret. Would you like to hold . . . uh . . . receive Joseph?"

"Oh yes, very much. And I would also like it very much if you would call me Maggie," she replied as she reached out for Joseph.

Up close, I could see the brocade blanket in her arms was covered in an intricate pattern of small winged creatures. Hummingbirds? I carefully placed Joseph into her arms and watched in amazement as Mother's receiving blanket dissolved into the brocade blanket. It wondrously emerged as vibrant golden strands in the fabric's design. When Maggie folded the blanket around Joseph, the birds' wings fluttered as if joyful at their part in welcoming this dear child. She gazed into Joseph's face and he stared back. For a moment, they seemed lost in the familiar blue of each other's eyes. Maggie kissed him on the forehead. Joseph exhaled a contented sigh.

She then raised him high over her head and we turned to face the Gate. A rush of great happiness enveloped us. I jumped up and down, excited to be part of such a beautiful and momentous occasion. Gregory lifted his hands high in the air and spun around in circles like a whirlwind, shooting multicolored glints from his garments and rings. Joseph joined the merriment with a hearty giggle as the Dove filled with light swooshed out above him and alighted on the edge of his blanket. He grew still.

The kind, resonant voice spoke the words I had heard before: "Welcome home, My son. Welcome home."

The Dove lifted and fluttered right over Joseph's face. They gazed at each other, much like Joseph and Maggie had done moments before. Joseph reached out his hand, which sent the Dove spiraling upward. A snowflake-like trail followed Him and floated down on Joseph's face. This sent him into more delighted giggles.

When at last he quieted, Maggie said, "It's time for us to go. There are others waiting in the place prepared for Joseph."

"What will you and the others do there?" I asked, hoping to keep them close for a few more moments.

"We will care for Joseph and see that he grows strong. He is a pure one who will only ever know the ways of the King and the Great City. There is a great deal to learn here, and many will teach him. He will be in great hands, Pearl."

"Will he be among other babies?"

"Yes, dear one." She seemed to sense my reluctance to let them go. "We all need friends in order to grow and learn and enjoy life. He will have many, many friends. Of this you can be certain."

"Can I go with you to this place and meet his friends and help him grow stronger?"

Maggie glanced at Gregory and tilted her head slightly, as if to say, "Can she?" I wanted more than anything to walk through the door to the Secret Place. I longed to see the marvelous things prepared on the other side. I looked eagerly to Gregory.

"Do you want to go through the door with Joseph and Margaret?" he asked.

"Yes, yes, yes," I cried as I clapped my hands and bounced up and down. "Yes, with all my heart I want to go."

"Are you sure?"

I stopped my happy dance.

"Why do you ask me that? Isn't that why we've come all this way?"

"My instructions were to bring Pearl the Baby Catcher and Joseph to the Gate and to the line of Puah so Joseph might be received. I did not get instructions about your reception."

My heart wobbled.

"What do you mean? Do I not get welcomed and received the same as all the rest? This is home. I know it. I don't want to leave."

But as the words *home* and *leave* left my mouth, a haze began to settle around me. It cut off my view of Maggie and Joseph. Gregory alone remained clear to me. The door, the Gate, the wall, and the road disappeared. Abruptly, I found myself moving swiftly down a long, foggy tunnel once again. Soon all I could see was haze and Gregory. He held my hand. He had not done this before.

"What's happening, Gregory? Where are we going? Are we going to a different gate? Can I at least say goodbye?"

He scanned the space just above my head and said only, "Yes."

"Yes? Yes, what? Yes, we're going to a different gate? Yes, I can say goodbye? Yes. what?"

But he repeated simply, "Yes."

He wasn't talking to me. He was responding to a voice I had not heard. As I gazed into his beautiful face, it, too, became enveloped in the haze and faded from my sight. His hand remained in mine.

"Don't leave me," I whispered.

"You are never alone, Pearl. Soon we will be face-to-face again. Soon you will meet the King and see beyond the Gate. Soon and very soon. But right now, you have work to do and people who need you to be you. Be strong. Be courageous. Be gentle. Be true."

INTERLUDE: ILSA

She enters my study at a trot, the excess silken cloth of her sleeves billowing out like miniature parachutes at her shoulders. The blueprints scattered across my desk rustle from the breeze that blows in behind her.

"John, I saw her! I saw her!" she says, throwing both hands in the air before spinning around once and breaking into what could only be described as a jig.

I lean back in my well-appointed office chair, amused by her enthusiastic arrival.

"It's nice to see you, too, Ilsa," I laugh.

"Oh John!" She sweeps over to greet me with a kiss on the cheek. "I had to tell you. I knew you'd want to know."

She bounces up and down before me like a child before a stack of unopened presents on Christmas morning.

"Okay, I'll bite," I say. "Who did you see?" The possible answers are endless.

"Guess," she giggles like a schoolgirl.

"Ilsa," I sigh. She loves this game.

"Just guess," she says. "Okay, one clue: family."

Why she would be so excited to see a family member, I can't imagine. We gather together regularly. But I play along with the game.

"Well, obviously, it's a she. So, uh, let's see . . . my mother?"

"Nope. Guess again."

"Your mother?"

"Edna? No. But she was there, and she saw her too."

"Uh . . . Aunt Hazel?"

"Think younger than yourself," she says, urging me on.

"Younger? That can't be."

Ilsa continues her jig, punctuated by a singsong.

"Oh, but it can, oh, but it can, oh, but it can."

I cross my arms atop my lustrous mahogany desktop.

"Okay, I give. Clearly this is someone beyond my expectations."

She stops mid-circle and faces me.

"Isn't that just like Him? Doing things beyond our expectations."

She's right.

I stand up from my chair and step around the desk.

"Come, sit, and tell me who you saw," I say, taking her by the arm and guiding her to the settee near the fountain.

I hope the soothing splash of the water might settle her. She sits on the settee's edge. I lean back into the plush upholstery.

"I was just doing my job right beside mother and all the usual workers," she begins. "I walked through the double doors on my way to the assigned spot." Her hands demonstrate her movements. "I happened to glance to my left to see how the others were doing. It's always so fun. I love my job."

"Of course you do," I say. "But who exactly did you see?"

"Well, I wasn't sure at first, because she wasn't expected. And she had her back to me." Ilsa's voice fades to a whisper. "But when she turned—oh John! She's getting to be so lovely."

"Who, Ilsa? Who?"

"Your youngest."

I scoot forward, joining her on the edge of the settee.

"Pearl? At your work? Are you sure? Why would she be there? Are you certain it wasn't my oldest?"

Ilsa shakes her head, amused by the suggestion.

"I think I know one granddaughter from the next."

"But that makes no sense. Why wasn't I notified that she was coming? Why weren't we all notified?"

It's her turn to settle me down. She pats my hand.

"Perhaps because she didn't stay. She was there and then she was gone."

Ilsa relaxes fully into the settee and stretches her feet out onto the stonework surrounding the waterfall. I stare into my mother-in-law's satisfied grin.

"Here and gone?" I say. "Why didn't she stay?"

ON THE THIRD DAY

"*I'm here, Pearl.* I'm here. You're not alone. We've been here all along. We won't leave you," a voice drifted through the haze. It wasn't Gregory's.

"Mother! Mother, come quick! She's waking up!"

My eyes fluttered open. I found myself staring into my sister Susan's eyes. She sat next to me, her hands wrapped around my hand. Tears shone in her blue-green eyes behind the lenses of her glasses. She tried to smile. I tried to focus.

"Susan?" My voice sounded distant and hoarse. "Where am I?" I squinted and blinked. "Where's Gregory?" I attempted to speak again, but my mouth was dry and my lips chapped.

"Where's who?" Susan leaned forward. "Do you mean David? He can't be here right now, but I'm here, kiddo. I'm right here. Don't try to talk—just relax. I'll get you some water."

She retrieved a water cup from the bedside table. She placed the straw in my mouth. I took a sip; the water tasted divine. I sipped some more. Someone else came close and grabbed my other hand. A familiar touch.

Mother's touch. I turned to see her, and pain shot up my neck. I winced and closed my eyes.

"Take it easy, sweetheart. Don't move too quickly. We're here. We love you." Mother's soothing tone reached through my pain. "Welcome back."

"Where am I?" I croaked in a groggy voice.

I tried to open my eyes wider, but they were heavy. So very heavy. There was no haze, no Gregory, no Gate, no Joseph. Just sleep.

☐

The next time I opened my eyes, the room was dimly lit. No one held my hand, but there was pressure on my forearm. I glanced down. Mother was fast asleep in a chair, leaned over with her head lying next to my leg. One of her arms was crossed underneath her forehead, the other stretched out to hold my arm. I looked up and studied the room around me. Nothing was familiar.

"Mother?" I said, making an effort to push sound across my vocal chords. She didn't move. I lifted my hand and laid it on her head. "Mother, wake up. Please wake up."

Her head lifted briskly. Immediately she was alert, focused, and present. Someday I needed to figure out how she did that.

"I'm here. What do you need, sweetheart?"

"I need to know where I am. I don't recognize anything. I've been somewhere . . . but I can't remember where. And I don't know how I got here."

"Shhh, shhh, it's okay. You're okay." She stroked my arm. "I know where you are, and I'm right here with you. Everything's fine. You're going to be fine."

She reached up and placed her hand on my cheek. Her touch comforted me. I closed my eyes and took a deep breath, then another.

"Pearl, can you look at me?"

I opened my eyes and focused on her face—her lovely, familiar face.

"Good," she said. "I want you to *slowly* look around the room. It's rather dim, but I don't want to hurt your eyes. Tell me what you see."

"Okay. I'll try." I looked slowly to my right. "Well, I see you and a machine blinking red and green numbers and stuff next to you. There's a metal pole and a bag of liquid hanging from it. There's a plastic line leading into my hand—which kinda hurts, by the way. Do I have to keep this stuck in me for long?"

"Just a little while longer. We need to keep you hydrated and get you stronger before we can remove the IV. What else do you see?"

I looked in the other direction.

"I see a window with shades pulled down. I see a curtain hanging from the ceiling." My eyes traveled past the end of the bed. "There's a white sink and a mirror. And, uh, this bed with metal rails."

"Okay. Very good. Think for a minute. What sort of room has all those things in it? Do you know a place like that?"

"Of course I know a place like that. It's called a hospital." I paused as this information sank in. "Am I in a hospital?"

"Yes, sweetheart, that's where you are," she said, sounding relieved. "You are in a room at County General."

"Why am I here? Am I sick?"

"Not exactly. Do you remember the pain in your head?"

I nodded carefully, remembering well the pain my sudden movement had caused me.

"You had an accident. You hit your head. Do you remember that?"

I thought for a moment. My mind filled with colors and lights and snippets of songs I couldn't quite catch.

"No. I remember other stuff, but I don't remember anything about that," I said. "How did I hit my head? When? Was it before I went to the Gate?"

"The gate? No, there was no gate, just a long driveway. We were at the Furness farm together—you and me and Violet. Do you remember being there?"

Violet? The Furness farm? I tried to remember, but my thoughts were detached and disorganized. Chaotic pictures darted across my mind.

"Did something bad happen there?" I said. "Why do I feel scared?"

"It's okay. Don't worry about it," Mother said as she caressed my hand. "It will come back to you when you're ready. Just rest. We'll talk tomorrow."

Suddenly I felt overwhelmed and tired. My eyelids drooped, and sleep pulled me under once more.

☐

Sunlight streamed through the windows onto the speckled linoleum floor when I awoke. Papers rustled. Susan sat in a reclining chair next to my bed, reading the newspaper, her blond tresses swept up in a ponytail on top of her head, her bangs fortified with hair spray. The cutoffs and T-shirt she wore made her look like she was still in high school. She was one of those people who always appeared younger than her age, a fact she had always disliked, although Mother repeatedly told her that one day she would be thankful.

I rubbed the sleep from my eyes.

"Hello, Susan," I muttered.

The newspaper dropped from in front of her face.

"Well, hello, yourself," she replied. "You look bright-eyed this morning. Are you feeling better? Are you hungry?"

"Yeah, I think I feel better," I said. "And now that you mention it, I'm starving. Can you get me something to eat?"

"You bet," she replied as she folded up the newspaper and set it on the bed. "Give me a minute and I'll track down a nurse. You okay by yourself for a sec?" she asked with a tug on my covered toes.

"Sure, I guess. Where's Mother?"

"She went home to freshen up and change her clothes. She's been in the same outfit for three days. Wouldn't leave your side until she knew you were going to be okay."

"Three days? I've been here that long?"

"Yup. You arrived here early Wednesday morning. I got here on Thursday, and today is Saturday. Had us all pretty worried for a while."

"Why can't I remember what happened?"

"Well, you hit your head pretty hard. Knocked you unconscious and caused some internal bleeding. The doctors induced a medical coma to stabilize you for a day or so. They let you come out of it on your own. Your brain will recover when it's ready. Be patient."

"Okay," I said. "Now please, can you get me some food?"

She laughed and rose.

"I can see you're definitely on the road to recovery. I'll be right back."

I used the gadget connected to the bed to tilt myself to an upright position in anticipation of the promised food. I looked around. A cut-glass vase with bright-yellow daisies sat on the windowsill with a little, pink balloon that said, "Get Well Soon," sticking out the top. Several cards stood next to the bouquet, cheery and colorful. They were pretty. I realized I was hungry for something besides food. I scanned the room, searching for something, though I couldn't say exactly what. My eyes landed on a side table next to the bed.

Propped up behind a water glass and a packet of saltines was an abstract watercolor in shades of pink, purple, silver, and green. A sunset sparkling on a lake? Or maybe a close-up of the inside of an oyster? The vibrant colors lifted my spirit. Next to the watercolor stood a card with a butterfly sketched in charcoal on the front. The wings were so lifelike, they seemed to actually flutter. I soaked in the beauty. Then my eyes settled on a solid object in the middle of the table, nearly hidden behind the saltines.

I reached over and picked it up. It was a colorfully striped stone that fit easily into the palm of my hand. It was smooth, lustrous, and almost soft to the touch. When I flipped it over, I discovered a delicate flower etched into the surface. Its petals flowed with the stone's natural lines. The artistry refreshed my soul. Tears stung my eyes.

Susan entered the room with a nurse carrying a tray behind her.

"Your food has arrived, princess," Susan announced with a slight bow.

The nurse smiled and played along.

"On the royal menu today: lime Jell-O cubes, toast, and milk. Nothing too exciting, but it'll get you started."

Setting the tray down on the rolling table-shelf, the nurse turned to check my IV bag.

"Let me know if you need anything else," she said before heading out the door.

"Thanks," Susan replied as she pulled the table over my bed. Spying the stone in my hand, she said, "I see you've discovered your gifts from your fellow artists. They are quite lovely. Such talented people right here in St. Gerard. Who knew? Did you read the card yet?"

"Nope. Not yet," I replied as I scooped up a spoonful of the Jell-O cubes.

The smooth flavor exceeded my expectations. I closed my eyes and relished the sweet sensation of the cubes sliding all the way down to my belly.

"Do you want me to read it for you?" Susan asked.

"Yesss, pleassse," I sloshed out over another mouthful of gelatin.

"Let's see. It says:

Dear Pearl,

We were so sorry to hear about your accident. Hope you are on the mend and that you will be back in class soon. You have been missed. We start pottery next week. Our thoughts and prayers are with you.

P.S.—We thought you might need some pretty things to contemplate when you woke up.

They all signed it: Teacher Anne, Mrs. Wilson, Mrs. Grant, and Fritz. And they included a Bible verse over here. Psalm 27:4—'One thing I have desired of the Lord, that will I seek: that I may dwell in the house of the Lord all the days of my life, to behold the beauty of the Lord, and to inquire in His temple.' Very thoughtful friends you have there, short stuff."

"Mm-hmm," I agreed, my mouth full of toast and my heart full of beauty and love.

"I'm sure your friends are anxious to see you. Maybe Mother will throw a little reception for you when you get home."

A reception?

The toast stuck in my throat. I grabbed my milk and gulped.

MEMORY GAMES

Mother breezed into the room an hour later, looking refreshed and attractive in her polyester sundress. Susan commented on her appearance.

"Thank you very much," Mother replied. "I feel almost as if I've been born again . . . again." She set her straw purse and navy blue sweater on a chair and turned to me. "I see you've eaten. Feeling better today?"

"Yeah. I think so. I'm not quite so fuzzy. How long do I have to stay here?"

"Depends on what the doctor says. He'll be in to see you this morning. The nurse wants to get you out of bed to walk a bit. Are you up for it?"

"Sure. I don't want to stay here any longer than I have to. I want to go home."

Suddenly vivid images flashed through my mind. An overwhelming longing flooded my heart. I leaned back into the pillow, staggered by the power and pull of those thoughts.

Susan rushed to my side.

"Hey, are you okay? You don't have to walk if you're in pain."

"She's right, sweetheart, there's no need to push things," Mother said.

"I'm okay," I assured them. "I just thought of something—uh—something else. But I'm okay. I want to walk. Can I try?"

Mother and Susan exchanged a concerned look.

Mother shrugged and said, "Okay. But only if you're sure."

"I'm sure."

Mother nodded to Susan, who hustled out the door. She returned in a few minutes with a stout, middle-aged nurse in a crisp, white uniform. Her rectangular, black name tag read "Nurse Judy."

"So now, young lady, you ready for a bit of a stroll then?" Nurse Judy asked as she approached my bed with short, efficient strides.

"Yes ma'am. I think so."

"Okeydokey," she said as she moved my IV pole close so I could grab it. "Lizzie, you wanna assist? I know you've done this a time or two."

Mother nodded and moved to my side. She gripped my forearm and elbow, easing me off the bed to an upright position. A wave of nausea swept over me. The room wobbled. Or was it me wobbling?

"Easy now," said Nurse Judy as she grabbed my other forearm. "You okay?"

I took a deep breath and blew it out. Everything within and without settled down.

"I'm good," I said.

"If you get dizzy or nauseous or have any pain, you must let us know right away," Nurse Judy ordered.

I didn't say anything about the wobbling; I figured she meant in the next minutes and not the past moments. I wanted to walk.

"I'm good," I repeated.

"Okay. Here we go, then."

I shuffled across the room in my rough, blue hospital socks with my escorts. At the door, Nurse Judy fell back beside Susan and let Mother lead me into the hallway, where several nurses greeted me with smiles and encouraging words.

"Want me to come along, Lizzie?" Nurse Judy asked.

"I think we're okay," Mother replied. "We won't go far."

"Okay, then. Just holler if you need me. I'll be close by."

"You're doing great, kiddo!" Susan cheered me on from the doorway as Mother and I moved cautiously forward.

My legs felt heavy. Walking took more effort than I had imagined. Halfway down the hallway, I stopped.

"Can we go back?" I said, out of breath. "What's wrong with me? It's just walking. I feel like a dork."

"It's okay. You've done well for your first time out," Mother said. "You've been unconscious for three days, remember? Your body has spent all its energy on recovery. That takes a lot out of you, even when you're twelve years old. You need to be patient. We'll go a little farther next time. Maybe soon we can walk over to Violet's room."

"Violet? Who's she? Why is she here?"

Mother didn't answer right away.

"Let's go back to your room. We'll talk there."

I didn't argue. Something told me the answers to those questions were at the heart of my situation. As we made our way back, I struggled to remember why the name Violet should stir up such an uneasy feeling. But I had to abandon that line of thinking in order to focus on putting one foot in front of the other. Nurse Judy, who had been chatting with Susan in the hallway, met me at the door to my room.

"You did real good, hon, but let's get you tucked back into bed before you fall over," she said, having assessed my weariness from afar.

It took all my energy just to comply to her wishes.

"There ya go now." Nurse Judy patted the side rails after she locked them into place. "Take a good long sip of this," she said, handing me the cup of water from my bedside table. After checking my vital signs, she gave me a thumbs-up and Mother a wink. "Looks good," she said before heading back to her station.

Mother opened a packet of saltines and handed them to me. I munched them down. Susan rejoined us.

"What did Judy say?" Mother quietly asked Susan.

"She said go ahead and try, as long as she's not too worn out," Susan replied in an equally hushed tone. "It will give the doctor more to go on when he gets here."

The two of them drew chairs up on either side of the bed.

"Hello, I'm right here," I said. "Try what?"

Mother glanced at Susan, then zeroed in on me.

"We are going to try to jog your memory about the night of your accident. If you're too tired, though, we can try later."

"Do I need to be able to remember everything before I can go home?"

"No," Mother said. "But it will help us understand how your brain is recovering if we can poke and prod it a bit."

"Then let's do it," I replied.

Susan led the way.

"First, I need you to relax. Take a few deep breaths."

I complied.

"Good," she continued in a calm, steady voice. "Now close your eyes and think back. Tell me what you remember about Wednesday night, the night of the accident. Do you remember anything at all?"

I closed my eyes and tried to retrieve any memories. Wednesday night seemed distant. My mind remained blank. No images. Not even any colors. Only noise—barking and howling.

"Do sounds count?" I asked, hesitant to say it out loud.

"Sure," Susan replied. "Sounds can often link us to past events. What did you hear?"

"I think maybe I remember a dog barking . . . maybe."

"Hmm, interesting," Susan responded. "Anything else?"

I let the sound bounce around my brain. A grainy image appeared. I chewed my bottom lip and focused on sharpening the image. Then there it was. I sat up straighter.

"I remember the neighbor's dog barking and running along the fence," I said as the picture played in my head. "Mother and I were backing down the driveway. It was dark and windy . . . I think. Am I right?"

"Yes, you're right." Mother clasped my hand. She leaned forward. "Is there anything after that?"

I closed my eyes and searched my memory banks.

"Uh, I remember rain and branches flying across the road. And Mother was driving really fast," I recounted with growing certainty.

I opened my eyes in time to see Mother nod.

"Why were you going so fast?" I asked her.

"Can you remember why?"

I closed my eyes again. I didn't see a thing.

Frustration set it.

"It looks dark," I said. "All I see is darkness."

Mother squeezed my hand.

"It *was* dark. Do you remember why?"

"It was dark?" Something clicked. "Yes, it *was* dark. It was dark because the power was out. We could barely see the house, because all the lights were out. That's right, isn't it?"

Mother nodded.

"You're exactly right."

My pulse began to race. Susan continued to guide the process.

"Do you remember what happened in the house?"

I scrunched my forehead and concentrated.

"I remember a lady opening the back door. And I remember sitting in the kitchen by myself—in the dark. But I don't remember why we were there."

Out of the blue, a scene popped into my mind. Treetops swaying in the wind. Rain pounding on the roof. A blanket wrapped around my shoulders. Blankets? Baby blankets.

And then I knew. The entire night played back to me like a movie, from Mrs. Furness's mother running across the yard to the eerily lit bedroom to towels and blood and Mother and Violet—and Joseph!

"Joseph," I squealed and sat upright.

A jolt of pain accompanied my sudden movement and I clamped my eyes shut. Mother and Susan grabbed my arms. I shook them off and blinked away the pain, determined to continue with the revelation.

"We were there to help Violet have her baby," I said. "Her mother left, and I had to help with the towels and the leg and the baby. And he was tiny and so still. And Mother, you tried and tried to get him to breathe. But he wouldn't. And Violet needed you, so you handed him to me. You told me to pray. He didn't look so good. But I swaddled him tight and I held him like you told me to."

My tumbling words slowed to a crawl as I relived those moments in the thin place.

"And then I saw Mother. She was kneeling on the floor. She looked up and cried out 'Help! Dear God, help!'" I turned to Mother. "I wanted to stay and help you, but he said it would be okay. I saw the ambulance coming and the white pickup truck. I knew you were going to be okay, or I never would have left. But they needed me to go. We had to get Joseph to his reception."

Susan and Mother stared at me.

"What's wrong?" I asked. "I'm right. I know I'm right."

They shared a look.

"Yes. Yes, you're right," Mother said. "I was there to help Violet with her labor and delivery. You did have to assist me. You are correct."

She spoke carefully. Too carefully.

"Isn't that what happened?" I asked.

"Well, yes, that's pretty much what happened." Mother paused and took a deep breath before she asked, "But, sweetheart, who is Joseph?"

Was she joking? I studied her face. Nope, definitely not joking.

"Joseph is Violet's baby boy. He's the baby I wrapped up in the blanket. I held him in my arms all the way to the Gate of the Great City. I never put him down until it was time for him to be received."

Again, Mother and Susan stared at each other. There was a long, awkward silence.

"Do you want me to be more specific?" I asked. "Do you want me to tell you about Gregory? Or the wall? Or maybe the rest of the escorts? Or how about Joseph's reception? What do you want me to tell you?" They remained silent. "Okay. You're kind of tripping me out here. I start to remember everything, and you stare at me as if I'm an alien."

"Oh, Pearl, we're so sorry," Mother said. "You're doing great. All the things you're remembering—it's just," she paused and stole a glance at Susan. "Well, some things are different than what actually happened."

"What do you mean, *different*? Different how?"

I eased back against my pillow and crossed my arms.

"It's okay, Mom. I'll tell her," Susan spoke up.

A sense of foreboding crept into my gut as Susan cleared her throat.

"Uh . . . well, there's no easy way to say this, so I'll just say it." She smoothed a wrinkle out of my blanket before resuming. "Violet's baby boy was, uh . . . stillborn." She paused and studied my reaction before she went on. "He never took a breath, Pearl. Mother tried to revive him, but she couldn't. You saw that, didn't you?"

"Yes, I did," I said. "I saw how tiny he was and kinda grayish. I saw all that when I first wrapped him in the blanket and sat down to hold him."

"Okay, good," Susan said. "So why do you talk about him as if he's, well, you know . . . alive? And why do you call him Joseph?"

"I talk like he's alive because he *is* alive," I stated, growing more and more annoyed by her strange questions and attitude. "And I call him Joseph because that is his name."

Period. Exclamation point. End of story. I was tired of the let's-jog-Pearl's-memory game.

A knock on the door interrupted the growing tension in the room. A doctor strode in. Mother and Susan scooted their chairs back and stood up. The doctor was an older man with silver hair and brown eyes crowned by fuzzy, white eyebrows. A stethoscope hung around his neck, one end tucked into the breast pocket of his crisp, white lab coat, which fit snugly around his generous belly.

"Hello again," he greeted Mother and Susan with a brusque nod. "I see my patient is awake. Heard a report from Nurse Judy that she's even been up and about."

"We did go for a little walk down the hallway," Mother replied.

"And she is making some interesting progress with her memory. I'd say she's, ah, improving," Susan added.

I detected grains of skepticism in their reports.

"Hmm, well, I'll be the judge of that," he said as he turned his back on them. "Good morning, young lady. I'm Dr. Brown."

He held out his hand and we shook. He did not let go.

"Is that all you've got?" he asked as he tightened his grip, a challenge in his eyes.

I clamped his hand as hard as I could and returned his stare.

"Not bad," he said, releasing my hand. "Not bad." He moved to the end of my bed and pulled a clipboard with my files from a metal slot on the footboard, his movements efficient and sharp. "Let's see what we've got here," he said as he pored over the nurses' notes. "Hmm, well . . . okay."

I forced myself to shake off the agitation from my conversation with Mother and Susan. Dr. Brown was the one writing my ticket out of there.

"Dr. Brown," I said. "I am feeling much better today. I've started to remember lots of things. My mother and sister have been really helpful in jogging my memory."

"Hmm, interesting," he muttered without looking up.

Well, that went well, I thought.

Another minute passed before he finally turned and approached me.

"How's the head feeling?" he asked.

He set the clipboard down on the side table and moved closer to check the dressing on the side of my head. He pressed around the wound he had stitched up— apparently my head had split open on the jagged edge of the metal lantern on Violet's bedroom floor. His touch was gentler than his bedside manner.

"Any pain when I do this or when you move your head around?"

"No, not really," I assured him. "Only if I do somersaults."

One bushy eyebrow cocked. He continued his questions. As he checked my vital signs, Mother and Susan huddled together near the window. Their conversation was hushed. Susan's hands fluttered up and down. Mother nodded. Susan pressed in closer. Mother shook her head. I tried to interpret their body language, but Dr. Brown demanded my full attention. He had lots of questions. He wasn't exactly warm and friendly, but at least he didn't treat me as if I were from Mars. In fact, by the time he finished his examination, I felt quite sane.

"Doctor, do you think I might go home soon?" I asked. "I am feeling sooo much better."

"Your vital signs are quite good, and you are making progress," he answered as he jotted a few notes on my chart. He rose and placed the clipboard back in its place. Then he stuffed his hands into the oversized pockets on his lab coat and rocked up onto his toes and back onto his heels, as if the motion might settle the information he had acquired. "I'm pleased with what I see. In fact, I am quite surprised by how far you've come, based on what I saw when you first came in. Head trauma can be a tricky thing. Never quite know how someone is going to respond. I need to confer with the nurses and your mother. I'll combine all the information, and we'll go from there. Fair enough?"

"Fair enough," I replied.

Something told me the results of that conversation would not be in my favor.

Mother and Susan followed him into the hallway. When they returned to the room a few minutes later, I knew by the looks on their faces that the outcome was not good.

"He's not letting me go home, is he?"

"No, he's not," said Susan in her I'm-studying-to-be-a-doctor voice. "He has a few concerns, and he wants to keep you here a little longer for observation."

"Observation of what, exactly?" I blurted. "To see if I'm going to grow antennae or turn green?" I knew my attitude was sliding from irritated to sassy, but I was incapable of stopping the decline. "Why are you both acting so weird? You know what—I don't want to talk about it anymore. I'm tired and I'm hungry. Do you think it might be possible to get something more for me to eat? Even aliens have to eat, you know."

Mother raised her eyebrows along with her voice.

"Young lady," she enunciated crisply. "We are not trying to treat you strangely. We are trying to understand the things you have told us. You may need to be patient with us, as we have been patient with you. Am I clear?"

"Yes, ma'am." It wasn't easy to push Mother's buttons. But clearly, I had. I let my hackles settle down. "But I *am* really tired, and I *am* really hungry."

"I'll rustle up some grub for you," Susan said and marched out of the room.

Mother picked up the newspaper and folded it brusquely. Straightened the chairs. Threw away saltine wrappers. Put fresh water in the flower vase and rearranged the cards on the windowsill - her eyes carefully averted from mine.

BE STRONG

The rest of the day passed without any more talk of things remembered or not remembered. After lunch, I slept for several hours. I woke in time to see Susan enter the room with her backpack slung over one shoulder and my tote bag hanging from her hand.

"Hey there, kiddo," she said. "Have a good nap?"

I nodded groggily. She plopped the bag beside me on the bed.

"Thought you might need a little distraction. I rounded up your sketch pad and colored pencils."

"Thanks," I croaked in appreciation of her thoughtfulness. For the first time, I realized I hadn't really considered what it might have taken for her to be there. "How long can you stay? Don't you have to be back at school or work or whatever?"

"I have a few more days before I start my next rotation at the hospital," she answered, setting her backpack down. "This isn't exactly how or where I would have chosen to spend my break, but I'm glad it worked out. Mother needed some reinforcements. She was really worried."

"Yeah, I feel kinda bad about that," I admitted. "Thanks for being here and everything. I'm glad it worked out too."

She sat in the vinyl reclining chair, unzipped her backpack, and pulled out a textbook and notebook.

"I need to catch up on some reading, though. Hope you don't mind if I make this a study hall for a while."

"Nope. Go for it," I said, digging into my tote bag. "Where is Mother, anyway?"

"She went over to the maternity clinic for a while. She had to check on a client."

We spent several hours in companionable silence. She studied and I sketched, interrupted only by the occasional nurse checking my vital signs. I knew right away what I wanted to sketch—actually, *who* I wanted to sketch: Joseph. It took all my focus and skill to bring his image to life on the page. The hardest thing to get right was his eyes. No matter what color of blue I chose, I couldn't seem to find the perfect match. I blended and blended until I was satisfied that I had found the closest shade possible.

Dinnertime came and went. Summer twilight still glowed through the window. Susan munched on the leftover apple slices from my dinner tray while she continued her studies. I had just finished the final touches on Joseph's rosy cheeks when Mother arrived. She came bearing gifts: a cup of steaming coffee and a brown paper bag with "Oak Street Bakery" printed on the side.

"Hello, you two," she greeted us. "I see you've been busy," she noted as she nudged my pencils over on my table tray and set down the paper bag. As she turned to hand the coffee to Susan, she added nonchalantly, "I spoke to David on the phone."

"You did?" I blurted.

Susan nearly dropped the cup Mother handed her, but she managed to slosh only a few drops of the steaming liquid onto one of her opened books.

"Yes, I did," Mother responded with a smile, handing Susan a napkin. I couldn't tell if she was happy because she had chatted with her son or because she had shocked her daughters. "Well, I was at home for a few minutes when he happened to call," she continued. "He was a bit surprised to find me at home, for some reason. I think he was hoping to maybe catch his older sister who he seemed to know was home to take care of his younger sister, who was in the hospital. Any idea how he knew all that?"

Susan busied herself with mopping the pages of her textbook before she responded.

"I thought he should know," she said, keeping her eyes on the smeared pages, but with a note of defiance in her tone. "I called him before I left the Cities, and I've been keeping him updated once a day." She looked right at Mother and added, "Just because you're not talking to him doesn't mean I can't. Sorry if you had an awkward conversation. I totally spaced that I had told him I would try to be home this afternoon."

I was eager to find out what was in the Oak Street Bakery bag, but I was equally eager to see how Mother might respond to Susan's confession. Silence ruled for a few uncomfortable seconds. Mother met Susan's challenge with a steady gaze.

"I have no problem with you talking to your brother," she said. "In fact, I am pleased that you thought to inform him of what's going on here. My head has been in such a swirl that I honestly just forgot to call him. And you're right; he does deserve to know. I'm sorry if I've made you feel like you shouldn't be talking to him. The issue we have is between us, not between the two of you."

Susan sipped at her drink, acknowledging Mother's words with a slight tip of her head.

"We had a very civilized conversation, if you must know," Mother said. "At least once we got over the initial surprise of hearing each other's voice. World peace may not have been completely achieved, but at least the cold war has reached a temporary thaw. We kept our discussion focused on Pearl. He's quite concerned about his kid sister," she said, turning her attention to me. "He says to tell you he's sorry he can't be here. And he wanted to make sure you were getting all your 'vital nutrients.' I believe that's what he called it. So that," she said, pointing to the bakery bag, "is his idea—not mine."

I grabbed it and peered inside. A burst of sugar greeted my nose, wafting up from the chocolate-glazed doughnut and maple bar nestled in the bottom. I set the bag on my lap and clapped my hands. I didn't want to be too loud and attract the attention of the nurses, but I did feel the need to celebrate.

"Thank you, thank you, thank you! Just what the doctor ordered. Doctor David, that is."

"Doctor David the Sugar Pusher," Mother quipped.

"Doctor David the Concerned Older Brother," Susan corrected.

Mother nodded.

"You're right," she agreed. "He's a good brother, and I'm glad you kept him in the loop. Thank you."

"You're welcome," Susan replied.

I could feel the peace settle back into our midst. I paused before pulling out the first doughnut.

"Do you want one, Susan?" I asked, hoping she would say no but making the offer in an effort to keep with the spirit of harmony.

"Nah," she answered. "You keep 'em both. I'll enjoy my coffee."

She turned back to her books.

"How about one now and one later?" Mother suggested.

"Okay," I agreed, instantly torn between which to eat first.

Mother brushed my bangs aside and bent to kiss my forehead.

"Good to see you regain your appetite. Have you been sketching something? May I see it?"

I hesitated, unwilling to stir up the unease again. But there was no good way to evade her request, so I handed over the pad.

While Mother took her time examining the sketch, I blindly stuck my finger into the paper bag, deciding that whichever doughnut I hit first would be the winner. The maple bar won. I pulled it out and bit off a large, luscious chunk.

Mother leaned closer to the light fixture on the wall by my bedside to study the sketch more intently. Her back was to me, her expression hidden from my sight. Nervously I waited for her reaction. I took another bite.

"This is very, very good," she said, turning around to face me. "The colors are remarkable, and this face is so sweet. He seems sort of familiar." She returned her gaze to the sketch. Her head tilted quizzically. She peered back at me. "Is this Joseph?"

My mouth full of maple sweetness, I just nodded. Susan raised her head from her book, peered over her glasses, and reached for the sketch.

"Wait. Did you say this is Joseph? Can I see that, please?"

Mother handed it to her while continuing to stare at me.

"Wow. It's so real looking," Susan commented. After a moment, she glanced up at me and asked, "Are you telling us that this is how you saw Violet's baby?"

I nodded, wary of how they might respond. Mother pulled up a chair, sat down, and stroked my leg.

"Well," she began with a sigh, "do you think we might start all over? Would you be willing to tell us the whole story? I have a sense there is more to what we've heard so far. Am I right?"

I swallowed and returned her gaze.

"Yup. There's a lot more."

"Can I ask you something before you begin?" Mother leaned forward.

"Sure," I replied, hoping I had a good answer.

"How did you know what I said when I knelt beside you on the floor in Violet's room? What you described is exactly what happened, but you were unconscious. You had a strong pulse and respiration rate, but you were out cold."

I set the maple bar down. The rest would have to wait.

"I know what you said because I heard you say it." I licked the last remnants of frosting from my fingers. "I saw you kneeling next to someone. I couldn't see who it was. But you moved and I saw it was me. And you looked up to the ceiling. You were crying, and you said 'Help! Dear God, help!' I asked Gregory if I could stay and help, but—"

"Wait, wait, wait," Susan piped up. She set aside her book. "Who is this Gregory fellow? You mentioned him before. If you're going to tell us what you saw, you need to go step-by-step. Start from the very beginning, okay?"

I took a deep breath and closed my eyes. A fresh image of Gregory filled my mind. His last words to me echoed in my thoughts: "Be strong. Be courageous. Be gentle. Be true." When I opened my eyes, I was ready to begin. Mother sat straight up, hands in her lap. Susan stretched her legs out on the recliner, closed her book, and crossed her arms over her chest.

"Okay. I'll begin with leaving Violet's room. And with Gregory."

So, I started the story of my journey to the Great City with Joseph and Gregory. All the details reappeared in my mind's eye, clear and fresh. I described every awesome sight and sound I had encountered along the way. Mother and Susan's expressions ranged from perplexity to wonder, but they did not interrupt. When I came to the part about the lines headed by Shiphrah and Puah, I spoke directly to Mother.

She gasped and clapped her hands in front of her mouth, her eyes as big as saucers.

"You mean *the* Shiphrah and Puah? The Hebrew midwives? You met them? You talked to them?"

I giggled at her reaction. You would have thought I'd met Elvis. When I revealed that her heroines knew who she was and admired her work, tears filled her eyes.

"I never expected such a thing was possible," she said, bowing her head.

"I never expected any of it," I confessed. "It was all way beyond anything I ever imagined." I folded my legs crisscross applesauce and leaned forward. "One of the most important things I learned there is that the work you both do—this baby-catching thing—it's really important to the King. He loves each and every baby, no matter how big or small. No matter if they come from a poor family or a rich one. No matter if they are wanted or unwanted. Each one is received with so much love and excitement. It's hard to describe."

I stopped for a moment, spellbound as I remembered the atmosphere around the Baby-Catcher Gate. Both Mother and Susan sat in silence. I wasn't sure what they were thinking or if I even wanted to know. I plunged ahead with a description of Joseph's reception and Maggie—how beautiful and kind she was—and of the door to the Secret Place and how it stood wide open without revealing anything beyond it. I told them how I had begged Gregory to let me stay and go through the door with Joseph.

Mother stopped me.

"Did you really want to stay there when you knew how desperately we would miss you here?"

I wasn't sure how to answer her. The last thing in the world I wanted to do was hurt her. But I had to be honest.

"When I stood next to the Gate, I was totally content," I explained. "I didn't long to go home, because it *was* home. I didn't miss you or Susan or David or my friends. My heart was so full, there was no room for loneliness. Does that make any sense? When I saw you kneeling on the floor in Violet's room, all I wanted to do was stay and help you." I stared out the window at the deepening evening sky. The stars had begun to appear. "But when I saw all the stuff, all the wonderful things the King has prepared for us, everything and everyone else faded away." I turned back to Mother. "If I had thought about causing you pain, it would have brought me pain. And there is no pain there. I don't understand how it all works. It's hard to explain."

"I can see how that might be difficult. But thanks." Mother squeezed my knee gently as she spoke. "It does help. I've never seen or experienced all you have described. But I have seen enough in the thin places of my life to recognize that what you say is possible. Heaven is not far. In fact, it feels very close right now."

A gentle rap on the door interrupted us.

"Sorry to cut this short," the night-shift nurse said. "But visiting hours are over. Actually, they've been over for about fifteen minutes. You were having such a nice time together; I hated to shut it down."

"Perfectly okay, Delores," Mother replied. "We're about done, anyway."

"We'll get out of your way and leave this kid to get some rest," Susan added while she packed her books into her backpack.

"Will you be spending the night here again, Lizzie? I know the recliner isn't all that comfortable, but I can at least get you some clean blankets," Nurse Delores offered.

"No, I think our patient will be okay by herself tonight. Especially with you on duty." Mother smiled at Delores, gathered her purse, and bent over to kiss me on the forehead. "Good night, sweetheart. I think you are well enough to spend the night by yourself. My friend Delores will be right outside in the hallway all night. Is it okay if I go home with Susan? I sure could use a good night's sleep in my own bed."

"Have you been sleeping here?" I asked.

She stroked my cheek lightly.

"The hospital lets me stay with you overnight if I want. Which I have been doing. But tonight, we will leave you in the hands of your very capable nurse, okay?"

"Sure. I'll be fine," I said, trying to sound brave.

"You bet she will," Nurse Delores chimed in from the doorway.

Mother squeezed my hand and turned to go.

There was no further mention of what I had told them. I think they were trying to process it all. I couldn't blame them; I was just grateful they had heard me out.

Susan bent over to kiss me good night.

"Sleep tight, kiddo. Love you."

"Love you too."

That's all we said. It was enough.

☐

Mother and Susan arrived the next morning alongside Dr. Brown. He approached my bed briskly and began his list of questions, tests, pokes, and prods. After he consulted with the nurses and Mother, he signed my discharge papers.

"Okay, young lady," he said. "I am sending you home. But you are going to have to stay off your bike and out of the swimming pool for two weeks. Understood?"

"Yes, sir," I replied.

"I also advise you to take it easy on the somersaults for a while," he added with an unexpected twinkle in his keen, brown eyes. "But other than that, you are good to go."

I was excited to go home. A lot had happened since the last time I had been in my bedroom sketching bird wings. Had it really only been a few days?

Once we arrived home, Mother heated up a tater tot hotdish someone from church had cooked for us. We ate lunch around the kitchen table and discussed everyday stuff – Susan's classes, Mother's work, and my upcoming school year. It felt good to do normal things.

But then again, what was normal? My perspective on life had changed. How could it not?

After lunch, Mother changed into her scrubs and headed back to the hospital for an afternoon clinic. Susan began to pack her belongings to head back to the Cities. The move from hospital to home had worn me out, and I was ready for a nap. But I didn't want Susan to leave without talking with her about some things, so I sat on the front porch step and watched her load her bags into her rusted, yellow Toyota Corolla. The outdoors was intoxicating. The sun on my face, the breeze in my hair, and the aroma of freshly mown grass—I savored it all.

Alongside the house across the street, Mr. Schmidt was winding his garden hose. He swept a handkerchief across his brow and tugged his Twins cap back into place before noticing me.

"Feeling better?" he yelled.

"Yes, sir," I yelled back.

"Glad to hear it."

He gave me a thumbs-up and returned to his duties. He was as friendly as his wife was grouchy. I wondered what he saw in her—it had to be something the rest of us didn't.

When Susan finished packing, she sat down next to me on the porch. For a minute or two we sat in silence, enjoying being home, enjoying being together.

"Can I talk to you about something?" I asked.

"Sure, what's up?"

"Well, I didn't want to tell Mother, cause I thought it might upset her. I think I've caused enough upset lately. But I need to talk to someone who understands what it is to be part of this family. So, you're elected."

"Okeydokey. Shoot."

"Remember when I told you about meeting Puah?"

"Yeah, sure."

"I sort of left out one teensy part of that conversation. When we got to the front of the line and Puah read from the scroll, it said, 'Baby Joseph and Pearl the Baby Catcher.' I told her I wasn't a baby catcher. You and mother are baby catchers, but not me. But she checked back on the scroll. It definitely said 'Pearl the Baby Catcher.'"

I hesitated, uncertain of what to say next. She waited.

"I'm not a baby catcher," I blurted. "I don't ever want to be a baby catcher. I'm not like all of you. I hate being around women in labor and all that birthing stuff. I passed out at Violet's house because I couldn't stand the smell and the sight of blood. There was so much blood, Susan, and I just couldn't . . ."

My throat tightened, and tears stung my eyes. Susan scooted closer and put her arm around my shoulder. I leaned into her side, into the comfort of her and the familiar smell of her Herbal Essence shampoo. She patted my arm and waited for me to calm down. When she pulled away, she lifted my chin. We were face-to-face.

"For as long as I can remember, I've wanted to be a baby catcher," she said. "I wanted to be involved in all the things Mother and Grandma did. I loved going with them and listening to their stories. I loved being near mothers and their babies. It challenged and fascinated me. It satisfied something deep in my soul."

Her gaze shifted to her waiting car.

"In the middle of my classes and work, I have to remember those things. No matter how tough the process is to become an ob-gyn—this is who I am."

She returned her eyes to mine.

"You're different from me. You always have been. I mean, look at us. Even from the outside, we're different. I look like Mother—blonde and blue eyes. And you look like Daddy and David—brown hair and hazel eyes. We are very different. No one expects you to follow in my footsteps or Mother's or anyone else's." She put her hand on my shoulder. "You are awesome just as you are, Pearl. I'm not sure what your conversation with Puah means for your future. Maybe your definition of *baby catcher* is too narrow. Maybe you need to remain open to something broader. You'll find your place. It just might take some time."

I took a deep breath.

"I guess you're right. As usual."

"I want you to hear something else. . . . Your journey or vision or whatever you call it has challenged my thinking."

Her eyes swept out over the Schmidts' roofline. When she resumed, her words were quiet but firm.

"Daddy's death devastated me. You were only three, and I'm not sure what you remember about him, but he was a great dad." Her features soften. "He was funny, hardworking, kind. He was also really good at sketching and drawing. Same as you. When he died . . . the way he died . . . I couldn't figure out how a loving God would allow that to happen to such a good man." She shook her head and turned back to me. "I was furious. I slammed the door on God and faith and church. I didn't want to think about heaven. People who told me he was in a better place only made me angrier. I knew the best place for him was here with us."

She sighed and fiddled with the zipper on her sweater before she continued.

"I've been angry for nine years . . . and I'm tired. Tired of thinking of ways I might've changed the night he died. Tired of trying to make the world and life and death all make sense. I want to believe there's a hope I'll see Daddy again. But that's not so easy for me," she said, then paused. "I guess I've been afraid to hope. Afraid that hoping makes me vulnerable. The same way loving does."

Her words dropped. I let them sit. They were heavy.

I wasn't sure how other families operated, but in my family, we didn't talk much about our deepest feelings. Mother attributed it to our German roots, which I thought was strange since nobody in our family had lived in Germany for over a hundred years. I attributed it to just doing what we were used to doing. And we were used to not talking about difficult topics—especially this topic. Besides that, the age difference between Susan and me had pretty much prohibited any real sharing of our inner worlds over the years. This was the first time I felt like a sister and not just a little sister. I wasn't sure what to say. Mother's advice for such situations flitted through my mind: "If you don't know what to say, say nothing. Even a fool who keeps silent is considered wise." I kept silent.

"All the things you described have given me the courage to at least begin a journey back toward hope and faith." A slow smile spread across her face as she reached over to tousle my hair. "Thanks. Thanks a bunch."

"Sure. You're welcome." A burning sensation rose to my cheeks. It felt great to be my sister's confidant, but a little strange too. We sat quietly for a moment. "Uh, since we're on the subject . . ." I hesitated, uncertain of how far I could push this open-communication thing. "Is David mad too? I never hear him even talk about Daddy. And I know he stopped going to church a long time ago."

"Well, that's a good question," Susan said. "He's been pretty quiet about the whole subject since the night of the accident. But I did have an interesting conversation with Miranda this morning when I called to give David the update on your condition."

"You did?"

"Yup. David wasn't home, but Miranda answered and she asked all about what was going on with you. She seemed well-informed. I told her the latest news and then we just started talking." She shifted and leaned back against the thick wooden post of the porch rail. "I don't know her all that well, but we talked for over an hour. I can see why David likes her so much. She's a great listener. Naturally, we got on the topic of David. She told me that he has talked to her for hours about Daddy. About the accident. About how lost he felt. About his anger at God and Mom. About everything. I was amazed. It was stuff I'd seen in David but I'd never actually talked to him about."

"Wow, that's really cool," I said, hungry to hear more. It's funny how you can live in a family your whole life and not realize what's brewing underneath the surface of those you love the most. "Did she say anything else?"

"Quite a lot. But some of it is none of your business," she replied, drawing a line in the sisterly confidence sand. "I can tell you, however, that when I told her about your journey with Joseph and everything, she was very intrigued. Said she'd tell David."

"I hope he doesn't freak out."

"Ah, so what if he does, short stuff? A little stirring up is good for us every now and then."

"I'm glad I'm good for something in this family," I said, trying to lighten the mood. I had reached my capacity for in-depth sharing. I got to my feet and said, "Hey, you can't call me short stuff anymore." I rose to my full five-foot-five-inch height. "I'm taller than you are."

She popped up onto the step above where I stood.

"Not from where I'm standing." She laughed and drew me close in a tight hug. "I don't care how tall you get; you will always be short stuff to me. I love you, Little Sis."

"Love you too," I muffled into her shoulder.

She headed down the steps.

As she walked to her car, she turned and said, "Tell Mother I'll call when I get to the Cities. And you—no bike riding or swimming. Got it?"

"Yeah, I got it."

She got in her car and backed down the driveway. I waved at her until she disappeared.

How could there possibly be anything more to being a baby catcher than catching babies?

I need a nap.

THE POTTER'S WHEEL

Wednesday arrived and I strolled the ten blocks to First Presbyterian Church. My tote bag swung from my shoulder, my sketchbook tucked inside. My mind wandered as the sun dipped in and out of the clouds. Dusty whirlwinds spun in the sandlot next to the old creamery, kicking up dried leaves and bits of newspaper. A yellow-breasted warbler hopped from tree to tree, following my progress. I stopped. It stopped, too, puffed up its chest, and warbled a merry tune.

"Well, thank you. That was lovely," I said.

The bird twitched his head from side to side as if to acknowledge the compliment. I reached out my hand with a finger extended like a perch. It was something I'd learned from David, who had told me that Daddy had a knack for getting wild birds to come to him. David and I had tried repeatedly over the years to lure one in, but with no success. Even bread crumbs only drew them so close before they flew away. But I kept hoping and trying.

"I won't hurt you, Mr. Warbler," I promised.

He eyed me for a moment.

I held my breath.

And then he flew away.

Disappointed but not surprised, I continued on my way, wondering once again what life would be like with a dad. In my reverie, I managed to miss my turn on Madrone Street and had to circle back around the block.

When I walked into the fellowship hall, my classmates were already gathered around a potter's wheel at the far end of the room. They each wore aprons that covered them from neck to knee. Teacher Anne sat at the wheel with a lump of clay on the center of the wheel plate, her hair piled on top of her head in a twist with a pencil stuck through the middle. A bucket of water sat on a shelf that jutted out from the wheel, a sponge and other tools next to it. As she talked, she dipped her hands into the murky water. She wrapped them around the clay, and the wheel began to spin. Everyone was so engrossed that they didn't notice my entrance. The room buzzed with questions and answers between students and teacher.

I stood and watched, surprised by a sudden rush of emotion. I loved this class. Maybe this was what Susan meant when she talked about being with Mother and Grandma. I took a breath and shook off my sentiments, not wanting to be caught in my choked-up state. Teacher spotted me as I walked toward the circle. She smiled and continued to shape the clay, muddied water flowing between her fingers.

"Well, hello, young friend," she said. "Welcome back. There's an apron on the table behind you," she indicated with a thrust of her chin. "Might want to get it on before you get splattered by clay."

"Oh Pearl, we didn't see you come in." Mrs. Grant stepped over and gave me a quick hug. "Are you feeling better, then?"

"Yes, ma'am, I am."

"You gave us a scare. Of all the people in this class, you were the least likely to wind up in the hospital," said Mrs. Wilson with a laugh. "Welcome back."

"Thanks. It's good to be back."

Fritz stepped closer. He tried to say something but only managed a nod.

"I sure love the rock you carved for me. I carry it with me wherever I go," I said, pulling it out of my pocket.

His eyes lit up.

"Good. That's real good. Glad you like it."

I pivoted to the others, stuffing the rock safely back into place in the depths of my pocket.

"Thank you all for the beautiful gifts. They're all just perfect."

Tears filled my eyes. I dropped my chin and reined them in.

"Sometimes art is the best medicine," Teacher Anne said, the wheel still whirring under her hands. "Ready to get to work?"

I set down my tote bag and donned my apron. The others returned their full attention to the wheel, the potter, and the clay. Teacher talked as she worked.

"Remember, as the potter, you are in charge of the clay. You move and shape it to your intentions. However, you will find when you sit at the wheel that the clay will seem to have a mind of its own. The wheel's spin is strong. You will need to learn how to work with its force. You will also need to learn how to work with the piece of clay in your hands. It's not always easy to get it to conform to the image in your head."

We watched as she demonstrated. First, she drew the clay up with her palms. She then pushed down slowly from the top.

"See how I'm pressing down." She looked at us to make sure we saw her movements. "This is to make sure the clay is securely attached to the center of the wheel. This is a vital step. Don't skip it."

Then she drew the clay upward with a combination of fingers and thumb on her right hand while she pressed inward with the thumb pad of her left.

"Now we can shape the clay. The pressure you exert with your fingers or palms will do specific things to the clay," she continued.

The clay responded to her touch. A smooth, symmetrical bowl emerged under her expert molding.

"Oh, that's real pretty," Mrs. Grant exclaimed.

"Well, thank you. I have done this a time or two. But here comes the tricky part—lifting your piece from the wheel. Pay attention. It is a shame to get this far and then ruin it," she said while she scraped away excess clay from around the base of the bowl.

She picked up a wire strung between two handles and ran it under the bottom of the bowl. It began to slide along the wheel's wet surface. Teacher carefully lifted the piece up.

"Voilà," she proclaimed when the bowl sat safely on the table, ready to dry.

We clapped.

Then it was our turn. One by one, we plopped our clay on the wheel. We attempted to put into practice the things we had observed, but it was not as easy as it looked. We learned from one another's mistakes and applauded one another's successes.

When it was my turn, I instantly fell in love with the oozy texture of wet clay between my fingers. Teacher allowed me to test the limits of the clay and my knowledge. I failed quite miserably on my first go-around but loved the challenge. My second try met with better results, as did almost everyone's. Fritz's bowl was the closest to resembling Teacher's model. But it didn't really matter. We all had fun and we learned a great deal.

As we scrubbed the clay off in the deep kitchen sinks, Teacher asked if she could see my sketch from the prior week. Everyone else had already shared theirs. When we circled back to the table, I retrieved my sketch pad and took out my bird drawing.

"It's not quite finished," I explained. "I was in the middle of drawing when I had to leave with Mother last Wednesday night. And, well, I didn't get back to it."

They didn't seem to mind. Their remarks were encouraging as they passed it around. Fritz handed it back to me and I returned it to the pad. As I did, the sketch of Joseph slipped out. It skidded on the floor, landing next to Teacher's feet. She picked it up.

"Can you tell me about this sketch, Pearl?" she asked.

I wasn't sure I wanted to talk about it. I didn't want her to think the bump on my head had jarred something loose.

Teacher added, "You don't have to tell me if you don't want to. That's okay. But this is quite good."

She held it up for the others to see.

"Wow, will ya look at that," Mrs. Wilson commented.

"Real good," Fritz said as he stared at it.

"So lively and colorful," Mrs. Grant chimed in.

Their kind words gave me the courage to speak.

"His name is Joseph. He's the baby boy born the night I was hurt."

Teacher's head bobbed up and down.

"I see. Well, clearly you connected with this little fellow. The colors and the lines are very good. But the best part is the way you caught this baby's life and essence. I feel as though I know him simply by looking at this drawing."

The others murmured in agreement.

Her feedback astonished me. Had I really caught a baby on paper?

Just then, Mother appeared in the doorway by the stairs.

"Am I interrupting?" she asked.

Teacher turned to see her but didn't say a word.

"Figured Pearl could use a ride home." Mother took a few steps into the room and stopped. "Are you done?"

"Yes. Sure. Come on in, Lizzie."

Teacher urged her forward with a wave. Mother stayed put. I turned to retrieve my picture from Teacher's outstretched hand. She was staring at Mother with a funny, strained smile. Mother looked down and fumbled for something in her purse.

"May I?" I tugged gently on the sketch.

"Oh, certainly," Teacher said, still gripping it firmly.

It seemed as if she wanted to ask me something else, but then she smiled and let it go. I slid it back into my bag, said my goodbyes, and walked out, following Mother into the bright sunshine.

☐

Mother allowed me to stay in bed until eleven o'clock the next morning. With school days right around the corner, the opportunity for lazy, recuperative mornings would soon be gone.

Since I had come home from the hospital, she tried not to hover but I knew her mother-nurse eyes were always assessing me. The truth was I felt quite normal— apart from the shaved spot on my head where Dr. Brown had stitched me up. The hair was growing back. It itched like crazy, and I still had two more days before the stitches could be removed. But I figured that wasn't worth complaining about, considering everything that had happened.

Since I was under strict orders to not ride my bike, I had called Mel and El to see if they could hang out at my house. The weather forecast called for a warm, sunny day.

I told them to wear their swimsuits so we could run through the sprinkler in the backyard. Mother said she would make us a picnic lunch; it was the best I had to offer. They accepted.

I slid out of bed and stretched with the kind of stretch required after a good, long sleep. I donned my yellow bikini, pink smiley face T-shirt, and orange flip-flops. I brushed my hair carefully to avoid the stitches and drew it up into a high ponytail.

The sounds of Mother humming and making lunch lured me into the kitchen. She stood by the counter, chopping celery for our tuna salad sandwiches.

"Good morning, Little Mary Sunshine," she said as I plunked down at the kitchen table. "Why don't you get some paper plates and napkins from the pantry? I need to head off to an appointment shortly."

I pulled myself back up and headed to the pantry. I came back out with what I had gone to retrieve plus a box of Fig Newtons and a bag of chips.

"Can we have these too?"

"Sure. Just make sure you clean up the garbage when you're done."

The doorbell rang. I set down the picnic supplies and went to the front door to usher in my friends.

Mel rushed in, dropped her beach bag—which was overflowing with copies of *Teen Beat*—and hugged me fiercely.

"Holy cow, Pearl. I was so worried about you." She pulled back and held me at arm's length while inspecting me from top to toe. "You pretty much look exactly the same."

She swept into the kitchen in a blur of orange terry cloth to hug Mother. Perpetual motion—that was Mel. Or as Mother would say, "a force of nature."

"Uh, thanks, I guess," I replied to the space she had occupied.

"She means you look tremendous."

El walked by, draped from shoulders to shins in a striped caftan. She propped her beach umbrella against the wall. Her oversized book bag thudded as she plunked it down. She came back and gave me a side hug.

"We were quite apprehensive about your ability to recover from your accident. But it would appear you are thoroughly recuperated."

Despite the expansive vocabulary, I knew what she meant. El was officially the smartest person in our class; I was not. But ever since first grade, El and I had had an easy understanding.

It went back to the day I found her in tears on the playground. She had been born with one leg shorter than the other. A lift in one shoe made it almost unnoticeable, but when she ran, which she seldom did, there was a definite hitch in her giddy up. That day Reggie Dumfrey had mimicked her galloping gait for his buddies. I found her sobbing next to the monkey bars.

"Hey, Elspeth, are you okay?" I said to her. "Reggie's just a big, ole bully. He makes fun of me all the time."

She looked at me with alligator tears dripping down her freckled cheeks.

"Why?"

"Cause of my name."

"What's funny about Pearl?"

"Dunno . . . he calls me granny."

"He calls me Elf Spit," she said, wiping her sleeve across her nose.

We made a pact that day to defend each other from any and all bullies.

Things became easier for her when we abbreviated her name to El. She sympathized with me because I didn't really have that option. Mel, who joined our antibullying club, decided she would shorten her name also. Her reason? Melissa was too ordinary—the very thing Elspeth and I longed for.

El and I joined Mother and Mel in the kitchen.

"Hello, El. Care for some fresh-squeezed lemonade?" Mother said. Mel was already sipping from a tall, sweaty glass.

"Yes, I believe I would," she answered. "Thank you."

The ice cubes crackled as Mother filled our glasses with my favorite summer beverage. She untied her apron and hung it behind the pantry door.

"Your lunch is ready," she said. "I am headed to an appointment. I will be home around four o'clock." Before she reached the hallway, she turned and added, "There are fruit-juice pops in the freezer. Please keep the music down to a dull roar. We don't want Mrs. Schmidt calling the authorities. And don't stay in the sun too long, you two." She pointed to Mel and me, fully aware her warning was unnecessary for El.

We acknowledged her instructions, grabbed the girls' belongings from the hallway, and headed through the sliding doors to the fenced backyard. We each grabbed a beach towel from the stack on the patio table next to my blue Panasonic radio. Mel and I arranged our lounge chairs in the yard for the most sunshine possible. El arranged hers for the least, dug her umbrella into the sod next to it, and snapped it open. We returned to the kitchen to fill our plates and pick up our lemonade.

I tuned the Panasonic to 98.3 FM—the cool rock station. When "Waiting for a Girl Like You" came on, Mel dropped her sandwich and sprang to her feet. As she began to lip-synch, El and I grabbed our imaginary microphones and took our place as her backup singers. Mel danced as if born to a career onstage. El and I swayed awkwardly and giggled. The song ended. Mel grabbed our hands, raised them skyward, and pulled us down into a dramatic bow.

"I guess you really are okay," Mel remarked as we returned to our lunch. "I thought maybe you might be . . . you know . . . sort of different or slow or something."

"Honestly, Melissa," El spoke up. "Can't you be a bit more gracious?"

"It's okay, El," I said. "I get what she means. Head injuries affect people in all kinds of ways. I guess I'm lucky. I'm pretty much just the same old Pearl." As I said it, I knew in my heart that wasn't exactly true. "Just some stitches on the back of my head, which will soon be covered by hair."

"Ooh. Can we see it?" Mel asked.

"Sure."

I took out my ponytail and parted my hair to reveal the spot. They both leaned in.

"Hmm, not all that impressive," El declared.

"That's for sure. It hardly looks like anything. Well, that is a relief," Mel concluded, wiping the crumbs from her mouth. "Let's run through the sprinklers. I'm hot."

And so we did. The hours skipped by in carefree summer fashion. We pored over Mel's magazines, picking out our favorite hunks. I was tempted to tell them about Gregory but decided against it. They were my best friends, but neither one of them was very spiritual. Mel's mother never went to church. She called herself an agnostic (El said that meant she was someone who doubted that God even existed). On occasion, however, I had seen her father slip quietly into the back pew of Our Savior's by himself. Mel never came with him. El went to the Catholic church with her mom and brothers, but mostly only at Christmas or Easter. She said it was because her mom felt embarrassed about being divorced.

I knew I'd tell them all about my experience sometime. I just didn't know when . . . or how.

Mel kept the conversation flowing with talk about life in junior high, Scott Baio's latest girlfriend, and other important topics. We consumed the entire bag of chips and all but one of the Fig Newtons. Before long it was time for them to go home. They packed their stuff and hugged me before heading toward the front door.

"Can you guys come back tomorrow?" I asked.

"Maybe," Mel said. "I'll have to check with Dean and Francis."

"Who?" El and I said at the same time.

"The parental units," she said on her way outside.

"What about you, El?"

She stopped and faced me.

"I am required to go out to my Dad's."

She paused. A darkness washed over her face.

"Is he okay?"

"He seems, uh, unsettled . . . more than usual, even."

"Why? Are you sure you should go?"

"I don't have a choice." She tried to smile. "But don't worry. I am quite sure it has nothing to do with me or my brothers. From what I could gather from the latest quarrel between my parental units, something unfortunate has happened to his latest girlfriend."

"Oh. Uh, sorry," I said, not really knowing what to say.

She grabbed my hand.

"I'm really glad you're okay. I don't know what I would do without you."

Her emotions had reduced her to the use of ordinary words. I choked up. We might have cried had Mel not burst in from the bottom of the steps.

"Hey, Els-Bells," she hollered. "Let's skedaddle. I gotta get home."

El rolled her eyes.

"I am taking my leave, Melissa," El proclaimed. "Hold thy horses."

She descended the steps in regal fashion. Mel bent forward in a mock bow. We laughed. They headed to their bikes on the side of the house, arm in arm.

☐

By the time I heard Mother's car pull into the driveway, I had the yard mostly cleaned up. I walked past her in the kitchen on my way to the garbage can. She greeted me but didn't comment about the pink on the end of my nose. She seemed a bit preoccupied. I went to finish the cleanup. She moved to the coffee maker. How adults drank hot stuff on hot days was beyond me.

I came back in, towels draped around my neck and the last Fig Newton hanging from my lips. I dropped the magazines Mel had loaned me on the counter and headed to the laundry room while consuming the cookie hands free—a trick I had learned from David. When I came back, Mother stood next to the kitchen sink, staring out the window.

"Did I forget some stuff out there?" I asked.

She spun around.

"Huh? Oh, no . . . no. The backyard looks fine. Thanks for picking up. Did you girls have fun?"

"Yeah. It was nice. I'm gonna take a shower."

"Okay, fine, good idea," she said. "Uh, say, when you get done, can we chat?"

"Sure." I started across the kitchen, my flip-flops smacking and whacking against my heels. I paused in the hallway, then turned around and went back. "Are you okay? You seem kinda worried. I can wait to shower if you want to chat right now."

"Guess I'm not hiding my concern too well," she said with a soft exhale. "I would appreciate that, sweetheart. Let me pour a cup of coffee. Do you want more lemonade?"

"No, I'm fine," I said as I flip-flopped back to the table and sat down. "But you're starting to freak me out a little. What's going on?"

She picked up her coffee. As I plopped onto the vinyl kitchen chair, I wished I had one of the beach towels I left in the laundry room; my nose wasn't the only pink part of my body. Mother leaned against the kitchen counter.

"The client I went to see this afternoon was Violet Furness."

She sighed. I waited for her to go on. She didn't.

"How's she doing?" I asked. "Is she at home?"

She looked right at me, but her thoughts seemed far away.

"Yes, she's back at home. She's fine physically, but her mother is quite concerned about her emotional well-being. And rightly so." She paused. "I wouldn't tell you this, except I think maybe you can help. Violet is physically capable of being up and about, but she refuses to get out of bed. She doesn't eat. She won't let her mother open the curtains or turn the lights on in her room. I understand she's grieving and she needs to grieve. But something has me troubled. I have this sense . . . she's trying to die."

My eyebrows shot up. This was serious.

"I am intimately acquainted with the pain of traumatic grief," said Mother as she sat at the table across from me. "I know what it is to wish you could die to stop the pain. But do you know what kept me alive after your daddy died?"

I shook my head. Mother had never talked with me about her grief. Was she about to tear out her German roots? I sat very still.

"What kept me breathing was hope," she began slowly. "It wasn't the fact that other people needed me or loved me. Somehow, that wasn't enough. At least, not at first." Her words gained momentum as she talked. "The thing that got me through the first days of loss and shock was the hope that one day your daddy and I would be reunited. I am not sure I would have survived without that hope."

I nodded, solemnly acknowledging her confession.

"Humans are not designed to have our love and our lives interrupted by death," she said. "Even though these bodies we live in wear out and die, there is a part of us that is eternal. And that part cannot accept separation from those we love. That part needs hope to continue." She took a sip from her coffee and gazed out the window. "Violet doesn't have any hope."

I began to wonder what this had to do with me.

As if in tune with my every thought, she asked, "Would you be willing to go with me out to the Furness farm? Would you talk to Violet? Could you tell her the things you told us? Especially about her baby. About Joseph."

Could I? It was hard enough getting Mother and Susan to believe me. What would other people think? But Violet wasn't just anyone. Maybe she deserved to hear it more than anyone.

"I guess," I started hesitantly. I put my arms on the table and hung my head. "But I'm not so sure. Maybe she won't listen to me. I'm just a kid."

"I know this is a lot to ask. But I can't think of anything else that would be more helpful for Violet than to listen to what God has done for her baby." She reached over and touched my forearm. "You can keep your experience to yourself if you want. Or you can use it to help others. It's up to you."

I closed my eyes to think. Instantly, Gregory popped into my mind. He'd said I had work to do and people who needed me to be me. I opened my eyes and looked at Mother.

"Okay. I'll try."

WORK TO DO

Mother sat on my bed. "Sleeping beauty," she said while brushing the hair back from my face. "Time to wake up."

I blinked, struggling to rise through my sleepy haze. She rubbed my back and waited. It was a peaceful way to emerge from dreams into reality.

"I need to go to the hospital for a morning clinic," she said when my eyes were open and focused. "I've arranged for us to go out to the Furness farm at one thirty this afternoon. I'll pick you up by one o'clock. Can you be ready to go?"

I nodded, ready to slip back into slumber. One thought kept me above the brink of sleep. As Mother got up to leave, I managed to mutter, "Should I take the sketch with me?"

She stopped and turned back to me.

"Do you want to?"

I hesitated a moment.

"What if she wants to keep it?"

"Well, she might. Are you willing to let her have it?"

"I'm not sure. It is her baby . . . but I like to be able to look at it."

Mother came back and sat down next to me.

"How about this?" she suggested. "What if I take the sketch to work and make a color copy at the hospital? We have a high-quality copier in the main office. Let me talk to the secretary and see what she says. Okay?"

I nodded and pointed to my sketch pad atop my dresser. She tousled my hair quickly before I snuggled back under the covers.

I was out of bed, showered, and ready to go long before one o'clock. Once fully awake, I wondered if this was such a good idea. What if I just made things worse? What if Violet got mad that I saw her baby alive and she didn't? What if she got embarrassed or irritated that a twelve-year-old helped deliver her baby? What if she thought it was my fault he was stillborn? My mind raced through all kinds of scenarios, none of them good.

I tried to watch TV, but the talk shows and soap operas only fed my anxieties—too much drama. I tried flipping through magazines, but those people's lives looked too perfect. I tossed them aside and made a peanut butter-and-jelly sandwich. Real life, I concluded as I licked the peanut butter from the knife, was mainly lived in between the two extremes of drama and perfection. I dropped the knife into the sink. It wasn't going to be an in-between kind of day. But which way would it swing? I didn't know.

I took my lunch out onto the front porch and sat on the top step, happy for the shade the overhang provided. It was a muggy August day. I munched my potato chips, which were a bit on the soggy side from all the humidity. A welcome breeze pushed puffy clouds across the summer sky like a heavenly flotilla.

"Lord, please help me today." I directed my plea into the clouds. "Help me make things better and not worse. And if You think this is a really bad idea, please tell Mother. I am willing to call the whole thing off."

Our car pulled into the driveway as I finished my last-ditch prayer.

Mother rolled down the window and yelled, "Let's go, Pearl."

She was sticking with the plan. I resigned myself to the task before me and took my dishes back into the kitchen. She waited while I locked the front door. As I settled into the passenger seat, she pulled out a manila file folder and handed it to me.

"Look inside. I think you'll be pleased," she said, putting the car into reverse.

I buckled my seat belt and opened the folder. Inside lay my original sketch and two colored copies. I held the original up next to a copy. Some of the texture of the original was lost, but the colors were accurate. Even Joseph's eyes shone with the blue I had worked so hard to capture. Mother glanced in my direction.

"What do you think?"

"Pretty good," I replied.

"I got an extra copy for Susan. Don't you think she would like that?"

"Yeah, she might."

I hadn't told Mother about my last conversation with Susan. Maybe she knew more about Susan's struggles than I knew—as mothers usually do. But I wasn't going to risk breaching a confidence I had so recently gained by volunteering information.

We were quiet for the rest of the drive, each locked into our own thoughts. Two miles past the city limits, Mother tuned the radio to the local news. We listened to the sports scores, the farm report, the stock exchange numbers, and Paul Harvey. I fantasized for a moment about hearing my story on his broadcast one day. The story of Pearl, her mother, the delivery of a baby one stormy night—and the rest of the story.

Before long, we turned into the Furness farm's long driveway. The day was bright and soft, nothing like the last time we had been there together. My stomach still tumbled at the sight of the house as we drove past the grove of trees. I truly had no idea what the rest of the story would be, but we were about to find out.

Violet's mother, dressed in elastic-waisted jeans and a striped cotton blouse, stood in the back doorway, shielding her eyes and waving. I tucked the original sketch into the folder and left the two copies on the seat as I got out of the car. Mother strode toward the house. She carried a small briefcase she called her follow-up bag. I wasn't sure what was in it exactly, but I felt better knowing she was prepared. I still wasn't convinced my part in this scheme was the best idea. But I was in too deep to back out.

As I entered the kitchen, Mrs. Furness's mother greeted me with a firm handshake.

"Pearl, I don't think we were ever properly introduced the other night. I'm Mrs. Peterson—Violet's mother. I sure am glad to see you up and about. You look a whole lot better than the last time I saw ya lying next to Violet in the ambulance. Wasn't sure what was gonna happen to either one of ya. Just said my prayers and trusted the good Lord to figure it all out. Come on in."

I moved into the kitchen and set my folder on the table. Mrs. Peterson shut the screen door, leaving the other door open. She dabbed a finger across her beaded upper lip.

"Hopin' we might catch a breeze if I leave that open," she said. "It's real stuffy in here, and the one fan we got ain't workin'."

I slowly soaked in the room's details. Everything appeared so different in daylight. It was actually a cheery little kitchen. Neat and tidy. A wildflower bouquet arranged in a mason jar sat on the windowsill above the sink. The window was raised, and the checkered curtains puffed up and down with the hoped-for breeze. It didn't seem like the same room I had been in the night Joseph was born.

Mother and Mrs. Peterson conversed in hushed tones while Mrs. Peterson poured them each a cup of coffee.

"Would ya like some Kool-Aid, Pearl? Or maybe a glass of water?" Mrs. Peterson asked.

"Water would be fine," I replied.

Mother winked her approval.

We each took a seat by the table. A plate of snickerdoodles sat in the middle.

"Help yourself," Mrs. Peterson said, pushing the plate across the table to me. "Baked 'em yesterday. They're Violet's favorite. Was hopin' I might get her to at least take a bite."

I checked with Mother. She nodded. I took one.

"Thanks. These are one of my favorites too."

Mother shook off the offer with her hand.

"No thanks," she said. "Coffee's good."

I took a bite but could barely swallow. My mouth was dry as a desert. I drank my water and set the rest of the cookie aside. Mrs. Peterson and Mother sipped their coffee. We sat silently. No eye contact. A tension lay among the three of us; I wasn't the only one wondering how it was all going to go. Finally, Mother spoke up.

"Mrs. Peterson says Violet is much the same as yesterday. She still is refusing to eat and will only drink when urged to do so. She has been told you and I would be here this afternoon and that you, in particular, have something special to tell her. She has not responded to this information. So, what she has processed regarding our visit is unclear at this point." She paused. She sipped. She squared her shoulders. "I think it best for me to go in alone at first. I'll check her vital signs. I will reiterate that Pearl is here. Hopefully I can get her to agree to listen to what she has to say. How does that sound?"

I shrugged. I didn't have a better plan.

"Give it a go," said Mrs. Peterson,

Mother picked up her briefcase and went down the hallway to Violet's bedroom. She left the door open. I could vaguely make out her instructions to Violet as she took her heart rate, temperature, and blood pressure. Mrs. Peterson and I didn't talk. I took another bite of the cookie. Any other day, the sweet morsel would have been devoured, but my nerves had somehow deadened my taste buds and dried up my saliva glands. I took another swig of water.

Mother finished her exam but remained in the bedroom, talking to her client. Her tone shifted. It became less professional, more personal. She was doing all she could to reach Violet. The minutes dragged on, and still I heard Mother's tender pleadings. I was so entrenched in my eavesdropping that I jumped when Mrs. Peterson patted my hand.

"So, what's that there in your folder, dear? Is it your artwork?" she asked. "Your mother tells me you're in an art class this summer. Mind if I have a peek?"

I kept my gaze down. I hesitated. She patted my hand again.

"It's alright, dear. No need to show me. I was just curious."

The wall clock ticked above us. A tractor rattled by on the highway.

"Seems your Mother is having a hard time of it," she said, swatting at a fly that buzzed above the cookies. She covered the plate with a napkin. "I've been so hopin' maybe you two might get through to Violet. I haven't been able to. She's in a dark place, she is. Don't know how to reach her. It's a hard thing for a mother to watch her child suffer."

Her focus drifted to the back bedroom. Tears swam in her eyes. I opened the folder and held up Joseph's picture. She turned to it and stared in bemusement. I had seen others react to the picture, but never with such utter bewilderment. Neither one of us spoke. She reached for the picture while pulling up her glasses, which hung from a chain around her neck. Placing them on the end of her nose, she examined the sketch like a surveyor poring over a map.

"Where did you get this picture?" she asked, peering over the top of her glasses.

"I drew it."

"How? Were you copyin' a photo?" she said, still staring at me.

"I, uh, drew the sketch from memory."

"From memory?" She looked back at the sketch, then back at me. "You couldn't possibly have seen this baby unless you saw an old photo. Course, the hair ain't quite the right color . . . but the eyes . . . my, my, my."

"No," I replied, trying to remain polite but still firm. "I didn't see an old photo. I actually saw this baby." A trickle of sweat ran between my shoulder blades. "This is Violet's baby."

Mrs. Peterson pulled her glasses off her nose and stared at me. Her look was so intense that it scared me. She put the glasses back on. She methodically examined the picture a second time.

"Excuse me, Mrs. Peterson, but did you think the picture was of someone else?"

She faced me and removed her glasses. They dangled from their beaded cord. Her face softened, and tears brimmed her eyes again, threatening to overflow. She reached for my hand and squeezed.

"Did you know that Violet has a twin brother?" she began. "Vernon is his name. He lives about two hours west of here. He's been callin' every day, checking on Violet. Wants her to come stay with him and his family. Anyways, when Vernon was a baby, he looked just like this here picture. His hair was real blond, though. Not quite so coppery. Maybe Violet's got a photo around here of the two of them when they were small." She scanned the photos stuck on the fridge. "If I can find one, you'll see what I'm talkin' about. Course, you won't be able to see the colors, seein' as those pictures are probably black-and-white. But believe me when I say this color here," she pointed at Joseph's eyes, "this is the exact blue of Vernon's eyes." She gazed at my drawing and shook her head. "But you're tellin' me this is Violet's baby boy?"

"Yes, ma'am. That's the truth."

Footsteps sounded in the hallway. Mrs. Peterson and I turned our heads. Mother stopped in the doorway. She set her briefcase down on the counter and sighed.

"I haven't been able to get Violet to respond at all, let alone agree to listen to Pearl. I'm sorry," she said to Mrs. Peterson. "I wish I could've done more."

Mrs. Peterson took in the report with an understanding nod. The sketch of Joseph was still in her hands. She glanced from Mother to me. Our eyes met over the top of the drawing.

"Would it be okay if I took your picture back to Violet?" she asked.

"Yes, ma'am. If you think it might help."

Mrs. Peterson stood up. She headed past Mother down the hallway, a hint of hope in her stride. Mother looked at me quizzically, walked to the table, and sat down.

"Want to tell me what that was all about?"

I recounted all that had happened while she was in the bedroom. She listened intently, then shook her head.

"Isn't that something? Well, maybe a picture can do what a thousand words couldn't."

We listened for any response from down the hallway. Mrs. Peterson's voice was soft, but certain words were discernible, like "Pearl," "sketch," "Vernon," and, finally, an emphatic, "Look, love. Just look."

All went quiet. Mother bowed her head and wrapped her hands around her coffee mug. Her lips moved in prayer. I found a good fingernail to chew on and stared at the flowers on the windowsill. Silently, I added my prayers to Mother's. It was nothing too eloquent, just, "Help, Lord. Please help." I returned to gnawing my nail.

A new sound filtered down the hallway. A sound unlike any I had heard before—at least, not from a person. It was more like the sound of an injured animal, a low, pain-filled moan that came from somewhere deeper than a soul should ever have to go. The hair on the back of my neck stood to attention. My chewing stopped along with my heart. I glanced at Mother, wondering if this was good or bad. She lifted her head.

"It's okay. It seems your picture has reached her."

Violet's moans grew in intensity until they became a wail. Not a siren sort of wail, but more like a raspy, birdlike wail. Mrs. Peterson's encouraging words mingled with her daughter's cries in a strange harmony.

"Okay now. That's it, love. That's it. I'm here. I'm right here with ya."

Mesmerized by the intensity of the emotions spilling from the bedroom, I was suddenly embarrassed. It was a private moment, and I was an intruder. Mother sat quietly, her head bowed, lips moving. As a nurse, I knew she had seen her share of grief and suffering. But I was quite unused to the sheer force of it.

"Mother," I whispered.

No response.

"Mother," I whispered louder.

She raised her eyes to me.

"Are we in a thin place?" I asked.

A faint smile crossed her face. She nodded.

"Yes, sweetheart, we are in a thin place. God says He is near to the brokenhearted. So, you can rely on this: where there is sorrow, there is also an extra measure of God's presence. Do you feel the weight of the atmosphere in the house?"

I stopped and thought for a moment. She was right. The air felt heavy. "I do feel it," I said. "I thought it was only my nerves. I'm not sure I like it."

"The raw emotions of grief can make us uneasy, but God is not put off by it," she continued in hushed tones. "No, He comes rushing into these places. Especially if we invite Him. Times of suffering are a peculiar mixture of the depths of human pain and the breadth of divine love. God always wants to do something in these times. I've seen it over and over again. Do you know God is sometimes called the Comforter?"

"Yeah, I've heard that before."

"Well, now you will see the Comforter in action," she said. "We just need to wait and pray."

The whole time we carried on our whispered conversation, the cries from the bedroom continued along with Mrs. Peterson's constant flow of comfort.

All at once, Violet cried out, "My Joseph! Oh, my sweet, sweet Joseph!"

Shivers ran along my spine. I turned to Mother, who had returned to her quiet prayers. I reached over and shook her shoulder. "Mother, did you hear what Violet said?"

"Of course."

"But did you tell her?"

"Did I tell her what?"

"Did you tell her his name?"

She paused.

"No, I never mentioned his name to either Violet or her mother. I assumed you told Mrs. Peterson when you talked about the sketch."

I shook my head.

"No, I didn't. I never said his name was Joseph—not once."

BE COURAGEOUS

Mrs. Peterson appeared in the doorway. Underneath her puffy, red eyes, her face shone with a peculiar mixture of sorrow and love. Somehow, it was beautiful.

"Violet wants to talk to Pearl," she said.

"Uh, can, uh, Mother come too?"

I was prepared to do what I could, but not by myself.

"Sure, you bet. I didn't mean to say ya had to come by yourself only meant that Violet asked specifically to talk to you. Your picture has drawn her up . . . " She swallowed down a lump in her throat. ". . . drawn her up out of a dark place. I'm most grateful. We've got a long road to walk, but at least we've taken the first steps."

It seemed a long walk to the end of the hallway. I wasn't sure how I would tell Violet about Joseph or about all we had experienced together. It suddenly felt like a distant dream. Mother and Mrs. Peterson preceded me into the dimly lit bedroom. The shades were pulled down and the curtains drawn. Not one ray of the day's golden sunshine was allowed in. Only the hooded lamp over the headboard shed light into the room. The two older women helped Violet sit up. They tucked pillows behind her and a sheet around her. In the midst of the fuss, she clung to the sketch of Joseph as if it were a lifeline.

I snuck a glance around the room as my eyes adjusted to the dimness. Vanilla and pine candle scent lingered. It didn't take much for me to conjure up the pungent smell of blood, too, in the room's stuffy atmosphere. Sweat beads popped up all over my body. Sudden images of the night Joseph was born flashed across my mind. My heart pattered wildly inside my chest. My head started to feel like a balloon filling up with helium. I longed to retreat to the cheery kitchen. I did not want to repeat my performance as the Fantastic Fainting Pearl, but as I started to backtrack, something bright on the far side of the room caught my eye and brought me to a halt.

I peered into the corner, where a golden haze was beginning to spread. I glanced back at the bed. The others paid no attention to me nor to whatever was appearing in the corner. The haze grew brighter. Flashes of light spurted from its center and glittered on the ceiling. I couldn't detect a shape, but a strong feeling of complete peace poured across the room. I closed my eyes and let it soak into my soul. When I opened my eyes, a misty hand reached toward me out of the haze. On its fingers sat the source of the glittering flashes: four rings with beautiful gems and a fifth with the signet of a crown.

"Gregory," I whispered, my hand stretched outward to touch his.

My fingers encountered only air, but my heart filled with a rush of love. Though I couldn't see him fully, Gregory's presence felt as real as my own skin. His words came back to me: "Be strong. Be courageous. Be gentle. Be true." I wanted to run to him.

"Pearl, are you okay?" Mother said.

I dropped my hand to my side.

"We have a chair ready for you next to Violet. Come and sit down."

I glanced back at Gregory. The beautiful, golden glow remained, but no one else seemed to notice. His nearness strengthened me and clarified my thinking. Our journey together was no longer a far-off dream.

I sat in the chair pulled up beside Violet. Mother took a chair near the door, and Mrs. Peterson went around the bed to climb up beside her daughter. Violet stared at my sketch, seemingly unaware of my presence, her eyes shiny with tears. Her dark-brown hair hung limply around her face, dull and lifeless from days of neglect. The tired, mustard-colored sweater she wore hung off one shoulder, revealing her bony collarbone.

I didn't know if I should wait for her to ask me a question or just begin. A hushed minute passed. I wetted my lips.

"Your son Joseph is very handsome," I said.

Violet continued to stare straight ahead but nodded almost imperceptibly. More uncomfortable seconds ticked by.

At last she whispered, "How do you know his name is Joseph?"

"Well, that's sort of a long answer," I said. *Lord, where do I start?*

"Just begin. I will lead you."

The voice was so clear, I wondered if the others had heard it. They sat unmoving as breathing statues.

"On the night Joseph was born," I began, "Mother asked me to hold him, cause you needed her help. So, I did. I sat in that chair right where Mother is sitting. And I held him real close and stared at his face." I wiped my palms on my shorts. "Then the room started to feel stuffy. When I looked up to see what Mother was doing, I got really dizzy. I guess I fainted and hit my head. I don't remember that part. The next thing I knew, I was moving up and away from this room. Your baby was still in my arms. But we weren't alone. We had an escort."

I snuck a peek into the corner. The golden haze remained. I marveled that the others could be unaware of it.

"I guess he must have been an angel, but he never called himself that," I continued. "He just told me his name was Gregory and that he was here to escort us to our destination. Shortly after we left here, the baby started to move in my arms. I looked down into two clear-blue eyes. They looked back up at me. Your son was alive. I was so excited. And that's when Gregory said, 'His name is Joseph.'"

For the first time since I'd entered the room, Violet turned her gaze to me. I was prepared for her to question my story, but she seemed to have accepted it all as fact until this point.

"But how did he know?" she asked. "I hadn't told anyone. I only decided on his name the night before he was born. The one person I told was the doctor at the hospital who asked me what name I wanted on the death ... "

She stopped, unable to continue. Mrs. Peterson softly rubbed the threadbare sheet that lay over her daughter's legs.

"Gregory told me the name came from The Book of Life. He said all the babies were given the name already written there."

Violet's eyes fixed again on the sketch.

She nodded and whispered, "I'm glad God already knew his name and that it was written in a book of life before it was written on ... a certificate of death. I like that a lot."

I didn't know where to go next, though I need not have worried. Violet herself led the way. She turned to me with a perplexed but eager look. It was remarkable how much younger she looked with life in her eyes.

"Did you say you were being escorted to a destination?" she asked. "Where were you going? What was it like?"

So, I began to recount the whole adventure. I added every detail I could remember about Joseph. I also told her about the other babies and their receptions, about the Gate, the Dove filled with light, the wall, the lights, the aroma, and the music. Although she remained silent, she seemed to soak up every word. At times she closed her eyes as if picturing it all herself. At other times, she focused on the sketch of her son, caressing his face with her fingertips.

When it came time to tell her about Joseph's reception, I started my story with the lines of Shiphrah and Puah. I described the scrolls and the names of the places prepared for the little ones: the pavilion called Marvelous Kindness, the fortress called the Secret Place, and the refuge named Under His Wings. I recounted my conversation with Puah, carefully sidestepping the title she had given me, since I hadn't disclosed that information to Mother yet. Then I told her about Joseph's assignment to the Secret Place and described the lone figure who awaited us at the gate.

Violet stopped me.

"Why was only one person there? Didn't the others have whole groups of people waiting for them?"

"Yeah," I replied. "Others did have groups, but at the lines for the preborn, only one person was assigned to be the receiver. Gregory told me it was so these little ones could be whisked quickly into their prepared places, where many people waited to care for them. I never got to meet those people. I just met the one lady who received Joseph. Her name was Margaret." I let my eyes drift to the corner. "Gregory said she was part of Joseph's family. She was so beautiful and sweet. I wanted to stay and be her friend forever."

"Did you say Margaret?" interjected Mrs. Peterson.

"Yes, ma'am."

"What did she look like?"

"Oh, she was gorgeous, with thick, black hair that hung down to her waist. And she had blue eyes just like Joseph's. She asked me to call her Maggie."

Violet turned to her mother, who had bowed her head.

"Do you think it could be her, Mama? Oh my goodness. Of all the people I could wish for to care for my Joseph, I can't think of anyone better than Auntie Maggie."

Violet slumped against her mother, who drew her close. They wept. I turned to Mother and mouthed, "What did I say?" She shrugged and shook her head. We sat and waited. After several long, mournful minutes, Mrs. Peterson looked up. She placed her chin on top of Violet's head as she spoke.

"Well, that is something," she said. "That is surely something. I have . . . *had* a younger sister named Margaret. We all called her Maggie. She had crystal-blue eyes and long, black hair that fell in waves down to her waist."

She sighed, lost in a memory and seemingly unable to continue.

"What happened to her?" Mother urged her on.

"Well, she was the baby of the family—a full fifteen years younger than me. My mama was sickly after Maggie was born. So, I took that little baby under my wing. She became my special pet." A small smile broke through the pain on her face. "When I got married, Maggie came to live at my house. She was just ten years old when my twins were born—Vernon and Violet. But she was a great help. She loved those babies with her whole heart. She helped me feed 'em and change 'em and put 'em to bed. She didn't complain about havin' to spend her time takin' care of 'em. It was as if she was born to do it." She stroked Violet's hair with her fingertips as she spoke. "No one could pull a giggle out of 'em the way Maggie could, and no one could lull 'em to sleep the way Maggie could. I thought for sure she'd grow up to be a baby nurse like your mama, Pearl. Or maybe a preschool teacher or someone like that. But she never got the chance. Never got to be all she was supposed to be."

She took a ragged breath and paused. When she resumed, she spoke in a low, controlled monotone.

"Maggie was eighteen when we lost her to leukemia. Six short months and she was gone. All her potential, all her beauty, all her joy . . . just gone . . . lost forever."

Her chin slipped off Violet's head. The two figures on the bed melted into a bundle of shared sorrow and comfort. I snuck a fleeting look at Gregory. A glint of light shot in my direction. I heard one word: "Courage."

"Ma'am, uh, Mrs. Peterson," I started, "I'm sorry about your sister. I really am." I gulped down some air and blew it out. "But, well, Maggie is doing exactly what you thought she would be doing. Gregory told me that only people who loved to work with babies on earth are chosen to receive the babies at the Baby-Catcher Gate. Maggie was chosen to receive Joseph not just because she's a family member, but also because she's the perfect one to care for him. She definitely knows her job. Her potential wasn't lost—or her joy or her beauty. None of it was lost. It's all just been . . . well, it's been relocated."

Gradually, the mother and daughter drew back from each other. Mrs. Peterson wiped her eyes and nose with a hankie she pulled from her pocket. I plucked a fresh tissue from a box on the nightstand and offered it to Violet.

"I wanted to stay," I said to her. "I longed to get to know your Auntie Maggie. With all my heart, I wanted to go through the door to the Secret Place and be one of those who cared for Joseph. But it wasn't to be." I looked down into my lap and pulled at the hem of my T-shirt, which had begun to cling to my sticky skin. "I've wondered why. Why am I here and they're not? Why are they there and I'm not?" I returned my gaze to Violet. "I don't have the answers to those questions. But I think maybe my being here with you today to tell you all these things . . . maybe that's part of the why. The King wants to comfort you, and I think He's using me to do that."

Violet's chin quivered. Fresh tears surged up and over. She shook her head.

"I don't understand. I thought I was being punished." She swallowed and took a ragged breath. "Why would He want to comfort me? After all I've done . . ."

"Shh, now." Mrs. Peterson stroked her cheek. "There's no need to go back over all that." She pulled Violet close. "Remember what we talked about? You ask, and He forgives. Ain't no punishment left to give."

Violet nodded.

"I know . . . I just wish it could all be . . . different."

"We all have those wishes about some things in our past," Mother said. "But dwelling on what might've been or could've been doesn't help. It just keeps us chained up to our pain and regrets." She rose, knelt beside the bed, and grasped Violet's hand. "It seems to me that a loving heavenly Father has gone to a fair amount of trouble to bring you comfort and to help you see how precious you and your Joseph are to Him. Let's choose to dwell on that. Okay?"

Violet nodded and blew her nose.

"Okay."

Mother stood and hugged her.

"You're gonna make it," she said as she pulled back. "Pearl, I think it's time for us to head home."

Mrs. Peterson scooted off the bed, and the two of them headed down the hallway. Just as I turned to leave, Violet grabbed my hand. Her grip was surprisingly strong.

"Thank you, Pearl. You're a real courageous girl."

I stood speechless, digesting the moment. I peeked into the corner. The haze had disappeared. I was sad Gregory had left but glad he had been there. He had bolstered my courage. Maybe in reality he was still there, but I just couldn't see him. Maybe he was always there. All at once I was exhausted. I had done all I could do.

Violet dropped my hand and returned her gaze to the sketch of her son.

"You can keep that," I said.

She lifted her head. Her tearful smile rewarded me more than any dollar price she might have paid.

Mrs. Peterson saw us out the back door with hugs and words of thanks. The sun still shone warm and bright between the billowy clouds, although it was a bit lower in the sky than when we had arrived. Mother wrapped her arm around my shoulder. We strolled back to the car, crunching over the gravel driveway.

"Pearl," Mother said, "you did a good thing in there today. I am proud of you."

Immediately on the heels of her praise, a profound whisper rumbled inside my heart.

"Me, too, My daughter. Me too."

I glanced up into the battalion of summer clouds that drifted in formation above our heads. The ones emerging from behind the row of tall spruce trees were darker than the ones directly overhead. A sudden wind swept past us and lightning flashed on the horizon.

"Hmm," said Mother. "Appears to be something brewing in those clouds."

INTERLUDE: WILLIAM

From across the strip of jade-green lawn, I observe William and his classmates on the grand stairway in front of the great hall. A group of twenty or so scholars are gathered around a stately figure I immediately recognize as Jacob the Patriarch. He must be telling an engrossing story, for the teenaged boys and girls all have their heads tilted toward him like hummingbirds sipping from the nectar of a flower. Suddenly, his hands fly upward in their midst and the group breaks into spontaneous laughter and applause. I smile at the sheer pleasure of seeing my son engaged with one of the eminent teachers of all time and eternity. Is there a greater joy than this, to watch your child walk in truth? Perhaps there is, or at least one equal to it.

My mind slips back to that moment of discovery. The inexplicable joy. The overwhelming love. The instant bond with the son I never knew I had.

The scene plays out again in my mind's eye, all the family and friends gathered before the Gate at my reception, reunion after reunion, until from the back of the bunch came Grandmother Edna. A small, blond boy was clinging to her hand. At the sight of him, my heart flip-flopped. He looked so like Lizzie.

"John!" Edna began the introduction with barely contained excitement. "I would like you to meet William." She bent down to the lad, her eyes twinkling. "William, this is your daddy."

My face must have registered my bafflement, for many in the group spoke up, affirming her words and patting me on the back. Had we been in another realm, no doubt cigars with blue ribbons would've been passed around.

"It's true."

"He's yours."

"Isn't it fantastic?"

William launched himself across the space between us and wrapped his arms around my legs in a ferocious hug. Momentarily stunned, I simply let him. Then I slipped my hands under his arms and scooped him up into my embrace.

"A son? My son?" I whispered into his neck, trying to fathom this revelation.

He drew back his head and peered at me with his aqua eyes.

"Hi, Daddy," he said. "I've been waiting for you."

"Hey, Dad," a more mature version of the voice in my head interrupts my reverie. "Ready to go?"

The same aqua eyes. The same pure pleasure at the sight of them. I put my arm around his shoulders.

"Let's go home. Wanna walk, ride, or blink?"

Travel in this realm can be accomplished in many ways. My favorite is the blink—a mere thought of one's destination, and in a blink of the eye, one arrives. But William, having never known the limitations of time and space, often prefers the "old-fashioned" modes.

"Let's walk," he says.

I am not surprised.

"Great choice."

"I just have so much to tell you," he says, knowing that I probably would have chosen another option.

"It's okay, Son. I am totally fine with walking," I respond as we set out down the trail that winds through the forest, past my favorite lake and beside an open field of wildflowers.

To walk and chat and enjoy each other's company in the middle of paradise—who wouldn't be okay with that?

"So, was Jacob your teacher for class, or was he just hanging out on the steps, waiting for some young scholars to appear?" I ask.

"He was one of the teachers. We got to hear from all his sons too."

"Wow, that is a loaded lesson. What did they talk about?"

"At first, the brothers were all kidding each other and telling jokes. They were really funny. I think they enjoyed making us laugh. Jacob had to finally get them to settle down so we could get around to the actual teaching."

William repeats verbatim the entire lesson as we walk, including his teacher's hand gestures and accent. Having sat under Jacob's teaching myself a time or two, I am amused by the accuracy of his imitation. Then, suddenly, he stops and reaches out his hand. A bright-red bird lands on his finger, a twig in its mouth loaded with berries.

"May I share with you?" William asks his feathered friend.

The bird nods, and Will plucks a succulent berry from its stem.

"Want one?" he asks me as he harvests another.

"Sure." I plop the berry in my mouth. The bird takes flight.

"Thank you very much," Will says to its retreating form.

We walk in silence for several paces along the softly carpeted forest floor under the aromatic pines and cedars.

"It's hard for me to imagine," Will says.

"What's that, buddy?"

"That animals could be terrified of us and us of them."

"Here, that is hard to imagine. But there, things are a little different," I say, nodding.

It has become one of the themes for our walks, William's curiosity about how things operate on earth. It isn't like he wants to leave his heavenly home, but there is something in his humanity that longs to connect with the everyday experience of life on the planet. I almost envy him (if that emotion were even possible in this sphere), for he is blissfully ignorant of the darker side of mankind. He has never suffered an illness or trauma or tragedy. He will never know abuse or catastrophe, loss or lack. Grief, death, and dying are only concepts taught in his Humanity 101 class. Yet I have to admit, in the knowing of such things— experientially knowing—there is an undeniable bond formed. A commonality. A compassion. A comfort.

"Know what else is hard for me to imagine?" Will continues.

I shake my head, wondering where his inquisitiveness will lead us next.

"What it's like to have siblings."

"Well, that isn't something I'm very well versed on, Son. I was an only child, as far as I knew. Wasn't until I arrived here that I met my siblings. It was almost as big of a surprise as meeting you."

Normally a reference to our first meeting would get him to smile, and we would engage in a lively reliving of our first meeting. But not this time.

"I guess listening to Joseph and Rueben and Benjamin and Judah and all those guys got me thinking about it," he says, shuffling his feet over the soft moss. "I mean, I know that everything between them wasn't perfect while they were on the planet, but they sure seem to love each other now. And the stories they tell of everything they went through, well, it makes me wonder what it would be like . . . what they're like."

"You mean Susan and David and Pearl?"

We have been down this rabbit trail before many times, but like a kid with a favorite bedtime story, he never seems to tire of it.

"Tell me again."

And so, I rehearse for him all the qualities I can remember about his older and younger siblings. I don't mind. It is a pleasure to speak of them with someone as eager as I am to love them. Stories about Susan and David flow from the archives of my heart fully and freely.

"What about Pearl?" he asks, as always.

And as always, I scramble to fill in all the details I can remember about the baby girl I left so soon. No less precious to me, just less known.

"I don't know what it is," Will ponders aloud, "but for some reason, I feel most connected to Pearl. Why do you think that is?"

"Maybe because she's your baby sister. Sometimes big brothers can be very protective."

"That's what Rueben said. Guess he sorta stepped in to save Joseph's life."

"And Joseph, in turn, became the person who saved all their lives during the great famine."

"Funny how that all works."

"What's that, buddy?"

"How the younger kid gets chosen to rescue the older ones."

I nod.

"I think the King delights in shaking up human concepts of who can do what."

We walk out from under the enormous cedar trees onto the stepping-stones that lead around the lake. My bench, or what I have come to call my bench, is just around the bend.

"Up for a race?"

William's eyes light up.

"To the bench?" he asks.

"First one there gets to choose what's for dinner. But no blinking. Okay?"

"Okay."

"Ready, set, go!"

We speed down the path, our feet barely touching the smooth cobbled path. I run with all my might to keep ahead of my growing boy. This race is not an automatic win anymore, and I revel in the joy of this, too—my son is becoming a man. How that is even possible in a realm beyond time is one of the many mysteries I have yet to solve. As we reach the final stretch before the bench, I am only slightly ahead of him. Will lets out a piercing whistle and lifts his arms, then two of his mighty feathered friends lift him up and whisk him to the bench ahead of me, where he stands with a grin as I trot the final few yards.

"Hey, no fair," I remark, pulling to a halt next to him.

"You said we couldn't blink. You didn't say anything about calling for assistance," Will says.

I laugh.

"True enough."

"I think I'd like Mazimbaki food tonight."

"Mazimbaki? Again?"

"It's my favorite."

I can't blame him. It's a variety of food found only in heaven, and it is just that—heavenly.

"Fair enough. Mazimbaki it is."

He grins triumphantly, gives a brisk, satisfied nod, and heads down the path toward home.

"Dad?" he says over his shoulder.

"Yes, Son," I reply, wondering what else is brewing in his curious mind.

He turns to face me.

"Jacob said there's a ladder that reaches from here into the earthly realm, where angels ascend and descend. Do you think humans could go up and down on it too? Do you think maybe we could?"

CHANGED BY FIRE

My classmates and I spent the final art class of the summer preparing our clay bowls for firing. We lightly sanded the surfaces to remove any small bumps before waxing the bottoms in order to prevent them from sticking to the bottom of the kiln. As we worked, Teacher continued to instruct us on what to expect next.

"Your bowls have already been in the kiln once, which has helped remove impurities from the clay as well as harden it," she said while holding up her bowl from the previous week.

She set it down and picked up a glossy, green vase.

"The next round of firing will be at a slightly higher temperature, right around 1,900 degrees Fahrenheit. This extreme heat accomplishes several things. First, it continues the transformation of the clay from a fragile substance into one that is extremely durable and impervious to liquids. And second, it turns the glaze into a shiny finish like you see on this vase which adds beauty and additional protection."

She placed the vase on a table and picked up a binder.

"Now, when you choose which glaze you want, you need to make your decision based on the finished color samples you will find in this binder and not the dull, chalky color in the jars. You must trust the firing process for the transformation from one to the other. It is sort of a leap of faith, I know," she added with a chuckle.

Once our bowls were sanded and waxed, we all gathered around the binder with the charts of sample glazes. Mrs. Grant and Mrs. Wilson quickly decided upon warm, earthy tones, and Fritz went with deep blue and yellow. I chose a rich burgundy color for the outside of my pot and a soft eggshell blue for the inside. Teacher helped us locate the numbered jars containing our choices. We retreated to our chairs to begin the painting process. She walked around the room, checking on our progress, ready to assist with any difficulties. When she reached my station, she sat down next to me and watched as I painted.

"Fascinating color combination, Pearl. Mind telling me why you chose it?" she asked.

I thought for a second.

"I guess I chose it cause I like both these colors and I wanted to see them next to each other. Plus, I kinda like the idea that seeing the outside of something doesn't mean you know what's on the inside."

"Ah, good insight. I appreciate how you are using your art to express an idea."

"Well, I suppose it's something I learned from coming to this class."

I continued to paint as we chatted.

"Oh really? And why is that?" Teacher prodded.

"Well, the first day I walked in, I wanted to turn around and walk right back out. What I saw was a group of old people . . . uh, no offense."

I peeked up at her.

"None taken," she said with a wave, as if to erase the very notion. "Go on."

"Well, I wasn't sure I would fit in. I was worried you wouldn't want a kid in your class. But you wouldn't let me disappear. You pulled me in, and I'm glad you did, cause what I found on the inside of this class is way different than what I saw on the outside."

"And what did you find on the inside?" Teacher asked.

I mulled it over for a second before I spouted anything else that might possibly be offensive.

"I found I love art more than I thought I did. And I found it doesn't matter how old you are; there's always more to learn. I also found out that art can do more than just add pretty things to the world—it can build friendships and help people heal."

"You are an excellent student, my dear," Teacher remarked. "And a superb classmate."

She got up to resume her rounds. When I glanced up, I noticed the others had paused in their painting. They were looking in my direction and smiling. I must have been talking louder than I'd thought. They wordlessly returned to their projects. Teacher patted my shoulder before continuing to her next student.

□

As summer melded into fall, life sped back up. Mother and I shopped for number-two pencils, spiral notebooks, and folders at Thompson's Drugstore in town. She believed in supporting local businesses. But for school clothes, we drove sixty miles to the closest Sears.

There was one women's clothing store in St. Gerard—Francine's on Main Street. The sign above the door read "Women's Fashions." I had been in there just one time with Mother. The word "Fashions" was a stretch. I was relieved they didn't carry juniors' sizes. And I wasn't exactly fond of the owner, Miss Francine. She strolled through the aisles of her store as if it were a kingdom and she the queen. If any hanger was ajar or shirt unfolded or purse askew in its display, she was on it. Her cat-eye glasses and perfectly coiffed beehive bubble hairdo may have been the height of fashion in some other era, but not in the 80s. She looked like a photograph out of Grandma's *LIFE* magazines.

The one time I had accompanied Mother as she shopped for a dress at Francine's, I had placed myself on the wrong side of Her Majesty. How was I to know that poking my head under the door of the wrong dressing room in search of Mother would send some poor lady dressed only in her undergarments into hysterics? Mother had insisted I apologize to the lady, who did accept it in good humor once fully clothed. But Miss Francine had not been so easily soothed, even though Mother had bought a dress she wasn't crazy about in an effort to keep the peace.

"Perhaps you should think of leaving this young one at home next time you shop with us," Miss Francine had advised Mother as she folded the dress in pale-pink tissue paper. "At least until she has reached a higher level of ma-t-urity." She'd articulated the *t* in *maturity* with regal airs.

Either I had not yet reached the desired level of ma-t-urity or Mother simply no longer felt the need to support that particular local business. Whatever the reason, we were both content to shop at Sears. It wasn't exactly high fashion, but at least it resembled what my friends and I saw in magazines. And it was where everyone else bought their school clothes—except Mel. She and her mom drove all the way to the Cities to shop.

Amid this normal back-to-school activity, something deep inside me felt different. I was still only twelve years old. I still lived in the same house on the same street in the same town. But my view of who I was and what was important in life had been altered.

It was uncomfortable at times when I hung out with my friends. Not because they were weird or different. They were the same. I was the one who had changed. I didn't care so much about the latest album or style of jeans or newest hairdo or cutest boy. (Well, maybe a little about the cutest boy.) My thoughts were wrapped up in life and death, art and beauty, love and loss. I was afraid if I talked to Mel and El about my thoughts they might think I was off my rocker. Which might have been okay, since I knew that eventually they would take it all in stride. But what happened if they told someone else? Even if they pinkie promised not to tell, this sort of thing had a way of leaking out of even the most sealed lips, and I knew that not everyone was as accepting as Mel and El. I was okay with starting off my junior high career as the awkward, artsy girl, but not as the lunatic, laughingstock girl. So, I kept quiet and floated through my days, interacting as best I could on a superficial level.

One day, El caught me in one of my spaced-out moments in the middle of math class.

"Solving the issues of quantum physics? Or quantifying the number of holes in the ceiling tiles?" she wrote in the note she slipped across the aisle to me.

"No great thoughts. Just a bad hit on the head a month ago. Ha, ha, ha," read my return note.

She cast a doubtful look my way.

Her response read, "You are equivocating."

I wasn't quite sure what that meant, but she had used it often enough that I knew it was something like "beating around the bush."

"Two more minutes to finish up," our math teacher announced.

His stroll around the room headed in our direction. I slid the note under my textbook, relieved to have a good excuse to not answer El. I didn't feel good about not telling her everything. But I just wasn't ready.

One glossy day in mid-September, I came home from school to find a plain cardboard box tied with twine by the front door. A card lay tucked under the knot on top of the box. My name was written on the envelope. I dropped my backpack on the porch, picked up the box, and sat down on the top step. I didn't recognize the handwriting. Intrigued by the possibilities, I savored the mystery for a moment. Then I ripped open the envelope.

The front of the card was awash in color and movement, a field of brilliant orange poppies swaying in the breeze. I recognized the artist—it was Teacher Anne's work. I sat and enjoyed the beauty before opening the card.

Dear Pearl,

I meant to get this to you a few weeks ago, but life kept getting in the way. Please forgive the tardiness. Your bowl has been sitting on a shelf in my studio, awaiting delivery, and I have enjoyed its presence. Each time my eyes land on it, I remember our conversation regarding your color choices. Know that the reasons behind your choices still inspire me. I hope the fired version meets your expectations. I was surprised to see that you had added gold flecks to your glaze. Didn't know I had anything like that in my inventory and didn't notice them until after the firing. Magnifique!

I am truly glad you were part of my class this summer. You are not merely a talented artist but also a thoughtful student. I hope you will continue to discover your abilities and the ways your art can influence our world.

Teacher Anne

P.S.—I will be leading an art appreciation night the second Tuesday of every month. It will be at 7 p.m. in the high school cafeteria starting in October. Different artists each month will come to share their work and their thoughts. I have invited all your summer classmates. I hope you and your mother will join us.

Her note refreshed me. Even though I hadn't spoken a word, it felt like my first real conversation in weeks. And the possibility of an art appreciation night each month with my "old" friends made me a bit giddy.

I was so excited, I almost forgot about the package. I set the card aside and turned back to the box. Gold flecks? I didn't know what Teacher was talking about, but I was eager to see for myself.

The twine untied easily, and I lifted the flaps with anticipation. My bowl was nestled inside a mound of shredded paper. As I removed a handful from the middle, a glint of eggshell blue captured my attention. I was astonished at how radically different it appeared from the soft matte paint I had applied. I delicately pulled out the pot, eager to see the burgundy exterior. It, too, was richer than anticipated, and all along the brim were flecks of gold that shimmered in the sunlight. I was amazed at how the firing process had changed the dull glaze into something so vibrant, but I was dumbfounded by the gold. It looked as though someone had turned the bowl upside down and dipped the rim in gold dust. But it wasn't me. And evidently it wasn't Teacher. Who then?

Before I could come up with even a remotely feasible answer, my thoughts were interrupted by Mother's arrival. She got out of the car and greeted me with a warm hello as she approached the steps.

"What've you got there?"

"It's my pottery from art class," I replied. "Teacher dropped it off. I found it in a box by the front door."

"May I see it?" she asked.

I handed the bowl to Mother, who examined it slowly and deliberately. As she held it, I noticed the many flaws of a novice potter. Its shape and curves were far from perfect. But Mother seemed to see only the beauty. I have since learned this is what mothers are good at—seeing beauty in all our awkward beginnings.

"It's delightful," she declared "The colors are unexpected together, but they're suited to each other at the same time. And this gold rim . . . it's just remarkable."

I nodded. It was more remarkable than she knew, but since I had no explanation for it, I kept my mouth shut and simply let her enjoy it.

"I love it, sweetheart. Where shall we put it?"

I gathered my backpack, the card, and the box full of shredded paper and followed Mother into the house. We tried various locations for my latest art piece. At last, we settled on placing it in the middle of the coffee table in the living room. We agreed this vantage point showed off both the inside and the outside of the bowl while showcasing the sparkling brim. Pleased with ourselves, we sat on the couch and admired our choice. Only then did I remember to pull out the card from Teacher. I showed it to Mother.

When she finished reading it, she said, "I'd say we need to put the second Tuesday of every month on our calendar."

I nodded, unable to speak. Mother understood the change in my twelve-year-old soul, and I loved her afresh for it.

"Interesting," Mother said.

"I know. I think it will be really interesting."

"Well, yes, I believe that too. But that's not what I meant." She held the card open, as if rereading every line. "It's just interesting that she'll be sticking around."

"Who?"

"Anne . . . Teacher Anne. She usually heads to Florida for the winter."

BOY CRAZY

A crisp wind from the north blew into town on the second Tuesday of October, causing leaves to chatter on the branches and scatter across yards. A brilliant autumn sun broke through and warmed the daylight hours. That afternoon, the sweaters we had worn in the morning hung tied around our waists as Mel, El, and I walked home from school. We chatted about our classes, teachers, homework, and the new boy in town. We couldn't agree on what his name was. I thought it was Bart. Mel thought it was Ben. El insisted it was Bradley. What we could agree upon was he was cute.

"Okay. Big question." Mel ran a step in front of El and I. She turned, thrust her arm straight out, and signaled us to halt. "Where do you rank him on your Top Five Cutest Guys list?"

"You first," El challenged Mel.

"I have him a close second behind Steven Jenkins," she responded without missing a beat. "Your turn, El."

"I concur with your placement," she replied. "However, Steven Jenkins has descended on my list to number four after he slept through the entire last hour of *To Kill a Mockingbird* in Miss Wells's class. Not attractive."

"Whatever, El. He's still super cute," Mel said. "So, who do you have as number one?"

"Mark Pawkowski is my current front-runner," El announced.

"Mark Pawkowski?" Mel and I blurted in unison.

"El, he's a sophomore in high school," I said.

"And he's a total nerd," Mel added.

"I am unfazed by your opinions," El responded, her chin held high. "Perhaps I am drawn to older, intellectual types."

"Oh jeez." Mel rolled her eyes. "Of course you are. What about you, Pearl?"

"Well," I paused dramatically.

"Come on, Pearl," Mel urged. "Spit it out."

"Okay, okay," I laughed. "I put Bart or Ben or Bradley or whatever his name is at number three."

"Three?" they both shot back. It was my turn to face the music.

"I need to have an idea of what's on the inside before I give too much weight to the outside," I said.

"This is true," El agreed. "But I am willing at this point to overlook a few internal flaws based upon the excellence of the external presentation."

Mel and I stared at her and burst into laughter.

"Sometimes, El," Mel gasped, "you really crack me up."

When we recovered our breath, El held up her pinkie finger and said, "Let us make a solemn pact before we part ways."

Mel and I lifted our pinkies, too, shoulders back, faces constrained from further laughter.

"Okay. What's the pact?" I asked.

"We agree to compare notes about any internal personality factors or other pertinent details regarding Mr. Bradley Ben Bart that come to light with the other members of this pact," she declared.

"Agreed," Mel and I replied.

We took turns pinkie shaking and resumed the walk home. Mel and El turned left onto Quince Street.

"See you tomorrow," they echoed over their shoulders as they went.

I smiled as I walked the last few blocks solo. It was nice to be absorbed by normal seventh-grade matters. My mind wandered back to the new boy. We didn't get too many new families moving into town. I wondered why they would come to St. Gerard of all places. Mel and El would probably find everything out before me. El had more classes with him, and Mel was more aggressive in her investigative tendencies than I was. Maybe *nosy* was the proper description.

I walked into the house and headed straight to the kitchen for a snack. As I opened the fridge, I glanced at the calendar on the corkboard next to it. Until that moment, I had somehow forgotten that it was the night for the first art appreciation gathering. Excited by the reminder, I grabbed a granola bar and settled at the table, determined to finish my math homework before supper so I could fully enjoy the evening ahead. This was more difficult than I anticipated. My mind kept flitting backward to a certain boy and forward to the night's event. I finally solved the last story problem just as Mother came through the door.

"Tonight's the night," were the first words out of her mouth. "Are you excited?"

"For sure," I responded, reluctant to tell her I had actually forgotten about it.

"I am truly looking forward to it," she said. "Let's get some supper and then we can get ready."

As we ate, we speculated as to who the speaker might be and what sort of art we might see. We finished up, cleaned up, and spruced up before heading out the door at 6:45 p.m. Several other cars pulled into the high school parking lot at the same time we did. We had to snake through the rows, searching for a vacant space to park. I hoped all the cars weren't just there for a wrestling match or something. We hurried through the nippy evening air into the school and followed the Art Appreciation Night signs that pointed toward the cafeteria. The hum of human interaction and the aroma of coffee enticed us onward.

As we entered the cafeteria, the far wall grabbed my attention. It was covered with an array of photography. People were already walking up and down the wall's length, viewing the artwork. The round cafeteria tables were dressed up for the occasion with white tablecloths. Sprays of multicolored fall leaves encircling wooden bird houses served as centerpieces. Mother unbuttoned her woolen coat, but I kept my jean jacket securely fastened. The jacket really wasn't warm enough for the night's plunging temperatures, but I had insisted on wearing it. Mother had muttered something about paying a price for fashion as we had gone out the door. I was beginning to understand what she meant; I was chilled to the bone from the short walk from the parking lot to the school.

I searched the room for Teacher Anne. She was standing in the front near a podium, speaking to a young man. They were engrossed in what appeared to be a sound system issue. I scanned the rest of the room, hoping against hope to find one or two kids my age in the crowd. There was one table completely occupied by high school students slouching in their chairs. They already looked bored. I recognized Mr. LaMoure, the new, young art teacher, who sat in their midst. He was hard to miss. No other guy in town wore a ponytail or a pale-blue sports coat with shoulder pads. He was engaged in conversation with a female student I recognized as the artist who, according to the local paper, had designed the homecoming buttons several years in a row—an honor I hoped to inherit one day. The rest of the class appeared to be in attendance solely due to a few promised extra-credit points or some such bribe.

At the table next to them, a group of young mothers sat drinking coffee and nibbling on cookies, engaged in small talk. Two of them had infants swaddled across their fronts in a sling-like arrangement. Two were noticeably with child. One woman at the table, whose head stuck up several inches above the rest, was talking to no one. When she turned to pull something from the purse slung over the chair back, I recognized her. It was Miss Wells. She was my English teacher as well as the girls' volleyball and basketball coach. I liked her a lot, but for some reason I didn't want to go and say hello. It was always weird to see a teacher outside of school hours, being forced to deal with the fact that they had lives beyond the confines of the classroom.

"I'm going to grab some coffee," Mother said, interrupting my people-watching moment. "And then I'm going to say hello to Dr. Brown over there."

She pointed to a table on the far side of the room, where my doctor sat at a table, studying a flyer of some sort, his tweed blazer accessorized with a natty, golden pocket square. The only other person at the table was Coach Spencer, the junior high PE teacher, whom I barely recognized without his sweat suit. His hulking figure was stuffed into a plaid dress shirt that looked like it might burst at the seams with any sudden movement. It was surprising who showed up at an art event. Even Mr. and Mrs. Schmidt were in attendance.

"Do you want to come with me?" Mother asked.

Dr. Brown seemed much more approachable out of his doctor regalia, and I might have gone with Mother, except at that moment another person sat down in one of the vacant chairs at his table. It was Miss Francine.

"I think I'd prefer to go see the photographs," I replied.

Mother smiled knowingly.

"Okay. I'll let you off the hook."

She headed toward the refreshments before embarking on her social call. I almost followed her. The dessert plates were piled high. But the possibility that she might change her mind and prod me to go with her overruled the temptation. I walked straight across the room to the display wall. My decisive discipline was rewarded several minutes later when Mother caught up with me and offered me an oatmeal raisin cookie.

"Thanks. How's Dr. Brown?" I asked.

"Good. He asked how you were getting along."

"What'd you say?"

"What do you think I said?"

"I don't know. Sometimes you still treat me like I'm a fragile doll or something. You're always hovering," I said.

"It's called being a mom. I told him you were just fine."

"And Miss Francine?" I poked. "Did she ask how I was doing?"

"Honestly, Pearl. Give Miss Francine a break. I'm sure she's a lovely lady . . . most of the time," she said with a wink. "Now let's enjoy these pictures."

We stopped in front of a collection of photographs arranged to form a human face. I bit off a chewy chunk of cinnamon-y goodness as I pondered the display. Each photo captured a small part of a person's face: an eye, a nostril, an eyebrow, a cheek, a lip. Clearly the photos represented separate individuals, because a variety of skin tones, eye colors, and hair types were evident. Yet when they all fitted together, they formed one large and surprisingly attractive face.

Suddenly the PA system squawked loudly, causing people to jump and laugh nervously at their own startled responses. Teacher tapped the microphone, and the young man next to her adjusted the knobs on an amplifier.

"Why don't you all grab a seat and we'll get started in just a moment," Teacher Anne said.

As we headed to the tables, a familiar voice cried out, "Pearl, come join us over here."

Mrs. Wilson stood next to one of the tables, beckoning us with a wave. Already seated at the table were her husband, Mr. and Mrs. Grant, and Fritz. They had saved two chairs for us, and we gladly took them as we shared our greetings.

"Ladies and gentlemen, welcome to the year's first art appreciation night," Teacher Anne began. Several in the audience applauded. "I am pleased to see you all here."

She paused to allow the hubbub of people getting settled to subside.

"You are in for a special treat tonight. I see many of you have already been enjoying our guest speaker's work, and you will have time after his talk to enjoy it some more. But right now, let me introduce you to our artist. His name is Scott Stewart, and he is a professional photographer."

She donned a pair of magenta reading glasses and glanced down at a piece of paper in her hand.

"He earned a Bachelor of Fine Arts Degree from Fulton Institute of Art and Design in Boston, Massachusetts, where he received instruction from some of the top professionals in the field of photography today. Last year he was awarded the Kenton Case Award for excellence in photography by the American Photography Association. He recently relocated to the Cities, where he has opened a studio and school of photography."

She removed her glasses and looked back out over the crowd.

"You may recognize him, since he graduated from this very high school in 1975. We are extremely proud of his accomplishments and pleased he could join us. Of course, it was serendipitous his father's fiftieth-birthday party was this past weekend, which helped draw Scott back up into the north woods. All I had to do was convince him to stay a few extra days and bring along samples of his work."

The crowd laughed appreciatively.

"As you listen to Scott and the journey he has taken with his art, I hope you will find more than just a talented photographer—although he doubtless is that. I hope you will also find a young man with a heart to use his talents for good. So, let's give Scott a warm hometown welcome."

Applause broke out and Teacher moved back to her table at the front. She scooted her chair around to face the speaker. As she did, I caught a glimpse of who was sitting next to her. It was Brad or Burt or Bart or whatever his name was. He sat at Teacher's table, next to a woman I assumed to be his mother, based upon their similarity in appearance. He wasn't slouching or sulking like the high school boys at the table next to him. He sat forward in his chair, his elbows on the table and eyes focused on the guest speaker. I missed all of Scott Stewart's opening sentences as I strained to get a better view.

Mother tapped my shoulder and redirected my attention to the speaker with her eyebrows. Outwardly, I switched my focus. Inwardly, though, my mind remained fixed on this latest addition to the night's agenda—at least, *my* night's agenda.

However, Scott Stewart had an appealing way of talking, and soon I was absorbed by his tale. It didn't hurt that he was handsome, despite a nose that appeared to have been broken a time or two. He described his journey from our small town to the big city of Boston, driven by his love for photography. As a kid, he had dreamed of becoming a professional hockey player.

Explained the nose.

In high school, he was recruited by several universities before a knee injury sidelined him at the beginning of his senior season and crippled his hopes.

"I was completely devastated at this turn of events," he confessed to us. "And I struggled to make sense of it. I went through months of physical therapy, hoping to recover my former abilities, but I never quite got there. Didn't lace up my skates the entire season. It was during this time I began to focus on photography. I was already on the school's yearbook team as a photographer. But when I was sidelined by my injuries, I got the opportunity, however unforeseen or undesired, to expend more time and energy taking pictures."

He paused and looked intently at the people seated at the table next to Teacher Anne.

"Before I go any further," Scott said. "I really need to acknowledge some of the people who encouraged me and cheered me on through some of those tough times. First of all, my parents, Andrew and Ellen Stewart." He pointed to them and they raised their hands and waved. "And, of course, Coach Libby and Mr. Johnson, who are both still teaching right here." They, too, stuck up a hand and waved. "Truly, I owe such a debt of gratitude to each of you. Thanks for being here tonight."

He walked over, gave his dad and mom hugs, and shook the hands of his teachers. The audience applauded. The new boy turned around to follow Scott's movements. As he did, our eyes met across the room. He smiled. I wanted to smile in return, but my face was paralyzed.

Mother nudged me and said, "There's some good upbringing."

"Huh?"

"Are you okay?" she said, reaching over to touch my forehead. "You're all flushed."

"I am?" I felt my cheeks. "Guess I'm a little warm."

"Take off your jacket," she whispered.

"Oh, yeah . . . no, I'll be fine."

Scott returned to the podium and resumed his speech. He told of how he began to take a camera with him everywhere, even to physical therapy sessions, where he documented the painful recovery process.

"I got so obsessed with my camera, my therapist asked me to leave the darn thing at home so I could focus more on the actual therapy than on the images of the therapy," he said, laughing at the recollection.

Near the end of his senior year, he put together a montage of photos depicting his shattered hockey season. Unbeknownst to him, Mr. Johnson, the yearbook faculty adviser, entered it into a statewide photography contest.

"One day I got a notice in the mail that I'd won $150, a new camera, and a chance to participate in a summer photography workshop in the Cities. I almost threw it away because I didn't even know I'd entered."

Scott paused and pointed to the back corner of the cafeteria.

"If you want to see the original montage, it's back in the corner, along with pictures from the summer workshop. I didn't have to carry those with me—my parents still have them hanging in their family room."

He chuckled and shook his head as if embarrassed by his parents' pride, but he added quickly, "Although it is not my best work, it may be my most important, because it changed the whole course of my life."

Scott went on to describe how he got a scholarship to Fulton, and he spoke of the training he received. He experimented with a broad scope of photography techniques as well as subject matter there. But no matter which direction his education took him, he found gravitated back to human subjects.

"Capturing people's diversities and complexities with the lens continually fascinates and challenges me," he said. "My new studio in the Cities is a portrait studio. My goal is to capture a person's personality and spirit with my camera. So sometimes I photograph them while we're talking or while they're doing something they enjoy.

Whatever it takes to get at their core. One of my first customers was a guy who loved to volunteer his time at a homeless shelter downtown. I followed him one day when he was serving and took a ton of shots of him in action. Watching him give his time and energy really got me thinking: What was I doing to serve my community? Could I possibly use my passion for photography to give back in some way?

"I approached the director of the shelter to see if I could come and take pictures of anyone who wanted one taken. Free of charge. She loved the idea. I went back one Saturday and spent the entire day taking portraits. It was a blast. Sobering at times, but still super fun to interact with the people. When I came back the next week with their developed portraits, the peoples' responses were amazing. Some of them wept. Some laughed. Some just grabbed their picture and went into a corner. One guy said it was the first picture he had ever had of himself since elementary school, besides a mug shot.

"I still go back once a month. And I've branched out to a couple of hospitals and one inner-city school. Some of the most valuable experiences of my career thus far have been on those shoots." He pointed to a far wall. "A group of photographs over there at the end of the wall are from my volunteer days. I hope you'll pay special attention to them."

He finished with a short spiel about his photography school and invited us to pick up the flyers laid out next to the coffee and refreshments. Teacher went to the front to lead us in a round of appreciative applause for our speaker. She encouraged us to mingle, linger, and enjoy.

Mother, Mrs. Wilson, and Mrs. Grant gathered their purses while we chatted about Scott's talk. Out of the corner of my eye, I saw Teacher approaching our table, the new boy and his mother close behind her.

"I'm glad I caught you all together," she said when she reached our table. "I'm sure you want to go see Scott's work, but I wanted you to meet my new neighbors. This is Sandra Bradley and her son Ben. They just moved back into town to care for Sandra's father. Ben is in your grade, Pearl. He is also an eager young artist, so I thought it would be great for you two to connect. Sandra grew up here. Her dad owned the car dealership in town. He was the one who used to paint those fabulous pictures on the huge showroom windows for every sale and every season. Remember those?"

"Oh my, yes," Mrs. Grant said. "Those were marvelous."

"She says the artistic gene passed her by and landed on Ben," Teacher added. "But I've seen her knitting projects, and if that's not art, I don't know what is. They are remarkable. Aren't you selling them through a catalog?"

Sandra Bradley answered and gamely fielded more of the group's questions about her knitting. I wasn't really paying attention.

His name was Ben Bradley and he was standing right next to me.

My mind wasn't functioning too well.

Mother prodded my elbow and suggested, "Pearl, why don't you take Ben over to the displays? You young people probably want to check out the photographs. We'll be right behind you."

My mouth went dry. I managed an audible "okay" before departing from the circle of adults.

Ben Bradley followed me silently.

I was glad I'd worn my jean jacket.

SEEING THINGS

I approached the back corner of the cafeteria, acutely aware of the human walking behind me. When we reached Scott's high school montage, I screwed up enough courage to speak.

"Is it okay if we start here?"

Ben came alongside me, his eyes focused on the photographs.

"Sure."

We stood before the montage for several minutes in total silence.

"Want to see some other stuff?" said Ben.

I shrugged.

"Sure."

We ambled in silence past more of Scott's work. We wove around other viewers until we reached the end of the wall. At the corner, we faced the last set of photographs. These were the pictures from Scott's volunteer outings. Each photo's label told the specific location where it had been taken. We both slowed our pace. Scott was right; these photos were different.

"This one is cool," Ben said, pointing at a picture of three small boys.

They were seated on a cot at a homeless shelter, arms around one another and grinning from ear to ear. Each one wore an identical pair of Superman slippers. They must have been brand-new. Shredded wrapping paper and empty boxes lay on the floor beneath them. Joy glowed on their faces.

"They don't look very old," I commented.

"Nope. Maybe four or five," Ben said. We stared at those boys, and they stared at us. "It's neat the way the photograph pulls you in and sorta tells a whole story."

"Makes me wonder about those boys' lives."

"Do you think they're brothers? Or maybe cousins? They look alike, don't they?"

"Totally. I wonder why they're in a homeless shelter."

"Good question."

Our thoughts spilled out, and we shared with an ease that surprised me. We didn't talk about ourselves, just the photos. But I found out a great deal about Ben Bradley. He was kind of shy, but he wasn't afraid to express his opinion. He listened to my thoughts. He had a quirky sense of humor. He enjoyed art. And, on top of all that, he was even cuter up close than from across the room.

Ben was focused on a photo from a soup kitchen when I moved on to the next pictures, which were labeled *Children's Hospital*. I wasn't sure I wanted to see pictures of sick kids, but I forced myself to look. Miss Wells and Coach Spencer stood side by side, viewing the photos. Actually, quite closely side by side. Coach coughed and nudged Miss Wells when he saw me approaching.

"Hello, Pearl," she said, discreetly sashaying away from Coach, her face blooming pink under her tortoiseshell glasses.

"Hello."

I slipped in beside them, pretending not to notice their discomfort at my presence. Apparently I wasn't the only one uncomfortable with acknowledging a life outside the classroom. They moved on to the next picture.

The photo in front of me showed two small feet cupped in a sturdy hand. The hand appeared to be unusually large. After inspecting it for a moment, I realized the hand was normal; it was the feet that were unusual. They were tiny, not more than an inch long. I was mesmerized by their teeny perfection.

Suddenly, as I stared at the feet, the entire baby appeared before my eyes—a little girl with a crown of curly, black hair. Her eyes were velvet brown. She had skin the color of caramel that darkened in the creases of her neck. Her lips puckered, ready for a kiss. Her hands clenched in miniature fists. The satiny, white gown she wore flowed around her in overwhelming ripples. She was absolutely adorable. She turned her face to me, blinked, and let out a funny squawking noise.

My breath came in short gasps. I shook my head. Closed my eyes. Took a deep breath and counted to three.

One Mississippi. Two Mississippi. Three Mississippi.

I opened one eye cautiously. Then the other. There was only the big hand holding two tiny feet. That was it. But I could not erase the little girl's image from my mind.

Ben stepped into place next to me. He glanced at me, at the photo, then back at me. He waved one hand in front of my face.

"Hello. Anyone home?" he joked. I continued to stare straight ahead, unable to respond. "Hey, Pearl, seriously, are you okay?"

Miss Wells noticed his distressed tone and stepped back over to where we were.

"Is everything okay here?" she asked Ben.

"I dunno," he said.

"She looks a little upset," Miss Wells said. "Are you okay?" she asked me.

I tore my eyes away from the pair of little feet.

"Huh? Oh, yeah, I'm fine," I replied. "I just, uh, found this one to be very, uh, dynamic."

"Okay. Well, you look like you've seen a ghost," Ben said with eyebrows raised. "I can get you some water if you want."

"That's a great idea," Coach Spencer commented as he joined the little evaluation party. "We'll wait here with her 'til you get back."

"Thanks," I said.

Ben gave me a look that said, "I'm not totally believing what you just said," but he headed toward the refreshment table nonetheless. I turned to Coach and Miss Wells.

"You don't have to stay," I said as calmly as possible, hoping to convince them of a sense of normalcy I did not feel. "Ben will be back in a second, and I'm really just fine."

"Well . . ." Miss Wells hesitated and glanced at Coach.

"She seems like she'll be okay, Beth, uh, Miss Wells," he stammered. "But maybe you should sit down, Pearl. You look kind of pale."

"Oh, that. I'm naturally sort of that way."

"Are you sure you'll be okay?" Miss Wells asked.

"Totally, for sure."

She looked at Coach. He shrugged as if to say, "What can you do?" and took her by the arm as they moved away. Had I not been so baffled by my own situation, I might have counted the revelation of their friendly relationship as one of the most interesting tidbits of the evening. But it paled in comparison to what I had just seen.

I took a few deep breaths and tried to erase the vision in my head of the baby girl in the white, satin dress. I decided to move away and view other photographs, hoping to fill my mind with new images.

The next picture was a large black-and-white photograph. In it, a petite hand wrapped around the pinkie finger of an adult hand. Then it happened again—the full baby appeared. Clothed only in a diaper, he had rosy skin and fuzzy, strawberry blonde hair that stood straight up and shot out in all directions. The eyes that peered at me were deep blue, almost purple. With his free hand, he reached out to me, imploring me with those eyes to extend my finger for him to grasp.

My hands flew up and covered my face. I shook my head and blew out my breath.

One Mississippi. Two Mississippi. Three Mississippi. Four Mississippi. Five Mississippi.

I lowered my hands and peered over my fingertips. Only the little hand wrapped around the pinkie finger remained. But I knew who the hand belonged to. I had seen him. He was precious.

"Pearl, are you okay?" This time the question came from Mother. "Ben asked me to bring this water to you. He and his mother had to leave." She paused. "What's going on? Was he mean to you?"

I gathered myself as best I could.

"No, no," I assured her. "He was very nice. I just got thirsty, and he offered to get me some water."

"Well, that was kind of him."

She handed the plastic cup to me. I reached for it, unable to steady my hand. The water sloshed as I brought it to my lips. Mother watched me with her eagle eyes.

"Are you going to tell me what happened? I realize Ben Bradley is an attractive young man, but I think you may be overreacting."

I gripped the cup with both hands, trying to control their shakiness.

"No, it's not him. Its these pictures. They're so . . . intense. They sorta hit me between the eyes."

"Yes, they are intense. I can see how you might have a strong reaction." She paused and looked at the pictures, as if caught up in viewing them. Without turning back to me, she continued her inquisition. "Is that all? Nothing else?"

I chewed my bottom lip. How was I to tell her that her daughter was seeing things? I sipped my water. Mother maintained her position, face forward.

"Can I tell you once we get in the car?"

She nodded slowly.

"Okay. We can do that. But I think it's time to go right now."

I nodded. We headed back across the cafeteria to the exit. Thankfully, the path to the hallway was clear. I swallowed the rest of the water and pushed the cup into the flap of the garbage can near the exit. We spoke to no one, not even each other.

My mind seesawed back and forth between the photographs and the visions in my head. One was as real as the other.

I went through the motions—getting into the car, shutting the door, buckling my seat belt—all on autopilot. Shivers ran through my body under my thin jacket. Mother started the car and cranked up the heat. We headed out of the parking lot, toward home. She was the first to break the silence.

"I had a very pleasant conversation with Scott Stewart and his mother. She and I have served on the hospitality committee at church through the years. Scott graduated right between Susan and David. I remember watching him play hockey when David was a sophomore. We used to sit on those frigid bleachers together, all bundled up. Remember?"

"Uh, kinda."

"I remember when he got injured." One finger tapped on the steering wheel as she drove. "Such a disappointment for him and his teammates and coaches. But obviously, God had another plan for his life. I knew he had gone off to a design school out east, but I wasn't aware he had moved back to the Cities." She hit the blinker and we turned left down 7th Street. "He asked about Susan and David, although I would say he was a bit more interested in finding out about your sister than your brother. I guess she and Scott worked on the yearbook together back in high school. He gave me his number to pass along to Susan. I guess I'd better call her. She's always so busy these days, but it might be nice for her to take a break and catch up with an old acquaintance. What do you think?"

"Maybe."

She was trying to draw me out. I knew the emotions and thoughts pent up inside me would gush out once I started. But the floodgates within me were still shut up tight.

We pulled into the driveway. Mother shifted the car into park but kept it running. She turned to me.

"Do you want to talk here, or do you want to go into the house? Something is clearly bothering you. It is not an option for you to go to bed without telling me what's going on. So, you decide—here or there?"

I picked at the cuticle around my thumbnail. She reached over and covered my hands with one of hers. It was cool from the steering wheel and the chilly night air. I surrendered to its tender pressure and peeked sideways. The greenish glow from the dashboard illuminated the concern etched on her face. Tears inexplicably filled my eyes. She squeezed my hands firmly. I blinked back the tears.

"I saw things."

"What do you mean by that?" she asked, her words measured and calm.

"I saw things that weren't in the photographs," I explained.

"Are we talking about the last photographs you saw or all the photographs?"

"The last ones—the baby pictures."

"Okay. You observed things when you looked at those pictures that no one else observed? Is that what you're saying?"

I nodded.

"Mm-hmm. I saw things."

"What kind of things? Can you tell me?"

I took a shaky breath. Images of the babies zipped across my mind.

"I saw the whole baby. The face, the hands, the skin, the hair, the clothes—everything. One was a girl and the other a boy."

Mother's hand remained on mine. Her head tilted forward as she repeated my words.

"You saw the whole baby. Everything? You saw everything. A boy and a girl. Well, isn't that something."

She spoke thoughtfully and slowly, as if she were talking to a skittish colt ready to bolt.

"Yes." Now that I had started, I was impatient to get everything out. "At first I just saw their little feet and hands and then—bam—I saw the whole baby. Oh Mother, they were so beautiful. The little boy's eyes were this deep, deep blue. And he had the craziest strawberry blonde hair that stuck out all over the place. He reached his little hand out to me. The girl's hair was all curly and black. And her eyes—her eyes were the color of milk chocolate. She was all dressed up in a shiny white dress that was about ten sizes too big for her. Oh, she was so cute. Then she looked at me. She looked at me as if she knew I was looking at her. And she blinked. And she squeaked."

My voice wound down to a whisper as I relived the moment, still astonished by its existence. The car was silent save for the engine's purr and the hum of the heat flowing through the vents. Mother turned away from me. She stared straight out the windshield. We sat quietly. After a long moment, it dawned on me that perhaps she was considering where to send me.

"You believe me, dontcha?" I asked.

She turned back to me.

"Sure, yeah . . . I believe you. I'm just, uh, you know, pondering what it all might mean. Thank you for telling me. I appreciate your honesty." She turned off the car and undid her seat belt. "What do you say we go inside and get a cup of tea? I'm a little chilly, how about you?"

I nodded. We headed into the house through the brisk night air. I was glad Mother knew. I wasn't so sure Mother was glad she knew, but it helped to have someone else pondering the impossible with me. We fixed our tea, sat at the kitchen table, and drank it while we chatted. Our conversation carefully skirted the elephant in the room— the moving baby pictures. Instead, we talked about the other photographs we had seen. About how nice it was to see my summer classmates. About how talented Scott was—not to mention handsome. We ventured guesses as to whether Susan might contact him or not. When the tea was gone, Mother kissed me on the forehead.

"Let's just pray about the things you saw tonight," she said. "And we'll see what the Lord has to say. He always has something in mind. We don't have to fully understand what that is right away. So, don't worry about it. We'll wait and listen and see what we hear. Agreed?"

"Agreed," I replied.

She shooed me off to bed.

☐

I was clambering up a hill covered in brilliant-green grass, a wicker picnic basket in my hands, when the dream started. A warm breeze blew through my hair as I climbed, making the grass dance in waves of shimmering green life. White wildflowers sprinkled the hillside. An occasional clump of resplendent red poppies lifted their heads above the sea of grass. On the hilltop, a grove of trees stood outlined against a brilliant blue sky spotted with billowy clouds.

I was alone, but I knew I was there to meet someone. I had no idea who. Halfway up the hill I stopped, set down the basket, and flopped onto the grass. It was softer than any grass I had ever touched, and it smelled minty fresh. I lay back, lifted my face heavenward, laced my hands behind my head, and crossed my feet at the ankles. The songbirds' chirps and trills descended from the trees in a wondrous melody. The leaves of the trees seemed to clap a constant percussive backdrop to their song. The entire scene was so joyful, I thought my heart might burst with gladness. I closed my eyes and let the sounds, the smells, and the textures flow through me.

A sound akin to rushing waters spoke my name.

"Pearl."

Was it a voice? Or was it a river? I kept my eyes closed and listened.

"Pearl."

This time, the sound of the voice shifted from that of a rushing river to that of a burbling brook. Was it water or was it laughter?

I opened my eyes and sat up. A friend sat next to me, robed in brilliant white. His hair hung down to His shoulders in shiny waves. Lightning flashed all around Him. Everything about Him was so bright, I couldn't see His face, even when I squinted and shielded my eyes. I was tempted to be scared of Him, except for one thing: He was chuckling. A very merry chuckle. A contagious chuckle. I began to laugh too. Soon we were both laughing so hard, we held our hands across our bellies and fell back in the grass. We laughed and laughed until finally only an occasional chuckle bubbled to the surface. My friend stretched His arms over His head and mimicked my previous state of repose upon the grass. I joined Him. We watched a few puffy clouds float by, bathed in silent contentment.

"Ah, so refreshing," He said. "There's nothing quite like a good laugh, don't you agree?"

"I do."

I was at ease with this friend, but He was a mystery.

More clouds drifted by. More birds sang in the trees. We lay there, comfortable in each other's company. He wasn't in a hurry to tell my why He was there, and I was content to simply be near Him. After some time, I sat up and pulled the picnic basket from its place at my feet.

"Should we find out what's inside?" I asked.

He sat up too.

"Are you ready?"

I glanced back at Him. Suddenly, I was able to see His fiery eyes. They were captivatingly intense and yet marvelously kind. A hint of merriment still crinkled at their edges.

"Do I know you?" I asked.

The crinkles grew deeper.

"I know you," He said. "Since before you were born, I have known you."

"Oh, I know who you are," I gasped. "You're the King of the Great City. I've been to the Gate of Your city, but I didn't get to go in. Gregory said he had to ask You if I could enter, but You said no. Why did You say no?"

"Ah, Pearl," He said with a tender smile. "There is a time for everything and a purpose for every activity. I make everything beautiful in its time."

He hadn't answered my question, but it didn't matter. He was the King, and kings do as kings choose to do.

"Is it a beautiful time to open the picnic basket?" I asked.

"That's why I'm here."

He reached forward and undid the silver clasp holding the top basket flaps in place. I got up onto my knees. The basket had grown in His presence. As the flaps opened, a glowing light poured out and flew away in a cloudburst of yellow butterflies. I clapped my hands as I watched the cloud flutter up into the sky. When I looked back, He smiled—a smile so dazzling, it took my breath away.

"Thank you. That was beautiful."

He grinned.

"That's not all. Look inside."

I peered over the edge. Cradled in plush blankets in the basket's bottom lay two babies, a boy and a girl. The boy had wild, strawberry blonde hair, and the girl had a crown of black curls. Their faces were healthy and full. The chubby little arms that reached out to me rippled with baby fat. I stretched my hand to them. The baby boy grasped my pinkie finger firmly.

"Their names are Timothy and Shavonne," the King informed me. "They asked to meet you. They wanted to say thank you."

"To thank me? For what?"

"Thank you for seeing them," the King replied. "For seeing their lives. For acknowledging that they were and that they are. For comforting their families. For being courageous and kind."

"Did I do all that?"

"No, not yet, but you will. And not merely for these, but for many. Remember, you are a baby catcher, after all."

He gave me a quick wink.

I peered back into the basket. Neither one of the babies uttered a word, yet their faces seemed to say, "Thank you. Thank you. Thank you." Tears stung my eyes. Their precious faces began to blur.

I woke with a start and sat bolt upright in my bed, searching for the picnic basket but finding only my crumpled blankets. I was wide awake and vibrating as I disentangled myself and padded out of my room, headed straight for Mother. When I reached her bed, I crawled under the blankets. She rolled over and opened her eyes. Unalarmed by my sudden appearance, she reached out her arms and drew me close. I snuggled next to her warm cotton nightgown. The scent of glycerin face soap enveloped us.

After a few minutes, I whispered, "I had a dream."

She whispered back, "Tell me about it."

And so, I did.

BE GENTLE

I drifted through my classes the next day, half aware of my surroundings and half lost in a rippling sea of green grass. More than one teacher attempted to pull me back into reality with questions like, "Are you with us today, Pearl?" or "Earth to Pearl. Any chance you might join the rest of us?" I tried to blend into the conversation at the lunch table, but I finally abandoned my efforts and simply let the chatter flitter around me. My friends didn't seem to notice. I guess they had grown accustomed to my occasional remoteness.

After school, I grabbed my things from my locker and beelined for the bike rack. I was relieved that I had ridden my bike to school, despite the dropping temperature. I didn't want to walk home with Mel and El and be subjected to closer scrutiny. I wanted to get home and sketch Timothy and Shavonne. In my haste, I bumped right into Miss Wells.

"Oh, Pearl. I'm glad I *ran* into you," she said with a small laugh (she enjoyed puns). "I've been meaning to talk with you."

"I'm sorry, Miss Wells. I guess I wasn't paying attention."

"And that is exactly why I wanted to talk to you," she said. "I've noticed you've had a great deal of difficulty paying attention in class lately. Today you seemed to be adrift on some far-off planet for the entire period. It's not like you. Is everything okay?"

I hesitated. She waited.

"I'm okay," I said. "A little tired, I guess. Didn't sleep too well."

"Does it have to do with what happened at the art appreciation event last night? Perhaps some of the photographs stirred up your imagination? Truth be told," she leaned in closer, "a few of Mr. Stewart's photographs shook me up a bit too. The images he captured were so lifelike, they seemed to jump from the frames."

If she only knew.

"Well, let's hope the solution is simply a good night's rest," she continued. "But you will let me know if there is anything I can do, won't you?"

"Yes, ma'am. I will. And I promise to try harder to not be so spaced-out in class."

"I know you will," she said, laying a hand on my shoulder. "But please be aware that I have a good listening ear if you need one—even for things beyond the *orbit* of my classroom."

I smiled despite my longing to escape her field of gravity.

"Thanks, Miss Wells."

I resisted the temptation to add, "Didn't mean to be so out to *launch*." It would only have fueled her trajectory. She had a reputation for being able to "outpun" most anyone. And I didn't have time for that.

Miss Wells retreated into her classroom. I bounded down the stairs and out the front doors. I was on my bike in a jiffy, zigzagging past groups of students who loitered on the sidewalk. Before I bounced off the curb and onto the street, I was already sketching babies in my mind. The entire way home I pedaled and pondered my project, eager to begin.

I flew up the driveway and leaned my bike against the house. I was so focused on my plans that I didn't see the other bicycle propped against the front porch until I was nearly upon it. It was a boy's bike, a ten-speed with curled handlebars. Definitely not Mel's or El's.

"Hello, Pearl," came a voice from the top step.

I dropped my backpack and shrieked. Ben laughed and I stomped my foot.

"That was not nice, Ben Bradley. You scared me half to death!"

My rebuke, however, only seemed to fuel his laughter.

"Oh, my gosh," he gasped. "You should've seen your face. That is the funniest thing I've seen in a long time. I thought you were going to take off running for the hills."

He held his stomach and doubled over. I was not amused. When he took a moment to glance at my face, he evidently became aware of this fact, because he attempted to subdue his laughter. He wiped tears from his eyes and offered a half-hearted apology.

"Sorry for, ah, catching you off guard. You must not get much company."

He took a deep breath, blew it out, and brought his outburst to a finale at last. I snatched my backpack from the ground but remained at the foot of the steps. I wanted to respond with a witty remark, but my mind was fixated on one thought: Ben Bradley was sitting on my front porch. I must have remained frozen for a few seconds too long, since Ben stood up and came down the steps.

"Hey, listen, Pearl, I'm really sorry I scared you. I didn't mean to. Are you okay?"

He appeared to be genuinely repentant. Finally, my brain and my mouth decided to cooperate.

"Oh, no big deal," I said, shaking off my embarrassed irritation. "I just wasn't expecting to find you sitting on my front porch."

"Yeah, sorry about that too," he added. "I tried to catch you at school today but never did see you. Were you there?"

"Yes, of course I was there. Hey, how did you find out where I live, anyway?"

"Jeez, the town's not that big. I can go if you want," he said as he picked up his backpack and moved toward his bike.

"No, don't go," I said, grabbing his arm.

Something like electricity shot through my hand. I gulped. He stared at my hand on his arm.

"Let's, uh, start over?" I said, slipping my tingling hand back into the pocket of my parka.

He shrugged.

"Okay."

As we headed up the steps, I added, "We'll have to stay out here, though. Mother doesn't allow me to have boys in the house when she's not home."

"Okay. Cool," he replied.

We settled onto the top step, a respectable foot and a half between us. Our backpacks behind us, we stared out at the street. Mrs. Schmidt stared at us from behind the blinds in her living room. I waved. The blinds snapped shut.

"Who's that?" Ben asked.

"Mrs. Schmidt. The neighborhood busybody."

"Good to know."

"Hard to avoid," I added.

He smiled. Dimples appeared.

I zipped my parka all the way up and stuffed my hands deep into my pockets. An awkward hush descended. It lingered until I could stand it no longer.

"So, are you and your mom doing okay, settling in and everything?" I asked.

"Yeah, we're getting used to things. It's different, but I think we'll be fine. Give it time. That's what my mom says."

"She's probably right," I said, trying to sound confident. "I've lived in this town my whole life. So, I can't exactly say I know what you're going through. But I can imagine it might take some time."

He nodded. Again, the quiet simmered. My mind went blank. My one attempt to break the ice had failed. Finally, Ben turned my way.

"I wanted to come by and find out what happened to you last night. When I went to get the water, my mom got a hold of me. She said we had to get home. Did your mom tell you? I hope you don't think I bailed on you."

"Mother told me. I knew you hadn't deserted me on purpose."

I stopped. How was I supposed to explain what happened to a guy I hardly knew? I didn't want to lose a friend before I made one.

"Ok. Good," Ben said. "Glad she told you. Did the water help? You seemed kinda freaked out."

I wanted to scream and run for the hills for real. Why should I tell him? I hadn't even told Mel and El. What if he thought it was a joke? What if he thought I was a wacko? What if he told the kids at school? If they thought I was strange before, this would put me on the Certifiably Crazy List, which, to my knowledge, only had two current members in all of St. Gerard: Mr. Navonavich, who was known to throw things out the windows of his spooky two-story brick house at any random passersby, and Miss Finnelson, who at the age of ninety-three had perfected the art of escaping from her room at the old folks' home and waltzing down Main Street in her silk pajamas. I was not eager to become number three. But in the midst of convincing myself what a bad idea it was to spill the beans, something deep in my belly, beyond my ability to put into words, argued back. It told me I could trust him. I took a deep breath and looked straight into his eyes.

"It's a long story," I began. "And once you hear it, you may not want to be seen with me. But you must promise me two things."

"Sounds interesting. What?"

"First, you must promise not to tell anyone—except maybe your mom," I instructed.

He nodded.

"And second, when I finish and I ask what you think, you must promise to be honest. Can you do that?"

Without hesitation, he put out his hand and answered, "I can do that."

I reached out my hand too. We shook on it. Then I began back where it all began—with Joseph and the Baby-Catcher Gate. He listened intently. From time to time he stopped me and had me repeat something, but it wasn't rude. It was more like he was trying to understand. When I started to explain the previous night's events, he leaned forward, elbows on knees and head in hands. I wasn't sure if I should include my dream from the night before. But then I thought, he may as well have the whole kit and caboodle, as Grandma used to say.

So he heard about the green pasture, the picnic basket with the bundled babies, and the laughing King. As I told him, contentment and joy washed over me. When I finally stopped, Ben was leaning back against the porch rail, his feet extended, his face lifted to the clouds, his hands lost inside his sweatshirt pouch. Neither of us spoke. It felt like a thin place.

"So," I asked, "what do you think?"

Ben aimed his words more at the clouds than at me.

"Honestly, I'm not quite sure what I think. You've experienced some pretty, uh, intense stuff. Sounds like a movie or a book or something."

He continued to stare off into the horizon. I wasn't sure what was going on in his head. But judging by his stillness, it seemed that my story had stirred something up inside him. I wondered if he would tell me what it was. It seemed as though he might. I waited.

"When I was seven," he said quietly, his eyes still focused on a point in the distance, "my daddy left me and my mom. He was a travelling preacher. He'd be home one week and preach at our small church. The next week he'd be gone, filling the pulpit at another small church in the area. Turns out he was doing more than preaching in the other town. He had a whole other family there—a wife, a daughter, and a baby boy. One day he decided going back and forth between the towns, the churches, and the families was too much. So, he stopped . . . stopped coming back to us."

He peeked at me from under his long, blond bangs, as if to check my reaction. Even though I wanted to drop my jaw in shock, I concentrated on keeping my face neutral. He seemed satisfied that it was safe to continue.

"Guess he thought a wife and two kids needed him more than Mama and I needed him. Or maybe he just liked them better. I didn't ever really know. When Mama went to find him, she found more than she bargained for. She came home by herself. Told me we were going to be a family of two from then on. The churches in both towns fired him when they found out what was going on. Daddy and his other family moved away. I didn't care. I hated him. I hated them. Every night when I went to bed I would hear Mama praying and crying in her room. I didn't understand how she could still pray to a God who would let such bad stuff happen to us. The only prayer I prayed was 'God, let them all die.'"

Ben sat up and hunched forward, his arms crossed on his thighs.

"One day I came home from school and found Mama sitting at the kitchen table with a letter in her hands. She was crying, which made me mad again. I wondered who had hurt her now. She told me it was a letter from her cousin who lived in the town my daddy had moved to. She thought we might want to know that he had fallen on some hard times. His other wife and daughter had left him after he had accidentally let the baby boy drown in the bathtub. He'd been drinking a great deal and had lost his job. Mama dropped the letter on the table and cried some more.

"I yelled, 'How can you cry for him? This is what he deserves. I hope he dies too!' Mama looked at me with such pain in her eyes. It was as if I had slapped her."

Ben spoke so softly, I leaned closer to make sure I didn't miss a word.

"Mama grabbed my hands and pulled me in," he continued. "She told me hate was a dangerous thing. She said I needed to find a way to forgive my daddy. If I didn't, it would poison my soul for the rest of my life. I didn't care. Hate was the only way I could punish him. If I forgave him, I would be letting him off the hook. He didn't deserve my forgiveness."

Ben stopped for a moment. I sat perfectly still, afraid any movement might distract him or deter him from continuing. It was strangely comforting to hear his story. Not that I enjoyed hearing of the painful events in his life. But by telling me, it was as if he were saying, "I don't really understand your story, but I accept it. Now, will you accept mine?"

We were going to be friends. In fact, we already were.

"One day," Ben resumed, "Mama left me at my friend's house for an overnight. She went to see my daddy. For a long time, I didn't know why. I was just relieved that when she came home she didn't have him with her. Turns out she had helped him get into a rehab center. Guess the church helped her out. I don't know the details; she doesn't talk about it. All I know is when she came back, she was at peace. Seemed like helping out the man who hurt her was her way of proving to herself and to him—and to me—that she would live what she believed, no matter how hard it was."

He shook his head as if still perplexed by her courage.

"I was sorta jealous of her peace, but I wasn't ready to let go of my hate. In a way, my hate helped me ignore the other thing I felt—guilt. I kept hearing a voice in my head saying, 'That baby boy died because you wanted him to die. It's your fault.' Whenever that thought came, I flooded it out with hate for my daddy. It was his fault, not mine. For a long time, that's how I fell asleep at night—a wave of guilt, a wave of hate, back and forth. Then one night when I was eleven, I had a dream. It was different from any kind of dream I'd ever had. It was so real."

He paused. He glimpsed at me as if to see if I was still with him. I was.

"In my dream," Ben continued, "a man sat on a chair near the edge of a cliff. The cliff overlooked a big ocean. As I walked to the man, I saw he was old and covered with green mold. Then he turned to me. I recognized him. It was my daddy. In a split second, hatred rose up in me and overwhelmed me. I grabbed him around the neck and began to strangle him. I wanted to kill him. But nothing happened. He didn't even put up a fight. It was as if he was already dead, but I kept squeezing anyway.

"Then I noticed the mold was beginning to cover my hands. It was moving up my arms, all the way to my throat. It was heavy. I felt as if I was suffocating. Then the earth beneath my feet crumbled, and the entire cliff disappeared in an instant. Daddy and I were falling into the sea, my hands still around his neck. I was scared. Then a voice said, 'Let go and you will live.' So, I let go. The mold left, the heaviness lifted, and I could breathe. I was still falling, but for some reason, I wasn't afraid. And I woke up."

He stopped and looked my way. I gave him a little smile. He forged ahead.

"I knew what the dream meant. So, I prayed right there in my bed, 'God, I don't want to be full of hatred anymore. I forgive my daddy.' It was that simple—a choice to let go. I fell back asleep with waves of peace instead of hatred for the first time in a long time." Ben dropped his head. "You're the only one who's ever heard that story besides Mama."

A small smirk crept onto my face as I replied, "Well, I guess we're even then."

I was rewarded with a dimpled half grin.

"Yeah, I guess so."

We sat in silence for a while, but it wasn't an awkward silence anymore. It was the silence of two old friends. I didn't want to break the peacefulness, but I had a question I needed to ask.

"Hey, you know how you said you used to fall asleep on waves of hate and guilt, hate and guilt?"

"Yeah?"

"Well, I'm wondering. I don't mean to be nosy, and you don't have to tell me if you don't want to. But you said the anger left once you forgave your daddy. But what about the guilt? Have you asked God to forgive you?"

"Only about a million times," he said. "But I don't think I deserve to be forgiven. Maybe if I hadn't prayed those prayers, my brother would still be alive."

"Hmm." I stopped to think about my next step. "Well, I don't think forgiveness is really about whether we deserve it or not."

Ben stared back down into his hands. He didn't say anything. When he looked at me, tears coursed down his cheeks. His face was so troubled and tender, he appeared years younger than his age. Tears welled up in my eyes. I scooted across the respectable foot and a half and put a hand on his shoulder. It seemed to help. I felt him shudder as he drew in a ragged breath.

"He was my baby brother," he said quietly. "But all I ever felt for him was hate. Now I'll never get the chance to know him. Maybe one day he and I might've been friends. But I asked God every night to let him die, and He did. He let him die." Ben shook his head. "No, I think I will have to live with the guilt. Maybe it's my way of keeping him alive."

I let my hand slip from his shoulder but remained next to him. I was at a loss for words. Then a still, small voice echoed inside my heart: "Be gentle." I waded into his pain.

"Well," I said, "your baby brother is alive. But your holding onto guilt isn't the reason why. To the King, everyone is living. We're simply not all in the same place at the moment. One day you will get to know your brother, but you must trust the King. He didn't let your brother die because you asked Him to. From what I know about the King, I don't think that's a prayer He takes too seriously. He knows you didn't really know what you were asking. Besides, He's a good King, and He can't do anything bad. I don't know why your brother died, but I do know it wasn't your fault. The King simply has a time for everything. He told me He makes everything beautiful in its time."

Ben remained staring downward, but his shoulders relaxed. When he raised his head, he put both hands to his face and wiped away the tears. He followed that with a brusque sweep of his sleeve across his nose. He looked twelve again. Maybe even thirteen.

"I'll think about that," he said. "Thanks, Pearl. And thanks for telling me about last night and everything."

He looked me right in the eyes. A funny shyness swept across his features and he dropped his gaze.

"I wasn't sure if I would find a friend in this town, let alone a friend as . . . well, let's just say as peculiar as you."

It wasn't exactly the word I was hoping to hear, but his voice was so sincere, my heart fluttered. I inhaled and studied my fingernails. A quick sideways glance revealed that he was studying me.

I was immensely relieved when he spoke up and said, "I better head home. And don't worry. Next time I'll give you fair warning before I show up on your front porch."

He stood and pulled up his hood, slung on his backpack, and leapt down the steps, landing catlike next to his bike. I sat and watched him pedal away. I smiled to myself.

"Peculiar."

GIRL TALK

After supper, Mother took the cordless phone into the front room. This meant she had a call to make that required a certain level of privacy. I sat at the kitchen table with my sketch pad before me, keeping one ear tuned to the living room to figure out who she was calling. I preferred not to think of it as eavesdropping—Mother didn't approve of that practice. I preferred to think of it as *valuable tidbit hunting.* Maybe it wasn't the right thing to do, but I figured if Mother truly wanted a private conversation, she would take the phone to her bedroom. I considered the front room fair game. Most of her calls were to clients, anyway. Those conversations didn't interest me in the least. But on occasion I gathered valuable tidbits when the party on the other end was a family member, a neighbor, or someone else who might be of interest to me.

Tidbit hunting proved challenging that night. I was still stirred up after my conversation with Ben. Plus, I was trying to focus on sketching Timothy and Shavonne. My mind flitted back and forth between the two equally compelling subject matters. And when I determined Mother was calling Susan, my focus was divided even further. Eventually, however, the baby sketches won my complete attention and I gave myself to the process of moving the images in my head onto my sketch pad. I began with Shavonne's tawny face and shiny, black curls. I labored over her puckered lips and dark eyes, so consumed that all was lost to me except the portrait of this precious baby girl. When I glanced at the clock, I was surprised to see an hour had flown by. I was equally surprised to hear Mother still on the phone; she didn't generally engage in lengthy phone conversations. Even long-distance calls to my sister or brother (which had resumed, thanks to my stay in the hospital) were usually kept under thirty minutes.

I set down the dusty, pink eraser and listened as I stood and moved to the sink to refill my water glass. It just so happened that the sink was closer to the opening to the living room, which may or may not have contributed to my sudden thirst. I filled my glass and sipped with my ears trained on the other room. I was rewarded with the name Scott Stewart and a phone number being read off. A very valuable tidbit. They must have been talking about the art appreciation night. I wondered if Mother had told her about my visions or hallucinations or whatever you called them.

"Pearl, as long as you're listening, would you care to chat with your sister?" Mother asked from the living room.

I was baffled. How did she know I was listening? Listening didn't sound like anything. Oh, maybe that's how she knew.

"Sure," I replied nonchalantly, setting my glass on the counter as I strolled toward the all-knowing one.

She handed me the phone.

"Keep it short, please. I've already run up the bill."

"Hey, Susan," I said as I plunked onto the recliner.

"Hey, short stuff. How're ya doing?"

"Pretty good. You?"

"Super busy, but hanging in there," Susan replied. "Sometimes I wonder what I've gotten myself into. There's so much to learn. It's overwhelming at times."

"Yeah, I'll bet."

"So . . . I hear you met Scott Stewart last night and saw his photography. What did you think?"

"I think you should call him."

She laughed.

"That's not what I meant."

"Well, it's what I meant," I said as I launched into my sales pitch. "He's cute. He's talented. He owns a business. He lives in the same city as you. He went to school with you. Why wouldn't you call him? Unless, of course, you've already got another hunk on the line?"

"Listen to you, you little matchmaker. It's not always so simple. My schedule is crammed to the max."

"You gotta take a break sometime. Anyways, I'm not saying you have to marry him or anything. Although that might not be a bad idea. I'm only saying you should give him a call and see what happens."

"Okay, okay, Dear Abby. Maybe I will," she said. "I confess I am a bit curious. And I could use a little fun."

"Great," I said, feeling pleased with my ability to close the deal. "Make sure I'm the first one you call after your first date."

"Hey, hey, hold on there. I said I'd call him. I didn't say I'd date him."

"Yeah, whatever. It's not what you said, but it's what you meant. True?"

The phone was silent for a moment.

"Okay," she responded.

"Okay, what?"

"Okay, if the phone call turns into a date, you'll be the first one I call."

"Yahoo!" I yodeled into the receiver.

She laughed. I kicked off my slippers and sprawled sideways across the chair, my feet dangling over one puffy stuffed arm and my neck over the other. Her laughter faded.

"Hey, kiddo," she began switching gears. "Can I ask you a serious question?"

I had an inkling I knew where this was going.

"Sure," I answered, my head still hanging upside down.

"Have you drawn the babies you saw in Scott's photos?"

My feet stopped swinging. Suspicions confirmed.

"I was sketching the little girl before Mother handed me the phone."

"I hope you're not upset she told me everything."

"Nah, it's okay," I said as I scooched into an upright position and blinked away the stars from my eyes, aware that I would need a clear brain for the rest of this conversation. "Saves me from having to repeat it. Sometimes I wonder if it's even real. But then I sketch, and it's like those babies come alive on my paper. And I know I'm not making it all up."

"Hey, listen," she said. "I'm convinced you're not making it up. I actually think it's pretty cool. Makes me think about things beyond my textbooks and labs. Bigger things. And guess what?"

"What?"

"Those thoughts give me peace and joy, sorta all mixed up with hope." She paused before adding, "Whatever happened to you—it's helped me. So, thanks for letting me in on it."

When an older sister thanks a younger sister for helping her, it's a topsy-turvy moment. It felt uncomfortably wonderful.

"You're welcome."

"Okay, I'd better go. But don't worry, if—and that is a big *if*—this Scott Stewart thing develops into anything, you will be the first one I call."

"Okay, deal. Good night, Susan. Love you."

"Love you too."

☐

I sat contentedly on the recliner, relishing the thought of Susan dating Scott Stewart as if it were an accomplished fact. What if she married him? Susan Stewart. Sounded nice.

When the phone rang in my hand, I jumped. The receiver dropped onto the floor. I scrambled to find it under the coffee table before whoever was calling could hang up.

I recovered it and yelled, "I've got it."

"Okay," Mother yelled back from the kitchen.

"Hello, this is Pearl," I answered from my hands and knees.

"Okay, Pearl, give me the scoop. What's he like?"

"Mel? What's who like?"

"Oh, come on. You know who 'he' is. We made a pledge. Remember?"

She was asking about Ben. I sat down on the floor, my back against the couch. With my knees drawn to my chest, I pondered what to tell her. A yellow flag popped up in my heart. I proceeded with caution.

"What do you mean, exactly?"

"What do I mean? I saw you on your front porch this afternoon with Ben Bradley. Didn't you see me wave when my mom and I drove by?"

I didn't want to tell her anything. But I knew Mel. She would never let me off the hook if I didn't give her something to chew on. Besides, we had made a pact. I wondered how much information was required to fulfill a pinkie's worth of promise. I was glad we didn't shake hands on it.

"Hello? Pearl? Are you there?"

"Yeah, yeah, I'm here," I said. "And no, I didn't see you drive by. Sorry."

"Well, it appeared as if you were in a deep conversation. What was it all about?"

"Oh, it wasn't much. He, uh, had a question about our history homework."

As I said it, I knew it was a lie, but somehow it seemed better than revealing the truth.

"A homework question? It didn't look like a homework kind of conversation."

"Well, it was. He was confused. Besides how could you tell what kind of conversation it was?"

"Jeez, you don't have to get all defensive. It looked like more than a homework conversation because you had your hand on his shoulder."

"Oh, that," I backed down. "Well, that was because, uh, because he's new here and he doesn't think he's going to find any friends in this little town."

Which was true, I consoled myself.

"Hmm." I swore I heard the wheels turning in her head. "So, does he think he's found a friend in you?"

Her question felt heavy with a jealousy I didn't want to feed.

"Maybe. Maybe not," I replied. "He told me he thinks I'm peculiar."

"Peculiar?!" A new voice joined the conversation.

"Tiff, I told you to stay quiet," Mel rebuked the unseen valuable-tidbit hunter.

"Tiffany? Uh . . ."

"Sorry, Pearl, for eavesdropping. But I just can't believe he actually said that to you. How rude," Tiffany blurted.

"Tiff is just hanging out 'til her Dad picks her up, and she was in the car when we drove by, and we just got super curious, and . . . I'm sorry, Pearl. I should've told you she was listening."

Of all people. Tiffany Paulsen. The class tattletale.

"Did he really say 'peculiar'?" Mel asked, sounding embarrassed both for herself and for me.

"Honest, cross my heart, that's what he said," I assured her.

"Well, Pearl," Tiffany jumped back in, "don't you worry about what he says. We all know you're, well, maybe slightly odd, but that's just you. Don't let some new boy upset you. He'll learn. Cause underneath it all, you're pretty much normal."

Although her words were kinda nice, I could tell she was relieved to think that the conversation between Ben and me had ended badly.

I'd given a pinkie's worth.

"Hey, Mel, I've gotta go." I intentionally omitted Tiffany in my sign-off.

"Yeah, okay," Mel said quietly. "And, Pearl . . . I really am sorry."

"Me too. I don't know if I even want to get to know a guy with such bad manners," Tiffany added, completely oblivious to the fact that she was the reason Mel was feeling sorry.

"See ya tomorrow."

I clicked off the receiver before she could add anything else to the already disastrous chat.

Mother stepped into the door, drying a pan with a checkered kitchen towel.

"What was that all about?" she asked.

"Nothing much," I said with a shrug.

Just the end of the world as I knew it.

INTERLUDE: THE KING

Ilsa's voice carries over the hubbub. "John, over here."Her waving hands barely visible over the sea of humanity that stretches out around me, I advance in her direction. I've chosen to walk to our designated spot so I can more fully absorb the spectacle around me. As I go, I glance over to the massive stone platform that rises about four stories tall in the midst of the throng. Its polished black surface shines like a deep, still pool and reflects the brightly arrayed crowd gathered around its base. A stairway carved into the side of the stone zigzags up to the top, where an enormous golden bowl stands on a white marble altar. Around the brim of the bowl, engraved in flowing script, are the words "On Earth as It Is in Heaven."

The atmosphere buzzes with excited chatter. Overhead, thousands upon ten thousands of winged hosts hover in brilliant finery. Spontaneous songs burst out here and there from the assembled masses, each one delightful in its unique melody. Some sweep like wildfire across the crowd, igniting a mighty chorus, colossal in power, overwhelming in goodness and joy.

Family and friends greet me when I arrive. William sidles up next to me, and I wrap my arm around his shoulder.

"Hey, buddy."

"Hey, Dad."

"This is really something, eh?"

"For sure." He nods, then suddenly points toward the platform. "Look. Look up there. The King is here!"

The entire assembly erupts in praise as the resplendent figure of the King appears on the podium. He is at once majestic and humble, familiar and foreign, ferocious and gentle—the Lion and the Lamb.

"How can He be so far from us and yet feel like He's right next to us?" Will asks over the sustained ovation.

Always full of questions, this one—my son, my William.

"He's mysterious that way," I say with a shrug. "Along with a bunch of other ways."

"That's for sure," Ilsa adds from beside me. "I always thought once we arrived here the mysteries of life would be explained. Turns out to be true on some levels, but by and large, the unsolved of this realm far outweighs the solved of the last one."

"Really?" Will asks.

"I suppose you wouldn't know," Ilsa says, caressing his cheek. "Trust me, you've got plenty of mysteries here to keep you occupied for eternity."

"I know. But just once, I'd like to go to the other side," he says, looking out over the crowd to the platform. "The King did."

He has a point.

Trumpets sound from above, and our attention pivots back to the center of the gathering. A holy hush settles over the throng.

"Do you know why we've been gathered?" Will whispers.

"Special occasion was all I heard," I whisper back before Ilsa shushes the both of us.

Twenty-four elders, robed in white and with crowns on their heads, begin to climb the stairs to the top of the platform in solemn single file. Clouds of incense drift up from the polished ceramic bowls that fill their arms, sending a spicy, sweet aroma over the assembly. Anticipation builds as the elders reach the platform's summit, bow their heads to the King, and form a circle around the base of the large center bowl. Twenty-four resplendent hosts descend from on high and lift the earthenware from the elders' arms. Upward they fly until they hover over the heart of the altar.

In unity, they face the King and wait. He turns to the east and all eyes follow His gaze. A dazzling flash lights the horizon, accompanied by a low rumble like that of a legion of timpani.

He turns back to the altar, lifts His hands, and commands, "Begin."

The crowd cheers as the winged hosts, one after the other, lift their bowls overhead and tip the contents into the gigantic receiving bowl. Multihued embers flare from its midst with each new deposit. And we, in turn, break into praise along with all the heavenly hosts.

"Blessing and honor, glory and power, be unto the Ancient of Days!"

Over and over we sing with gusto as the outpouring continues.

When the twenty-fourth host lifts his bowl overhead, the crowd falls silent as he turns back to the King and announces, "In Your presence and the presence of all those gathered here, I deposit the prayers of the saints and declare, by the authority of the Father, a season of overflow."

"Yes and amen," the King affirms in a resounding voice.

"Yes and amen," we echo in one accord.

The host raises his bowl, and as its contents flow into the amalgamation, a wondrous, smoky vapor of every color imaginable and unimaginable spills over the golden brim. Gushing and swirling, the glorious smoke envelops the platform and rushes out over the crowd with its heady aroma. The elders fall prostrate before the King. The hosts cover their faces with their wings, and every knee across the entire throng bends as the overflow shrouds us in weighty glory. Silence reigns.

When at last the vibrant vapor dissipates, we rise from our knees. The King and the elders are gone. Overhead, the heavenly hosts disperse in every direction, swiftly, purposefully. And the throng disbands in quiet awe.

"What happens now?" William asks as he, Ilsa, and I walk together.

"Wondrous things," I reply.

"Have you seen this before?" Ilsa says.

"Just once."

"And?" Will prompts.

"And we will have to see what He has in mind. From what I've heard, each season of overflow is peculiar unto itself."

"But what happened in the last overflow?" he asks.

"It's hard to describe," I say as we continue our homeward journey. "A thinness in the boundaries . . . unusual encounters."

"Do you suppose that's why she was here?" Ilsa asks.

"Could be," I say, nodding.

"Who?" William grabs my arm. "Who was here?"

I look at Ilsa. She looks at me.

"Pearl," we say in unison.

SPREAD THE WORD

Someone knocked at our front door early the next morning. Mother answered it since I wasn't fully dressed yet. I stuck my head into the hallway to listen.

"Uh, hi," he said. "I'm Ben Bradley . . . a friend of Pearl's."

My hand slipped from the doorframe and I stubbed my toe trying to catch my balance.

"Oh, yes, Mr. Bradley," I heard Mother reply as I hopped up and down in pain. "I remember you from the other night. Come on in."

"Oh, I don't need to come in. I was just wondering if Pearl wanted to bike to school with me."

"Well," Mother said, "you can ask her yourself. But you will need to come in, because she isn't quite ready yet."

"Okay," he replied. "I guess I am a little early."

"Not a problem," Mother said. "I'll go get her."

The front door closed and I hopped back into my room, scurrying to zip up my jeans, throw on my sweatshirt (which suddenly seemed frumpy and unsatisfactory), and brush my hair. Mother knocked and entered.

"So, I assume you heard all of that," she said with an amused look on her face. "Better get your bottom in gear if you want to ride with him."

I was surprised, delighted, and nervous as I smeared strawberry Lip Smacker over my lips before rushing out to meet Ben in the entryway.

"Hey," I said, slightly out of breath.

"Hey," he replied. "Wanna bike to school together?"

"Sure," I said.

I just stood there, like a dork.

"Uh, you ready to go?" he asked.

"Just about," I said, coming to my senses. I stuffed my feet into my clogs, grabbed a jacket off the hook by the door, and retrieved my backpack from atop the bookshelf. "I wasn't expecting you . . . again," I said with a laugh.

"Yeah, I should have warned you . . . again. Sorry."

"No biggie," I said. "But my house isn't exactly on your route to school."

He dropped his chin and shrugged.

"Yeah, well, uh . . ."

Mother joined us from the kitchen with my lunch.

"Well, I think it is quite chivalrous of him to make the extra effort," she said, handing me the brown paper bag. She checked her watch. "Time to get moving," she said and opened the door. Out we went.

I wasn't quite sure what "chivalrous" meant, but I did understand "extra effort." And I was pleased beyond words to think that Ben Bradley had gone out of his way to show up at my front door that morning.

We stopped at the corner of Quince and 10th to wait for Mel and El.

"Hey guys," I said as they halted next to us. "This is Ben Bradley. Ben, these are my friends Mel and El."

"Hey," he said with a quick wave. "Think we've got science together," he said to El.

She didn't respond.

"And aren't you in my English class?" he asked Mel.

She, too, remained in a state of dazed silence.

"Are they always this quiet?" Ben asked with a hint of mischief in his eyes.

"Trust me when I say this is a rare occurrence. Enjoy it," I said, pushing off and starting to pedal.

The others followed suit. Mel quickly pulled alongside me.

"About last night . . ." she said in a voice meant only for me.

"What's done is done," I said. "Don't worry about it."

"I am truly, honestly, completely sorry," she added.

I nodded and pedaled faster to catch up with Ben and El, who were chattering away. The moment of muteness had passed. By the time we had locked our bikes in the stand by the school steps, Mel had joined in the prattle, and they were all laughing like long-lost buddies. I was glad they were getting to know Ben, but I also kinda wished I could keep him to myself.

Inside the school doors, Mel and El peeled off to their lockers on the west wing.

"See ya at second lunch?" Mel asked while walking backward.

"I've got first lunch, sorry," Ben replied.

Mel's face registered her disappointment.

"After school, then?"

"Mel, watch—"

El's warning came too late to save Mel from running smack dab into Tiffany Paulsen, who was absorbed in her own conversation with Reggie Dumfrey.

Mel bounced off Tiffany and was saved from a complete face-plant by El's quick reflexes. Tiffany was not so lucky. She flew backward and landed squarely on her bottom before smacking up against a locker. Tears quickly filled her eyes and crimson flushed her cheeks. Ben ran to her side.

"Jeez, Elf Spit, can't you keep your friend from running over people?" Reggie barked.

El's cheeks flamed as red as her hair and fire lit her eyes, but her tongue stayed tied.

"And what about you, ya big bully?" I spit out before I could stop myself. "You were standing right next to Tiff and you didn't even try to catch her."

"Ooh, granny . . . or should I call you Peculiar Pearl? Gonna be all brave, are ya?" He loomed closer, his finger pointed at my chest. "Guess Romeo over there figured you out in no time. Peculiar Pearl the Airhead Girl."

My eyes blurred. Tiffany hadn't wasted anytime in sharing her valuable tidbit.

"She's not peculiar, she's just . . ." Mel tried to come to my aid.

"Just what? Super peculiar?"

Reggie leaned in and wagged his grinning mug in our faces. He seemed delighted to see us all flummoxed.

"Hey, you." Ben spun Reggie around and grabbed him by the front of his shirt, despite his significant disadvantage in size. "What are you saying about my friends?"

For a split second, Reggie was so stunned he couldn't respond. But that didn't last long. Enraged by Ben's audacity, he broke the hold on his shirt and shoved him against the lockers with a resounding bang.

Miss Wells dashed out of her classroom and into the midst of the fray.

"What is going on here?" she demanded, striking a formidable pose in the middle of the hallway.

Reggie unclenched his fists and pretended to smooth Ben's shirt.

"Nothing, Teach," he said. "Just a little accident."

Seeing Tiffany still leaning against the wall, Miss Wells bent to assess her condition.

Reggie took the opportunity to say right in my ear, "Be seeing ya, Peculiar."

"Everybody get to your classes," Miss Wells ordered. "I will take Tiffany down to the nurse's office. Now go, or you'll all get detention."

Mel and El retreated toward their lockers along with Reggie and the small contingency of onlookers who had accumulated. Ben and I headed the other direction.

"What was that all about?" he asked after we had distanced ourselves from the scene of the crime.

"Oh, it's just Reggie being himself—a big, fat bully."

"Why was he calling you peculiar? Did you tell him what I said?"

"Are you kidding? Of course not."

"Well, he must've heard it from somewhere."

The first bell rang. Thank goodness. I didn't want to have to tell him about my phone conversation with Mel and Tiffany. I hadn't really told them anything . . . actually, only one word. One lousy word. I could hardly imagine what Reggie might've done with the rest of the story.

"I'll explain later," I said, hoping against hope that I wouldn't have to.

☐

The day did not improve from there.

In first-period math, we had a pop quiz. I failed.

In biology, we dissected worms. I puked.

In health class, the boys left the classroom with Coach Spencer while we girls remained with Mrs. Weiss. It was time for the lesson on the birds and the bees, which left everyone all twitterpated except me—old news in my book.

In English, we were supposed to hand in our essays. Mine lay on the kitchen table, where I had left it in my haste to get out the door with Ben that morning. Not only that, but both Reggie and Tiffany were in that class. She was evidently fully recovered from her humiliation, and Reggie acted as if he had been her hero, boasting in hushed asides to his gang about saving her from Romeo and Peculiar, as if Ben and I were some comic book crime duo. Miss Wells had to shush him more than once.

Finally, when one of his comments sent too many ripples of laughter through his audience, she announced, "Mr. Dumfrey, meet me in the hallway."

He sat defiantly in his desk. She glared at him and strode toward him until all five feet and ten inches of her solid frame loomed over him.

"Move it, Reggie," she ordered.

Begrudgingly he did so, and she followed him out the door. When she returned, Mr. Dumfrey was not with her.

"If anyone else would like to join your pal in the principal's office," she announced, "just keep up your foolishness, and I will accommodate your wishes."

The remainder of the hour went by without incident, but by the end of it, I could compose myself no longer. I sat at my desk until everyone left, laid my head on my folded arms, and dissolved into tears. I didn't care if I missed lunch. I had lost my appetite.

A gentle hand touched my shoulder.

"Pearl, can I help?"

I lifted my head. Miss Wells was crouched next to me in the aisle. She handed me a tissue.

"Don't let him get to you," she offered.

I was glad she knew exactly what—or who—the problem was.

"I try . . . not . . . to," I said, attempting to bring my tears to a halt.

"He's just an insecure kid who thinks he'll feel better about himself if he can make someone else feel worse."

I nodded and blew my nose.

"I heard what he called you this morning," she said softly.

The waterworks started afresh. She handed me another tissue.

"Did Reggie throw something at you?"

I shook my head.

"No. Why?"

"Well, it's just that you've got glitter or something all over your shoulders."

"I do?" I looked down and sure enough, my shoulders were covered in gold, dandruff-like stuff. "What is it?"

"I don't know," she said, brushing some of the dust onto her hand. "But it's quite lovely. Look."

She held it up for my perusal and it glistened under the fluorescent lights. I had seen this before somewhere.

"It looks like my bowl."

"Your what?"

"Just some pottery I made this summer."

"Maybe you brushed up against it this morning or something?" she said, reaching for an explanation. It was better than anything I could come up with.

"Maybe."

"If I were you, I'd just leave it where it is. Gives you a certain peculiar glow."

Her eyes projected kindness, but the mere reminder of the word jolted me. Tears leapt back into my eyes.

"Hey, hey." She patted my arm. "I don't think it's a bad thing to be called peculiar. I know Reggie meant it in a mean way, but it can actually mean something really positive."

She pulled a thesaurus out from the desk across the aisle and squeezed onto the seat.

"Let's see," she said, thumbing through the pages. "*Peculiar* can also mean unique, special, individual, particular, and distinctive. That sounds pretty cool, if you ask me."

I pulled in a ragged breath.

"I think that's what he meant."

"Reggie?"

"No, Ben . . . Ben Bradley. He told me he was glad to have met someone as peculiar as me in this small town."

"Ah, I see. Well, I happen to agree with Mr. Bradley. You are a unique young lady. And I think you have some peculiar qualities that will make the world a better place if you will share them. We just need you to be you."

From there, the day got better. By the time the last bell had rung and me and my buddies were pedaling home, the knot in my stomach had untied itself.

Ben didn't push me for details about the origin of Reggie's knowledge. I hoped he would forget about it.

I knew Reggie wouldn't.

DINNER PARTY

The following week, Mel achieved a lifelong goal: she won a spot on the cheer squad. Then El debated her way onto the high school junior varsity debate team, where she was by far the youngest member—Mark Pawkowski was the captain. She and Mel were both thrilled to stay after school for their activities. So, after that first week of all four of us commuting together, Ben and I rode back to my house after school by ourselves.

Although I missed my gal pals' company, I was thrilled to have Ben to myself. The front porch became our hangout. Some days we talked nonstop. Other days we took out our sketch pads and drew. He was great at drawing birds and animals, but he preferred to draw cartoons.

Most of his cartoons were downright ridiculous, with crazy caricatures of everyone from the principal to the postman. But some were quite thought-provoking, like the one he drew on Arbor Day with Paul Bunyan setting his axe aside to plant a pine tree seedling.

On days Mother came home early, we went inside and sat at the kitchen table. She plied us with snacks like carrots, apple slices, and cheese sticks; having a health-conscious mother had its downside. Occasionally she surprised us with cookies or bars, but even those were full of raisins, oatmeal, and nuts. Ben never complained. He stayed and we worked on our homework while we munched on our snacks. Some kids teased us as we rode past them after school. We made a point of avoiding Reggie and his gang. The others were pretty harmless, and they didn't seem to bother Ben, so I decided I wasn't going to let them bother me either.

One day in early November we sat on the front porch with our parka hoods pulled over our heads. An icy north wind had whipped in from Canada. We realized that soon we wouldn't be able to ride our bikes to school or sit out on the front porch—at least, not without freezing. It wasn't a pleasant thought. Ben's mom said his grandpa needed complete peace and quiet, so we couldn't go there. We were discussing alternative hangouts, like the library or the bowling alley, when the phone rang inside. I jumped up to answer it.

"You can leave if you want," I told Ben. "But I shouldn't be too long."

I pulled off my gloves. They seemed to have done little in the way of actually keeping my hands warm. I fumbled the keys twice before succeeding in unlocking the door, then I rushed across the entryway into the kitchen to grab the phone.

"Hello, this is Pearl," I blurted.

"Hello, sweetheart. Are you okay? Are you and Ben sitting out on the front porch in this frigid wind?"

"Yeah. I guess."

"You guess? Are you or aren't you?"

"Yes, we are," I clarified. "Why?"

"I'm leaving work soon. If you want, you can invite him in for some Ovaltine. I will be home shortly. Just gonna stop by the Red Owl and get some groceries."

"Thanks. See ya soon."

I hung up and dashed back outside. Ben was still there, hunkered over with his chin tucked into his jacket.

"Hey, want some hot Ovaltine? Mother said you can come in if you want. She'll be home in a few minutes."

He popped up from the step and grabbed his backpack with an exaggerated shake of his limbs.

"Thank the Lord," he chattered. "Thought I was going to freeze to the step and you would have to chisel me free. Ovaltine sounds terrific."

We hurried inside, hung up our coats, and prepared our warm drinks. I scrounged through the cupboards, searching for possible snacks.

"All I can find is graham crackers," I said.

"Perfect," Ben replied. "My favorite."

Out came the box and off came the wrappers. We broke the stacks into halves, divided them between us, and sat down to indulge ourselves and chat about the day. Eventually we pulled out our homework and attempted to accomplish something productive. Just as my mind began to wrap around the questions on my science worksheet, Mother rapped on the door, her arms full of groceries. Ben jumped up and opened the door. He grabbed a precariously balanced bag as Mother maneuvered her way inside.

"Oh, thank you, Ben," Mother gushed. "I guess I overestimated my capacity. I hated to have to make two trips in this nasty wind."

"You're welcome," he replied. "I don't blame you. It's cold out there. Thanks for inviting me in."

I helped Mother pull groceries from the bags and put them away in the cupboards.

"Sweetheart," Mother instructed, "please leave out the chicken and noodles. I'm going to make a big pot of soup. I've invited Teacher Anne for dinner. You're welcome to stay, too, Ben, if your mom says it's okay. Why don't you give her a call?"

"Wow, thanks! That sounds great. I'll check. My grandpa has been pretty sick this week. She's had to run him back and forth to the hospital a couple times. Once it was the middle of the night. She didn't get home until after I left for school. She's a little worn out, I think."

"I'm sorry to hear that." Mother had stopped to listen. "I'll give her a call tomorrow and see if there might be something we can do to help. One of the benefits of living in a small town is that people know one another, and there's always someone willing to give a hand."

Ben gave her a grateful nod before he reached for the phone.

I wasn't so sure all the people in town would be willing to help. From where I stood, a fair number of them seemed grumpy half the time and not too inclined to get involved in somebody else's trouble. But if anyone could find a way to help, it was Mother.

Ben got the okay from his mom, and my mom put us to work.

☐

Teacher Anne rang the doorbell promptly at six o'clock. I greeted her at the front door.

"Hey, Teacher. Come on in out of the cold."

"Ooh la la! It is getting downright frigid out there," she said, coming through the door with a shiver. "But can't complain too loudly. It is November, after all. C'est la vie."

I offered to take her coat. She handed it to me and I hung it in the front closet. When I came back to her side, she was staring at the large family picture in the hallway.

"That's me," I said pointing to the chubby baby. "I was a year old."

"And adorable," she commented.

"That's my sister Susan, my brother David, and my daddy John," I added, assuming she could figure out which one was Mother.

She nodded slowly.

"Yes, I recognize them all. I know . . . uh, I knew your daddy quite well."

"You did?"

"Sure did."

I paused.

"I didn't."

She put an arm around my shoulders.

"And that is a shame, my young friend. John was a good man and a great father."

"That's what Susan says."

"Well, she is right." She gave my shoulder a quick squeeze. "Shall we find your mother?"

I led the way into the kitchen. Mother turned from the pot on the stove and wiped her hands on her apron. She took one step toward Teacher and stopped.

"Welcome," she said. "I am glad you could make it on such short notice."

Her voice was stiff and her greeting a bit formal. Teacher didn't respond right away. Her eyes grew moist. An uncomfortable silence descended upon the room. I looked from Teacher to Mother and back again. No one said a word.

Then they both spoke up at once.

"I should have called—"

"I meant to call after—"

They both shook their heads and smiled. Mother stepped forward and placed a hand on Teacher's arm.

"Let's not talk about it right now, Anne. I am so pleased to have you here again."

Teacher placed her hand over Mother's.

"And I am so pleased to be here again."

Ben tromped around the corner from the bathroom into the kitchen. Teacher jerked her head around.

"Mr. Bradley, I didn't expect to find you here. Are you joining us for dinner?"

"Yes, ma'am, I am," he said, looking back and forth between the two older women. "Uh, I hope you don't mind if I crash the party."

Teacher laughed. Ben's entrance had diffused the tension in the room.

"Not at all. Always nice to have a gentleman in the mix." She turned to Mother. "It smells absolutely divine in here. What are you making?"

"Oh, it's just a soup recipe my mother used to make on cold, blustery days," Mother said. "Pearl and Ben have whipped together some biscuits too. It will be simple fare tonight, but hearty and warm."

"Let me find my contribution," Teacher said as she dug into her voluminous leather purse. She pulled out an aluminum foil packet and handed it to me. "You can peek in there if you'd like. We'll save these for after dinner. They're fresh from the oven."

I unfolded one corner of the packet. Ben swooped over to peek inside with me. The scent of freshly baked chocolate chip cookies escaped into the room. We oohed and aahed at the golden stack we spied inside.

"This totally deserves a high five," Ben said, lifting his hand.

I slapped it with gusto. Teacher burst out in laughter at our enthusiastic reception. I wasn't sure she understood how much of a treat this was in our house.

Though we were only a party of four that night, something in the air wooed us out of the kitchen where Mother and I normally ate dinner and into the dining room—a room we reserved mostly for larger gatherings, like Thanksgiving or birthday parties. Mother pulled out the good dishes and linen place mats. Ben and I set the table. Carried along by the festive atmosphere, I dug through the drawer of the china hutch and found the crystal candleholders and two tapered candles. Before we sat down to eat, I lit them and dimmed the lights.

With steaming bowls of soup in front of us, we bowed our heads. Mother asked a blessing.

"For what we are about to receive from the bounty of Your hand, dear Lord, we are truly grateful. For the warm food before us. For friends at our table. For life and breath, we give You thanks. In Jesus's name . . ."

We all said amen in unison.

We all tucked into our food like laborers after a hard day's work, but between mouthfuls, the conversation flowed with surprising ease. It was different to see Teacher in our home as our guest. I wondered why we hadn't had her over more often. I figured it was probably one of those grown-up things that seemed to make life complicated.

After we finished our soup and Ben devoured the last buttery biscuit, we all pitched in to clear off the dishes. In the kitchen, Mother poured coffee for herself and Teacher. Ben and I filled mugs with milk. Teacher unwrapped the cookies she brought and arranged them on an etched-glass plate Mother handed her. When we returned to the dining room, Teacher set the plate in the middle of the table and proclaimed with a flourish, "Bon appétit!"

Ben grabbed two large cookies and began to dunk pieces in his milk. I closed my fingers around two cookies as well. But before I retracted my hand, I glimpsed at Mother, who nodded her permission. It was a festive night, indeed, for Mother to allow such sugar consumption. When she snatched two cookies for herself and looked in my direction with a grin, I nearly fell off my chair.

"Well, I never would've believed this if I hadn't seen it with my own eyes. Two cookies at one time," Teacher remarked in mock disbelief.

She did know.

"Your heavenly sweets have tempted me beyond what I could bear," Mother confessed, pretending to swoon.

As we lingered over dessert, Teacher cleared her throat and announced, "May I have everyone's attention, please? As you all are aware, our next art appreciation night is next Tuesday. The last one was a resounding success, thanks to the support of art enthusiasts such as yourselves. For our next event, I have asked a small group of artists to combine their work for a mixed-media collaboration of local talent."

"That sounds wonderful, Anne. Who have you asked to participate?" Mother asked.

"So far, I have asked Fritz, Mrs. Wilson, and Mrs. Grant."

I stopped midbite, half a cookie sticking out of my mouth. The only one missing from that list was me.

"Pearl, I'm wondering if you would be willing to enter the pieces you worked on this summer," Teacher said. "That way I can showcase our summer art class as a whole and stir up interest for upcoming classes. What do you say?"

I finished chewing. I was equal parts flattered and terrified. After I washed down the crumbs with a generous swig of milk, I answered with a question of my own.

"Will I have to say anything?"

"Only if you want to," Teacher assured me. "Mrs. Wilson and Mrs. Grant have agreed to say something. Fritz is more reluctant, as you might imagine. But I am hopeful he will say a few words. It's always helpful for an audience to become acquainted with an artist when they view their art. If you want, I can give you a few questions ahead of time so you can prepare your answers. If that's too much, though, I still would love to display your pieces. They are quite good. And it might encourage other young people to join the class next summer."

I glanced at Ben, who gave me a shrug.

"Why not?" he said. "She's right. You have some good stuff to show off—uh—I mean, display."

I punched him on the shoulder.

"It's not about showing off," I said. "It's about bringing enjoyment to people. And maybe helping them see the world in a new way. That's what I think, anyway."

He grinned back at me.

"I'm only teasing. I think you should go for it. And I think you should display your baby sketches."

"Your baby sketches?" Teacher interjected. "You have more than the one I saw this summer?"

I glared at Ben. He grinned as I replied.

"Yes, Teacher. I have a couple more."

"May I see them?" she asked. "If that's okay?"

I sighed and nodded as I got up to retrieve the drawings. I trusted Teacher, but I knew that showing her the sketches meant more than just looking at them—it meant explaining how they came to be. For some reason, it seemed like an invasion of privacy, a crossing of a line, a baring of the soul. Maybe that was a bit dramatic, but it was how I felt. I grabbed my folder from my dresser and brought it back to the dining room. Mother and Teacher were talking quietly while Ben consumed another large cookie.

As I sat down, Mother turned to me, a gentle pleading in her eyes.

"Sweetheart, Teacher Anne was asking me about the sketch of Joseph you showed her this summer. She is aware that Violet's baby was stillborn, which naturally has left her perplexed as to the origin of your drawing. Could you tell her the story?"

"Okay," I said. "But what about Timothy and Shavonne?"

Ben chimed in, "I can tell that story. Well, at least the beginning. I was there for that one."

Teacher Anne set her elbows on the table and placed her chin on her crossed fingers.

"To say I'm intrigued would be putting it mildly. However, I don't want to force you to tell me anything. I respect your right as the artist to divulge or withhold. Whatever you think is best."

Looking into her sincere eyes, a great pressure lifted off my chest, and I knew it was okay to tell her my story. Beyond that, I knew she needed to hear it. And so, with help from Mother and Ben, the stories behind the sketches spilled out.

Teacher sat in rapt attention. She seemed to capture each word picture I painted. She didn't check the tears when they came, but let them slide freely down her cheeks. Mother tucked a napkin into her hands. When the last word of the last sentence dropped from my lips, we all sat in hushed silence, the sputter of the candles the only sound in the room. Teacher dabbed her eyes and wiped her nose.

At last she said softly, "Thank you, Pearl. That is . . . amazing. I can't tell you how deeply your story has touched me tonight. Thank you."

"You're welcome."

"May I see them now?" Teacher asked with unconcealed interest.

I slid the folder with my sketches across the table and Teacher drew it reverently into her care, as though she were receiving the *Mona Lisa*. Her fingers trembled as she opened the folder. Fresh tears lit her eyes as she spread the sketches out on the table, all three in a row.

"Oh, Pearl," she whispered as her hands lighted tentatively on each one. "So much life in their eyes. Oh my goodness."

Ben kicked my foot under the table.

"Good job," he mouthed, giving me a thumbs-up.

I mouthed back, "Thanks." It wasn't time to talk out loud yet. We waited quietly, letting Teacher study the drawings.

"Could we possibly display these at the art appreciation night?" she asked, looking up at me. "You don't have to tell the stories behind them. Or you can, if you want. I just want people to see these beautiful babies. They are captivating. They exude such joy and life."

I hesitated to answer her.

"You don't have to give me an answer tonight," she added quickly. "Talk to your mother. You can let me know in a day or two. Okay?"

"Yeah, uh, okay," I replied.

"Fantastic. And thank you again for baring your soul. That takes courage. Your stories are safe with me if you want me to keep them secret."

"Would you—at least for now?" I said, relieved by her insight into my wariness. "I'm not sure what I'm supposed to do with all this just yet."

"I can understand that," she said, nodding her head. "It's quite a treasure trove you've been given. Wisdom is required to handle such a gift. But you have a mother whose middle name is Wisdom, so you should be all right."

"Oh, Anne," Mother said as she clasped her friend's hand. "It's been great to have you here. We need to do this again, and sooner rather than later. I'm so pleased you decided to stay north for the winter."

Teacher squeezed her hand and replied, "Truth is, I finally realized that the thing I was looking for in Florida was actually right back here all along."

"What's that?" Mother prodded.

"Don't get me wrong. I love Florida. The colors, the people, the food, the warm weather," she said with a sigh. "And for a season, it was a very healing place for me. But there came a day when I felt restless. I couldn't find peace. Not even in my art. I traveled back to Paris and spent a few months there, thinking maybe a change of scenery was all I needed. But one day as I stared at yet another painting in yet another museum, I realized that what I wanted—and needed—was to go back to my roots and take care of some of the tangled ends I'd left unattended."

Mother nodded. Teacher nodded. Quiet descended once more. And once more, I sensed there was more to their story than what I knew.

Teacher interrupted my ponderings. She slid the sketches carefully back into the folder and turned to Ben.

"Well, Mr. Bradley, it's probably high time you got home. Can I give you a ride, neighbor?"

"That's awfully nice, but I have my bike here, and I may need it in the morning . . . if it hasn't snowed a foot by then," Ben said.

"Oh, that's not a problem," she said with a wave of her hand. "I drove the Blazer tonight. We should be able to stuff the bike in the back end."

"Are you still driving that old thing?" Mother asked.

"Yeah, I can't seem to let it go. And it just felt right to drive it over here tonight. If you know what I mean . . ." Teacher's voice tapered off.

Mother stepped forward to give her a hug. I heard her whisper, "I do know what you mean, Anne. I do."

Teacher whispered something into Mother's ear. Mother shook her head and whispered something back before they pulled back to arm's length. They looked at each other with tearful smiles for a moment.

"Pearl, please get Teacher Anne's coat," Mother instructed.

I moved to comply, but I had questions.

I definitely had some questions.

GROWN-UP STUFF

When the candles were extinguished, the place mats put away, the dishes done, and the leftovers stashed in the fridge, Mother and I trekked down the hallway to get ready for bed. I ducked into the bathroom first and performed the usual nightly rituals. When I finished, I slid across the hall to my bedroom and hollered, "It's all yours," before I closed my door.

A chill seeped up through the purple shag carpet in my room. I dropped to my knees next to my bottom dresser drawer and searched in earnest for my flannel nightgown. Once located, I undressed in haste, tossed my clothes into a heap, and quickly slipped the soft nightie over my head. I leapt into my bed and burrowed under the covers, sticking my nose out for a breath of fresh air. When I peeped out above the blankets, I realized the overhead light was still on.

"Mother?" I shouted through the door.

"Just a minute," came the muffled reply.

True to her word, in just a minute she popped through my door, garbed from neck to toes in her flannel nightie as well.

"Yes? Something you need?"

"Forgot to turn off my light."

"Too nippy to venture out again?" she said, flipping off the switch. She remained in the doorway, silhouetted by the bathroom light. "You did a good thing tonight. I realize it's not easy for you. But your story is powerful. It brings comfort to people. We need to pray and see how God wants you to handle it."

"Yeah, okay." She blew me a kiss and turned back toward the bathroom, but before she could escape I blurted out, "Hey, can I ask you a question?"

She slid back into view.

"Of course. What's up?"

I wasn't sure what to ask. But I knew I had to get some answers, or I would fall asleep with speculations spinning in my head. I ran through several possible approaches.

"Pearl, you wanted to ask me something?"

"Yeah. Uh, I was just wondering, well . . . why hasn't Teacher Anne been to our house before? You seem like good friends, but you don't hang out very often . . . more like not at all."

Mother's head drooped slightly. She pushed the door all the way open and shuffled across the carpet in her hand-knit slippers.

"Well, funny you should ask," she started. "Scoot over and let me sit down if you truly want to hear the story."

"I truly do," I replied as I shifted to make room.

Mother flipped the beside lamp switch to on and went to turn the bathroom light off. She was not a fan of leaving lights on unnecessarily. Returning to my room, she kicked off her slippers and crawled under the covers. She grabbed a big stuffed bear from the end of my bed and plumped it up to use as a backrest.

"There," she said. "Two peas in a pod."

I smiled up at her from my Strawberry Shortcake pillowcase and waited for her to begin.

"Where to start?" she sighed. "First of all, Teacher Anne has given me permission to tell you this. And I think you're old enough to hear the story. Okay?"

I nodded solemnly. She settled back into the bear and crossed her hands in her lap.

"So, Anne and I first became friends because your father and her husband Rick worked at the mill together. Actually, those two guys were high school classmates— played on the baseball team together, went to the same church, and lived on the same block. Since your daddy was an only child, Rick was the brother he never had."

Her eyes grew distant. I lay perfectly still and waited for her to resume.

"Anne grew up just east of here, in a town even smaller than ours," she said. "She met Rick and your father one summer after high school when she played against their team in a coed softball tournament. One thing led to another, and she and Rick started dating. They got married later that same fall. I came into the picture a few years later when I married your father—my college sweetheart.

"Your daddy had been gone for years getting his engineering degree. After graduation, he had a hard time finding a job. We were already married, and I was pregnant with Susan. So, he decided to take a job back here at the paper mill. It wasn't exactly what he wanted to do, but it gave him a way to care for his family. Anyway, an extra perk for your daddy was reconnecting with his high school buddies—especially Rick. Anne and I became friends because those two guys were friends. We spent a lot of time together at softball tournaments, BBQs, and church picnics. Rick and Anne were our best friends. In fact, when Susan was born, we asked them to be her godparents. Bet you didn't know that."

She glanced at me. I shook my head.

"Did Teacher Anne ever have any kids?" I asked. "What happened to Rick? I never knew she had a husband."

"Let's take one thing at a time," Mother resumed. "Anne and Rick tried for years to have children but couldn't. Then when I got pregnant with David, Anne unexpectedly was expecting too. She and Rick were over the moon, and we were happy for them. Everything seemed perfect, until one day in her third trimester, she had a miscarriage. They were devastated. We all were. But Anne took it especially hard. No matter how Rick or anyone else tried to encourage her, she slid deeper and deeper into depression. She never left the house, didn't answer the phone, stayed in bed all day . . . pretty much stopped functioning."

Mother stared into the shadows in the hallway and sighed.

"I felt so helpless. And, although I tried to comprehend her grief, it wasn't until a few years later, when I miscarried a baby, too, that I truly understood what she was going through."

I gulped.

"You lost a baby?"

She nodded.

"Two years after David. I was only about twelve weeks along. In fact, I had just gotten the test results back, confirming my suspicions . . . when suddenly, it was over. I hadn't even told your dad I was pregnant yet . . . so I just kept the miscarriage to myself."

"Why?" I asked.

"I don't know exactly. Didn't want to burden him, I guess." She picked idly at lint balls stuck on my comforter. "I did confide in Grandma, who, of course, reminded me that it wasn't an uncommon occurrence. Just something women had to endure."

Another sibling? I was flabbergasted.

"Were you sad?"

Mother nodded.

"Very."

"Didn't Daddy wonder?"

"He did ask me what was going on, but I just told him it was 'female problems,' and he stopped asking," she answered with a shrug. "Maybe I should have . . . I don't know. But what's done is done."

The minute marker on my clock flipped. Outside my window, empty branches rustled in the wind.

"Do you know if it was a boy or girl?" I said.

She shook her head.

"No. Guess it's one of those things I'll find out when I get to the pearly gates."

I nodded, fully assured that this was indeed the case.

"But let's get back to Rick and Anne," she said, brushing my bangs back and peering into my eyes as if to check one more time that I was ready for this. I guess she was satisfied with what she saw, because the story continued. "Five or six months after Anne lost her baby, Rick decided she needed more help than what he could give. So, he enrolled her in a recovery program at a Catholic rehabilitation center a few hours away. Not only did she receive superb help at that center, but it was there that she discovered her love of art. The nuns used art as a form of therapy. It was exactly what Anne needed. She found that art gave her a reason to get out of bed in the morning. She also discovered that her artwork brought joy to others at the center. This new sense of purpose lifted her slowly but steadily out of her depression. When she came home, Rick built an art studio right on their property. She became so accomplished, she started to sell her work at fairs and craft shows all over the state. Eventually, her pieces were displayed in galleries down in the Cities and at some of the nicest resorts and restaurants.

"It was wonderful to see her happy. She and Rick still came over for dinner after church on Sundays or for birthday parties and such. But Anne had a hard time being around the kids. She never did get pregnant again. And for some reason, they decided against adoption. I think her art became her baby—her way to bring life into the world. Rick didn't argue. He was just thrilled to have his wife back."

Mother went silent.

"Wow, that's sad," I said. "But it's cool that art helped her get better. I like that." I could see that this was stirring up difficult memories for Mother, but I wanted to know the rest. "So, what happened to Rick?" I prompted.

She let out a deep sigh and squared her shoulders, as if to fortify herself for the rest of the journey down memory lane. I swallowed and tugged the blankets closer to my chin. Maybe I didn't really want to hear anymore. Maybe this wasn't the greatest idea. But maybe knowing hard things was part of growing up, and I did want to grow up. Just not right then. But it was too late—Mother hurtled ahead.

"Your daddy and Rick worked on the same crew at the mill as drivers and mechanics. They often worked the same shifts. Whenever that happened, they carpooled in the very same Blazer Teacher Anne drove here tonight."

She glanced at me. When she continued, a slight quiver entered her voice.

"The night of your daddy's accident, Rick was supposed to pick him up. But the Blazer wouldn't start, for some reason. So, your daddy went by himself. The weather was bad. Icy snow had been falling all day. I was relieved your father wasn't scheduled to drive a route that night. He was supposed to be on mechanic duty. But . . . he volunteered to drive Rick's route. And that's the night it happened. On a route that wasn't even his."

Mother brushed away a tear from each eye.

"I'm sorry for making you cry," I said, blinking away my own tears.

"No, sweetheart, it's okay. It's time you knew. It's just never easy remembering it all." She reached over and tapped the tip of my nose. "Your daddy adored you. I wish you would've had the chance to know him better. Do you remember what he used to call you?"

"Kinda. I mean, I remember cause sometimes David still calls me that—Pearl-i-cue?"

"Yep. 'Pearl-i-cue with the curlicue' he used to say when I pulled your hair into a curly spout on the top. Oh, you thought that was hilarious. So he would say it over and over just to make you giggle." A sad sort of smile crept across her face. "He could be very funny at times."

"I wish I remembered him more."

"Me too," she sighed, and our mutual longing ground us to a halt for a long moment.

"So, what happened next?" I broke the silence, spurred on by curiosity mixed with a growing sense of dread. "Something must've happened to Rick."

Mother laid her head back on top of the stuffed bear. She stared at the ceiling before she resumed.

"It's unfortunate . . . so senseless."

She looked back down and twirled the braided edge of my floral comforter, as though she was seeking the right thread to pull.

"Rick was so grief-stricken and full of guilt when your daddy died," she said softly, "he couldn't go back to work. He believed it should have been him in the truck that night. And nothing anyone said could make him think differently. He started to drink . . . a lot. Anne tried to get him to go to the rehabilitation center that had helped her so much, but he refused. Then one day, out of the blue, he changed his mind. Said he would go as long as he could drive there himself. She was so desperate for him to get help, she agreed. Of course, she checked to be sure he was sober. And she let him drive off."

Mother slid down the stuffed bear until her face was just above mine. Her voice wound down to a near whisper as she resumed.

"Several hours later, she called the center to make sure he had arrived. He hadn't. She checked every hour until late into the night. Then she called the sheriff's department. They said they couldn't file a missing person's report until he had been gone for twenty-four hours. She climbed into her Volkswagen Bug and went looking for him herself. She searched all night long but didn't find him.

"In the morning, she drove directly to the sheriff's office. She filed her report. They sent out a search party. Later that day, they found him. He had driven clear out to Round Lake. That's where he and your daddy used to fish. He'd parked the Blazer and was sitting outside in a snowbank with his back up against a tree—several empty whiskey bottles around him. He must've been there all night in the bitter cold. Drank himself into a stupor, passed out and . . . and, well, he froze to death."

The last sentence was barely audible. It was as if she wanted me to have the information, but she didn't.

She cleared her throat and pressed on, her eyes fixed on the ceiling.

"After Rick's funeral, Anne locked up her house and went to Paris. Stayed there for months. I was glad she could afford to do that. Knew she'd always wanted to go. And, selfishly, it was sort of a relief to not run into her all the time. Seeing each other was too full of grief and memories—of things that might have been or should have been. When she came back to the States, Anne got a place in Florida for half the year and poured herself into her artwork. I poured myself into you kids and my work. And our lives just went separate ways. We'd see each other around town from time to time whenever she was back from Florida. But our attempts at conversation were awkward and brief.

"When I found out she was teaching an art class this summer, I had an inkling you might be interested in going. So, I signed you up. Of course, I was excited for you to have a chance to learn from Anne. But I also hoped it might give us a chance to reconnect. I never imagined how important it would be for all of us."

She turned to me, her face soft and thoughtful.

"From the first class, you couldn't stop talking about Teacher Anne—how talented she is, how kind, how funny, how caring. When I saw her through your eyes, I remembered all the things I loved about her. And I found myself longing to renew our friendship. That's why I invited her here tonight. I wanted to see if we could maybe build a bridge over all the hard times and reconnect. I think that tonight we started that process."

My heart was a jumble of emotions. Life was strange. How could it be so terrible and so beautiful?

"Mother?"

"Yes?"

"Will you stay with me? At least for a little while?"

She leaned over and kissed me on the forehead before switching off my lamp. As she nestled down under the covers, I snuggled up to her back.

She whispered into the darkness, "This is going to be cozy."

☐

In the dream, the sun was high in the sky. I sat on the front porch, waiting for someone. No one came. Still I waited and waited. Shadows from the trees lengthened. A sharp breeze penetrated my cotton blouse, raised goose bumps on my arms. At last, I gave up my vigil and stood to go inside.

But just as I did, someone yelled from far away, "Pearl, wait up!"

I peered down the street in the dusky light. A person on a bicycle headed my way. It was Ben. He wore a large backpack, like one a hiker might take on an expedition into the Himalayas.

"Ben, I've been waiting for you all day," I exclaimed as he approached. "I expected you hours ago. Now it's too late."

He pulled in next to the porch and sat on his bike, perfectly balanced without pedaling or touching the ground.

"Yeah, sorry. I kinda got lost," he said. "There was a detour. I had to go way out to the highway and back around behind the school. But I'm here now. Please don't say it's too late. Evening is sometimes the best part of the day to hang out," he pleaded as his dimpled grin spread from ear to ear.

My heart softened.

"Well, okay. You can stay. But what's in your backpack? Are you going somewhere? Or are you moving in?"

"Yeah," he said. "Open it up."

I didn't quite understand his response, but I stretched my hand out to the backpack anyway.

"But I can't reach it. You're too far away."

"Okay. I'll pull up right next to the porch."

He came up close, his back to me. When I unhooked the backpack's top flap, a small baby head popped through the opening and grinned at me with a familiar grin.

"Well, hello little guy," I said with a laugh. "What's your name?"

Ben glanced over his shoulder.

"Oh, that's Daniel. Isn't he something?"

"Yes, he sure is. Not what I expected to find, but he's a cutie. Reminds me of you, except his eyes are much darker and his hair is super curly."

"That's because he looks like my dad."

"Oh, this is your brother?"

"Yeah, of course," Ben said. "Who else do you think I'd be carrying around?"

Daniel started to squiggle, trying to escape from the backpack. I reached over to stop him. That's when I noticed other eyes peering up from the bottom of the sack.

"Uh, Ben? Are you aware that there are several more babies in your backpack right underneath Daniel?"

"What? Nah, I don't know nothin' about them."

"Well, it can't be good for them to be sitting down there in the dark."

"Oh, don't worry, Pearl. Everything will work out. I just wanted to stop by so you could see that Daniel and I are good."

"You're good?"

"Yeah, we're good. Aren't we, Dan?" Ben lifted a hand, and Daniel slapped him a high five. "See, we're good. Thought you should know before I go."

"Before you go? Are you leaving? I thought we were going to hang out."

A hollow spot opened in my chest. Ben gazed at me with a gaze full of sadness, hope, pain, and love. Suddenly he seemed old and worn out. I wanted to comfort him, but he began to pedal away—far, far away. And he didn't look back.

"Ben, wait. Ben, don't go," I cried out. "Come back. Ben. Ben!"

I awoke to Mother softly shaking my shoulder.

"Pearl, wake up. It's just a dream. Wake up."

I blinked as Mother turned on the lamp. "Are you okay?" she asked, struggling to sit up and untangle my limbs from hers.

I was disoriented. For a moment, I couldn't figure out why I felt so disturbed. Then I remembered the image of Ben pedaling away.

I looked at Mother and with a strangled voice whispered, "He's leaving. Ben is leaving, and he's going far, far away."

I began to cry in deep, gut-wrenching sobs. I knew it was for more than just Ben. It was for Daddy, Rick, and Teacher Anne. For babies lost, siblings unknown, friendships interrupted, and the hard things in life. I couldn't fathom how grown-ups lived with all this . . . all this knowing.

Mother drew my head onto her lap. I wrapped my arms around her waist and clung to her like a buoy in a windswept bay. She stroked my head and quietly began to sing in her soothing alto voice.

Children of the heavenly Father,
Safely in his bosom gather;
Nestling bird nor star in heaven,
Such a refuge e'er was given.

God his own doth tend and nourish;
In His holy courts they flourish;
From all evil things He spares them;
In His mighty arms He bears them.

Neither life nor death shall ever
From the Lord His children sever;
Unto them His grace He showeth,
And their sorrows all He knoweth.

As each stanza of the familiar hymn washed over me, my sobs subsided. An inexplicable peace began to heal the bottomless despair in my heart. Mother handed me a tissue from the nightstand. She continued her calming lullaby, reminding me that I was still her baby—no matter how far I had traveled down the road to ma-t-urity in one night.

> Though He giveth or He taketh,
> God His children ne'er forsaketh;
> His the loving purpose solely
> To preserve them pure and holy.

> Praise the Lord in joyful numbers:
> Your Protector never slumbers.
> At the will of your Defender
> Ev'ry foeman must surrender.[1]

I lay exhausted but contented as she continued to hum and stroke my hair.

"Mother?" I whispered hoarsely.

"Yes, dear?"

"Could you sing it again?"

She could, and she did.

[1]*Children of the Heavenly Father*, written by Karolina Wilhelmina Sandell Berg 1858. Translated into English by Ernst W. Olson 1925.

DREAMSCAPE

Mother vacated my bedroom in the wee hours of the morning. I felt her leave but didn't protest. My need for her touchable presence had diminished, and the reality was that it was difficult for two people to sleep in my bed.

At 7 a.m. I peeked at my alarm clock, anticipating the usual 7:15 a.m. beeps. Fifteen more minutes. My head ached and my eyes were puffy. I longed for much more than fifteen minutes. Then a cheery thought bubbled to the surface. It was Saturday. In nothing flat, I was sound asleep, coldcocked by bliss.

☐

"Pearl, it's ten o'clock." Mother's voice penetrated my slumber. "You might want to get up and get dressed. Ben is at the front door with sleds in hand, looking for a sliding partner, and Mel just called a few minutes ago."

"Sliding?"

In my groggy state, I couldn't make sense of her announcement.

She walked across the room and pulled up the shades.

"First snow of the winter," she proclaimed.

I stumbled out of bed with my stuffed kitty in hand to join her at the window.

"Holy moly."

I peered out at the backyard. It had been transformed into a puffy winter dreamscape. I blinked rapidly at the excessive whiteness.

"It started right after midnight, and it's still coming down," Mother reported. "They say we'll have ten to twelve inches more before it's all over sometime tonight."

"Yippee!"

I threw my stuffed animal into the air and caught her by one paw as I spun around in celebration. All the night's sorrows evaporated, and joy erupted. I dropped to my knees and pulled out a drawer under my bed filled with my winter gear: wool socks, long johns, snow pants, scarves, stocking caps, mittens, etc.

Mother smiled at my enthusiasm.

"I take it you want me to ask Ben to wait?"

"Yes, please," I mumbled as I pulled my nightie over my head and prepared to dress for the adventure.

The metamorphosis from sleepyhead to snow bunny took less than ten minutes. When I opened the front door, Ben was stacking a good-sized snowball on top of a larger one. The two of them combined reached up to Ben's chin.

"Hey, need some help?" I asked.

"Sure. Still need a head," he said.

"I know, but what about the snowman?"

"Ha, ha. Very funny.

I shuffled through the snow on the steps and knelt on the ground, ready for action. I packed a small snowball and rolled it in the flakes. It was perfect snowman-making snow—sticky, but not too wet. Quickly it grew into the proportions for a proper head. I handed it to Ben for placement and then scrounged two dead branches off the shrub by the porch, which I stuck on each side of the middle snowball for arms. Ben brushed aside the snow from along the sidewalk and gathered enough pebbles for us to fashion a face for our creation. He embedded the eyes and the nose while I worked on the mouth. We stepped back to inspect our work.

"That is one fine-looking snowman, don't you think?" Ben asked, his hands on his hips, admiring our handiwork.

"Oh, the finest," I agreed. "What shall we name him?"

"Frank," he said without hesitation.

"Of course," I laughed. "Frank it is."

Satisfied that our work was done, we walked over to the porch and grabbed the ropes of the sleds Ben had laid there and began our trek to the sliding hill.

"See ya later, Frank," Ben hollered over his shoulder as we left. "Don't let Frosty talk you into any crazy side trips."

"Maybe we'll build you a girlfriend when we get back," I added.

Ben rolled his eyes.

"Girls . . . ya always gotta add romance to the deal."

I giggled. We slogged through the muffled streets, kicking up snow geysers and catching flakes on our tongues. The troublesome revelations of the previous night were smothered by blankets of pure white.

There was no question as to where we were headed. The biggest and best sliding hill in town was behind the high school. Of course, we weren't the only ones with sliding on our minds. It seemed half the town was there by the time we arrived.

"Pearl!" a voice cried out.

"Ben!" came a second wild shout.

Mel and El zipped past us on a toboggan. Ben and I laughed as they careened out of control. The rear end whipped past the front end and they sailed down the hill backward, screaming all the way to the bottom.

We climbed to the crest of the hill.

"Race ya," Ben challenged, taking a seat on his sled.

I ran three steps and flew onto my sled.

"Catch me if you can," I whooped as I shot past him.

"No fair!" he yelled, struggling to get started.

"Go, Pearl, go!" El hollered from the sidelines as I zoomed by.

Covered from head to toe in snow, it was hard to tell where El stopped and the hillside started. The wild red hair protruding from her stocking cap was the only telltale sign that it was her. I waved triumphantly to her, sure of my impending victory.

At the apex of my glory, a dip in the course caught the lip of my sled and catapulted me into the air. I landed on my bottom ten feet down the hill, discombobulated by the sudden flight. Ben sped by with an exultant grin, my unmanned sled skittering to the bottom behind him.

The most serious injury I sustained was to my pride. Ben rubbed it in for a while until he, too, landed flat on his face in a massive wipeout, with Mel on the toboggan behind him. The hill humbled us all—and we loved it.

The hours zipped by as we flew down the hill and trudged back up again and again. By the time Mel checked her watch, it was after two o'clock.

"Oh my gosh," she said. "I gotta get home. My mom volunteered me to babysit the neighbor twins. Their mom is at work and their dad needs to fix his snowblower. El, you comin' with me?"

El mopped her nose with her snow-encrusted mitten.

"The prospect of being housebound with you and those two whirling dervishes for hours on end is not all that appealing."

"Ah, come on," Mel pleaded. "Be a pal. I'll split the pay with ya."

"Dear, dear, Mel," El sighed. "I have no need of your petty bribes. I will join you out of the sheer goodness of my heart."

"And out of the hope of getting a glimpse of the other neighbor—Mark Pawkowski," I teased.

"Is it so hard to believe that I might have purely altruistic motives?" El said.

"Yes, it is," Mel replied. "Whatever all-tourist-stick means. Let's go."

She backed away, making sure El followed. El gave me a quick hug.

"If you have not heard from us by noon tomorrow, we have been consumed by cannibalistic two-year-olds."

She tramped behind Mel dramatically, as if being led to the stake.

"They can't be that bad," Ben said.

"Well, maybe not cannibalistic for real," I commented. "But they do have a reputation for biting."

"Yeesh, that's rough. Makes ya wonder if that snowblower is really broken or if the guy just needs a break."

"Ben," I punched his shoulder, which had little to no impact through all the layers of puffy down.

Having stood in one place for a while, I realized my toes were aching from the cold and my neck felt raw from the clumps of snow deposited there in my last wipeout.

"Hey, I'm getting pretty cold," I said. "How about you?"

"Nah, but I am starting to starve," Ben admitted. "Let's take one more run and then head home."

It was one run too many.

Waiting for us at the bottom of the hill were Reggie Dumfrey and a couple of his hoodlums.

"Well, well, well, if it ain't Romeo and Peculiar," Reggie said. "It might just be me, fellas, but I think these two have been avoiding us."

His buddies laughed.

"What's the matter, Romeo? Scared to finish what you started in the hallway?" Reggie sneered.

Ben's eyes began to blaze.

"Ben, let's go back to my house. He's just trying to get your goat."

I pulled on his sleeve and started back up the hill.

"Yeah, he ain't worth it," he agreed and began to follow my ascent.

But Reggie wasn't done.

"Ooh, going back to Peculiar's house. I'll bet all kinds of weird stuff happens there at the gypsy witch doctor's place."

I spun around.

"What are you even talking about, you ignorant brute?"

"Hey, Pearl, remember what you told me?" Ben tried to smooth my ruffled feathers.

"My ma says your ma is some sort of wacko hippie baby doctor."

Reggie contorted his face and pretended to smoke a joint. His pals slapped his back.

"Good one, Reg," they said, passing around the imaginary joint.

"Guess you and Elf Spit make quite a team." Reggie was on a roll. "Her dad goes around the county making babies, and your ma cashes in deliverin' 'em."

I would've charged down the hill and taken his head off if Ben hadn't restrained me.

"Easy now, Pearl," he whispered in my ear.

"Heard the last one didn't go so well, though." Reggie turned to his gang. "Probably made Old Man

Furness happy he wouldn't have to raise somebody else's brat."

The alarmed expressions on the hoodlums' faces came too late to save Reggie. The human projectile named Ben Bradley flew down the hill and into his back. Ben stuffed Reggie's face into the snow and held it there until Reggie's flailing arms and kicking feet began to still.

The surprise attack left the Dumfrey crew so dumbfounded, I was the one who had to pull Ben off Reggie's back.

"Hey Ben, that's enough."

Ben pulled Reggie's head up by the hair and hissed into his ear, "Don't ever say stuff like that again. You got it?"

Reggie tried to nod. Ben let go and Reggie rolled onto his back, gasping for air. His buddies looked at one another, turned tail, and ran.

"Let's get outta here," I said.

I pulled Ben up and grabbed our sleds. He stared at Reggie as we backed up the hill, just to make sure he stayed down.

□

We tramped wordlessly back to the house through the mounting snowdrifts.

"Thanks," I said at last.

"Welcome."

The rest of our journey was as silent as the falling snow as I thought about what happened. Was what Reggie said true? Did El know? Maybe it was just small-town gossip. Not having a Mother who participated in the village grapevine, I wasn't privy as to how one verified what was true or not. It was always crazy to me how so many people knew so many things about so many others. Or at least they thought they did. But how did you know if what they thought they knew was factual?

I wondered how long it would take before word of Ben's takedown of Reggie would hit the grapevine. A smile snuck up on me despite the seriousness of what had just transpired. Ben had been magnificent.

My mind was so busy, it wasn't until we had shed our wet snow gear and were sitting at the kitchen table, eating tomato soup and grilled cheese sandwiches, that I remembered my dream from the night before. As the images scrolled through my memory, a familiar despair gnawed at my heart.

"Hey—you," I heard vaguely as a crumpled paper napkin plopped into my soup.

"Ben!" I exclaimed as I scooped out the mushy clump from my bowl. "What are you doing?"

"I'm trying to get your attention," he said with a shrug. "You were totally zoned out. What's up with you?"

"Sorry. I was . . . uh . . . remembering something."

"Like what—the creation of the universe? Cause you looked like you were way out in space."

"No. It wasn't anything like that. It was sort of . . . personal."

"Ooh—personal girl stuff," he said, putting his hands up in self-defense. "Not sure I want to know."

"Ben, I'm serious."

"Well then, what is it? Are you gonna tell me or not?"

I didn't want to cry in front of him. But I figured he'd cried in front of me.

"I had a dream about you," I said quietly.

"That's it? Lots of girls tell me that."

I picked up the lump of wet napkin and threw it back at him. He ducked, and the gooey mess hit the fridge and seeped down to the floor. I didn't even care.

"Ben Bradley, you are a brat. That is not what I meant, and you know it."

He threw both hands in the air, his head dipped to the side to avoid any further airborne projectiles.

"Hey, hey, hey, I'm only teasing. Can't a guy tease anymore?"

"Not when I just told you it was personal."

He peered timidly at me.

"Maybe I'm not sure I want to hear your dream," he confessed. "You make it sound ominous."

"It's not ominous," I contended. "It's mostly good . . . and then kinda . . . kinda not."

"Great," he said, scooting his bowl aside to make room for his crossed arms on the table. "I guess I'd better hear it—the good, the bad, and the sad."

I started from the beginning. I told him how I had waited for him for hours because he'd gotten lost and that I had told him when he finally did show up that he was too late.

"And that's when you said, 'I'm not too late. Evening is sometimes the best part of the day to hang out.'"

"Hey, that's a pretty good line," Ben said, complimenting his dream image.

"True. But may I remind you that since it was my dream, I am actually the one who came up with it?"

"I guess," he conceded, and I continued.

As I described the large backpack he carried and told him what happened when I unhooked the top flap, he moaned.

"A baby? It's always babies with you. Why would I carry around a baby?"

"Actually, you had more than one baby in the backpack. There were a couple more down near the bottom. You said you didn't know anything about them, but the one that popped up . . . well, you knew him. You told me his name was Daniel and that he was your brother."

All the color drained from Ben's face.

"Daniel? Did I tell you his name was Daniel?"

"In the dream, you did."

"I know. But before that—did you know his name was Daniel before the dream?"

I shook my head.

"Is his name Daniel?"

"Yeah . . . Daniel James." He spoke as if he was trying to fathom the unfathomable. "What did he look like?"

"Well, he looked kinda like you, but not really—only when he smiled. Then he had the same dimples as you. But his eyes were much darker than yours and his hair was curly. You told me it was because he looked like your dad."

Ben dropped his head into his hands.

"This is weird. Really weird." After several long moments, he looked up and said, "I need to show you something."

He reached into the back pocket of his jeans and pulled out an old leather wallet. He undid the snap that held it closed and laid it flat on the table. There wasn't a lot in it that I could see: a couple pictures in their plastic flaps and a dollar bill peeking out. Ben pinched the wallet to reveal a hidden slot under the photographs. He slid one finger all the way into the slot and pulled out a newspaper clipping preserved in a cellophane slipcover. The cellophane crinkled as he carefully removed the newspaper clipping. It was about two inches wide and three inches long. He paused to study it himself, then handed it across the table to me.

"My mom's cousin sent this to us," he explained. "She cut it out of the newspaper. It's the obituary for my brother . . . for Daniel. That's him at the top."

I stared at the picture.

"This is the baby I saw." I gulped and read through the brief description of a brief life, then reverently set the clipping back on the table. "Ben, there was more. In the dream, you said the reason you came to my house was to tell me that you and Daniel were good. You were happy to have him on your back, and he was happy to be there. He even slapped you a high five."

Ben sat motionless for a minute before asking, "Was he really happy?"

I nodded.

"He was. And so were you."

"That's cool."

He reached across the table to retrieve the clipping. With infinite care, he placed it back into the wallet and returned the wallet to his pocket.

"So, there must be more," he said. "Cause I think what you just told me is the good part, right?"

"Yeah, that was the good part."

I took a sip from my glass of water, willing myself to not get teary-eyed as I told him the last part of my dream. But as soon as I opened my mouth, my eyes blurred.

"The sad part is . . . you left . . . and you didn't turn around when I yelled after you. You kept pedaling and pedaling until you were far way. And I knew you weren't coming back."

I looked down into my bowl of half-eaten soup, unable to meet Ben's gaze.

"Hey, it was just a dream," he asserted. "I mean, maybe parts of it are more real than other parts . . . maybe."

I knew he was trying to console me, but it wasn't working. I glanced at him, embarrassed by my tears.

The ring of the telephone interrupted our awkward moment. I couldn't seem to move to answer it. It rang again and again until Mother scurried into the room and grabbed the receiver on the fly. As she answered, she looked at me with a face that conveyed the question, Is there some reason you couldn't have picked up the phone? Her voice was calm, though, and her conversation short. She hung up and turned back to us.

"Ben, that was your mom. She wants you to head home." She paused to assess our quiet scene. "Are you two okay?"

Ben came to my rescue—again.

"We're fine. Just a little tired from all the fresh air."

"Okay," Mother said.

Her raised left eyebrow told me she wasn't buying that explanation. Nevertheless, she left the room and I helped Ben get geared back up for the walk home.

"Thanks for . . . well, for everything," he said as he opened the door to leave.

"You too."

The wind blew in a skiff of snow as Ben went out. I stood there and watched him plow through the drifts on the steps, unconcerned about the flakes collecting at my feet. He grabbed the ropes to the sleds and began to pull them to the driveway. He stopped to brush a layer of excess snow off Frank's grinning face as he passed by. After a few steps, he turned back.

"See ya soon Pearl."

I waved and shut the door.

Of course, I would see him soon.

Why wouldn't I?

CRYSTAL CLEAR

Sunday arrived, dripping in sparkling, white crystals like a designer evening gown. The sun's dazzling winter rays drove the temperature from the teens in the morning to near freezing by midday. Melting snow trickled from the eaves, forming long, glinting icicles along the roofline. Frank the Snowman's left eye slid an inch lower than the right, and his body listed slightly to the left.

Mother woke me early.

"Up and at 'em, missy. We're going to have to walk to church this morning," she announced.

Missing church was only acceptable in cases of documented illness, national emergencies, or natural disasters. I was not sick, the communists had not invaded, and a foot and a half of snow did not meet the standard for a natural disaster in our neck of the woods. So, we bundled up and trudged the mile and a half to Our Savior's, where a Dodge pickup with a snowplow blade attached to the front had just begun to clear the vacant parking lot.

Mr. Alder, the janitor and snowplow operator, waved at us as he scraped by, then pointed to the sidewalk leading to the front door. That must have been his first project of the morning, because it was free from snow and sprinkled with salt. We waved back and headed past the snowmobiles lined up along either side of the walkway.

Inside the first set of double doors, several sets of cross-country skis and poles stood propped up along the wall. I knew one pair belonged to Mrs. Swenson, the organist who lived five miles out of town. Whenever a winter storm blew in a fresh blanket of snow, this was her preferred mode of transportation. And judging by the tempo and volume of the first hymn, her morning expedition had produced its usual vigorous results.

The diminished congregation of about thirty or so responded to her leading with wholehearted, four-part harmony. Pastor Art called it "truly inspired." I thought the entire worship service was more spirited than usual. Maybe it was because only the most zealous members had braved the journey to church that day. But it was probably more directly related to the fact that we had all just had a glorious venture through the snow, regardless of our chosen mode of transportation.

Pastor Art preached on a passage from Philippians 4, which said we should not be anxious about anything, but instead we should pray and let God in on all our cares. As I sat in the pew next to Mother, I silently practiced what he preached. I offered up my list of worries—my dream about Ben, the fight with Reggie, the tidbits about El's dad, the upcoming art event, the anxieties about who was saying what about whom—and the peace that passes understanding slowly won out over all my circumstances. Despite my bulky snow boots, I felt ten pounds lighter.

We mingled with our friends and neighbors in the fellowship hall, swapping stories of inches measured, snowmen built, firewood chopped, and streets traversed. Then everyone suited back up for their journeys home. Mother grabbed a Styrofoam cup of coffee to go and I scooped up two brownies, carefully stashing one in my pocket, out of Mother's view. We stopped to watch Mrs.

Swenson strap on her skis and to wish her a safe journey as she shushed through the parking lot.

When we arrived home, we grabbed the shovels from the shed and shifted into our roles of snow-removal personnel. Mr. Schmidt's driveway was already immaculately clear, and he was busy pushing his snowblower up and down Mrs. Rundquist's drive.

"Why can't we just wait for Mr. Schmidt to help?" I asked.

"When you're eighty-seven and a widow like Mrs. Rundquist, you can sit inside and wave at your helpful neighbor. But for now, a bit of hard work won't hurt you," replied Mother.

We started on the front steps and moved methodically down the driveway. As we were about to declare the job finished, the city snowplow pushed down our street and deposited a hard mound of snow and ice at the end of the driveway. I groaned at the sight of it and flopped backward in despair onto the snow-covered lawn.

"Hey," Mother chided. "You can't quit on me now. We're almost done."

I swung my arms up and down and my legs back and forth in the pristine blanket of white.

"Oh, I see." Mother laughed. "You have decided this is the perfect moment to make a snow angel."

"Yup."

She moved across the driveway and offered me a hand.

"Come on, angel, let's finish up this job and get something to eat."

She pulled me upright and handed me my shovel.

Despite the heaviness of the snow, it didn't take us very long to clear a sizable opening to the street. As we finished, I turned to Mother with what had wriggled into my heart once all the worries had emptied out.

"I think I want to display the baby sketches," I stated.

Mother quirked her head to the side.

"What brought you to that decision? Did something tip the scales?"

"Well . . . I've got another baby to draw."

Her head popped upright.

"Really? What baby is this?"

"You know the dream I had the other night? The one that you had to wake me up from?"

She nodded.

"It was about Ben, but it was also about his brother—his baby brother who died. I saw him, and in the dream, Ben told me his name was Daniel. And then yesterday I found out that's his name for real."

"I see," Mother said as understanding lit her face. "Is this what the conversation at the table with Ben was all about?"

"Mm-hmm. He even showed me a picture of Daniel he carries in his wallet. It was the baby in my dream—the exact same one."

"Well, isn't that something," Mother spoke under her breath as she wiped beads of sweat from under her stocking cap. "So, seeing this baby—this Daniel—how did it influence your decision?"

I leaned onto the shovel handle.

"Well, I guess seeing Daniel and knowing that what I saw was actually true to life—I guess I'm beginning to understand that maybe this is a gift and not a weird disorder or something. I mean, I knew Joseph's name before anyone told me. But I also had seen what Joseph looked like . . . at least, pretty much. Even though seeing him alive was way different from seeing him . . . you know . . . like he was at first. And I know what I saw when I dreamed about Timothy and Shavonne. But I've never actually seen them. But with Daniel, I know what I saw and what I heard is the real deal. Why would God show me that? Maybe I'm supposed to share it. I think it could help people the same way it helped Ben and Violet. Right?"

Mother smiled and put an arm around my shoulder.

"I think what you're thinking is good thinking, sweetheart. Now let's go warm up and get a snack, then we'll call Teacher Anne. Deal?"

"Deal."

☐

It's funny how when you make a big decision, things start to happen. Some things seem to say, "Good decision. Go for it!" Others seem to say, "What the heck are you thinking? Abandon ship!" The hours between Sunday afternoon and Tuesday evening offered up some of each.

The first positive reinforcement came later that evening as I sat at the kitchen table drawing Daniel peeking out of Ben's backpack. Mother was puttering around the kitchen after supper, drying dishes and wiping countertops, when the phone rang. She dried her hands on the towel hanging from the fridge handle and answered the call.

I was surprised when she gave the phone to me.

"Your sister says she wants to speak to you first."

I dropped the cerulean blue pencil, popped up from my chair, grabbed the receiver, and moved hastily to the living room for a semiprivate conversation. I began my line of questioning before my rear end hit the couch's velour cushions.

"Susan, did you do it? Did you call him? Did you go out on a date?"

"Well, hello to you, too, kiddo," Susan said.

"Yeah, yeah. Hi. Now let's get to the good stuff. So, did you?"

"Wow, you are a no-nonsense girl, aren't you?" she commented and then paused, keeping me on the edge of the couch. "So, here's your no-nonsense answer: yes, I did."

"Woohoo!" I hollered as I flopped back against the couch and raised one arm overhead in elation. Mother stuck her head into the room. I shooed her away. She retreated to the kitchen with a shrug, and I resumed my examination.

"Where did you go? What did you do? Was it fun? Was he nice? Did he kiss you?"

"Good golly, Miss Molly. Calm down and I'll tell you."

For the next twenty minutes, she described her date with Scott Stewart. I curled up on the couch and pulled the crocheted afghan around my shoulders, ready for every detail. Scott had taken her out to eat at a cozy Italian restaurant. They sat and talked so long, the wait staff turned out the lights on them. Then he drove her home and they sat in his car outside her apartment and talked with the car running for another hour. While they were sitting there, it started to snow big, fluffy flakes. Scott asked if she wanted to grab some boots and go for a walk. She did. When she came back out of her apartment, she found him fully winterized with cold-weather gear he stored in his trunk. They walked and talked as the city turned into a magical, muffled winterscape around them.

"It was as if we were walking around inside a big, beautiful snow globe," she confided in a breathy tone.

I sat spellbound, living every moment in my mind's eye.

"How late was it when you got home?" I prompted.

She seemed to have gotten lost in the memory of her winter wonderland.

"Oh, I don't know . . . maybe around two o'clock or so," she said.

"And?" I prodded.

"And what?"

"And did he kiss you good night?"

If blushes could be heard, I'm quite sure I heard one over the long-distance phone line that night.

"Hey . . . some things are private," she asserted.

"Oh, so he did kiss you. I knew it. I knew you two would hit it off. You can thank me now, or you can thank me later, when you name your first daughter after me."

She giggled like—well, like she was my age.

"Okay, short stuff, enough prying. I've fulfilled my vow to you and reported on my first date with Scott Stewart. Truth be told, it wasn't our very first date. We went out once in high school . . . kind of . . . with eight other people from yearbook club to the Roll-a-Rena."

"Wait—what? You were an item in high school?"

"No, not really," she laughed. "I think it was more of a distant crush. He was two years younger than me. I didn't want to be accused of robbing the cradle. But that was long ago, and now two years doesn't matter. And I think maybe that crush thing isn't quite so distant anymore."

"Wow."

I had set up my sister, and it was love at first sight—or maybe second sight. But it was definitely love— or at least a serious like.

"But hey," Susan resumed in her regular grown-up voice, "there's something I need to ask you."

"Okay."

"You know those pictures you drew from Scott's photos at the art event?"

"Yeah. What about 'em?"

"Well, I'm wondering if you could send me copies like the one you sent me of Joseph. I told Scott what you saw that night. I hope that's okay. He's really curious. He'd love to compare your sketches of those babies to some photos he's got. He's a bit skeptical about the whole thing, but he's open to investigating. What do you say?"

She inhaled and waited.

I didn't blame him for being skeptical. It was a pretty wild thing to ask someone to believe. I probably wouldn't believe it either if I hadn't been there. And although I was a bit upset that she had told him without asking me, my curiosity outweighed my irritation. Would the sketches of Timothy and Shavonne be close to the real pictures?

"Yeah. Okay. I'll have Mother make a few copies and we'll send 'em to you."

"Great. Can't wait to see them. Do you know the story behind those photographs?"

"Just that Scott took them at Children's Hospital in some kind of volunteer work."

"That's right. He has a student whose mother is a nurse in the NICU at Children's—the neonatal intensive care unit. When she saw Scott's work, she asked him if he would be willing to volunteer his services there. They try to keep a photographer on call for families whose babies are failing or stillborn. It's a way to capture precious moments for those parents and give them something tangible to take home with them. Isn't that amazing?"

"Yeah, that sounds amazing . . . and super intense. I don't know if I could do that."

"Scott says it's one of the hardest things he's ever done and one of the most rewarding at the same time. I'm guessing it's one of those places Mother would call a thin place."

I cradled the phone against my ear.

"Hey Susan?" I said. "Maybe I should send extra copies in case Scott wants to give them to the parents."

Now it was Susan's turn to be quiet for a moment.

"Yeah, good idea. That might be a really cool thing for them to see." She paused and then added, "Thanks, kiddo. Now, can you put Mother on the phone?"

I handed the phone to Mother as I walked into the kitchen and sat at the table to resume my sketching. Daniel's face peeped up at me. He seemed to say, "Tag. You're it."

□

Negative reinforcement banged at our front door right around 8 p.m. Mother had just finished watching *60 Minutes* when the pounding started.

"Are you expecting someone?" Mother asked, switching off the television.

I shook my head. We headed to the front door together. A man's stocking cap was visible through the half circle of glass at the top of the door. Mother instinctively pulled me behind her back before opening the door about six inches.

"Can I help you?"

"Already helped enough," came the brusque reply. "You and that daughter of yours."

"Mr. Olson, I'm sure I don't know what you're talking about."

El's dad?

"Don't preten' like you don' know," said Mr. Olson, his voice growing heated.

"Dad, you promised you'd be nice," El pleaded from somewhere behind her dad.

I grabbed the door from Mother's hand and swung it open.

"El, are you okay?" I asked.

"I'm sorry, Pearl. He insisted I bring him. He promised he'd be reasonable."

"Mr. Olson," Mother took charge, "I am open to discussing any situation with you, but you must calm down."

He grabbed his hat from where it sat atop his carrot-red hair and wrung it in his hands.

"Sorry. Don' mean to be so mean . . . just that . . ." Suddenly, his anger melted into tears. "Can't seem to get over it. She's gone . . . and he's gone too."

He hung his head. Mother hesitated and then opened the screen door.

"I think perhaps you should come in."

El ushered her dad into the entryway. The smell of beer filled the air.

"Have you been drinking, Mr. Olson?" Mother asked.

He shook his head.

"Dad," El urged.

"Well, okay," he conceded. "Just a few Millers."

"Then let me put on some coffee. Pearl, show El and her dad into the front room, please."

I clutched El's hand and led the way.

"It's gonna be okay," I whispered to her, hoping that was truly the case. The moment had come to separate fact from fiction.

Mr. Olson unzipped his coat and plopped onto the couch. El and I scrunched together onto the recliner, our hands still intertwined and her coat buttoned to the top. She was shivering.

"While the coffee is brewing," Mother said as she entered the room, "maybe you can tell me what this is all about."

She pulled the other armchair from across the room to the side of the coffee table opposite from Mr. Olson and sat down.

"Won't be no surprise to you," he began, his hat still twirling between his thick fingers. "I'm here to talk about Violet."

Mother nodded. Her features told me that she was not, in fact, surprised to hear this. El gripped my hand tighter.

"Her baby . . . the one who died . . . he was my baby."

He looked into Mother's eyes, a mixture of defiance and pain written across his freckled features.

"I'm sorry for your loss," Mother said.

Her gentle response seemed to turn aside what might've been coming. He hung his head and wept again.

"I knew it weren't right and all," he said between sobs. "But I loved her. And that old husband of hers . . . he's a son of a b—"

"Mr. Olson," Mother cut him off, "in my house, such language is not allowed. If you want to continue this conversation, please watch yourself."

He blew his nose into a crumpled hankie he'd pulled from his coat pocket.

"Sorry, ma'am. But it's the truth. He ain't no good for her."

"That is not mine to judge. Why don't you compose yourself and I'll get that coffee?"

El leaned her head onto my shoulder as if she could hold it up no longer. I knew that drunken scenes were not uncommon for her and her dad, but for me it was a whole new world. I sat spellbound by the drama, fascinated and terrified at the same time.

Mother returned with a steaming mug.

"It's black," she said, handing it to him.

His big mitts wrapped around the mug until it almost disappeared. He stared into the blackness before taking a sip.

"Thanks kindly," he said.

We all waited for him to take the next step.

"She was gonna divorce him, ya know. And once that was all done, we were gonna go to Vegas and tie the knot. Make us a real family. Me and her . . . and the baby."

"I see," Mother said.

He took another sip and set the mug on the coffee table, drifting into silence.

"But that didn't turn out the way you had planned," Mother prompted.

He shook his head.

"Never even got to see him. Vi said he had hair just like mine."

Tears streamed down his face once more.

I don't know if it was the agony of watching a grown man cry or simply the need to feel useful, but I released El's hand and got up from the chair.

"I'll be right back," I assured her.

I left the living room and returned with my sketch of Joseph.

"Uh, Mr. Olson," I said, approaching the couch, "I don't know if this would help or not, but I did get to see your son. And, well, it's kinda a long story, but I drew a picture of him. Would you like to see?"

His bleary eyes looked at me as though he couldn't understand, but he reached a hand out for the sketch nonetheless. He stared and stared at my sketch for what seemed like half an hour, though it was probably more like a minute or two. Finally, he gazed back at me.

"Looks like he's alive. But . . . that cain't be."

I took a deep breath and sat on the couch beside him.

"Do you want me to tell you why he looks so alive?"

El leaned forward on the recliner and unbuttoned her coat.

"I do," she said.

"Okay," he said, his eyes glued again to the image of his infant son.

I glanced at Mother. She nodded her encouragement, her lips already aflutter in noiseless prayer.

Once again, I recounted the story of Joseph and the Baby-Catcher Gate. El and her dad listened intently. When I reached the end of my summary of that night, El came and sat on the other side of her dad.

"Can I see it?" she asked, pointing to the picture.

Suddenly Mr. Olson's eyebrows furrowed. He flung the sketch across the room.

"I don't believe it."

He stood up and kicked the coffee table, sending coffee splashing everywhere and my bowl flying into the air. Mother reached to stabilize the coffee mug. My bowl fell to the carpet, rolled, and smacked up against the TV stand with a sickening crunch.

I leapt up.

"Why'd ya do that?" I barked at Mr. Olson as I ran to retrieve my bowl.

"Sorry about that . . . Wait. What am I sayin'? I ain't got nothin' to be sorry 'bout. You're the ones that killed my boy!"

"Dad, stop."

El reached for his arm and he slapped her hand away.

"Don't you tell me what to do."

"Mr. Olson, you either get a hold of yourself or you leave. Right now."

Mother stood with both hands on her hips.

"I don't gotta listen to you, either," he said, stepping around the end of the coffee table. "Shoulda never let Vi go to you . . . you crazy baby catcher . . . and your crazy daughter. There ain't no gate in heaven for bastards."

He moved closer and closer to Mother. El gripped the back of his coat and tried to pull him back.

"Stop it!" she yelled.

He swung around and knocked her to the couch.

"Pearl, call 911," Mother ordered, going around the other side of the coffee table to pull El into her arms.

I ran to the phone and dialed, fingers trembling.

Mr. Olson stared at Mother and El for a long moment, then barged out of the living room and ran for the front door.

As he stood in the threshold, he yelled back at us, "Don't you be spreadin' your pack of lies around town. Or you'll be hearin' from me."

The door slammed. And he was gone.

☐

Mother drove El and me to school together the next morning red-eyed and exhausted. After talking to the sheriff and calling El's mom the night before, I'd rolled out a sleeping bag for El in my room and we'd talked until the wee hours. The few winks of sleep I had managed to get weren't very restful, and I suspected the case was true for El as well.

I was relieved to finally have all the cards on the table with her, but I certainly was not excited about the way they'd been dealt. The strange encounter with her dad had given me a new appreciation for my friend El and all the things she quietly endured. Turns out we both had secrets—ones that intertwined with one another in a peculiar fashion. I wasn't sure how good it would be for those secrets to get out.

Mr. Olson's threat echoed in my mind over and over. El had tried to reassure me that it was all just hot air, that her dad would never hurt a fly. But I wasn't so sure. I'd seen how quickly his temper flared. And even though he hadn't hurt El physically, he easily could have. Maybe that only happened when he was drunk, but how often was that? I didn't know, and I didn't care to find out.

All day long as I wandered through my classes, I seriously considered reneging on my offer to Teacher Anne. My fears were no longer just about what a bully like Reggie Dumfrey might do to sully my reputation if he found out all there was to know about me. Now they were about what a full-grown bully like Mr. Olson might do to physically harm me or my mom or El if my story about Joseph were to become public knowledge.

Of course, I would never divulge that Mr. Olson was Joseph's dad—though apparently that wasn't such a big secret, anyway. El begged me to keep it to myself. She was embarrassed that I knew, and she didn't want anyone else to know.

"No one else could possibly understand my situation," she had said the night before.

I knew that wasn't true. I looked for Ben throughout the day but didn't find him. I felt that El might find comfort in his story, but it wasn't mine to tell. The final bell of seventh period ended, and I was no closer to sorting out the pieces of my strange world than when I had gotten out of bed that morning.

Someone somewhere in a much higher place must've known I needed some encouragement.

When I got home from school and walked into the kitchen, the day's mail was piled on the table. Propped up against the napkin holder stood an envelope hand addressed to me. I snatched it up to see who it might be from. The label in the upper left corner said Peterson. The return address was in a town called Little Prairie.

My curiosity was piqued, but I forced myself to put it down while I grabbed a cheese stick and apple slices from the fridge. Then I sat down with my snack, ripped open the envelope, plopped an apple slice in my mouth, and unfolded the letter. It was written on crisp, white stationery fringed with purple and adorned with a clump of lilacs in the upper corner. A pleasant aroma wafted from the page. I took a sniff. Lilacs. I turned the sheet over. It was signed at the bottom, "With sincere gratitude, Mrs. Peterson." I stripped off a chunk of cheese and chewed as I read.

Dear Pearl,

I am writing to say thank you once again to you (and to your Mother) for how you helped this family get through a very tough time. Your care and courage have meant more than you know. I realize Joseph's birth was difficult for you and your Mother too. Am truly sorry it worked out the way it did for everyone involved. But we want you to know we do not blame his death on the care he received that night. Violet told me later that she had a feeling something was wrong. She had started spotting days before she went into labor, and the baby's movements had slowed way down. Don't know why she didn't let me or your mother know—something might have been done much sooner. Anyway, after the coroner examined Joseph's body, he let us know that Joseph had probably died just an hour or so before birth due to a "total placental abruption." (Your mother will know what that means.) He was pleased to hear that Violet survived. Thought you two might need to know this information.

Also wanted to let you know Violet has moved from her place and is now living with her brother Vernon and his wife on their farm. She wanted to get away and make a fresh start of things. I, too, am staying here for a few weeks to make sure she is settled. She helps around the house and has even gone out to help Vernon with his chores recently. This is good for her. She still has days when the grief takes her down pretty low, but she doesn't stay there real long. The picture you drew of Joseph is framed and hangs at the end of her bed, where she can see it first thing in the morning and last thing at night. Can't tell you what a great gift that is for her and for all of us. To see Joseph as he is—healthy and happy—and to know he is being taken care of with such love is surely a treasure. On top of all that, knowing my sister Maggie is there caring for him has freed my heart from a pain I didn't even know I still carried.

I know the bump on your head and the time in the hospital wasn't fun for you, but you need to know that the experience you had of life beyond this life is a precious gift, and your ability to capture what you saw on paper is a true gift as well. I am praying God will give you wisdom beyond your years to know how to share your gifts with others. Please give my most tender regards to your Mother.

With sincere gratitude,
Mrs. Peterson

I pondered her words as I munched another apple slice and skimmed back through the letter. She was right. I needed wisdom beyond my years—way beyond.

I set the letter down and went into the living room. The sketch of Joseph still lay on top of the stereo where Mother had placed it last night. But my bowl, chipped and fractured by the fall, was nowhere to be found.

INTERLUDE: PUAH

Shades of indigo, chartreuse, plum, and saffron saturate the garments of the small group of women gathered in front of Ilsa's home. Gemstones large and small glitter from the top of their heads to the tips of their toes. If women are breathtakingly beautiful on earth, as I know they are, then I have insufficient vocabulary to describe their essence beyond the pearl gates.

Their gay chatter reaches William and me as we cross the expansive golden boulevard and approach the group. Ilsa waves us into their midst.

"Come and join us," she urges. "This is my son John and grandson William," she says to the other women who have turned to greet us.

One holds a baby wrapped in a brocade blanket in her arms. Nearly hidden behind the other's skirt is a curly-headed little boy. He peeks at us from behind the purple fabric. William kneels beside him.

"Hey, there," he says to the young lad. "Wanna meet a friend of mine?"

The little guy looks up at me and shakes his head. Will laughs.

"Not that guy." He whistles and reaches out his hand. "I meant this guy." A bluebird appears from nowhere and alights on his finger. The little boy's eyes beam.

"You can pet him." Will holds the bird close enough for the boy to reach. "His name is Oliver."

A tiny hand reaches out from the skirt and touches the bird's head.

"Hi, Oliver," he says. "I'm Daniel."

The bird twitches his head to the side. Daniel leans in until he and Oliver are eye to eye. Then the bird opens his mouth and a warbling melody fills the air. Daniel claps his hands and jumps up and down.

"Do it some more! Do it some more!"

Oliver complies.

"He likes you," Will says. "Not everybody gets a song out of him as soon as they meet."

"And not everybody gets Daniel's name out of him at first meeting," the woman in the purple skirt says. "Well done, young man. You are more than welcome to join us Under His Wing if you'd like to help with some of the other youngsters."

William transfers his feathered friend to Daniel's outstretched arm. "Just pet him gently and he'll stay right there," he instructs the lad, who eagerly does as he is told.

Will stands up and turns to me. "I think I'd like that. Can I?"

I appeal to Ilsa, whose domain I know this to be.

"I'm sure that can be arranged," she says.

"Delightful." The woman reaches out her hand and shakes William's. "My name is Puah, by the way. You've grown up since you passed through my line at the Gate."

"Yes, ma'am," William replies. "I've heard a lot about you from Grandma. Can't say that I remember meeting you, though."

Puah laughs.

"No, most of the tiniest ones don't. And that is all fine and good. We like to get you connected to your baby catcher as quickly as possible and get you situated behind the Gate. Speaking of our work, let me introduce you to one of my finest coworkers."

She turns to the young woman dressed in cobalt blue who holds the bundled baby.

"This is Maggie. And the little fellow sleeping in her arms is her nephew Joseph."

"Hello," Maggie says as she sways slightly from side to side in her role as a cradle. "I like your bird," she says to Will.

"Wanna hold him?" Daniel says lifting Oliver upward. Maggie smiles.

"That's okay. I've got my hands full right now. But maybe later?"

"Okay," he says. "I'm really good at sharing."

"I'm sure you are," she replies.

"Are you ladies venturing out somewhere?" I ask.

Puah pulls a small scroll from her waistband.

"We've been summoned to Bethel," she says as she hands me the scroll.

I unroll it and William peers over my shoulder to read the words inscribed there.

"Is that where Jacob's ladder is?" Will asks her. "Jacob just told my class all about it."

She smiles.

"Yes. Bethel is the gateway between heaven and earth, where the heavenly hosts ascend and descend."

"Are you going to there to watch them?" William asks.

Puah shrugs.

"We don't know for certain. As you can see on the scroll, I was simply asked to gather these women and children and go to the gateway. Beyond that, I do not know. We will await further instructions once we arrive."

"Have you been there before?" I ask Ilsa, intrigued by this summons.

She shakes her head.

"Never. But I'm excited to go."

"Me too," Maggie adds.

"Any idea why the summons came now?" I say, turning to Puah, who is the head of the contingency.

"Not completely. But it has been my experience that activity at this portal seems to be particularly busy during a season of overflow."

Daniel tugs on Will's pant leg.

"Can you come with us? And Oliver too?"

William looks to Puah. She smiles.

"I don't see why not. And bring your dad too. The more the merrier."

"But the summons . . ."

I hand the scroll back to her.

"Did you read the fine print?" she asks, rolling it back up and returning it to its place in her waistband.

I look at William. He looks at me. We shake our heads. Puah chuckles.

"I have sat under Jacob's teaching, too, and if I learned anything from him, it was this—always read the fine print."

"What does it say?" Will blurts.

She speaks slowly and clearly, with a twinkle in her eyes: "For those who have ears to hear, let them hear."

"Does that mean us?" I ask, as eager as Will to be included in this venture.

"Do you see anyone else standing around asking questions?" Puah laughs and puts her hand on my arm. "It would appear that you have been summoned as well."

Daniel jumps up and down. Oliver flies above us in circles as William kneels to pull Daniel onto his back.

"Let's go!" Daniel prods Will. "I wanna see the big ladder."

"Everybody come in close, put a hand in the middle, and close your eyes," Puah instructs. We obey. "To Bethel," she whispers into our little circle, and we fly as one on the wings of her command.

ACCEPTING THE CALL

Ben wasn't at school on Tuesday, nor did he return my calls from the day before. I was growing concerned and might have been downright worried if I hadn't been so anxious about my own looming obligations in the hours ahead. I skittered through my day at school like a butterfly on Mountain Dew. Mentally I flitted in and out of classes and conversations, unable to focus or comprehend much of anything. I may as well have stayed at home, but that would have been disastrous; school at least offered legitimate distractions that held me back from a total panicked free fall.

As I walked through the door to Miss Wells's class, Tiffany pulled me aside.

"I heard what Ben did to Reggie," she whispered, wide-eyed with wonder.

I shrugged and glanced over her shoulder to make sure Mr. Dumfrey wasn't right behind her.

"Yeah, well, Reggie deserved it," I whispered back.

"I'm sure." She grabbed my hand. "I just wanted to say . . . I'm glad someone finally stood up to him," she said with a squeeze before beelining for her desk.

You could have knocked me over with a feather as I wandered to my seat. Just about the time I thought I had her figured out . . .

"Penny for your thoughts, Peculiar," Reggie said with a smirk as he passed by and slipped a piece of paper under my notebook.

I pulled it out and opened it.

"SOMEDAY ROMEO WON'T BE THERE."

The room started to spin. My heart sank to the vicinity of my kneecaps.

"Class, please take out your textbooks and open to page 142," Miss Wells instructed us.

I crumpled up the note and stuffed it in my pocket.

"We will continue our study of the hero's journey," she said. "Last week we talked about the first two stages, the call to adventure and the refusal of the quest. Who can tell me what the third stage is called?"

Tiffany's hand shot up.

"Yes, Miss Paulsen, go ahead."

"The third stage is accepting the call," Tiffany offered confidently.

"Correct. And that is where we will begin our discussion today. My goal for this week is for us to get through this stage and move on to the next two stages, which are entering the unknown and supernatural aid."

It was uncanny. If I didn't know better, I'd have thought Miss Wells had been camping in my bedroom and listening to my every cry.

Just the night before, as I lay in bed, I'd protested to my stuffed kitty, "They can't make me do this. I won't. I can't. I'm not gonna."

After I'd shed a few tears, a strange tingling presence descended on my whole body, like an electric blanket. I looked around for any telltale golden shimmers in the corners of my room but didn't see a thing. I lay there for a while, letting the tingling soak all the way into my heart. And then I'd whispered to the Presence that I felt all around me, "Okay. I'll do it. But please, please, please—help me. Let Your kingdom come and Your will be done on earth as it is in heaven."

I'd accepted the call, and I was about to enter the unknown. My sincere hope was that supernatural aid was on the way.

☐

After school, Mother picked me up and we drove home to get my art pieces and sketches.

"Have you seen my bowl?" I asked Mother.

I was searching the places I'd searched before, but with the same results.

"Is it missing? I'm sure it will show up. Let's get going," she said, handing me the box filled with the rest of my projects.

A bit miffed by her lack of concern, I grabbed the box and trudged to the car behind her.

We were headed to the high school cafeteria, where we would meet Teacher and the other exhibitors to organize the artwork for the evening. On the way, Mother told me she had seen Ben and his mother at the hospital that day.

"Is he all right?" I sputtered.

"Yes, dear, he's fine," Mother assured me. "His grandfather is quite ill, though. He was admitted to the hospital on Sunday, and it appears to be very serious. They don't expect him to recover this time."

"That's too bad," I said. My relief at hearing Ben was okay was tempered by the gloomy report about his grandfather. "Guess that explains why Ben hasn't called me back. I wish there was something we could do."

"We can pray."

"Yeah, I know, but what are you supposed to pray when someone is dying?" I asked, not really expecting an answer.

"You can pray for God's peace to be very present," Mother said without missing a beat. "And for physical pain to be removed. You can pray that the Holy Spirit will comfort the family. Ben's mom told me her dad has walked with the Lord for many years. The Bible says the death of a saint is precious in the sight of the Lord. This is a thin place for Ben and his family. Ask God to do special things for them in this time to help them know He sees them and cares for them."

I pondered her words, wondering if mothers everywhere possessed answers for everything or if it was just my mother.

When we arrived at the cafeteria, Fritz marched across the room to greet us.

"Need some help there?" he asked with a nod.

"Sure," I said, handing him my box.

The objects inside rattled as he held it. His hands were trembling.

"You okay, Fritz?"

"Oh ya, I'm fine," he said, tucking the box close to his body to stop the shaking. Halfway across the cafeteria, he pulled to a halt. The sadness I'd seen the first time we met darkened his features. "Honestly, I wish this was all over. I'm as nervous as a cat in a sinking boat."

I mustered up a smile I hoped appeared brave.

"Sounds pretty nervous."

"Ya, it is."

"Then I'd say you and I are in the same boat."

Something close to a smile touched his eyes. We resumed our trek together. I have heard that misery loves company. I don't know if that's true or not, but that day I found that nervousness sure does.

Teacher saw us coming and strode over to give Mother and me a quick hug.

"This is exciting, n'est-ce pas?" she asked.

It was more a statement than a question. Good thing, too, because my answer to her question would have been an emphatic, "No!" But she didn't wait around for my input. She took off across the room, Fritz and my box in tow. Mother and I followed the parade.

We greeted Mrs. Wilson and Mrs. Grant, who were pulling easels, fabrics, and other props from plastic bins beside the long tables set up for our use. They were old pros at this, having displayed their work many times before at various venues.

Teacher gathered us all together.

"Each of you will have one table to display your individual pieces. This table," she said, tapping the one she stood beside, "is for our summer art class. Why don't we start here, then you can go off to your separate tables?"

Under Teacher Anne's watchful eye, we began to arrange and rearrange our summer projects.

"Pearl," Mrs. Grant said in the midst of our activity, "where's your pottery piece? I've been looking forward to seeing the finished product, dontcha know."

"Uh, I kinda . . ." I struggled to come up with a simple answer.

Teacher pulled a box out from under the table and handed it to me.

"Why don't you open that up?"

I thought she was just giving me something to do, but when I lifted the corners of the box, I couldn't believe my eyes.

"My bowl. How did you . . . where did you . . . ?"

"Teacher Anne has had it in her repair shop," said Mother, who'd been sitting quietly while watching us work.

"Take a look. Just be gentle. The restoration is quite fresh," Teacher instructed.

I didn't know how she did it, but the chip had been set back in place, and the fracture along the side was nearly undetectable.

"That's a beauty," Fritz said.

"Lovely," breathed Mrs. Grant.

"Where'd you find the gold sparkles? I didn't see those among our glaze choices," Mrs. Wilson added.

I shook my head.

"I don't know. It just came out of the kiln that way." I looked over at Mother and Teacher. "Thanks."

"Our display wouldn't have been complete without it," Teacher said. "Here's a perfect spot for it."

She indicated a place among the other pottery pieces. I set the bowl down gently, and we all stepped back to admire our work. I had been anxious about having my art compared so closely to the others. But when we combined everything, the variety of interpretations and ability levels melded together into its own artistic statement, something like "Art for all ages, and all ages for art." I must have spoken it out loud, because Mrs. Wilson promptly urged me to put the phrase on a banner to hang on the table's edge. The others agreed.

Finished with the group display, we each moved to our tables. I was mortified to think of how little I had to show, compared with my classmates' work. But when Mother and I approached the table designated for me, we realized Teacher had prepared for this inequity. My table was small and round as opposed to long and rectangular. All their tables were covered in black tablecloths, but mine also had a layer of frothy white fabric that made it look as though a cloud had landed on top of it. Rising out of the cloud at various heights stood three silver easels. As Mother and I stood inspecting it, Teacher came up behind us.

"Let's see what it looks like with your sketches in place," she said, prompting me forward. "You decide where each piece goes."

"Okay, but, I, uh, actually have four sketches."

"You do?" Teacher said.

"Yeah. Another baby," I said with a shrug. "And another long story."

"How exciting! Let me check with the ladies and see if they have an extra easel," she said as she trotted off.

I opened my folder and contemplated what I should do. I placed Joseph's picture on the highest easel in the middle of the table, since he was the first baby I had captured on paper. Timothy and Shavonne sat side by side on easels to the left. I pulled them together at an angle.

"Here we go," Teacher said, raising a small, golden easel overhead as she trotted back to my table.

I set it opposite of Timothy and Shavonne and placed the picture of Daniel on it. I admired the way the frothy fabric curved up against the bottom of his picture. It looked as if the backpack's opening arose out of a cloud. I stepped back to check out my presentation.

"Ooh, la, la!" Teacher said as she leaned in for a closer look. "What a handsome young chap. Can't wait to hear the story behind this one."

Mother tilted her head back and forth.

"I think it's lovely. What do you think, sweetheart?"

As I chewed a fingernail, trying to decide what I thought, Teacher raised a hand and said, "Wait! I almost forgot." She swept off to the front of the room and came back with a black, velvet pouch in her hands. "Let's see what happens when I add these."

She pulled out a long strand of pearls and tucked them around the easels until it appeared as if pearly dewdrops were dripping from the cloud. She stepped back and stretched out her arms.

"Voilà!"

It was perfect. I looked into Teacher's sparkling eyes and simply nodded. I was so delighted, I forgot to be nervous for a minute. But my peaceful moment evaporated when Teacher pulled out a three-by-five card from her cardigan pocket.

"Now don't leave without this list of questions," she said.

I accepted the card from her hand and read the three questions.

What is your favorite type of art to make?
When did you start doing this?
Why is art important to you?

I glanced from the card into Teacher's face. I must have looked like a deer caught in the headlights, because she reached out hastily and put her hands on my shoulders.

"Pearl, if you don't want to talk, you don't have to," she said. "But I thought it might be good for you to have these questions in advance. Just take them home and think it over. Okay?"

I stared blankly at her. The butterflies that had been in my stomach all day metamorphosed into a herd of stampeding musk oxen. I dropped the card and sprinted across the cafeteria full throttle, thankful I knew precisely where the restrooms were located. As I fled, I heard Mother reassure Teacher.

"She'll be alright. She just needs some space to process."

Maybe Mother doesn't know everything after all, I thought before I crashed through the door marked "WOMEN."

☐

Only after I had emptied the contents of my stomach and washed my face did I see the scuffed, orange clogs. They were barely noticeable under the door of the last stall. I was embarrassed and about to make a quick, anonymous exit when I realized something—one sole was thicker than the other. I knew those clogs.

"El?" I asked tentatively.

No answer.

"El, is that you?"

"Pearl?" came the timid response.

"Yeah, it's me. Your favorite barfing friend."

I thought I might get a laugh. She remained silent.

"El, are you okay?"

Quiet sniffles. No words.

"Are you crying?"

Louder sniffles.

"Hey, open the door. It's just me."

Another minute passed before the latch slid back and the door opened. El sat fully clothed on the toilet. Her eyes were bloodshot and vacant. I approached her slowly and squatted down.

"What's going on?" I asked, placing a hand on her corduroyed knee. "Aren't you supposed to be at debate club?"

She began to sob. I reached up and pulled her into a hug.

"It's okay, El. Whatever it is, we'll figure it out together."

I spoke with more assurance than I felt. Since the scene with her dad, I had realized that her life was, well, complicated. Perhaps debate had nothing to do with her despair. Perhaps it was something way more complex than I was equipped to handle. I didn't know. But I had to try.

Her sobs subsided as I held her. She pulled back and grabbed a handful of tissue paper to clean up her dripping nose. I waited. She finally looked me in the eye.

"I can't," she said.

"You can't what?"

"I can't go back."

"Back where? Home?"

She shook her head.

"Debate club?"

She nodded.

"Why not?"

"Because . . . it's no use. I'm no good."

Her chin dropped. She blew her nose.

"Are you kidding me? You're the smartest, best debater in town. Everybody knows that."

"Not true," she said, shaking her head.

"What do you mean? How else did you get onto the JV high school team as a seventh grader?"

"I did, but . . . that was before."

"Before what? C'mon. Just tell me what's going on."

"That was before I actually had to debate someone. Last week, at the first meet, I froze. I couldn't defend my position. I couldn't even say my name."

"You? You always have words for everything."

"Well, apparently not when it matters."

"Oh, c'mon. It couldn't have been that bad. You just had a little lapse. You'll get over it. Just give it some time."

"No. I am not exaggerating," she insisted. "I completely lost it. Mark Pawkowski had to drag me off the stage. He dumped out the contents of his lunch sack and gave me the paper bag to breathe into. They stopped the meet and called the paramedics."

I swallowed.

"Wow, that's intense."

"Yeah, I know. They all said the same thing as you. 'Give it another try, El. It was just a fluke, El. You'll be fine next time, El,'" she said, mimicking their patronizing tones. "Well, next time was today. And the same thing just happened. Except this time, I got off the stage myself and ran . . . ran right here . . . to wallow by myself. Mark yelled in the doorway once, looking for me, but I didn't answer. I was finally pulling it together when someone came barging in and puked their guts out."

"Oh man," I said. "I'm so sorry. I was in a complete panic myself."

"About what?"

"Tonight—art appreciation night."

El looked chagrined.

"I'm sorry. I've been so engrossed in my own world, I completely forgot. Are you going to do it?"

I plopped down onto the floor.

"I thought I was . . . but I don't know if I can."

El put her hand on my shoulder.

"I've been thinking about all you said the other night."

"You have?"

"Yes, I have. And I think you should tell your story tonight."

"You do?" Another feather-knocking-over moment. "What about your dad? What about your family? I don't want to make things worse for you."

"I appreciate your concern, but let me state my case. People in this town are going to say what they want to say about my dad and Violet, even though they might not understand all the circumstances. And while I am not condoning their behavior, I believe that all of us have things we do that we are not proud of. No one has room to throw stones. People are also going to say what they want to say about you and your mother too. But who cares? I know, and everyone who loves you knows, that you are some of the kindest and most caring people on the planet. And those are the opinions that matter."

She may not have been able to debate on a stage, but seated on a throne in the bathroom, she was making quite an impact on her audience of one.

"What about your dad? Won't he be mad?"

El shrugged.

"Maybe. But he's always angry. And even though he talks big, I've never seen him carry through with any of his threats. Don't let him intimidate you. That's what my mother had to learn—and me too."

I pulled out the crumpled note that had been burning a hole in my pocket all day.

"What about this?" I handed it to El.

Crimson crept up her neck, absorbing her freckles all the way to her hairline as she read it.

"You must not back down in the face of fascist tyranny!" she stated emphatically.

"Huh?"

"Don't you see, Pearl? Tonight is your night to speak truth from a platform of influence. We cannot allow tyrants such as Reggie Dumfrey to terrorize us and keep us from enacting our right to free speech."

The door to the bathroom swung open.

"Pearl, are you in here?" Mother asked, peeking into the first stall.

I spun around and poked my head out.

"Down here."

She stopped, hands on hips.

"What on earth?"

"I'm okay," I assured her, standing up and stepping out into the room.

El followed me.

"What on earth?" Mother repeated.

"Hi," El said quietly.

"What is going on?" Mother persisted.

"It's my fault," I said. "I came flying in here, all freaked out. I threw up, and, well . . . El just happened to be in here. She's been calming me down. Helping me work through stuff."

"Well, that is very fortunate, to find a good friend in time of need," she remarked, turning to El. "Thank you for your assistance."

"The assistance has gone both ways," El said, looping her arm through mine.

"We need to be going, Pearl. Need to have some dinner and get ready for tonight," Mother said.

"Okay," I replied. "Can I just get a minute alone with El? It won't take long. I'll be right out."

Mother nodded.

"Do you have a ride home, El?"

"Yeah, my mom will be here soon," she said.

"Hope we'll see you tonight," Mother said as she exited.

"Is your mom really coming soon?" I asked once Mother was out of earshot.

"In about an hour, when the meet is scheduled to be over." She shrugged. "But it's okay. I should really go back to the auditorium and let everyone know that I have survived my disgrace."

"Alright." I took a deep breath. "Can you come tonight?"

"I will do my best to attend. Shall I see if Mel is free as well?"

"I'm not too sure what she'll think about it all, but sure. That would be great. Just seeing you guys in the room would be really helpful," I said. "And, El, I don't care what happened to you at the meet. I still think you're the best debater in town."

She laughed.

"I think perhaps in encouraging you, I have found the courage I needed myself." She gave me a Mel-like hug. "You are a true friend—no matter what."

I hugged her tight. "No matter what."

☐

The hours at home were agony. I tried to distract myself by making the banner for the group table, which worked for about half an hour. When I was satisfied with the outcome, I showed it to Mother.

"Very nice," she remarked before moving on to finish supper preparations. "We need to eat soon and get dressed. What are you going to wear?"

My mind ceased to function. My stomach twisted. I realized I had completely overlooked this major decision.

"I don't know. What do you think I should wear?"

"A dress or a skirt would be nice. Make sure to put on warm tights. It's going to get cold tonight. Go look in your closet. I'll call you when food is ready."

I drifted toward my bedroom in a stupor. Halfway there, I stopped and went back to the kitchen.

"Would it be okay if I ate after the event?" I asked. "My stomach is not currently accepting any donations."

"Of course. I'm just making chili, and that's easy to warm up. Go work on your wardrobe choices. I'll check on you after a bit."

I wandered into my room and slid open the mirrored closet doors. A colorful mass of pants, skirts, tops, and dresses hung before me. My eyes searched for a sign that said, "I'm perfect. Wear me." No such sign appeared. I decided to go with a skirt or dress as Mother had suggested, thus narrowing my choices. Still, nothing popped out at me. I'm not sure how long I stood there in abject indecision. Before I knew it, Mother was pulling options out and laying them side by side on my bed.

"These are your most appropriate choices. Any of them will be fine," she stated as she pulled my chin up and looked me in the eye. "You need to make a decision soon so we have time to do something with your hair."

She left me alone to ponder my alternatives. I tried on every piece of clothing lying on my bed, one by one. I stood before the mirror and promptly tore them off one by one until they were heaped in a pile of inside-out discards on the floor. I was generally not a girl given to histrionics, but at that moment, any resolve I possessed dissolved. I flopped to the floor, dressed only in my underwear and training bra (which wasn't truly necessary, but helped me feel hopeful). I sat crisscross applesauce, dropped my head into my hands, and cried out, "I don't want to do this anymore. I changed my mind. Don't make me do this!"

The picture of El breathing into a paper bag with paramedics by her side swiftly became a picture of Pearl breathing into a paper bag with paramedics by her side. I had retreated to the refusal of the quest. I began to sob.

Mother's high heels clicked down the wood floor in the hallway. I sensed her in my doorway but didn't lift my head. I wanted her to see me in my misery and gain the full impact of my meltdown. She sighed, moved toward me, and stopped. She didn't say a word. In my curiosity, I reined in my sobs and raised my eyes a skosh to see if she was being swayed by my demonstration. Her hand reached down.

"Pearl, get up."

Clearly Mother was not impressed. I took her hand and allowed her to pull me up out of my pity party.

"Go splash your face with cold water," she ordered. "When you come back, you will pick up these clothes and hang them back on their hangers. Then I will help you make a decision. Understood?"

"Yes, ma'am," I muttered on my way to the bathroom.

When I got back, I did indeed pick up all the discarded clothes and hang them back on their hangers. I laid them next to Mother, who sat on my bed, arms crossed, waiting for me to finish.

"Here's the deal," she began. "You committed to Teacher Anne as well as your classmates to participate in tonight's event. You will keep that commitment. I am hopeful you will be dressed in something more appropriate than what you currently have on. My suggestion is your jean skirt, your white Oxford shirt, and your lavender crew neck sweater. You always look very nice in that outfit. You have five minutes to come out of this room in whatever you decide. Are we clear?"

"As a bell," I conceded.

"One more thing," she said, unfolding a crumpled piece of paper. "I found this on the floor. Care to explain?"

No use trying to evade her.

"Reggie wrote it."

"Reggie Dumfrey?"

I nodded.

"Up to his old tricks. Who's Romeo? Ben?"

I nodded.

"I'll take care of this," she said as she stood up. "You just get ready." As she passed by on the way out the door, she muttered under her breath, "One day I'd like to take that young man and . . ."

Unfortunately, I was out of earshot before she finished her threat, but it helped me feel better to know that she was on high alert regarding Mr. Dumfrey.

I donned a pair of white wool tights, the jean skirt, the Oxford shirt, and the lavender sweater. I stood in front of the mirror. She was right. I slipped on my penny loafers and joined Mother in the bathroom. She leaned over the vanity counter toward the mirror, applying her makeup.

Without skipping a stroke of mascara, she glanced my way and commented, "Don't you look nice?"

I sat down on the blue-carpeted toilet seat to wait. Mother looked pretty in her slim, black skirt and long-sleeved, teal blouse caught in a bow under her chin. She'd softened the curls of her perm with a curling iron. The blond waves with traces of gray at the temples stood perfectly coiffed around her face.

I was resigned to the fact that I was going to participate in the art event, but I was still overwhelmed at the thought of it. I broached the subject again in a more reasonable fashion.

"I'm not sure I can do this. I feel nauseous even thinking about it."

"Sometimes the thinking about it is worse than the doing of it," Mother commented while she continued to apply her makeup. I felt a Mother Pep Talk coming on. "Maybe you need to get your mind off yourself for a minute and think about how other people will be blessed by the gift God has given you. Teacher Anne has repeatedly told you that you don't need to stand up and deliver the Gettysburg Address. Yet I do believe a few words from you could shed great light on the life behind your art. You have an opportunity tonight to let your story and your art bring honor to God and hope to people. In the Bible, it says that when you get called to stand before people, even very important people, you don't need to worry about what to say, because God will fill your mouth."

She spread a soft shade of plum lipstick across her lips and tamped down on a tissue to remove the excess. Then she grabbed a hairbrush and turned her sights on me.

"And this is what I know to be true: if we are bold enough to declare God's truth, He says he will confirm it with signs and wonders following. So, consider that while I tackle your hair," she said. "How about a French braid?"

I swiveled around to offer her the back of my head and relented to the stroke of the brush. She separated, tugged, and wove my hair into a tidy chestnut braid that ran down between my shoulder blades. The calm certainty of her movements soothed my agitated mind. For the first time that day, peace descended upon my heart.

As she secured the end of the braid with a silky lavender scrunchy, a still, small voice whispered into my inner most being, "Do not fear. I am with you always."

Once again, I accepted the call.

REINFORCEMENTS

When Mother and I arrived at the cafeteria at 6:30 p.m., Fritz was tampering with the sound system while Mrs. Grant arranged lemon bars, brownies, and oatmeal scotchies on platters on the refreshment table. Mrs. Wilson was scooping coffee grounds into the large, silver coffee makers perched on the stainless steel countertop behind her. Their husbands worked in tandem, unfolding black tablecloths and draping them over each table. We stood in the doorway, shedding our winter coats, when Teacher Anne appeared beside us, her arms laden with boxes of plastic cups and napkins.

"Anne, let me help you with those," Mother offered as she snatched two boxes from the top of the stack.

"Thanks, Lizzie. Let's get them back to the ladies at the refreshment table," Teacher said, heading in that direction. "You both look quite enchanting this evening. Love the French braid, Pearl."

"Thank you," I replied.

"You look lovely too," Mother added.

"Ah, merci, mon ami," Teacher said, her best French accent accentuating her artsy look. Her hair was caught up in a twist secured with a dowel stuck through a leather oblong. Silver hoops dangled from her ears nearly to her shoulders. A long, sleeveless cardigan hung past her knees over a soft, floral-print blouse and voluminous black pants.

"Is there anything I can do?" I asked.

"Sure is. Follow me, and I'll give you an assignment," she said over her shoulder, the familiar scent of Shalimar perfume wafting out behind her.

We trooped over toward the refreshment table.

"You can hang your coats right there," Teacher said with a thrust of her chin. "How's it going here ladies? I've brought some reinforcements."

"Hello, hello," Mrs. Grant greeted us as she sliced up another pan of bars. "Don't you both look pretty tonight?"

"Pearl, you look so grown up," Mrs. Wilson commented. "I almost didn't recognize you."

"Spin around. Let me get a gander at that hairdo," Mrs. Grant insisted.

I turned around, awkwardly aware that my cheeks had grown pink.

"I never could figure out how to do that with my girls' hair," Mrs. Grant remarked to Mother.

"Never had any girls to even try it on," Mrs. Wilson said with a wistful sigh.

"Tell you what," Mother said. "When that little granddaughter of yours gets older, I'll give you a tutorial."

"If I can get her to sit still long enough," Mrs. Wilson said. "She's a whirlwind."

Teacher Anne interrupted the small talk.

"Pearl, here's a job for you."

She handed me two cardboard signs with arrows on the bottom that read "Art Appreciation Night—This Way."

"Please take these and pin them up," she said, giving me a clear, plastic box of pushpins. "I need one posted on the bulletin board by the main entrance and one on the board at the end of the hallway leading to the cafeteria. We want to make sure our guests don't get lost."

I grabbed the signs and pins and headed out, glad to have a task to keep me occupied. In the entryway by the main doors, I stood beside the big bulletin board, deliberating where to place a sign amidst the clutter already occupying the space, when someone behind me called out, "Pearl!"

I swung around. Coming through the big, glass entry doors was Ben. The box of pushpins dropped from my hand and hit the tile. Pins exploded across the floor in all directions.

"Well, I can see my sudden appearance still brings out the best in you," he teased. "Let me help."

He bent down and started to collect the shrapnel from my pushpin-box bomb.

"Oh my gosh. Sorry about this mess. I can't believe I did that. I just didn't expect to see you. But I'm so glad you came," I babbled.

"That's alright," he said. "I should've warned you. But I wasn't sure it would work out. I've only got a minute. My mom is waiting outside. We have to go right back to the hospital."

"Yeah . . . I heard about your grandpa. Sorry about that too. We've been praying for you. How's he doing?" I asked, continuing to gather the pins and poking my fingertips repeatedly in my flustered state.

"Not so hot . . . they think tonight might be the night." Ben picked up more pins. "Uh . . . the night . . . you know . . . he passes."

We worked our way across the minefield of pins. We were silent, unable to talk casually in the face of his impending loss. We scooped up the last pins, snapped them into their plastic case, and stood in the middle of the entryway, a foot a part. When he glanced at me, the sorrow in his eyes squeezed my heart. I put a hand on his shoulder.

"I'm really sorry, Ben."

"Thanks."

We stood mutely for a moment. I retrieved my hand.

"I need to put up these signs. Wanna help?"

"I would, but I gotta go. I just came to give you this." He reached inside his jacket, pulled out a card, and handed it to me. "Thought you might need a little boost."

On the front, he had drawn one of his cartoons. It was an underwater scene with a closed oyster shell surrounded by rangy seaweed plumes. Above the oyster, it read, "For Pearl."

"Open it," Ben urged.

Inside was the same scene, except the shell was wide open. I sat in the middle of the oyster on a plush blanket with one baby on my lap, another peering over my shoulder from a backpack, and two more at my feet peeking out of a picnic basket. In the seaweed on either side of the shell, other babies peered in my direction. Every baby was happy. Some even appeared to be laughing. Underneath the scene was written, "The Baby Catcher." I stared at the picture in amazement. He had captured everyone in perfect caricatures—Joseph, Daniel, Shavonne, Timothy, and me.

"Who are all these other babies?" I asked, pointing to the seaweed.

He shrugged.

"Don't know for sure. The babies you have yet to catch."

Impulsively, I stepped forward and threw both arms around him.

"It's perfect, Ben. I love it! Thank you so much."

He stood stock-still with both arms locked down at his sides, pinned by my unexpected hug. I quickly drew back, fearing I had overstepped our friendship in my exuberance. But a glimpse of his eyes revealed an unmistakable spark of pleasure. He stuck his hands into his coat pockets.

"I'm glad you like it."

A car honked outside. Ben's mom was still waiting. He waved at her through the glass doors and turned back to me.

"I know you'll do great tonight."

He lunged forward, planted a kiss on my cheek, pivoted, and fled.

I nearly dropped the box of pins again.

My feet refused to move for several minutes. This was probably a blessing, since I may have wandered off into some unknown corner of the school, and Teacher would have had to send out search and rescue to find me. But eventually my mind returned to my body from the La-La Land of First Kisses, and I was able to complete my assignment. I was grateful it wasn't a job that required a great deal of brain power.

Ben Bradley kissed me! Over and over again this phrase washed across my mind, eliciting fresh rounds of butterflies. These were not the nervous variety, however, but rather the slightly delirious ones. Much more pleasant, but still a bit unsettling. As I pinned up the last sign, a new thought interrupted my delirium. Should I tell Mother? She might not approve.

Then, as if my thoughts were laid bare, Mother appeared at the cafeteria doorway. She walked briskly in my direction.

"Pearl, what have you been doing? Surely it hasn't taken you this long to put up two signs. It's nearly seven o'clock. People are arriving. We're almost ready to start."

In my haze, I hadn't even noticed the people walking past me in the hallway. If any of them had greeted me, I was oblivious to the fact.

"Sorry," I sputtered. "I didn't realize the time."

"It's okay, dear, but we do need to get inside and take our seats. Teacher Anne has places reserved for us at the front table with the others," Mother said. "What's that you're holding?"

Without realizing it, I was holding Ben's card with both hands pressed against my heart.

"Oh, this? It's just a card Ben made for me."

"Ben Bradley? When did you see him?"

"Well, that's what took me so long. Ben asked his mom to bring him here for a minute so he could give me this."

I gave her the card and waited for her reaction. She looked over the front and then opened it up.

"'The Baby Catcher'?" A smile tugged at the corners of her mouth. "It was very thoughtful of him to make the effort to get it to you tonight. Did you thank him and his mother?"

"Yes, of course, I thanked him," I responded, hating the flush that rose in my cheeks as I remembered my thank-you hug. "I didn't thank his mom. She stayed outside in the car. But I will when I get a chance."

Mother handed back the card, placed her arm around my shoulder, and steered me into the cafeteria.

"Okay, make sure you do. Now let's go."

☐

While I had been occupied with my task, the cafeteria had been transformed. Miniature pumpkins and yellow gourds in beds of brightly colored fall leaves filled the center of each table. Around the room, people stood chatting with friends and neighbors, their hands filled with coffee mugs and napkins laden with scrumptious morsels. Their coats were draped over the backs of chairs, sleeves stuffed like sausages with hats, gloves, and scarves. Some who had already staked their claim strolled the length of the room, stopping to examine the artwork at each table. I was surprised to see the sheer number of people who had arrived.

Mr. LaMoure and his art students entered the room in a chattering flurry and quickly filled up a table close to the front. Maybe it was just my imagination, but they all actually seemed excited to be there. The young mothers occupied the same table as the month before, passing around what looked to be a newborn with much oohing and cuddling. Dr. Brown stood at the far table and pulled out a chair for Miss Francine right next to Mr. and Mrs. Schmidt. It was pretty much the same crowd that had been at the previous month's event, except for one notable difference: there were more men in attendance. In fact, one entire table in the middle of the room was populated by middle-aged men.

Teacher Anne tapped on the microphone.

"Folks, why don't you freshen up your coffee, grab another cookie or bar, and make your way to your seats. The evening's event will be starting in just a few minutes."

As Mother and I headed for the front I heard, "Pearl, wait up."

I turned around. Mel and El rushed to me. El looked exactly the same as she had a few hours ago—except less crazed. Mel was in her black-and-gold cheerleading uniform. They fell on me in an enthusiastic group hug.

"I can't believe it," Mel raved. "If I weren't already here, I'd be so upset that I wasn't here."

El and I looked at each other and laughed.

"I'll meet you at the table, Pearl. Don't take too long," Mother said with a chuckle before leaving our little circle.

"We have arrived as authorized reinforcements," El announced. "Which is akin to being a cheerleader," she interpreted for Mel.

"I know that," Mel scoffed. "El picked me up straight from the wrestling meet. Haven't eaten dinner. Don't even know what this is all about, but El said it was a friendship emergency. So here we are."

"Thanks guys." Tears pricked my eyes. "I don't think there's room for you at my table, though."

"That's okay. I don't wanna sit in front, anyway. We'll find a spot," Mel said, turning toward the back. "Hey, are those brownies back there? I'm gonna grab about five of 'em."

She ran off. El remained.

"No matter what, Pearl. Remember?" she said.

I nodded. She followed Mel. I turned and headed to find Mother, but a commotion in the doorway grabbed my attention. Coach Spencer held a struggling Reggie Dumfrey by the scruff of his shirt collar and was dragging him in my direction like a disobedient puppy. Miss Wells was right behind him.

"Found this rascal skulking in the hallway," Coach Spencer said. "But don't you worry. He's gonna spend the evening next to me. Aren't ya, buddy?"

Reggie didn't answer.

"What's that Reg? Cat got your tongue?" Coach tightened his grip.

"Yes, sir," Reggie muttered.

"That's what I thought. Now let's find us a nice, comfortable spot." Coach steered Reggie past me and winked as he did. "Go get 'em, Pearl."

Miss Wells put a hand on each of my shoulders and peered into my eyes.

"Don't you worry about a thing. This is your night. You can do this. You were born for this."

She gave my shoulders a quick squeeze and ran off to catch up to Coach.

First Ben. Then Mel and El. Then Coach and Reggie and Miss Wells. It was an emotional roller coaster, and I wasn't sure what came next—an upward tick or a downward free fall.

I murmured to myself as I headed toward the front, "I can do this. I was born for this."

Mother sat at a table near Fritz, who was dressed in a white, button-up shirt and a silver- and red-striped tie. He was hunched over, staring at something in his lap.

"Hey, Fritz," I greeted him as I sat down next to him.

He didn't look up. His eyes were glued to a stack of three-by-five cards in his hands, studying them intently.

Mother picked up the pitcher on the table and poured water into some plastic cups.

"Want some water?" I offered. "I know I do."

Fritz looked up and blinked as if trying to refocus on the here and now. He reached for the cup I pushed in his direction and drank the whole thing down in one long gulp.

"Thank you. Mind if I get a refill?" he asked, setting the cup where Mother could reach it. "Guess I was thirsty," he remarked before taking another long swig from the refilled cup.

"It's best to have your vocal cords nice and moist before speaking," Mother reassured.

"I wouldn't know nothin' about that," Fritz said, "seeing as I generally avoid talkin' in front a folks like the plague. Now I remember why. It's silly. I've known most of these folks for years, and they're all the nicest sort you'd ever want to meet. It's not like they're takin' me out to a firin' squad . . . but it sure do feel like it."

I placed my hand on Fritz's forearm, careful not to wrinkle his shirt that was ironed to a starched crispness.

"Fritz, why don't you and I make a deal?" I said, trying to conjure up Miss Wells's encouraging tone. "When you're up there behind the podium, you can pretend you're talking just to me. And when I'm up there, I'll pretend I'm talking just to you. Then, if anyone else happens to hear our conversation, well, good for them. But if not, at least you and I will get to know each other better."

He reached out and laid his hand over mine.

"I reckon if you can do that, so can I." He turned to Mother and said, "You have a real-special young lady here."

"Thank you, Fritz. She even surprises me from time to time."

Mrs. Grant, Mrs. Wilson, and their husbands arrived at the table, chitchatting excitedly. They rearranged their chairs so they would all be facing forward.

"You've decided to say something?" Mother whispered in my ear amid the hubbub. "What changed your mind?"

"Some good friends," I whispered back. "And something I remember Gregory saying. He told me I would need to be strong and courageous. I guess when you're real scared is the time when that applies most."

She nodded and pressed my hand.

"I'll be praying."

"I'm counting on it."

ONE ACCORD

Teacher Anne strode to the front of the cafeteria and stood behind the wooden podium.

"Okay, everyone. It's time to get the evening rolling."

People converged on their seats. Shuffling, scuffling, and bumping of chairs underscored a flurry of last-minute conversations. Over the hubbub, she continued.

"I would like to welcome everyone to the second art appreciation night of the year." A smattering of applause as well as a few discreet shushes assisted Teacher in her attempt to settle the crowd. "Tonight, we have the pleasure of honoring some of our local artists. Some have been part of our art community for many years, and some are just joining our ranks."

She smiled directly at me. My mouth dried up like a sponge. I grabbed a cup of water and took a gulp.

"You will see some amazing artwork and hear some wonderful stories. I know because I have had the privilege of working with each one of these artists. They all participated in a community-sponsored art class I taught this past summer. The middle display table," she said, pointing in that direction, "holds the pieces we worked on in that class. The other tables are filled with each individual artist's work. There is quite a variety—a veritable feast for the eyes and refreshment for the soul. You will have more opportunity to view the art once we have heard from the artists. So, without further ado, I would like to bring to the podium a dynamic duo in both art and life—Delores Wilson and Helen Grant."

The audience applauded as the two women paraded to the front. Mrs. Wilson, clad in navy blazer and matching slacks with a yellow scarf at her neck, moved to take the microphone first. Dressed in a tan, corduroy jumper over a turtleneck imprinted with fall leaves, Mrs. Grant took up a post behind her friend. Mrs. Wilson grabbed her by the hand.

"Helen, you can't hide back there," she said, pulling her forward.

"Oh now, I'm okay back here," Mrs. Grant protested, pushing away her hand.

"Come on," Mrs. Wilson persisted. "We talked about this. One for all and all for one."

"You just go," Mrs. Grant said, not budging from her spot.

"Nope." Mrs. Wilson crossed her arms and waited. "Not starting 'til you get on up here next to me."

"Goodness' sake. Such a fuss," Mrs. Grant whispered as she stepped forward.

Her cheeks were flushed. Their little squabble was quiet and probably only audible to those of us in the front row. Mrs. Wilson stretched her long, athletic arm around her comrade's plump shoulder, maneuvered her into a spot right next to her, and gave a squeeze.

"There. Stay," she instructed.

Mr. Grant leaned forward across the table and whispered, "You look just lovely, honeybun."

The pink in his wife's cheeks blossomed into full-blown red. He sat back, his arms resting on the top of his generous belly, his face aglow, pleased as punch.

Mrs. Wilson adjusted the microphone and began.

"Is this alright? Can everyone hear me?"

A few claps and verbal affirmatives arose from the audience.

"Very good. Well, let's get started. As most of you know, I am Delores Wilson, and this dear lady standing right next to me," she said, smiling at Mrs. Grant, "is my friend Helen Grant. As you will see at the display tables, my main focus in art is watercolors, and Helen's is charcoal sketches. We hope you will enjoy viewing them as much as we have enjoyed making them. Teacher Anne has asked us to tell you a little about how we got started in art and why we believe art is so important. We thought the best way to do that was to tell you the story of our friendship."

Mrs. Wilson sashayed to her right as Mrs. Grant moved over and pulled the microphone down to her level. She placed her folded hands on the podium.

"First, let me say how nice it is to see you all here tonight," she said.

"A little louder, honeybun," Mr. Grant coached.

Mrs. Grant cleared her throat and eyed her husband before starting afresh.

"Thank you for coming out and showing your support for the arts in our community," she enunciated clearly and strongly. "And let me say an additional thank you to our dear Teacher Anne for being the spearhead behind this event. Anne, your passion for the arts is a true blessing to so many of us."

Mrs. Wilson cried out "Hear! Hear!" and lead a round of applause for Teacher Anne, who accepted the thanks by placing a hand over her heart. Mrs. Grant, tucking her neatly bobbed silver hair behind one ear, leaned back into the microphone.

"So, let me start at the beginning then. Delores and I were both young brides when we came to this community more years ago than either of us care to admit."

"Thirty-seven, to be exact," Mr. Grant piped up loud enough for all to hear.

"Harvey!" Mrs. Grant exclaimed. "If you're not going to behave yourself, I will have my teacher escort you to the back."

He raised his hands in surrender and chuckled. Many joined him.

"You can dress him up, but you can't take him out," Mrs. Grant said with mock despair. "So, as I said, Delores and I were real young when we arrived in this town. Our husbands had both been hired to work at the paper mill. At the time we moved here, I had one baby in arms and another on the way. Delores was pregnant with her first. We met at a summer barbeque sponsored by the mill. Our husbands already knew each other from work, but Delores and I knew no one. We had our families and our homes, which we loved, but we needed something more, dontcha know. Delores and I hit it off the very first day we met. We found that we had many things in common. I know that by looking at us, you wouldn't necessarily think we were a matched set."

The audience laughed at her good-natured humor. Their response seemed to bolster her courage, and she settled into her role.

"We soon found out we had similar perspectives on life, similar dreams, and a similar sense of humor. In short, we were kindred spirits. One thing we discovered early on was we both had an artistic bent. But neither one of us had any formal training. So, we went to the public library and began to check out books on learning to draw and paint and such. Of course, our little library didn't have too many books like that, so we got to know the librarian real well. Are you here tonight, Mary Lou?"

She scanned the crowd.

"Back here, Helen. She's right here," a voice cried out.

I craned around to see. Others did the same. I couldn't see who Mrs. Grant was talking about, but Mel and El caught my eye from their spot in the back. They sat right beside Dr. Brown and Miss Francine. I silently prayed that Mel would behave herself. As if on cue, she scrunched up her face and stuck her thumbs in her ears, wiggling her fingers wildly. Miss Francine averted her gaze. El waved apologetically. I waved back.

"Hey, friend," Mrs. Grant carried on, pointing to where Mary Lou was seated.

I caught a glimpse. I recognized the gray-haired woman with the thick glasses and ample bosom. She went to our church, but I didn't know she used to be the town librarian. And I had no idea her name was Mary Lou. I always thought she was probably named Pearl.

"Thanks for coming," Mrs. Grant continued. "Mary Lou retired a few years back. She's a little shy in public, but put her on the trail of a book, and she's a real tiger. She helped us order books from libraries all over the state and even the country. I don't think Delores and I would be standing here tonight without the assistance she has given us over the years."

"Amen to that," Mrs. Wilson chimed in.

"So, with our books in hand," Mrs. Grant resumed her story, "Delores and I scheduled one night per month for our husbands to be in charge of the home front—which eventually consisted of four kids per household—and we had "art night." Sort of like tonight, except we got our hands dirty trying all different kinds of arts and crafts. We didn't have much extra money, so we pooled our resources and got creative at making our own supplies. As the years went by, we started to get pretty good at some things. We discovered we could sell our work at arts and crafts fairs. This opened a whole new world to us. Plus, we began to see a return on our investment. Of course, this is about the time our husbands started to get excited about everything—when they saw us making money instead of just spending it."

The audience murmured appreciatively as the two husbands reached across the table and high-fived each other. Mrs. Wilson swapped places with her friend and pulled the mic upward with a creak.

"As you've heard," she said, "art became an important connecting point and source of great enjoyment for the two of us. But as you know, life isn't always smooth sailing. Sometimes it's downright hard, and our two families are no different than yours. We've experienced our fair share of upheavals and difficulties. It was during these times that art became something more to us than just a fun hobby or side business. It became a way for us to express things we had no words for.

"When our second son went off to Vietnam and never returned . . ." Her chin dropped. Mrs. Grant placed a hand on her shoulder. Mrs. Wilson blew out a breath, squared her shoulders, looked up, and continued. "I couldn't see the beauty in anything anymore. Stopped painting for three years. But during those years, my friend here"—she turned and spoke directly to Mrs. Grant—"she created a hand-drawn card for me every week. Every week for three years I'd come home and find one of her charcoal sketches on my kitchen table. And my spirits would lift." Mrs. Grant's cheeks blossomed anew. Mrs. Wilson redirected her comments to the crowd. "The beauty she captured helped ease my sorrows in ways I cannot explain, even to this day. I'd find myself going back to her sketches over and over again for encouragement and comfort. I still have every one of those cards tucked safely in a special box."

"You do?" Mrs. Grant blurted.

"Yes, I do," Mrs. Wilson nodded to her friend. "They are some of my most treasured possessions."

"Well, don't that beat all," Mrs. Grant muttered.

Mrs. Wilson smiled at her before turning her attention back to her audience.

"Then one day, at the end of those three years, I heard Helen's youngest was going through a rough patch. And I knew what I needed to do. I dusted off my paintbrushes and made a card. The look on Helen's face when I handed it to her is one I'll never forget. She knew and I knew that her cards had helped carry me through some rough waters and now it was my turn to carry her. Somewhere around that time, we started to think about what our little cards might do for others. We realized our art was more than a talent. It was a gift from God, and it needed to be shared."

Her words hit me right between my eyes. Their story differed from mine, but their conclusion about art was the same. I leaned forward, eager to find out what came next.

"So," Mrs. Wilson resumed, "we connected with our different churches—yes, ALC Lutherans and Missouri Synod Lutherans can be friends—and we asked if we could offer our artwork in the form of handmade cards for any who were grieving or ill in our community. Our pastors took us up on our offer. We have been making cards together for more than a decade now. Maybe some of you have received them. It has been our hope and prayer that in some small way they have brought you comfort or hope or joy or whatever you needed at the time."

"I still have mine framed and hangin' next to my bed," a clear, strong female voice from the right side of the room suddenly interrupted.

Mrs. Wilson turned to Mrs. Grant. They smiled.

"Mine is tucked into my Bible," came another comment from a man at the table next to us.

"Got mine under the glass in the coffee table," a woman shouted from clear in the back.

"Stuck mine on the fridge with magnets."

"Made mine into a laminated placemat."

"Sent mine off to a friend in the hospital."

"Saved mine for five years, 'til my dog ate it," added one more. "Might have to get sick again so I can get another."

The room erupted into laughter. Mrs. Wilson and Mrs. Grant grasped each other's hands and exchanged a tearful glance. Then, Mrs. Wilson leaned back into the microphone.

"No, please don't get sick. We'll make you one for being healthy."

Applause broke out. Teacher Anne stood up and gave the ladies each a hug. They moved back to their places.

I stared at the card from Ben that sat in my lap. I knew exactly what they were talking about.

BEAUTY FROM ASHES

"*Next on the agenda,*" Teacher Anne announced, "we have a rare treat. We get to hear from Mr. Fritz Schaeffer. Please warmly welcome him to the podium."

The audience applauded as Fritz rose and scuffled forward. I heard a quiet, "Attaboy, Fritz," from a man behind me and a, "Way to go, buddy," from another on my right.

"You've got this, boss," said Mr. Wilson.

"We're rooting for ya," added Mr. Grant.

"Yup, sure are," spouted another.

"Bring it on."

"Let's go now."

The prattle made it sound as if someone were stepping to the plate to take their turn at bat rather than taking the microphone to speak. I realized the extra men in attendance had come for this—to support Fritz. It was just what he needed. He shook his head and smiled ever so slightly as he tapped his three-by-five cards on the podium, adjusted the microphone, and cleared his throat.

"I sure do appreciate the support, folks," he said. "Most of you know I'd rather shovel Main Street by hand than stand up here and do this. In fact, I'd rather do most anythin' than this—'cept maybe run for office. Please don't ever ask me to do that."

A male voice from the middle table chimed up, "I'd vote for ya, Fritz."

Laughter helped ease the tension of seeing a man so obviously out of his element.

"Well," Fritz said, shaking his head, "that would be a waste of a vote, since I'd flee across county lines rather than hold public office."

Again, polite laughter rippled through the room. Fritz tugged on the knot of his tie and peered down at his notes for a moment. When he looked back up, he gazed straight at me.

"If the rest of ya don't mind," he said, "I'm gonna focus my attention on this pretty young lady at the front table. She and I agreed that we would pretend we were the only ones in the room. If you all overhear our conversation, well, so be it. But this is what I'm gonna need to do. Besides, I reckon most of what I got to say pertains to her, anyways."

I didn't quite know what he meant, but I gave him the most encouraging smile I could work up.

"Well, now, let's see." He glanced down at his notes. "I guess as far as art goes, my favorite things to do are carvin' and sculptin'."

He set down the cards, looked out above the heads of the people, and tapped his fingers on the podium as if pondering his next move. When he turned his eyes to me, it seemed he had made a decision. He stuffed one hand into his back pocket and launched out.

"So, when I was a young boy, my opa—my grandpa—lived with us. He taught me how to whittle. On long, cold winter nights we'd sit by the wood stove and he'd show me how to pick a piece of wood to carve. He said every piece had something inside of it waitin' to git out. It was the whittler's job to discover what that was and bring it to life. Sometimes the wood wanted to be somethin' useful, like a letter opener or a ladle. But other times the wood held things like critters or trees or people.

"For a long time, I didn't know what Opa was talkin' about. I just picked up a piece of wood and started hackin' away with my knife, makin' whatever I wanted to make. Opa would let me. He'd show me new ways to cut and scrape and mark the wood and so forth. But no matter how much he taught me, my pieces never came close to being as beautiful as his."

It was working. Fritz was talking as easily as if it was just him and me sitting in the living room. Not that he'd ever been to my house. Or ever really talked to me, for that matter. But I guess he'd been saving up his words. It seemed he had something he wanted to tell me.

"Then, when I was ten years old," Fritz continued his story, "Opa got real sick. Pneumonia in both lungs. Took to his bed for days, too weak to even hold his knife. So, in the evenin's, I'd sit by his bed just to keep him company and carve sorta aimless-like. Then one night, when he was startin' to feel a little better, he said, 'Enkelsohn, gif me dat piece of vood and come up here next to me.' I climbed up on the little bed next to him and handed him the chunk of pine I chose that night. He said, 'Put your hands next to mine on dis vood and tell me vat you feel.'

"We'd done this exercise before, and I'd never felt nothin' from the wood 'cept wood. So, I wasn't too eager to try again. But because he was sick and I knew better than to argue, I reached over and put my hands next to his. It wasn't a big piece of wood—about six inches long and four inches thick. 'Don't talk. Let's vait unt feel unt listen,' he told me. Then he took my hands in his and slowly moved them over the wood's surface, explorin' every nook and cranny. And all of a sudden, somethin' like electricity shot through my hands." Fritz threw both hands up to demonstrate his surprise. "And I dropped that piece of wood right onto Opa's chest. He started laughin', which caused a coughin' jag so fierce I jumped off the bed to git him a glass of water."

Fritz was on a roll. I was enthralled.

"When he caught his breath, there was a twinkle in his eye as he whispered, 'Vat did you feel? Vat did the vood tell you?' I thought for a moment about the current that had shot through my hands. 'Opa,' I said, 'I think this wood wants to be ein bärenjunge—a bear cub.'

"Oh, he clapped his hands in delight," Fritz said, chuckling at the memory. "Opa said, 'Dat's it! Dat's it, mein bärchen. Dat's vat the vood vants. Go unt get started, but be careful to listen as you go.' And, by golly, I whittled out the best lookin' bear cub ever. It was like the wood cooperated with my cuts and scrapes because that's what it wanted all along."

Fritz's words ground to a halt. Discomfort begin to creep in, trying to push out the ease he had acquired in reliving the moments with his opa. I didn't want him to give in to fear. I wanted to know the rest of the story.

"What happened next, Fritz? Did you keep on carving?" I asked.

My voice seemed to jar him back into the present.

"Yeah, boss, don't drop us now," Mr. Grant urged.

"Got us hangin' on tenterhooks," Mr. Wilson concurred.

Fritz managed a nod in their direction, then looked back at me.

"Well, I sure did keep on carvin'," he said. "For years, actually. All the way through my time workin' out at the mill. Had a pretty good little side business set up selling my carvin's too. The Mrs., God rest her soul, was my best marketer and salesman—er, saleswoman. We'd set up booths out at the county fair each summer. Even went down to the state fair a few years. She'd talk to folks and seem to know just what they were lookin' for. She said I heard what the wood had inside of it and she heard what people had inside of them. She had a real way with folks."

Fritz's voice trailed off again. He hung his head as he shuffled his three-by-five cards. I grabbed a cup of water from the table and stepped to the podium.

"Here you go, Fritz. You're doing great."

Memories played across his eyes as he took the cup and sipped.

"Thank you, Pearl. Sorta got lost there for a minute. So, then, let's see here." Fritz set down the cup and flipped over a few of his cards as I slipped back to my seat. "I know I've already said more than you expected, but I hope you'll hang in there a bit longer," he said with a brief glance out at the crowd.

"You're doing great, boss," Mr. Wilson piped up.

"Take all the time you need," added Mr. Grant.

"Keep 'er comin'."

"We're with ya."

His fan base kept up their chatter.

"Well," he said nodding his head, "as most of these folks here know, the Mrs. and I never had no children. So, the boys at the mill sorta became our kids. I was foreman over the mechanics and truck crews for twenty-five years. That's long enough to see boys turn to men, get married, have kids and even grandkids. I took pride in treatin' those boys like family—always wantin' the best for them and always expectin' the best from them. When the Mrs. got the cancer and died so sudden, those boys kept me goin'. Sorta took me under their wings and watched over me."

He paused, took a sip of water, and resumed.

"Durin' that whole time I kept whittlin' and carvin', but after her passin', I didn't sell anythin' no more. Just did it for my own comfort mostly and to give away as thank-you gifts when some of you kind folks invited me to your family gatherin's and such."

He glanced up and acknowledged the crowd.

"I never really tried any sculptin'—never felt the need to. I was content to be a wood-carver all my days. But that all changed after the accident—the one where we lost your daddy, Pearl."

Our eyes locked. He took a deep breath and blew it out, maintaining eye contact. A steely determination rose up in him. Suddenly, I wasn't so sure I wanted to hear what was next.

"I was the foreman that night," he confessed, "and I was the one who made the call that it was safe enough for him to drive. Never been more wrong in my entire life. I've regretted that decision every second since." He dropped his glance from me and then turned his gaze to Teacher. "Then, of course, we lost Rick and, well . . . you can imagine the weight of responsibility I felt for him too. None of it ever should've happened. But it did."

The room was silent except for the pounding of my heart in my ears. I stared at Fritz in disbelief. His chin hung down, leaving me a view of his shiny, bald head and the halo of white fuzz around it. A big tear slid down my cheek. Mother reached over and put her hand between my shoulder blades and rubbed softly. I turned to her and asked silently, Did you know? She smiled tersely and nodded. She knew. She'd always known.

Fritz cleared his throat and I turned my attention back to him.

"Pearl, I'm real, real sorry. I've talked to your mama and Teacher Anne over the years 'bout all this. They've always been real gracious and forgivin'. More than I deserve. But I never had the nerve to tell you. Course, I hardly knew you 'til we took the art class together this summer. There were times I wanted to tell you, but I couldn't quite find the words. So, please forgive me for doin' this so publicly. I hope one day you'll find it in your heart to forgive me for all you've lost because of me."

I was speechless. He paused. Quiet sniffles and soft wiping of cheeks surrounded me.

"I guess the reason I'm doin' this tonight at this gatherin'," he continued, "is because that time in my life not only changed me, but changed my art forever. After we lost those boys, I couldn't keep workin' at the mill. Just didn't have it in me no more. So, I took an early retirement and went home, not sure what I was gonna do. I tried carvin' again, which had given me some comfort after the Mrs. passed. But I couldn't do it. Couldn't carve a thing. I was real, real low one day, sittin' in my woodshop, thinkin' bout your daddy and Rick and relivin' every moment, when I heard a voice say, 'Pick up that rock.'

"It was so clear, I thought someone had snuck into the shop. But when I looked around, no one was there. I figured since there wasn't a body around, it must've been the Almighty. I hadn't ever heard His voice before. And I wasn't sure why He might want to have anythin' to do with me. But I thought I'd better do what He said. So, I picked up a chunk of granite I had sittin' on my workbench. I'd used it as a paperweight for years but never really paid no attention to it. Then the voice said, 'Hold it. Feel it and listen.' It was like hearin' from Opa all over again. I didn't resist, just took my time holdin' that rock—didn't have nothin' else to do. I held it and felt it and listened for hours until I knew—there was a rose inside that chunk of granite. The voice said, 'That's it. Make something beautiful out of something hard.'

"It took me a day or so to round up the proper tools, and when I did, I had no notion of how to begin. So, I asked the One who had told me to pick up the rock, 'How do I do this, Lord?' And I tell you, as sure as I'm standin' here tonight, I felt Someone's hands cover my own and teach me how to chisel somethin' delicate and beautiful out of that hard chunk of granite. As we worked together, He spoke to me about things—hard things. He showed me how to find treasures in darkness. He told me about riches stored in secret places.

"Sculptin' for me is God's healin' balm for my broken heart. It's my connectin' point to the Almighty. It's where He still speaks to me in every piece I do. I think the reason people seem to enjoy my work is because when they look at it, they don't see my skill so much as they see the handiwork of God."

He stopped, reached down inside the podium, and pulled out a chunk of granite. He stepped over to me and set it on the table with great care.

"So, Pearl, tonight I'd like to present this piece to you," he said. People all around me strained forward to hear what he was saying. He didn't seem to care if they could hear him or not; his words were for me. "It's sat on my workbench for nine years as a reminder to me of God's faithfulness and goodness even in the hard times. I want you to have it."

It was the rose—so lifelike, I half expected to catch a whiff of its perfume wafting up from the rocky petals. I stared at it, trying to absorb its beauty, trying to comprehend everything I'd just heard. Somehow, this art appreciation night had turned into a thin place.

I closed my eyes for a moment and a warm, weighty presence sent tingles up and down my spine. When I opened my eyes, Fritz stood directly in front of me, agony and tenderness carved into the crags of his face. I don't remember deciding to jump up and fling my arms around his waist, but suddenly, that's what I was doing.

"I forgive you," I said for his ears only.

He wrapped his arms around me and squeezed. We clung to each other mutely.

Then one person behind me began to clap, then another and another, until everyone was applauding and people were standing. No chatter or prattle from the peanut gallery. Just hands clapping. Fritz bent down to kiss the top of my head.

"You are a treasure, Pearl. A true treasure," I heard him say before we separated and took our seats.

In my haste to jump up, the card from Ben had fallen to the floor. Fritz saw it and bent to pick it up. He handed it to me.

"Appears as though you've got a fan," he said.

I nodded.

"Truth is, you've got quite a few," he added. "And I'm guessin' you're about to get a bunch more."

INTERLUDE: THE FATHER

To call it a ladder is a vast understatement. Maybe at the bottom of wherever the rungs lead it looks like a ladder, but up here where it begins, it is more like the entrance to a massive stairway. I calculate that from where our little group stands at one side of the stairs to the other side must be at least a mile. And it is a busy place. The bustle of activity is beyond anything I have experienced anywhere, ever. Heavenly hosts fly in and out, up and down, over and around with breathtaking speed. Vehicles and creatures and clouds and all manner of transport whisk humans to and from the translucent platform at the stairs' edge in a constant blur of arrivals and departures. And at the center of it all, seated on a glorious sapphire throne that seems to hover on a shining cloud above it all, sits the I AM.

"He's here," William whispers in awe.

Puah nods.

"The Father loves it here at Bethel."

I inhale deeply and try to resist the urge to fall flat on my face.

"What do we do now?"

The question isn't even off my lips when three mighty escorts appear before us. Joseph, awake and alert, squeals and reaches out his arms toward the golden one.

"He's excited to see you again, Gregory," Maggie says, handing him to the stately figure.

"And I him."

Gregory scoops the little fellow up and tosses him into the air, which elicits a wellspring of giggles from Joseph. Then he hugs Joseph close to his chest and kisses the top of his head.

"He has grown so strong," he says as he sets him back in his auntie's arms.

"Of course he has," says Puah. "He's in expert hands."

She pats Maggie's arm before turning to the two other escorts, one cloaked in brilliant blue and the other in deep purple.

"I'm certainly delighted to see you two," Puah remarks.

They smile at her but remain silent. The one in blue stretches out his hand. Puah pulls the scroll from her waistband and hands it to him.

He reads it silently, then says, "Come."

My heart pounds. William lets Daniel slide down his back. He looks up at us with glowing eyes the size of planets.

"Can Oliver come too?" Daniel asks, pulling the bluebird from his pocket.

"You brought him along?" I say.

"He said he wanted to come," Daniel replies matter-of-factly.

"Bring your feathered friend along," says Puah as she kneels in front of him. "The I AM is the Father of all creatures great and small."

Daniel wraps his free arm around her neck, and Puah stands with him riding easily on her hip. Oliver perches on Daniel's shoulder. Ilsa holds Maggie's hand and steps in line behind Puah and our three escorts. William and I follow. We maneuver at an incredible rate of speed toward the epicenter of all the movement—the sapphire throne. It is impossible to comprehend how, but the Father is instructing and dispatching every creature—human or heavenly—at the precipice of the great ladder with mind-bending alacrity. Before I know it, our group kneels in tandem at His feet.

"Ah, my precious ones. Rise," He says with unfathomable kindness.

We stand.

"It is a joy to have you here again, Puah. And with a group of novices," He says with a smile.

Puah laughs.

"Yes, Abba, a fresh group of diligent seekers. Those You love to reward."

"Yes, My daughter. Thank you for delivering them here."

He proceeds to cradle each of our faces in His hands and greet us by name. Such love envelops us that I am uncertain where I end and He begins. It is as if He has drawn us into His very heart.

"Ilsa, John, and William, I have chosen the youngest and the least from among your people to bring change. She will bind up the brokenhearted and set captives free. Go to her with a fresh wind of hope, a deep river of joy, and a stout measure of boldness. My love makes a way where there seems to be no way."

He turns to Maggie and Joseph.

"You, too, will deliver a great measure of courage and love as you go. Ready to take a journey down the ladder?"

Joseph claps his hands and kicks his little feet.

"It would appear that Joseph certainly is," Maggie says. "And I am honored to take him."

"Abba, Abba," Daniel pipes up. "Can I go down the big ladder too?"

The Father bends forward, picks him out of Puah's arms, and sets him on His lap.

"That's precisely what I had in mind, young man," He says. "But who is this sitting on your shoulder?"

"That's Will's friend, Oliver. Can he come too? He's really nice," Daniel pleads.

"I think that's a good idea." With one finger, He strokes Oliver's feathers. "Go as a carrier of light."

Oliver flaps his wings, breaks into song, and flies back to Will. Daniel squeals in delight and wraps his arms around the Father's neck.

"Thank you, Abba."

The Father holds him close, kisses his cheeks, then places him back in Puah's outstretched arms.

"Now, dear ones, I send you." He turns to the golden escort. "Gregory, you know the way. Lead on and go in my peace."

He breathes upon us, and we are swept over the edge on a carpet of love.

BE TRUE

With the room still echoing with applause, Teacher went to the front and motioned for everyone to take their seats. In a quiet reverence I had only ever experienced in church, we all settled into our places. Teacher stepped to the podium.

"Well . . . this has turned into quite the evening," she said. "I think I speak for everyone when I say thank you, Fritz, for sharing your story so candidly. Every time I hear the way God has given beauty for ashes, I feel the healing balm you described being applied to my heart as well. So, thank you for stepping out of your comfort zone to be a speaker tonight."

Fritz sat still with his hands folded in his lap and nodded once. When Teacher turned her gaze on me, I realized I had been so busy pulling for Fritz that I had forgotten what came next—until that moment. A wave of nausea flooded me.

Mother leaned over.

"Pearl, you can do this. Be strong and courageous. Remember?"

Teacher must have sensed my hesitation.

"We have one more exhibitor tonight," she said, "as I am sure you have all noticed. She was the youngest participant in the summer art class—by quite a long shot. At first it was not comfortable for her to hang out with us old folks. But Pearl persevered, because she truly desired to grow as an artist. As her instructor, I will tell you that it was a delight to see her skills develop. She was an eager student and a reliable classmate. Even when she faced some health challenges and wound up in the hospital for a few days, she came back to class ready to go. But beyond all that, she is a gifted artist. I have asked her to share a little so you can hear what's behind those remarkable sketches displayed on the round table in the back. Pearl, will you come and share?"

I sat stock-still, certain that someone had vacuumed the breath out of me. I heard what she said but couldn't respond, couldn't move a muscle. Mother tapped my elbow.

"Sweetheart, are you okay?"

Then just as the silence grew unbearable, a gentle breeze blew across the room, starting from the back corner. It rustled napkins and ruffled hairdos as it swept toward me. Low murmurs followed in its wake.

"What's that?"

"Someone open a window?"

"What's going on?"

When the breeze reached me, it flipped open Ben's card that lay on the table in front of me. I stared at the picture of me in the oyster shell surrounded by happy babies. The breath returned to my lungs. My heart found its rhythm.

I don't know how I got to the podium. But suddenly there I was, seated on the high, wooden stool Teacher Anne had set in place for me. I eyeballed the people. They eyeballed me. A hush fell. I contemplated escape.

Suddenly, Mel popped up and waved both arms overhead in true cheerleader fashion.

"Go, Pearl, go!" she yelled before El yanked her back down with a glare.

Miss Francine covered her mouth with a gloved hand. Mrs. Schmidt shook her head. People about-faced to figure out the source of the outburst. It was a relief to have all eyes shifted elsewhere. They murmured and pointed at my friends. I smiled and shook my head. Mel blew me a kiss. El buried her head in her hands.

And that's when I saw them. Just over Mel's head, near my display table.

David and Miranda stood against the back wall. Hand in hand. Their coats still on, unbuttoned and hanging open. Right beside them stood Susan and Scott. Susan lifted a hand and waved. David offered a terse smile.

When did they arrive? Why didn't they tell us they were coming? Did they hear Fritz talk?

I looked at Mother. Her head was turned to the back wall, her spine rigid. She'd seen them.

Emotions of every variety leapt up and collided in my heart. Stars flashed across my vision. I struggled to regain a semblance of composure, but the stars kept flashing. Then, to my surprise, a golden haze enveloped the stars and swept them off into a far corner beyond the refreshment table. I stared in amazement. The haze grew brighter and brighter. Then, on either side of it, a purple haze and a blue haze appeared.

I looked at Mother. She had returned her gaze to the front.

"Do you see them?" I mouthed to her.

"Yes, yes, I see them," she whispered. "I didn't know they were coming."

She had seen my siblings, but she hadn't seen what I had seen.

Teacher cleared her throat.

"Pearl, are you going to be okay?" she asked from her seat.

Suddenly a great and awesome peace flooded my heart like a river.

"Yeah," I replied. "I think I am."

I glanced down at Fritz. He gave me a thumbs-up. I looked over the crowd at my siblings. David, too, offered a thumbs-up. I breathed in deeply. I opened my mouth. Amazingly, it was full of words.

"Well, as you all know by now, my name is Pearl. My favorite thing to do is draw, and my favorite thing to draw is babies. I guess . . . you could call me a baby catcher. I come from a long line of baby catchers, but I never wanted to be one, and I never wanted to be named Pearl. Funny how God can turn that all around."

And so, my story rolled out. A cocoon of love enveloped me and gave me the courage to look beyond Fritz to the entire crowd. The people laughed, cried, oohed, and aahed in all the right places. I felt their encouragement. I didn't question why some parts of the story were left out and others included. I went where I was led, and as I did, shivers ran through my body in electrical currents. It was the same feeling I got when I sketched my babies. I had come to think of it as feeling the King's good pleasure. I knew He was pleased with my art. But I never expected to feel His good pleasure in my words.

It felt so exhilarating, I wanted to throw my head back and laugh. But I contained myself. Evidently, Gregory and his companions were under no such restraint, for in a twinkling, the room lit up with flashes of gold, purple, and blue. The lights danced across the ceiling and bounced from wall to wall. They spun in pirouettes on the tabletops, humming in glorious harmonies. It was like the aurora borealis and the Concordia Choir had burst into the room.

People looked up and around in startled confusion. I could hardly believe it—but it was true. I was no longer the only one with eyes to see or ears to hear. The entire crowd had become aware of the heavenly invasion.

"Where're those lights comin' from?"

"Who's that singing? We got a choir somewhere in here?"

"Is this one of those laser shows?"

"Oh my, isn't this pretty?"

Some scanned the ceiling and walls, seeking the source of the lights and music. Others sat dumbstruck in wonder. Still others reached for the lights, like kids trying to catch lighting bugs. At one point, the blue and purple lights merged together and stopped right above Mother's head. She looked up in utter amazement. They began to spin faster and faster, shooting out dazzling colors like a disco ball. Mother's hair stood up on end, all the careful curls undone.

My attention shifted from Mother's stunned but shining face when the three lights converged and darted to the front. The gold, blue, and purple hazes stopped right in front of me at the podium. They started to twirl. I was glad my hair was snugged tightly into a braid as the wind began to swirl around me. Bursts of every color shot out from the spinning cloud. Fresh exclamations arose from the audience as if they were admiring fireworks on the Fourth of July.

"By golly! That's a beauty."

"Ah, did you see that?"

"Oh my stars and garters!"

"Holy mackerel!"

I'd seen this sort of display before.

"Gregory!"

The word shot out of my mouth and through the speakers.

"Did she say 'Gregory'?" asked Mrs. Wilson.

"I believe she did," replied Mrs. Grant through the fingers covering her gaping mouth.

"Angels in our midst," said Fritz, his face awash in wonder like a kid in a candy shop with money in his pocket.

And the word bounced from table to table.

"Angels!"

"They're angels."

"I hear they're angels."

"Did you say 'angels'?"

Gregory continued dancing like he had at Joseph's reception, and his angelic friends did too. The wordless melody they sang together as they spun was so irresistibly joyful that I threw any sense of propriety to the wind and leapt off the stool. Jumping and spinning with all my heart and strength, I flung my head back and laughed.

It was as if I'd set a match to an oil slick. In a flash, people all over the room leapt to their feet and started to dance. Those who were able spun around and jumped in the air. Some who hadn't danced in decades tapped their toes, clapped their hands, and tried a few awkward arm motions. The moms'-night-out ladies organized a line dance. Mr. and Mrs. Wilson gathered up Mr. and Mrs. Grant and did an impromptu square dance. Teacher pulled Fritz to his feet and they began to polka—slowly at first, but soon they oompahed across the room like professionals. Much to my further astonishment, Dr. Brown and Miss Francine waltzed right past me, her carefully coiffed bubble undone and flowing around her shoulders. Following in their wake came Mr. and Mrs. Schmidt, both grinning from ear to ear. Coach Spencer and Miss Wells held hands and jumped up and down in circles as if they were kids on pogo sticks. And wonder of wonders, Reggie Dumfrey was right beside them, doing the twist like a man possessed with happiness. On one side of the room, Mel was cartwheeling and flipping with unbridled zeal.

And El . . . El ran. She ran around the perimeter of the room, her hair streaming behind her like the afterburners on a jet. She ran as I'd never seen her run before—swift, strong, and beautiful.

Laughter broke out here and there until it boiled over into a full eruption of glee. There were chortles and chuckles, snickers and titters, cackles and giggles, guffaws and snorts. People held their stomachs and slapped their thighs. They gripped chairs and tables in an effort to stay upright. The entire group of high schoolers and Mr. LaMoure were on the floor rolling around in tears of glee.

I stopped my happy dance to soak it all in. Then, in the midst of the euphoric chaos, a bluebird appeared overhead and flew in circles of light over the crowd. Flakes of shimmering gold drifted down from his flight path and settled on lashes and shoulders and outstretched hands. The bird flew toward me, and I lifted my finger for a perch. He descended and, much to my utter delight, alit with a final golden flap.

"Where did you come from, little friend?" I asked.

He twitched his head from side to side. I ran one finger down his glossy, blue back. He opened his beak and began to warble a blissful song. Like a key in a lock, the tune peeled back what looked like a curtain in the middle of the ceiling, and a heavenly ladder was revealed. There on the bottom rung stood Puah and Maggie with Joseph and Daniel in their arms. The boys were both clapping and giggling. Puah and Maggie smiled so radiantly, my eyes could scarce take them in.

A young man stood on the step just above them, his blond tresses aglow in a glorious haze. Two others were positioned behind him on a higher rung, but their faces were obscured by the bright aura surrounding the ladder. The young man looked right at me and waved. Did I know him? My hand shot up to wave back, and the bluebird took flight, circled the room, and landed on the young man's outstretched hand. When he smiled, he looked . . . well, he looked just like Mother.

My heart skipped a beat. Could it be?

Then, as quickly as they had appeared, they all disappeared. The curtain fell back, and the ceiling was just a ceiling.

I looked out at the people still dancing and laughing as the lights and the music began to fade. They seemed oblivious to the heavenly vision I'd just seen. I scanned the crowd, searching for my family. Not in the back. Not among the dancing couples. Not on the floor. Then I spotted them. In the midst of the twirling and swirling they stood motionless, rooted to one spot in the middle of the room. David had one arm around Miranda and the other around Mother. Susan and Scott held hands beside them. All stared heavenward. Tears streamed down their faces. Glory lit their eyes. And I knew.

They had seen it.

They had seen them.

THE NIGHT

The night became known in our town as the Night the Angels Danced. People demarcated their lives by whether something happened before or after that night. Eventually it became so much a part of our native lingo, we simply called it the Night. Conversations around town were sprinkled with phrases like, "Now let's see, that happened before the Night, so it must have been '81," or, "The twins were born nine months after the Night. Happiest babies you've ever seen."

The atmosphere in our small town was altered by the Night. Churches that had been half empty were suddenly full. Youth groups that had been puny doubled and tripled overnight. Pastors who had been on the verge of boredom and despair were bombarded with phone calls.

"Pastor Joe, got time for a cup of coffee?"

"Pastor Beth, did ya hear about the goin's on at the high school?"

"Can I bend your ear for a minute or two, Pastor Art?"

The editor in chief of the paper was present at the Night, and he ran a front-page piece about it. The headline read:

Angelic Disruption at Art Night
Euphoric Eruption Ensues

The article was chock-full of firsthand accounts. The stories weren't just descriptions of the lights, the sounds, the laughter, the art, or even the angels. They were testimonies of miraculous happenings in individuals' lives. Some told of physical aches and pains disappearing instantly. One lady who had been diagnosed with breast cancer said the lump simply vanished. Others testified that depression and anxiety that had plagued them for years were eliminated.

The article quoted Dr. Brown as saying, "My mother always told me that laughter does good like a medicine. Never gave it much credence. But from now on, it will be high on my list of remedies."

Mr. Wilson reported, "The grief from losing my son all those years ago lifted. I slept through the night for the first time in ages."

Fritz said, "After dancin' the polka for over an hour, I felt fit as a fiddle and ready for more. Haven't had so much fun since the Mrs. passed."

"I woke up the next morning with the energy of an eighteen-year-old," Mrs. Grant said. "Along with some pretty sore stomach muscles."

"The evening was effervescent—sparkling, exhilarating, and bubbling over with life," said Miss Wells. "I could just burst with joy!"

Even Reggie Dumfrey didn't walk away the same.

"Guess what I felt was love," he said. "Yeah, that's it. It was big time love."

My favorite quote, though, was from Mel.

She said, "If I'd known God was so fun, I'd have gone to church years ago!"

El didn't make any remarks for the printed page. But she told me on the phone the next day that her short leg was no longer her short leg. Her mother had taken out the yardstick and measured.

"I now have identical appendages," she bragged.

The newspaper reporter asked Mother for a quote. She declined. I did too. I figured I had already said enough. Besides, I really wasn't sure how to put into words what had taken place. Mother called it "transformative," which is probably as close as words could get. It certainly described what happened in our family.

That evening when we got home from the school, David and Mother spent an hour behind closed doors, talking. Susan, Scott, and Miranda kept me company in the front room. Miranda in particular was full of questions. Nothing in her background had prepared her for such a heavenly perspective on life, and she was eager to know more. Of course, those of us who'd spent our whole lives in church weren't exactly prepared for what we'd experienced either. Susan and Scott sat on the couch, wiping gold flakes off each other's shoulders and hair and dropping them into my bowl, which I had restored to its place on the coffee table. They, too, were excited to mull over the night's happenings, even though they had to return to the Cities by morning. I couldn't believe they had all made such an effort to be there.

"Wouldn't have missed this for the world," Susan said. "It's just what family does."

"Was that family on the ladder, do you think?" I asked her.

Her eyes brimmed with tears.

"I don't know who the ones in the front were, but I'm pretty sure I saw Dad and Grandma in the back row."

"You did? And what about the young guy in the middle? Did you recognize him?"

She shook her head.

"Seems like I should've . . ."

By the time Mother and David emerged from behind closed doors, I felt as though Miranda and Scott were part of the family. Turns out, she actually was. Besides coming to support his kid sister, David had taken time off work and journeyed across two states with Miranda to inform Mother that they had eloped. And they were wondering if she would be present in about six months to help deliver her first grandchild. What grandmother/baby catcher in her right mind could turn that down?

Although Mother looked slightly undone, with her hair still askew and her makeup smudged by tears, an inner peace shone from her eyes.

I hugged her with all my might and she whispered in my ear, "Another bridge rebuilt."

It was a night to remember, for sure. A night bursting with goodness. Miss Wells had captured it—it was "effervescent." It tapped a wellspring of joy in our community that did not exist prior to it and persisted long after it.

Before the Night, I wouldn't have described the people in our town as mean. Grumpy, maybe, but definitely not malicious. They genuinely cared for each other. But there was sadness in our midst—a heartache that ran like an undercurrent through the streets. I didn't know if it had to do with layoffs at the paper mill, or boys who hadn't come home from Vietnam, or rising gas prices, or my daddy's accident and Rick's suicide—or if all those things were just chapters in one long saga of loss and hardship.

I did know that after the Night, there was a new skip in the collective step of the town. People laughed more easily, hugged more freely, danced more often, and hoped more deeply. They prayed like they were heard, cried like someone cared, and looked for the good even in the toughest situations and hardest hearts. And they found it—the good, the light, the wonder, the beauty, the joy, and the life that come from encountering the goodness of heaven.

I'm not sure why the Night the Angels Danced happened in our little, two-stoplight town in the boondocks of northern Minnesota. But it did. If I had to speculate, I would say Fritz baring his soul to me and receiving forgiveness had something to do with it. I think the way Mrs. Wilson and Mrs. Grant expressed their love for each other, their families, and their community was a major ingredient. Perhaps it had something to do with my story as well. I didn't really think of myself as being a hero, but I definitely had been on a journey, and maybe it's just what happens when you accept the call and step into the unknown—supernatural aid shows up. Maybe it was like Mother said: when God's truth is spoken boldly, He confirms it with signs and wonders following.

Or maybe—and I've never said this aloud to anyone before, but I've wondered on my bed at night—maybe there just comes a moment when the thing so many have asked for so many times for so many years simply comes to pass—the Kingdom comes on earth as it is in heaven. All I know for sure is that a thin place developed as art and light and love merged into something beautiful.

So, the angels came down and danced.

And we danced with them.

AFTERLIFE

Thirty-five years later, I am once again mulling over the Night and praying for another visitation from heaven. For I am in another thin place, sitting in a hospice room by Mother's bedside, surrounded by family members.

David is here with some of his family. Susan is here as well. And Scott should be here soon. Yes, they actually did get married. Their children, children's spouses, and a few grandkids are also in attendance.

Teacher Anne sits in a rocking chair right next to Mother's bed. Over the past few weeks this has been her spot—close by the side of her dearest friend.

We moved Mother down to the Cities four years ago, after I received an urgent text from Mel—or Pastor Mel, as the members of River of Life Fellowship up in St. Gerard now call her. She was our eyes and ears on the home front to keep us abreast of Mother's health and welfare.

Her text read:

Found M in car asleep at wheel in church parking lot. At least not found by SRD in middle of road this time. ☺ Took her home. Doc checked on her. Please call. There is a time for everything.

"M," of course, stood for Mother, and "SRD" was Sheriff Reggie Dumfrey—in his second term at said position and doing quite a fine job, from all I'd heard. "There is a time for everything" was our agreed-upon phrase. Not sure why we thought a secret code was needed to say, "Your Mother's health is failing and she can't live by herself anymore." Guess in some ways we never outgrew relating to each other as childhood friends. Or perhaps we just liked the sound of the secret phrase better than the harsh words of reality. Whatever the case, the words motivated my siblings and me. We moved Mother down to David's remodeled daylight basement. He had moved back to the Cities years ago, after Miranda's final bout with cancer left him by himself with a house full of kids.

He wasn't quite sure how he and the one little chick left in his nest would manage Mother's care, but he was willing to give it a go. We prayed all would go well. And, as God so often does for Mother, He answered our prayers in a way that seemed perfect for her. A few weeks after we had Mother safely tucked into her new digs, Teacher Anne called.

"Does Lizzie have room for a roomie?" she asked. "Florida has gotten lonely."

Teacher's second husband had passed away suddenly from a heart attack, leaving her to ramble around her large condo in Coral Springs by herself. Mother was delighted by the prospect of being able to assist her grieving friend, and we were thrilled for Mother to have a companion. So, we moved Teacher in as well.

She and Mother have tottered around that apartment together for the past four years, with occasional breaks when Teacher has spent a week or two back in Coral Springs. They've listened to their old albums, watched movie classics, cooked family dinners, and told their favorite stories to any who would sit down long enough to listen. Of course, their best told tale is the story of unseen things above—of angels and pearl gates and colors and music and the good, good King of the Great City. It's a story that has won the hearts of each of the grandchildren, one by one.

Then, six weeks ago, Mother fell on the ice and broke her hip. At first it appeared she would recover, but then she caught a nasty cold that turned into pneumonia. The doctors have tried everything they know to do, but every part of her body has slowly been shutting down. So here we sit today in a hospice room, waiting for the gates of eternity to be opened for this precious woman—my amazing Mother.

A nurse wades through the crowded room and taps me on the shoulder.

"Excuse me, but there's a woman at the front desk who wants to speak to you," she whispers.

"Could you tell her this is not a good time?" I whisper back. "Please get her contact information. Tell her I will call her back in a few days."

"I'm sorry. I already tried that, Mrs. Bradley. She is quite insistent that she talk to you."

☐

Oh, yes. I did marry Ben Bradley—but only three years ago. After his grandpa died, he and his mother moved back to their former town. Ben and I wrote letters for a while and tried to sneak in occasional long-distance phone calls, but our efforts grew further and further apart, until they ceased altogether. I moved down to the Cities right after high school to work with Scott at his studio. Ben graduated from college, got married, and moved out to the East Coast. No surprise—he became a political cartoonist. I followed his career from a distance. Our local paper carried his syndicated work. He was very good. I was happy for him.

As for me, I was excited about my work with Scott, especially since he steered all the baby photography my direction. I loved it, and I created quite a name for myself in the region for baby portraits, both photographs and sketches. I also loved being part of a team of photographers who worked with the NICUs around the Cities. We volunteered our time and talents for families with infants in crisis.

My work was incredibly rewarding and my life so full, I didn't have much time for a serious relationship. I dated a few guys over the years, but for various reasons, nothing serious ever developed. The older I got, the more distant the idea of marriage became. I focused on my work, my art, and my ever-expanding troupe of nieces and nephews.

One day four years ago, a message popped up on my Facebook page. It was from El, who is a professor of English literature at New Brighton College in Poughkeepsie, New York. Her message read:

> Attended a publisher's function in NYC last week. Guess whose path intersected with mine? #3 on your list—Ben Bradley. Turns out my father is now a resident at the rehab facility where his father is the chaplain. Small world. He inquired about you. Thought you might be intrigued by this valuable tidbit.

I stopped chewing my Caribou Coffee croissant to digest that information. And I nearly choked when she added, "By the way, he's single."

I admit, I had taken a peek at a few pictures of Ben on Facebook. But although I was curious about his life and family, I didn't allow myself to become a stalker. It was just too hard on my heart. Maybe the biggest reason my dating relationships hadn't turned more serious was because I was always searching for someone just like Ben. But there was only one Ben. And he was married. At least, that's what I thought until the day El's message arrived.

At that point, I threw caution to the wind and became a bona fide stalker. I found out he had been divorced for many years and was a single dad of two college-aged girls. I thought about my dream with Ben and Daniel and the babies in the backpack.

Unbeknownst to me, after bumping into El, Ben had been stalking my social media as well. And one morning as I sipped my chai tea and checked my email, another message popped up on Facebook.

It said, "Am I too late? Evening is sometimes the best part of the day to hang out."

He certainly had taken a long detour. But he obviously remembered the dream, too, and he was hoping he wasn't too late.

He wasn't.

Once we reconnected, it was as if the feelings I had for him that had been carefully bottled and put on a shelf had been taken down, uncorked, and poured back into my heart. After just a few months of long-distance romance, he moved back to the Cities and we took up where we left off; hanging out in the evenings until our hearts were so crazily intertwined that we knew marriage was the only reasonable option.

And so here we are today. He's sitting right next to me. His six-month-old daughter is in his lap, sound asleep.

That would be the other major development. My own late-in-life baby—Annabelle. The light of our lives.

☐

"You'd better go check it out, babe," Ben says softly. "I promise I'll come and get you if anything changes."

I lean over, give him a kiss, and run a finger over Annabelle's plump cheek.

I pick my way through the somber assembly, giving little squeezes of encouragement to the hands of those who seem particularly distraught. It has been a long day already, and it's only noon . . . I think. Actually, I'm not sure what time it is. I check my phone. It's 1:45 p.m. Later than I thought.

As I plod down the hallway, I see a young woman standing with her back to me at the front desk. I have no idea what this is about, but I want to get it over with and get back to Mother. I walk up behind her. She doesn't seem to hear my approach.

I clear my throat.

"Excuse me. I'm Pearl Bradley. Are you the one asking for me?"

She turns around. A radiant smile floods her face. She is a beautiful, young woman with tawny skin and curly, black hair swept into a thick ponytail. The plaid scarf around her neck is undone. Her puffy winter coat is unzipped in concession to the warmth of the waiting room. She appears to be thirty years old or so, maybe younger—I'm not sure.

"Oh, yes, Mrs. Bradley. I'm sorry," she says. "I was lost in thought. Yes, I'm the one who asked to speak with you."

"Do I know you?" I ask.

"Well, not exactly," she replies. "Although from what I've read, we have met before under fairly unusual circumstances."

"From what you've read?" Now I am truly befuddled. "I don't mean to be rude, but this is not a great time for me. My mother is dying, and I would sincerely like to be by her side. Now what can I do for you?"

"I'm so sorry, Mrs. Bradley, I know this is an extremely inconvenient time, but I fly back to Houston in a few hours. I'm just here visiting my folks. I'll be quick. I promise." She reaches into her bag and pulls out a newspaper. "This morning after church I was looking through the Sunday paper when I came across the article about the work you and Scott Stewart do. Your photography of babies and families in crisis? And I noticed this sketch you drew years ago of one of the first crisis babies Mr. Stewart photographed."

She hands me a section of the Sunday paper. It is folded back to show the feature article written about *In the Arms of the Angels*, the nonprofit organization Scott and I now run. I forgot it was being published today. But there it is.

"I called the studio on a long shot to see if I might locate you," she says. "Mr. Stewart answered the phone, even though he says you're always closed on Sundays. I guess he thought it might be an important call. He said he was just there to gather some paperwork. Anyway, when I told him my story, he told me where I could find you. He said I should come here and ask to speak with you. Even though it's a bad time, I think you'll be glad I came."

"Okay. So, what's your story?"

She points to one of my sketches featured in the article.

"That's me. I'm Shavonne. Shavonne James." She pauses to see if I'm getting what she's saying. "I was born very prematurely," she continues. "All the doctors thought I was going to die. So, the nurse called in Mr. Stewart to come and take pictures. My parents were grateful for his service, but they were convinced the doctor's prognosis for me was wrong. They let Mr. Stewart take the pictures, but they believed they were not going to be my last pictures. I stayed in the hospital for weeks—alive but not thriving. Then one day my parents received an envelope from Mr. Stewart's studio. They thought it was going to be another photograph that had been forgotten. But when they opened it up, there was this sketch—the one in the newspaper—the one you drew."

Recognition floods my mind. Shavonne. As in Shavonne and Timothy.

"When they looked at that sketch they saw life—my life." Shavonne says. "And the hope they had been clinging to turned to belief. From that day forward, I began to thrive. Within a week, they were able to take me home and, well, here I am today."

She pulls a manila envelope from the bag on her shoulder, withdraws a piece of paper, and hands it to me. I gasp and put one hand to my mouth. The paper is aged around the edges but still vibrant with color. It is the copy of my sketch I sent to Susan to give to Scott those many years ago.

"Mrs. Bradley," Shavonne says, "I thought you should know—I lived. And your vision or dream or whatever it was of me as a living, breathing baby wasn't just a dream. It was reality waiting to happen."

Tears sting my eyes. All my frustration with the timing of her visit vanishes. I reach for her and pull her into an embrace. She melts into my arms. She lived. She lives!

I lean back and study her face, comparing it to the face that lives indelibly in my memory.

"Shavonne James, I am very, very happy to see you again. Thank you for making the effort to find me. Thank you for telling me your story. I would love to know more."

She reaches back into her bag and digs out a business card. It reads, "Shavonne James, LM, CPM—Hands of Love Midwives Group, Houston, TX."

"You're a baby catcher?" I ask.

"Yes, ma'am. Certified for five years now."

"Oh, we have much to talk about . . . "

"Pearl," a voice calls from down the hallway.

I turn and see Ben standing outside Mother's room. My breath catches.

"Pearl, we need you now," he says tenderly but firmly.

I am momentarily frozen.

"Mrs. Bradley, you should go," says Shavonne quietly. "You can call me whenever you're ready. Thanks for hearing me out."

I try to smile as I hand back the sketch. I have no words. She seems to understand. I turn back to Ben, who waits for me.

Here I am again, Lord. In a thin place—this place between life and death, heaven, and earth, arrival and departure. How do I do this?

A still, small Voice nudges my heart. It is a Voice that sounds like rushing waters. A Voice I have heard many times throughout the years. A Voice I love.

"Soon she will see me face-to-face."

Hope penetrates my soul. I am infused with peace so unexpected, it takes my breath away.

I take my next step.

INTERLUDE: LIZZIE

"**Lizzie**."

Her eyes flutter open at my voice.

"John?"

"Hello, love. Ready to go?"

Her face lights up and she takes my hand.

"I'm so happy you came for me."

"Me too. Truth be told, Ilsa wanted the assignment, but the King asked her to stay with William."

"William?"

"Our son, Lizzie. Our amazing, beautiful son. Wait 'til you meet him. He's at the Gate with your mom and everyone else, eager to welcome you."

"What are we waiting for?" she says with a laugh.

I am enthralled all over again with her beauty. "The waiting is over. Let's go home."

A THIN PLACE

As Scott hurriedly enters the room, he scans the scene in front of him, seeking answers. The rest of the family misses his entrance. But from my vantage point standing next to Mother's bed, I notice it. Our eyes meet over the hugging figures that fill the small hospice room. I muster a gentle smile through the tears streaming down my face and mouth.

"She's gone," I say.

He stops in his tracks. His head falls to his chest. All the energy of trying to get there on time courses out of his dangling fingers.

I rub Susan's shoulder. She sits next to Mother's still body on the bed. She glances up, and I nod in the direction of her recently arrived husband. She rises and makes her way to his side, where they fall into each other's arms.

I slip out of Ben's arm, which has been wrapped around my waist, and sit down in the spot my sister occupied. I reach out to caress Mother's face. Her skin is soft and smooth. The wrinkles that were so prevalent hours ago have nearly vanished. I am shocked at how cool she has become.

It is the first hour of my entire existence without her, and already I feel lost. It's not as if Mother was afraid of dying or I am afraid of never seeing her again. Just last week she asked me to tell her again, to tell her about the golden road and the singing stones and the swirling colors. Every detail of my journey to the Baby-Catcher Gate seemed to delight her afresh, even though she had heard it a thousand times. She knew her time to step off the planet was approaching, and far from dreading it, she was full of eager anticipation. Her faith was about to become sight. I am thankful she is where she longed to be, yet even so, my heart is heavy with the agony of parting. I wonder how long it will be before I breathe without pain.

Across the bed, a small movement catches my eye. I look over at Teacher Anne, who holds her namesake, little Annabelle, on her lap. For hours my baby girl has slept peacefully, but now she is stirring. Her chubby arms stretch up toward the ceiling. She seems to be reaching for something or someone. Teacher bounces her up and down, hoping to keep her content. Ben moves to scoop her up, unwilling for her to disrupt the solemn atmosphere in the room.

Before he can gather her up, Annabelle's plump hands begin to clap, and her pudgy legs begin to kick. Ben steps back in surprise. Then, quite unexpectedly, Annabelle sits bolt upright, reaches for something, and bursts into laughter, her little belly shaking with mirth.

Heads swivel as tear-filled eyes turn to this suddenly giggling infant girl. It is so incongruous with the setting that I am taken aback. I reach across the bed to take her and calm her down. Teacher Anne shakes her head.

"Let her be, Pearl. Look."

She runs her finger across Annabelle's cheek and then stretches it toward me. It is glistening with gold flakes.

Annabelle's laughter doesn't stop. In fact, her giggles blossom into a full-blown belly laugh—the contagious, viral, irresistible, full-of-life-and-joy type. I look to the ceiling where Annabelle is focused but am unable to see the source of her amusement. When I look into her eyes, though, they shimmer with a divine golden light—a light only she can see—a light that has tickled her funny bone and won't quit.

Then, maybe because our emotions are so raw—or maybe because the laughter is so captivating—or maybe because Mother wouldn't have it any other way—the entire room suddenly erupts in a fountain of laughter.

Laughter mixed with a wellspring of tears.

It is exhilarating.

It is exhausting.

It is exactly what Mother would love.

It is a thin place.

The End

Acknowledgments

Foremost thanks go to my Lord Jesus Christ who prompted me to start writing, enabled me to keep writing and provided people every step along the way to believe in my writing: my mom Doris, sister-in-law Karen and cousin Gisele, Joy and the Kona ladies' writing group, Rhoda, Sarah, Brennan, Chrisi, Martha, Carmen, Gail, Anne, Joe, Kathy, Cheri, Jennifer, Denise, Margot and The #1 Ladies Book Club members – all of whom read early drafts and urged me on despite the many flaws. Your feedback and encouragement were priceless. Special thanks: to developmental editor Natalie Hanemann for her patient tutoring and provoking suggestions, to copy editors Lori Baxter and Hannah Comerford at The Scribe Source for their scrub of the superfluous and erroneous, to midwife Stephani Young for her expert advice about the birthing scene, and to Delaney Cerna who not only designed the book cover but posed for the photo many years ago. Finally, my deepest gratitude goes to my family – my parents who not only gave me life but gave me a wonderful life, my brothers who protect, entertain and challenge me even to this day, my husband and children who cheer me on and allow me to spend hours holed up in my computer nook with fairly limited requests for food or attention. Their love, support and pursuit of their own creative outlets have been gentle but firm goads to my backside to keep me pressing onward. Way to go family, way to go. You are my highlight daily and forever.

About the Book

Life took an unexpected turn for my family on Friday, April 18, 2008. It was the day my niece, Taryn Leigh, was killed in a car accident on her way home from a college visit in eastern Washington. She was eighteen. Just about to graduate from high school. Just about to begin life. A life full of her special brand of wit, compassion, beauty, and spunk. A life, we were all convinced, would pack a powerful punch far beyond the reach of her diminutive five-foot-nothing frame. And it did. Just not like we thought it would.

Yes, she was 'just' my niece. To those who live outside the web of relationships in what I fondly call "The Cerna Nation", it is hard to explain the depths of what that word means. I have many nieces and nephews as well as great-nieces and nephews – right around seventy currently. Each one is precious, interesting, valued, amazing. But Taryn held a special spot in my heart. She and her family came to live with my husband and me for a while when she was six months old. It was before I had any children of my own. Unlike my husband, I had not grown up in a family where new babies appeared almost monthly. I was inexperienced and slightly intimidated by Taryn's presence in my home. But she was the kind of baby every person with baby fears should learn from –funny, easy, and adorable.

When my son entered the world a year later, Taryn and her older brother became his favorite people. When we broke the news to him when he was three years old that they were not in fact his siblings but his cousins, he was devastated. Eventually, I had three children of my own and a sister was added to Taryn's family. The lives of these six cousins were intertwined at school and church and family events throughout their childhood.

So, it was with great sorrow that we received the news of Taryn's death on that day in 2008. An enormous hole opened up in our hearts and none of us were quite sure how to fill it. For me, the only comfort I found was in pressing into my faith. I believed in the promise of eternal life in Christ. Believed in the hope of heaven. But this sudden loss produced an urgent need to know more of the reality of life beyond this life. I scoured the scriptures and devoured testimonies about heaven. I sat quietly for hours in the Lord's presence not even knowing what to ask. I had no words. Yet He met me there and led me through the valley of the shadow of death via a heavenly route. The eternal perspectives I gained there soothed my soul. Then a day came many months down the road – I'm not exactly sure when – that my heart was whole again. Not the same as before. Never the same. But whole. And, hopefully, better.

Years later, I was reading my Bible and praying, as is my habit in the morning. I was in a new season in life. My children were growing up and heading off to college. I was feeling lost. Small. Uncertain as to where I should expend my time and energy. I asked God, "What do you want me to do now?" He responded with a question of His own, "What do you want to do?" I was taken aback. What *did* I want to do? It took me a while to formulate my desire into a simple statement. "I want to do something creative that binds up the brokenhearted and sets captives free." A pretty broad stroke, I know, but it was true. It was what I wanted to do.

Fast forward to January 16, 2015. Once again, I was sitting with the Lord in the morning and He said to me, "There is a baby-catcher gate in heaven." Nothing more. Just that. I pondered His words for a moment and then said, "Thank you for that interesting nugget of information. What would You like me to do with it?" He promptly replied, "Write a book." To which I replied, "Well, that should be interesting since I have never written a book and I don't know what You're talking about." He answered,

"I have and I do." How could I argue with that? The next evening, I sat down with a yellow legal pad and a pen and prayed, "Okay, Lord. Here I am. I give you my pen. I give you my imagination. I give you whatever gifts I possess and ask that you fill in whatever I lack." And, in faith, I began to write. To my utter amazement, a story unfolded before my eyes. A story woven from the heavenly treasures I had unearthed in my time of great sorrow after Taryn's death. Over the course of the following months as I continued to write, I realized that this just might be the thing I wanted to do – something creative that binds up the brokenhearted and sets captives free.

I did not know I wanted to write this book. I did not know I could write this book. But apparently, He did. It is my prayer that in this story you might find a breath of hope, a whisper of comfort, a ray of joy in imagining the things that are beyond our imagination – the things God has prepared for those who love Him. And in so doing, may your broken heart be mended and your soul set free.

Taryn would love that.

For Her

They might've complained about the color of the
cummerbund or
the complexity of the cuff links.
They might've grumbled about her choosing the hottest
day of the year
for wearing such a get-up.
They might've tugged at the staid collar or
mumbled about their scrunched-up toes
But
They would've worn tuxes *for her.*

Instead
They wear freshly purchased suits of somber
black or navy blue.
They are too young to have them hanging at the ready
in their closets.
They stand in a semi-circle with shoulders hunched;
sober fabric strained across broadening shoulders.
They stuff their hands in pockets unable to reconcile
the load they've just carried.
They stare straight ahead willing the solid veil that encases
her to part;
to see her one last time.
They don't shuffle their appropriately clad feet
rooted into the sod like a fresh crop of grief.
They've fulfilled their solemn privilege *for her.*

Now they cannot fathom how to move again.
They can only watch and learn as a more mature navy
figure

approaches her hidden form.
He reaches toward her burnished veil,
in-laid angels adorn her shoulders and feet.
He reverently leans over and places first one hand and
then the other
 in a final father/daughter dance.
He hangs his head and speaks words meant only *for her*
as he lovingly hands her to the Bridegroom clothed in
splendor and light.

*For Uncle Randy and the young men who carried Taryn that
day in April 2008.*

About the Author

Born and raised in a family of educators in Minnesota, Wendy Jo travelled to the University of Washington in Seattle to complete her Bachelor's degree in Theatre Arts. In 1986, she married her college sweetheart. They settled in Bellevue, WA to run their contracting business and raise their three children. In 2009, she received a Master's degree in Psychology which she has used to educate and counsel hurting people in a variety of settings. In writing her first novel, she has found a way to combine her love of the arts and education with her passion for healing the brokenhearted.

Something Sweet

In the upper Midwest where I grew up, there are these desserts called 'bars.' Pronounced *bahrz,* they are a ubiquitous part of gatherings from coffee parties, to church potlucks, bridge clubs, sewing circles, high-school graduations, birthday celebrations, family dinners and everything in between. 'Bars' are not confined to one type like brownies or one flavor like lemon. They are as varied as the imaginations of the bakers who bake them. And so, as a grand finale to this ode to my homeland where a meal is never complete without dessert, I leave you with something sweet – a few of my favorite recipes for bars.

<u>Pumpkin Bars</u>
2 c. sugar
4 eggs
2 c. pumpkin
1 c. vegetable oil
2 c. flour
2 tsp. baking powder
1 tsp. soda
½ tsp. cinnamon
½ tsp. salt
1 cup nuts chopped (optional)

Mix sugar, eggs, pumpkin and oil together. Mix well. Add sifted dry ingredients and nuts. Pour into 9x13 and 9x9 inch baking pans. Bake ate 350° for ½ hour.

Frosting:
3 oz. cream cheese
½ cup butter
1 tsp. vanilla
2 c. powdered sugar
Mix together and spread on cooled bars.

Oatmeal Carmelitas

32 light colored caramels
5 T. milk or cream
1 c. flour
1 c. quick cooking oats
¾ c. brown sugar
½ tsp. soda
¼ tsp. salt
¾ c. butter (melted)
1 c. chocolate chips
½ c. pecans (chopped)

Melt caramels in cream in double boiler. Cool slightly. Combine all remaining ingredients except chips and pecans in bowl. Stir until all butter is absorbed and mixture is crumbly. Press half of this into a 7x11 inch pan. Bake at 350° for 10 minutes. Sprinkle with chocolate chips and pecans. Cover with caramel mixture. Sprinkle with remaining crumbs. Bake 15-20 minutes longer. Cool.

Final Exam Brownies

4 squares baking chocolate
1 c. margarine or butter
2 c. sugar
4 eggs (room temp)
1 c. flour
1 tsp. vanilla
2 c. mini marshmallows
1 c. chopped nuts
1 c. chocolate chips plus ½ cup for topping

Melt chocolate and margarine. Add sugar in large bowl. Beat in eggs. Add flour and vanilla. Stir in rest of ingredients. Pour into well-greased 9x13 inch pan. Sprinkle with ½ cup chocolate chips. Bake at 350° for 40-45 minutes.

Made in the USA
Middletown, DE
07 March 2019